AN UNSUSPECTING SPY

Geoffrey B. Lewis

*To Maureen
With best wishes
Geoff Lewis*

Octavo Publishing Ltd

An Unsuspecting Spy

© 2016 Geoffrey B. Lewis

The Author asserts the moral right to be identified as the author of this work. All rights reserved. This book is protected under the copyright laws of the United Kingdom. Any reproduction or other unauthorised use of the material or artwork herein is prohibited without the express written permission of the Publisher.

The story contained within this book is a work of fiction. Names and characters are the product of the author's imagination and any resemblance to actual persons, living or dead, is entirely coincidental.

British Library Cataloguing in Publication Data.
A catalogue record for this book is available from the British Library.

No part of this book may be reproduced, stored in a retrieval system, or transmitted in any form or by any means, electronic, electrostatic, magnetic tape, mechanical, photocopying, recording or otherwise, without the written permission of the Publisher.

Published in the United Kingdom by
Octavo Publishing Ltd, UK.
www.octavopublishing.com
Twitter @Octavo_Books
Facebook.com/octavobooks

Trade paperback edition ISBN: 9781786152954
POD paperback format ISBN: 9781786153944
Ebook format ISBN: 9781786153937

First Edition: July, 2016
Category: Spy / Memoir

In memory of my big sister Jeannette.

CONTENTS

PROLOGUE	1
BRYNMILL DISTRICT	15
THE PARK	28
FLOSSY, TREES, AND OTHER STUFF	37
THE ART OF FISHING	58
THE MAN WHO DRESSED IN TWEED	66
SAINTS AND SINNERS	71
IMPRESSIONS OF SCHOOL	81
THIS OLD HOUSE	100
OLD SMOKEY	105
THAT'S ENTERTAINMENT	114
YOUNG GENTLEMEN	126
WHEELS AND THE COAL HOUSE DOOR	139
THE LAUGHING CAVALIERS	159
POND LIFE AND AN ANGRY COW	179
SPLISH SPLASH	183
ROYSTON MY MENTOR	191
ALL LIT UP	216
A NEW FRIEND	223
CLAY IS A GRAY AREA	235
OVER THE GARDEN WALL	243
THE SECRET	248
AERONAUTICAL ENGINEER	257
CRASH LANDING	271
THE EXHIBITIONIST	276
DOWN BY THE DOCKS	283
NAILED	301
AN AFTERNOON AT MARKS & SPENCERS	307
STANDING BEHIND THE LEVERS	311
THE PERFECT DAY	330
LOOKING TO THE FUTURE	344
SCOUTS, SPIES, AND FLYING SAUCERS	360
THE MISSION	366
FOOTPRINTS TO NOWHERE	371
ON THE BEACH	375
FLIGHT	379
THE DREAM	389
LENINGRAD	399
COORDINATES AND A CHRISTMAS CARD	402
A FATHER'S SON	408
INFORMATION OBTAINED	415
DUPLICITY	422
EPILOGUE	428

PROLOGUE

I've got myself into a bit of a mess. But I'm not really worried... more like I'm terrified. I'm terrified about what I just found out and what it means. It's not that I think people are going to come after me or anything like that, but nevertheless I am concerned. I don't think anybody is going to come after me because those members of the police force, and possibly the navy, directly involved at the time are long since dead.

So now you might be wondering why I am worrying about something that happened such a long time ago that nobody else is left alive to care. Good question. The reason is that I only recently discovered what we really did, and now that I know about it I cannot leave things as they are. I feel it is my duty to tell the authorities what I now know. That is what terrifies me; what they are going to think when I reveal their town's dirty little secret, and what they are going to brand me. Me and only me because I am the sole witness remaining to the events in question. For too many years I have kept quiet about what took place on that miserable night because I didn't think it mattered. Just a schoolboy prank, I thought, but there was far more to it than I could have imagined. So I need to explain, and to do that I must go back to the beginning, because that's when it happened; way back when we were schoolboys growing up in the seaport town of Swansea not long after the end of the war. The three of us: Gordon, Trevor and me.

Lying at the southern end of Wales, Swansea was a natural target for Hitler's Luftwaffe and was heavily bombed on a number of occasions. I grew up in the years following the war as the rubble was cleared and a new town grew out of the devastation. It was because of all the extra activity that rebuilding generated around us in addition to the normal experience of just growing up, that those schoolboy years were an especially exciting time, and given the choice I would still prefer to have lived through that period rather than being born into the highly charged and complex twenty-first century world of today. For me I was born at the right time.

So let me tell you about those happy, relatively irresponsible, carefree days of my childhood and how I grew up as a schoolboy in a different, more innocent age. Let me share with you some of my friendships, experiences, and cherished memories of that time and how over fifty years later I found out that one of those memories was not what I thought it to be; an episode that had the most profound consequences, consequences I could never have imagined as a boy or even as a fully grown man. What I, what we did, will change Swansea's recorded history forever, although the City officials don't know it yet and there's going to be a real hullabaloo when they do. I'll explain in due course. But before I do, you need to know the full story. You need to know how I grew up, because when everything kicks off and hits the proverbial fan, as I'm

sure it will, I am going to need you to be on my side.
My name is Bernard Andrew and this is how it was.

PART ONE

PART ONE

DRUSLYN ROAD

I was born in the seaport town of Swansea during the Second World War. Emerging from the trauma of these years Swansea and its people gradually got back to industry and commerce along with the business of clearing the rubble and rebuilding the bombsites. It was the rebuilding of the town which influenced my ultimate direction in life but before that there was a great deal of boyhood fun.

I was born in the West Cross district of Swansea in a house that stood at the top end of a long sloping hill known as Druslyn Road. West Cross was five miles away from the main town and at the west end of the bay where my parents, together with my big sister Constance who was born four years earlier, had moved in order to avoid the bombing. Swansea was under siege mainly because of the docks which were near the town centre and the target for the Luftwaffe, and the residents of West Cross bore witness to the Blitz on many nights as they watched Swansea burn from across the bay.

Fortunately no bombs ever fell on West Cross but legend has it that I was born on the same day that the last bombs were dropped on Swansea town. According to official records there was a raid late in the evening following my birth in the afternoon, after which there were no more. Thus it was that my coming brought peace to Swansea. Not a bad start.

The house where we lived was opposite a piece of waste ground on which the older boys who lived nearby would fly their rubber powered model airplanes. It fell away steeply to one side and was adjacent to a large field at the top of the hill that formed part of what we called Collier's Farm. In its long and well fertilised meadow grass grew clusters of giant buttercups dog daisies, dandelions, cowslips, clover and all sorts of assorted wild flowers. It was a field which just invited children to play and there were many children in that road who would crawl up its grassy bank, duck under the wire fence and invade their own adventureland. We were the future and the residents made sure no harm came to us. We spent many happy hours chasing butterflies and dragonflies in that field in summertime wondering how many we could count. Occasionally however, the tables were turned on us and we ourselves got chased by Mr Collier's flock of geese, fortunately without casualty to either side. When we could be sure of no intervention by cows or mother goose and her kids it was also an ideal place to have a picnic.

At the top boundary of the field was an embankment and gently sloping gully which in the spring would be filled with a carpet of bluebells, some of which I would occasionally gather and take home as an offering to my mother. I also collected another kind of trophy because where cattle grazed would be left much bovine evidence on the ground for me to transfer in to my little wooden wheel barrow, all nicely patted down by hand, to deliver home to 'help daddy's potatoes grow'. At the top end of Druslyn Road a long sloping lane led down almost to the main Mumbles Road before turning away up an incline into the Mayals housing estate. Going along the opposite side of the lane a short distance in the other direction towards the farm was another field secured by a tall wooden gate. Sometimes we would be taken there for a walk and lifted up in turn to stand on its cross bars to look across the meadow, beyond the Mayals housing estate with its growing prefab population and out across the bay. Occasionally the pull of my childhood roots has taken me back to the area but of course the idyll of such a long time ago no longer exists.

Much has changed in the intervening years and opposite our old house there is no longer any waste ground and Mr Collier's field and farm have long gone. Where the Druslyn Road kids once played is now occupied by bungalows, the lane has become a road, and beyond that the meadow is now a large housing estate.

The nearest community to get household essentials was the village of Oystermouth with its castle and local shops. One shop I remember in particular was Greenslade's the grocer, which used to stand on the corner of Castle Crescent. It always seemed to be well stocked with fruit and vegetables and had a bacon slicer which always terrified me. At the time of course being so young I did not realise that there was a food shortage with ration stamps to be handed over in order to obtain your allowance, and the shelves were not as full as they could have been. That old grocer's shop is still there, but its use has changed many times since the 1940's.

The best shop in the village as far as kids were concerned though was Fortes ice cream parlour where you could get a sophisticated ice cream covered in bright red raspberry sauce, presented in a silver metal bowl to be savoured while sitting at one of the tables. A plain cornet or wafer could be had to lick away outside but having an ice cream sitting down was deemed a special treat and real posh. At the entrance to the establishment, which stood on a corner, was a display cabinet in which were placed enticing options to choose from if dad was awash with money. One of these tongue tickling delights was a very expensive looking arrangement in a tall glass called a Sundae; an unattainable ambition since dad's pocket was never quiet deep enough to pay for one. These mouth-watering displays were not actually labelled so when Constance told me what it was called I wondered why it was named after the first, or was it the last, day of the week. It was confusing. In my mind I still see it spelled as Sunday; the day on which I was obliged to dress tidy and attend chapel.

It was on the expanse of ground behind Forte's ice cream establishment that Oystermouth also had a stop for the Mumbles train, alongside The South Wales Transport bus terminus, where it paused on its way to the end of the line at the Mumbles Pier further around the bay.

The buses coming from the east end of the main town used the terminus to turn around for the return journey and it also acted as the hub for their single decker fleet ferrying passengers to and from Langland, Ratherslade and Caswell bays; top attractions of the area with Langland being a regular favourite of our family for many years.

The water at Langland was clear and there were many rock pools to explore, looking for crabs and shrimps after they had been exposed by the receding tide. When it was out far enough you could also walk around to the adjoining cove at Ratherslade where the beach had a lot more stones and pebbles than sand so that you couldn't build sand castles like you could in Langland. We had many seaside picnics sitting on hired deckchairs when we feasted on tomato and cheese sandwiches flavoured with the occasional pinch of windblown sand that grated your teeth when chewing.

Langland also had tennis courts, still there today, which could be hired by the public and where tournaments were held in the summer alongside the bus terminus from where the fleet of single-deckers ran to and from Oystermouth. When it was time to go home there were always long queues to contend with for the return journey with the hairpin bend halfway up the hill leading out of the bay where you could get your last look back at what had been your day out.

One visit made to Langland was at night time, taken by my aunt when still very young. As we walked along the promenade we were invited by a small group of people to look at the moon through a telescope. It was a full moon that night, it shone brightly and seemed exceptionally close, looking as though it was actually resting on the hill at the end of the bay. It was the first time I had ever seen the craters on the moon's surface, or even the moon through a telescope, and I was exceedingly impressed.

All these events of course took place a long time ago and are not necessarily in their correct chronological order, but occasionally some stand out because they can more or less be pinpointed in time. The first one, albeit vaguely, was the victory parade that took place in Oystermouth at the cessation of hostilities at the end of the war in 1945.

The parade, as I recall, marched up from the main Mumbles Road and then Newton Road, and was led by a small tracked tank vehicle with various members of the armed forces marching behind as people stood on the pavement either side cheering them on, an event which was taking place all over the country. Constance tells me that there was a street party afterwards with tables stretching all the way down the street.

By the time I was six we had moved much closer to the town centre at the eastern end of the bay so it must have been not long before the next memorable experience occurred. In April 1947 a major tragedy occurred off the Welsh coast when the cargo ship Samtampa was driven onto the rocks at Sker Point during a severe gale. The Mumbles lifeboat went to the rescue but was unable to reach the stricken vessel and also driven onto the same rocks where it too was smashed with all crew perished.

The funeral was a very public affair, the cortège proceeding from the main Mumbles Road and then up Newton Road, passing the school which my sister attended and a large house on the right hand side standing in its own grounds. The house belonged to a man by the name of Kyle who was our family doctor. The grounds were fronted by a long stone wall along which we stood with many others trying to shelter under trees from the torrential rain which lasted through the whole proceedings. There was very little shelter to be had however and by the time the cortège had passed, we were all soaking through to the skin resulting in hot baths when we got home.

During the war years my father worked on dockyard security and after cessation of hostilities returned to his peacetime role as a railway property inspector based at High Street railway station. I never thought to ask him but he must have used the Mumbles train to go most of the way there each morning walking down West Cross Lane and taking a short cut at the bottom of the hill to get to the West Cross stop and stand to wait with the full sweep of the bay in front of him. The Rutland Street terminus at the town end of the railway was also the depot and workshop, situated on the opposite side of the road to the running line. Whenever we caught the tram from there I would watch in fascination as they slowly rumbled and bumbled across the road from the depot onto the running line and got hitched together to run as a pair by important looking workmen in greasy overalls. It was an almost unique feature of the Mumbles tram that they could be run in tandem and these early scenes of transport I'm sure influenced my lifelong interest in all things involving mechanical engineering.

By 1948 we had moved from West Cross back nearer to the town centre. It was far more convenient for my father to be at that end of the bay than having to commute from West Cross, and the location we moved to allowed him to catch a bus, within walking distance of the house, that would drop him almost opposite his High Street Station office. Constance and I were of course reluctant to leave all our friends but it had to be and we spent a week with my grandfather and aunt in the Danygraig area of Swansea while the move took place.

Their house in Bay Street was on a hill overlooking the King's Dock which in those days was extremely busy and I watched and listened in total fascination as I was introduced to industry and commerce by the sight and sound of steam engines shunting and whistling and cranes playing lucky dip to offload cargo ships on the quayside. As I watched and listened mum and dad upped sticks and moved to the other end of the bay from West Cross to Brynmill.

After an eternity, the new house was eventually declared ready for inspection and one sunny Saturday morning, after the holiday at Bay Street, grandpa took us for our first look. We got off the bus at the top of Rhyddings hill, walked down Rhyddings Terrace to the group of shops by Locks Bakery, into Bernard Street and next left into Glanbrydan Avenue where stood our new home.

It was four houses down from the corner and was having its doorstep thoroughly scrubbed by my mother who was dressed in the apron and wrap around headscarf housewife uniform of the day. In the 1940's and 50's doorstep scrubbing was almost a religion. A dirty doorstep was, according to housewife legend, a sign of a dirty household. Scrubbing brushes were in demand and many of these, as well as other common domestic tools, were provided by door to door salesmen dressed in forces demob suits carrying a suitcase full of the necessary wares. I can remember on a number of occasions trying to get my mother to purchase a wire brush which on demonstration by Mr Demob would clean up a dirty penny to perfection. That was about its only use however so the offer at 'a very reasonable price' was always declined. This was very frustrating. The things a small boy could have found to do with a wire brush were endless. Mr Demob didn't always go away empty handed however. Mum would when needed, after some banter, offer to buy a duster or brush to help him on his way and lighten his heavy looking suitcase.

It was a joyous reunion as we were quickly given appropriate refreshment after the bus journey from the other side of town and then a guided tour of the house where my sister and I were to live for the foreseeable future. I don't remember a great deal about the house at Druslyn Road. I do remember that it was fairly small, had a sort of porch way out the back yard next to the kitchen where I pedalled around in circles on my tricycle, and that there was a long upward sloping garden which had a lawn on one side and a vegetable patch on the other. The vegetable patch was where my father anointed his potatoes with the manure I had gathered and patted down by hand from Mr Collier's field.

Whereas the houses at Druslyn Road were compact semi detached, the ones at Glanbrydan Avenue were arranged in blocks of terraces as were the dwellings over the whole district. They were also much larger inside than they looked from the outside; reaching further back than the width of the frontage would tend to imply. Four bedroomed and brick built throughout, ours had on the ground floor a front room, middle room, a dining room and kitchen with a long hallway leading from the front door.

At that time, I don't know why, the kitchen was

always referred to as the scullery and in one corner was the pantry used for food storage. In the immediate post war days of 1948 and for some time to come refrigeration was a concept unknown to domestic life in Britain. With a tiled floor, two outer scullery walls and another adjoining the coal house, the pantry was quite cold and ideal for the purpose.

Occasionally the scullery would be the scene of great drama when there was trouble with the boiler. This was the time for dad to put on his battered trilby hat and move mum's wooden work table aside so he could attack the water pipes causing the problem and which ran down the wall directly behind the fire place. They formed part of the hot water system and occasionally would need bleeding. Constance and I would stand 'out of the way' and watch while all the excitement took place and water taps were opened to run gallons of foaming water into a bucket. I can remember thinking: if he was bleeding it off why wasn't it red? Once a sufficient number of buckets full of water had been emptied down the drain outside the kitchen door the table was pushed back against the wall, mum reclaimed her domain, dad went back to reading the paper and we kids went back to play.

Outside at the back of the house was an outside toilet and a small coalhouse next door to it. Central heating was a long way off with coal fires being the standard method of supplying warmth for comfort and heating the boiler for domestic water with, like many others of the period, fireplaces in all the downstairs living rooms and the upstairs bedrooms. The rear garden was set some four feet below the level of the service lane at the back however, not very large with no space for produce like potatoes or cabbages like the old house. There was just a postage stamp size of lawn and relatively narrow borders just sufficient for mum to plant an ever changing array of flowers.

This was because the previous owner had built a timbered floor garage of full width mounted on supporting brick piers. With a corrugated roof and sides it was very roomy inside and although we didn't have a car it found many uses particularly for odd jobs that could still be done when it was raining and also as a hobby workshop where I used to mess around trying but not often succeeding in making something useful.

It also featured a couple of loose floorboards at the rear next to the lane that could be lifted out to gain access to void beneath. The space was unfortunately open to the garden so there were no secret rooms to disappear into but the layout inspired our imagination and we soon utilised the possibilities when we got together with our friends to play invading forces. While gallant defenders held the front door against entry from the garden steps, invaders used noisy stealth to sneak in through the floorboards at the back. The ground beneath the garage was in time also to become the last resting place for my good buddy Smokey – the family cat.

BRYNMILL DISTRICT

Today the West Cross district has grown considerably in size with housing development and its character has greatly changed from how I knew it as a child. Mumbles however and particularly the Oystermouth district, for me at any rate, although altered by the demise of the Mumbles Tram Railway, have retained much of their original charm and are a regular target for tourists and more geographically local residents of South Wales. The Brynmill district, with its greater choice of schools for the future, other amenities and closer proximity to the town, could not have been more different and had I remained at West Cross my horizons would have without doubt been far more limited.

As it was, the move opened up a whole new world for me that I would not otherwise have enjoyed. Although densely populated it was extremely well served by Brynmill Park which was just two minutes' walk from our front door and Singleton just a few more minutes than that. At the junction where I had first rounded the corner to see my new home stood a telephone box and within a short walking distance a variety of shops spread out along the street with several more at the next junction along.

They included a bakery, butcher, and a fishmonger next to cobbler and directly opposite on the other side of the road a chip shop. There was a post office, newsagent, grocery shop, hair dresser, chemist and ironmonger with a second grocery cum tuck shop selling Dollar bubble gum, sweet lollipops and other goodies to children on their way to and from school.

I remember Lock's the corner shop bakery in particular. They had a middle aged 'bakers boy' who would spend his days calling and delivering bread from a van all around the district; knocking on doors taking the order, collecting whatever kind of loaf was required there and then from the back of his van. When he brought it to the customer's front door he would take payment, and then give change, rattling and shaking up the coins in a leather bag that hung around his neck. It was almost door to door, jumping back into the van, moving it a bit further and repeating the same procedure time and time again before moving onto the next street. That man really used to work hard. At the end of his day he must have been exhausted.

It was at Lock's that I also watched completely fascinated as sacks of flour were delivered to their bakery kitchen. The sacks would be hauled up from the back of the miller's vehicle to the top attic by pulley and tackle suspended from an arm jutting out from above the access door. When the flour reached the topmost point the workman receiving it would lean out and haul it inside. I was always expecting him to fall out or a sack to break but fortunately neither event happened while I was watching.

They tempted us with halfpenny buns (and then the price went up to a penny), plain iced buns, iced Chelsea buns and other goodies; and, as food rationing ceased, they brought out even more tempting fayre.

If you couldn't find what you wanted in this little cluster of shops a ten minute walk in the other direction would take you to the 'The Uplands' which had a much bigger choice of suppliers that included Thomas The Bookshop. This was where we always got our newspapers and also very importantly sold spare parts for Meccano, which with the progress of age and growing model ambitions became a more frequent section to visit.

Occasionally they would put a large 'Official' Meccano model in the window and it would often draw a number of enthusiastic schoolboys around, encouraging them to build one of their own. One of the regular display models was of the Blackpool Tower. Thomas's also became popular every November when it sold fireworks, for Guy Fawks night and we would spend a lot of time rumaging through assorted shapes and colours before deciding which ones we would eventually purchase.

The key to my new life however was the park, which had a small gated off area for swings and roundabouts and later a slide. It was always full of children from the surrounding area jostling for a turn and occasionally trying to push each other off, most of it good natured physical banter. Outside this gated play area was a large expanse of open ground bordered by trees and bushes on two sides, which with railings also served to separate the park from roads which ran alongside. There was also a bowling green and a red brick building which served as a members' changing room at one end and, most importantly, at the opposite end a café which served ice-cream and sweets to the many children.

It was a beautiful park which was well tended throughout. In the spring in particular I remember the myriad of rhododendron bushes seemingly all over the place filling the park with colour, particularly after a refreshing shower of rain. Beyond the open expanse was the biggest pond I had ever seen. It had in former years been a reservoir but was now used as a swimming ground for ducks and swans and a watery home for several species of fish. Further into the park there was a monkey house, rabbit house and a wildfowl menagerie with various exotic bird species and peacocks that would regularly fan out their tails for visitors.

However, Brynmill was not the only park in the area. Almost adjoining it at the bottom end was one of the several entrances to Singleton Park, a very much bigger venture with a lot more open ground and woodland stretching for many more acres, providing a whole new haven for adventure. A playground which really came into its own on Saturday mornings because that was when the Saturday Morning Cinema Club was held for boys and girls of up to junior school age who could find their way to the Odeon Cinema in the Sketty district of Swansea.

Living in the same street a few doors away from my new home was Peter, another boy of my age. We had quickly become friends and although I think it was Constance who first took and introduced me to this wonderful children's social club, he soon took over the duty with several other boys in the area and we ended up going as a regular gang.

Absolute busloads of kids turned up from all parts of the town and how the staff coped I just don't know. The show always used to start, I think, at around ten o'clock with the national anthem which we may or may not have joined in with. I can't really remember because it was sung on the screen by a schoolboy choir with very serious faces before the main programme began. When it did start it was usually a Bugs Bunny, Terry Toons or a Tom & Jerry cartoon which always had us in fits of laughter. I think occasionally there may have been a Mickey Mouse but they were not so much fun as the others.

Singleton Park's Sketty entrance gate was not that far from the Odeon cinema and after the morning's showing it would funnel the considerable number of Brynmill and other kids through it into the woodland beyond where imagination would run riot. The weekly adventure films and serials would all be re-enacted in the upper reaches of its forest and for an hour or so it would become a wild west town, a ranch, a prairie, a scene of pitched battles featuring King Arthur and the Knights Of The Round Table, Robin Hood and his merry men, bank robbers fighting the police, a World War Two battlefield, or even another planet with battling robots and tele-transporters that would carry you back and forth from Earth to the Moon or distant Mars in the blink of an eye.

A weekly serial with very definable goodies and baddies led each episode to a cliff-hanging climax with us all wondering what deed of daring-do the hero would perform to extricate himself, the good guys, and the accompanying heroine out of danger. I know for a fact that they cheated on this part of the plot and must have assumed that kids were stupid and didn't have very good memories because the sequence of events leading to disaster at the very end of each episode was usually a bit different when it was replayed for the following one a week later.

One of the regular baddies was a stockily built American actor by the name of Ted De Corsa who could be relied on to get hordes of kids screaming at him by the time he came to a sticky end. His demise would often arrive as he was exuding a vast amount of menace towards the victim while demanding the answer to leading questions about who, what, where or when. The individual under threat would then reply saying something like "I guess you're never going to know the answer to that question" as off screen a gunshot was heard and 'Uncle Ted' would grunt and slowly sink to the floor expired.

Not being worldly wise to the way films were made I had great difficulty at first understanding how it was that he got shot in one serial and then appeared alive and well in another story some time later. The plots were obviously far too realistic for me to think of them other than just that: -real. A similar conundrum occurred in another series about a character called Brick Brabazon and his sidekick Sandy. Apart from the cartoons most if not all the films then were in black and white and I remember that Brick was always dressed in a white shirt and something like grey jodhpurs while Sandy wore dark coloured corduroy trousers and check patterned shirt. I think this story was the first one where I really noticed the deception with linked episodes being different.

Brick was in the back of a pickup truck having a fight with the baddie as it approached an overhanging tree branch. WALLOP! The tree branch caught him and then a brilliant white star filled the screen with a dramatic banner headline 'Next Time: What happens to Brick? Can he survive?' At the start of the next episode he has no contact with the overhanging branch at all.

We see Brick jump clear just in time and the baddie he was fighting got clobbered by the branch instead. It was a swizz. We all saw it, and as one, were disgusted. Well the girls didn't see it but us men did of course and let our feeling be known in no uncertain terms; a loud groan of contempt. Did they take us for idiots? The matter was discussed very seriously on the way home.

As we made the homeward journey through Singleton we were no longer schoolboys. We had all morphed into our favourite film heroes of the day. Buck Rogers with his space ship crew, Buck Jones riding stage coach shotgun, Hopalong Cassidy, Roy Rogers or John Wayne to name but a few. A number of toy shops sold cowboy cap guns which we took with us to the Saturday Club. We were the legends. Nobody thought to frisk us so we entered 'tooled up' or 'carrying' ready for later conflict except for the occasions when an over keen warrior started waving his wooden sword around. These if seen would be held by the management until the transgressor joined his gang for swordplay elsewhere at the end of the show. Some really went in style wearing their guns in holsters.

There was an essential piece of clothing to start with, even if it was a fine day. This was a dark blue or black Macintosh. As we poured out of the cinema arms would slide out of their sleeves and the 'mac' would be draped around the shoulders like a cape and the top button secured. All swordsmen wore capes and we were no exception. Old cornflake packets would be worked on in the week, maybe with the help of an amused parent, carefully fashioned into a knight's helmet or maybe even a silver bucket type helmet to put over your head and transform the wearer into a space robot. Saturday activities received due diligence.

This was serious stuff and the order of whatever replayed battle was often planned forehand. Those who were to die in action had to give their best performance. Now if you're a guy reading this you will appreciate that except on very rare occasions it was boys only. Playing with girls was considered sissy. Things could occasionally get rough but that wasn't the only consideration. The simple fact was that a cap gun sounded pretty unrealistic to us so we all made up our own sounds. These would be made deep in the throat and varied to suit the type of weapon being fired. A cowboy revolver would have a different sound to a bank robber's automatic for instance. There would also be a modified throat sound for a rifle.

Girls were useless at it. Really pathetic and we couldn't have that, particularly if you were in a tank or engaged in an air battle flying a spitfire fighting a Messerschmitt 109 with machine guns. This was a man's world. Girls just couldn't cut it. There was no limit to which the imagination of hordes of laughing and screaming kids could transform the bushy playground. My Druslyn Road paradise couldn't compete.

The thing which made it really work for us was the length and depth of the woodland which was approached up a sloping bank at the Sketty end. Here it was just more or less open ground but the further on you went into it the denser the trees and bushes became until eventually the trees thinned out and the area became more populated by bushes. These spread out across a natural stream towards the open pasture which filled much of the park. At the bottom end of this forest a wooden bridge crossed the stream leading to a gated exit which was opposite the bottom entrance to

Brynmill Park and also next to the start of Brynmill Lane. The lane ran from that point all the way up between both parks and exited on to the main Sketty Road, not far from the top entrance to Singleton.

It was in fact a narrow road that would only just allow two cars to squeeze past at any given point and was bordered for most of the way on both side with a high stone wall. The wall might have been tall but it was no match for our climbing skills. It was a great source of pride to us that on even on some of its highest points we were able to climb over it as a short cut when transferring from Brynmill instead of going all the way down to the gates. There was however a third way for the adventurous, but not used often because not many would dare.

At the top end of Brynmill Park adjacent to the lane was an old farmhouse separated by a surrounding wall. Although inhabited when I first arrived in the area, over time it became abandoned, collapsed and eventually overgrown. Next to the grounds there was what must have at one time been some kind of mill pond bordering the lane and a sluice gate for draining it. Next to the sluice was the entrance to a large pipe of around thirty inches in diameter used for the run off from the pond. This led directly under the lane and came out several feet the other side of Singleton's boundary wall into a wooded area with high earth banks either side.

It was rather cramped, dank and gloomy inside the pipe but if you squatted on your haunches and balanced on your heels you could waddle through to the other side with no problem. It was however not for the faint hearted and on a couple of occasions there were panic attacks necessitating the awkward exercise of turning around in the cramped space and retracing the duck walk; but of those brave explorers that did venture into the pipe, very few turned back.

It is quite illuminating now looking back at some of the cinema space adventure stories to see how naïve they were in depiction of space technology. Buck Rogers and Flash Gordon both had rocket motors that looked like spluttering squibs leaving trails of smoke in their wake and all crews wore helmets and dressed in an assortment of capes and clothing reminiscent of medieval crusaders and peasants. Control stations were wonderful creations with levers and dials and the background sound was beset with unintended thuds as microphones gathered up extraneous noises on the set.

There was absolutely no comparison to present day Star Wars style technology. Time travel through space to another planet using teleportation featured in one story line but without the slick special effects seen in today's Star Trek films. One such transfer was from Planet Earth to a colonised moon with operational headquarters located in some sort of castle. Guarding the ramparts were a bunch of robots that looked more like dustbins with attitude. They wouldn't even have made the grade as Star Wars' R2-D2's Neolithic grandfather. If anyone approached, the robots would extend their arms and move them up and down to prevent passage.

Peter and I were so impressed by them we held long intellectual conversations about their arm action, attempting to emulate it as we tried to stop each other going past our respective front doors. The robot heads were such a simple design that Peter actually soon made a cylindrical bucket mask just like it and wore it as we raced home, capes flying, through Singleton woods. It had slits for eyes and mouth with a triangular projection for the nose just like the original and was very effective until he tripped over a tree root and knocked the nose off. He only put it on afterwards to try and startle Constance when he came to call for me but failed miserably. She only giggled because she recognised the bright red jumper that he wore with his short leisure time corduroy trousers and school socks resting easy around his ankles.

I think the show lasted around two hours with an interval in the middle to get an ice cream or drink. Then after the interval there would be another short film before the last feature. Sometimes the 'shorty' would be some kind of magazine with an on screen book cover opening to take you to places of interest or show some kind of craft like weaving, corn milling, wood turning etc. The feature film was very often a western, with William Boyd as Hopalong Cassidy a firm favourite and Roy Rogers with his horse Trigger a close second. Randolph Scott sometimes appeared looking amused and Lash Larue also put in the occasional guest appearance with many other kinds of stories.

The one thing that always puzzled us in the cowboy films was the chase. Goodies chase the baddies for miles across rocky terrain and a long curved, often very curved, dirt road or track. With the object of the chase being to catch those in front why did the chase party never take a short cut across the curve?

There were comedy films with the likes of Old Mother Riley, Buster Keaton and many others but the one that always drew the biggest laugh were the Laurel and Hardy films. They still make me laugh. Occasionally some of the action characters which were popular in comics were also brought to life on the silver screen like Superman, although I can remember very few films when he was featured. One hero character that was run as a serial was Rocket Man. As I remember it he always looked like a middle aged doctor or businessman dressed in a shabby suit; and I may be wrong about this but I'm almost sure he also used to wear a trilby hat. No fancy dress, cape or super powers either.

What he did have was a leather jacket with a rocket motor on the back and a bullet shaped enclosed helmet which had to be placed over his head like a diver's. In time of need the rocket jacket was put on, the helmet put over his head, usually with the assistance of a distressed female, and he would run out into a field. There always seemed to be a field just when he needed one. With arms outstretched Rocket Man would take a run, adjust the controls on the front of his jacket and dive up into the air as the rocket ignited to power him to wherever he was required to find the bad guys; often tackling them as he came in to land while wearing the full outfit.

A battle would usually ensue with both sides knocking each other around in a fist fight. Kung Fu and Karate round house kicks were a long way off into the future. Well that's the way I remember it anyway. I also remember the copycat attempts at rocket flying with groups of friends on the way home and at other times in Brynmill Park as we followed each other diving into the air one after the other with our makeshift mac capes flying. Were we Rocket Man or Superman? Who cared? Any adults watching must have seriously wondered what we were doing. Were we trying to catch flies?

The Superman depicted in the films of that era bore absolutely no resemblance to the slick portrayals of today. For one thing, when we watched the few movie episodes we saw at the Odeon it was always in black and white, not colour. We never ever saw him change from Clark Kent into Superman like Christopher Reeve did; spinning around in a telephone booth or ripping his kit off while running. Whenever I see that some really silly questions go through my mind like: What happened to the clothes he ripped off ? Are they just left lying around for somebody else to pick up off the floor? Did he get regular easy-rip replacements from a gentleman's shop? What about Clark Kent's glasses? And what about those little red boots that he wears? He must have them concealed inside his shoes and socks and I just keep getting a mental picture of him hopping around on one foot trying to get a shoe off with his cape caught in the telephone box door. Is it just me -or did you ever wonder about those things? It's an image I just can't seem to shake from my mind.

THE PARK

I cannot really stress enough the importance of Brynmill Park and the influence it had on the lives of all the children who lived in the area. Apart from family life it was central to our existence and one of its most abiding features and memories must be the large expanse of open grass with surrounding trees and bushes which abounded there and were central to our play in a safe and traffic free environment.

Peter and I would always play football or cricket there, either by ourselves or with any other boys that were knocking about. If it was a group of us our coats would usually be pulled off and dumped to act as goalposts or failing that some other kind of markers used.

Once a group had assembled, sides had to be picked. This was usually OK, because each of the team captains would have their particular friends, so it wasn't often that there was one left over that nobody wanted – unless they were unknown or completely useless, in which case they would either act as a substitute or take turns on each side. This was not deliberate spite. It was just the natural result if there were an odd number of boys. Nobody was ever deliberately sent into the wilderness. Everyone played when the game started.

Although not a big football fan I did get fitted out with shirt, boots and socks and dad went to great pains to demonstrate how to apply Dubbin wax onto the boots so they would last. I was also given a proper ball one Christmas which I didn't really make proper friends with; it not always obeying my foot commands but seeming to have a mind of its own and where it wanted to go. Playing football did teach me two lessons however; if you can't play well, at least try to look good, and if looking good doesn't get you picked, then lend them your ball!

The balls we played with were not always made of leather but a kind of hard rubber or suitable man made compound .Whatever they were made of didn't matter to most of the players but it did to me because the one thing I found couldn't do was head it without jarring my neck. They bounced off some boy's heads like they were made for each other and it always looked good if a goal was scored. Whenever I tried the result was a headache.

There was no such problem when it came to cricket however. Playing with a proper red leather ball like a real cricket team had its own attractions. Like the satisfying solid sound of it being struck with the bat. Well that is except perhaps for one occasion when it sort of unintentionally got caught it in my mouth when it made a different sound: squashing the top lip onto my two front teeth while making a sort of crunching noise as they snapped in half, spraying blood everywhere as their remains cut through flesh. Mum and dad were not best pleased and for a few days afterwards until dental repairs had been carried out there was a large gap and a constant draught. A group of us had been playing in the lane at the back of a friend's house and learned that fielding slip position standing too close to an inconsiderate batsman was not the ideal place to be. The experience took its toll making me a nervous wreck and I didn't play cricket again particularly with a hard ball, for some considerable time.

In the summer months cricket had quite a following because of the proximity of the grounds at St Helens which was only a few minutes' walk away from anywhere in the Brynmill area. The Glamorgan team had quite large fan base amongst schoolboys because the clubhouse entrance was easily accessible from Bryn Road where we would stand in groups trying to catch members of the two teams for autographs before and after the game. If it was before the match we would then go into the grounds to shout appropriate encouragement to our favourite stars.

When very big games were being played and the grounds were full, or when payment for a ticket was not possible or to be avoided a lot of spectators elected to watch, albeit from some distance This was from the 'The Slip' bridge that crossed the road and railway lines for the LMS and Mumbles train onto the beach.

There were times when it had more spectators using it than people going to the sands.

Playing with Peter in the park we would have a tennis ball and use one of two particular trees to play against as the wicket. They were the only two I remember as being suitable and it was useful to have the pick of two in case one of them was already in use. The best one was positioned by the entrance gate on Oakwood Road.

There was a small cluster of trees there and the one

nearest the path had a narrow trunk and stood nice and straight. It only had one disadvantage and that was if it had rained. It was such a popular tree for cricket that the ground in front had been worn away by the tramp of many feet with the resulting dip collecting rainwater in a large puddle just in front of where the batsman stood and where the ball was supposed to bounce before meeting the bat.

The other tree we used was further across the stretch of grass alongside the bowling green at the Knoll Avenue gate. A much thicker tree it was an easier bowling target and also had a lot of topside foliage which spread out high over quite an area. It was thus in addition to providing a wicket a good tree to practice throwing over and catching. We played many games at both locations taking turns pretending to be England against Australia for 'The Ashes'. Both sides made some surprisingly low scores. Out for a duck was not unknown.

When a group of boys got together it would usually be with a hard ball so that we could be like 'real cricketers' and the game would be played with proper sets of wickets and pads. We all thought we looked good as we strutted out to the wickets, posing at the crease; looking around, eyeing up the fielders and enjoying the moment. I think eventually authority came to bear and hard balls were disallowed. Not so much out of consideration for players but for the presence of other children and members of the public being hit by ambitious boundary strikers.

Most of us had our own favourite position to play, dreaming we had the potential to be as good as the legends of the day like Len Hutton, The Bedser brothers or the legendary old Brylcreem man himself:

Dennis Compton. Some were very keen to bat and would prepare for their moment by swishing the bat through the air in classic boundary smashing strokes or defensive blocking moves.

Bowlers warmed up by performing artistic little flicks of the hand arranging and re-arranging finger grips around the seam of the ball in order that they might deliver the secret googly, deadly off spin or unexpected leg break. Some bowlers, trying to put on a show and frighten the batsmen before actually releasing the ball, started their run up from some distance away, speeding up gradually to run full pelt before letting go. Others, more subtle in their approach, lulled their victims into a false sense of security with just a couple of quick steps and a slow lob to generate the ideal situation for the keen fielder to catch the unintended gift of a miss-hit ball. There was one individual however who was obsessed with wicket keeping. He wasn't local but we saw him occasionally. We heard through the grapevine that he had a regular place in a school junior team. His name was Elliot and he was a real Glamorgan enthusiast, talking cricket even during the rugby season and could recite numerous obscure facts that nobody else was interested in or could even begin to query. It seemed he was always like that from the moment he started playing with us.

What was more interesting however, were the antics he got up to when he was alone behind the hedge of his front garden on Sketty Road. It was a high hedge but it had gaps and he thought nobody could see him - which was a mistake. Two of our cricket crew went to call for him one evening when we were short of a man. He was throwing himself around, diving to catch imaginary balls and then posing behind imaginary wickets to snatch an imaginary 'nicked' ball before sweeping the bails off. We had, I suppose, all done something like that at one time or other but not, as far as we were aware, under the amused gaze of spying spectators. Deciding not to embarrass him the crew changed their minds and just reported back. After hearing about his antics we nicknamed him Stumpy. It wasn't out of spite, we just thought it would be funny and seemed the natural thing to do. It actually backfired on us because nobody remembered that his surname was Woodman and instead of becoming insulted he considered 'Stumpy Woodman' to be a sophisticated play on his name and an accolade to his prowess.

Funnily enough he never grew very tall but did develop a some what rotund figure as he got older thus growing into the name instead of around it and eventually, we heard, taking the title into his adult life because he was so enamoured with it. When he'd actually fielded as wicket keeper he wasn't bad; maybe even good at times but always seemed to look a bit smug. I don't think it ever dawned on him that we were taking the mickey because nobody ever told him they'd seen him play acting in his front garden.

The meadow on which we played had a pathway running along side between the grass and the bushes, and standing waist height to an adult, a wire boundary fence provided a physical barrier. This was a tempting prospect for any athletic types who fancied their chances jumping over it without falling flat on their faces and we would occasionally have a jumping competition to see who would succeed or fail.

Depending from which side you jumped there could be a soft or hard landing. From the pathway would mean a sideways sort of jump with a scissor action of the legs, which wasn't easy to get right and could mean bottling out at the last second. Jumping from the grass was easier because it allowed a good run at it. Fortunately there weren't many times that the top of the fence caught a lazy foot and on the odd occasions that it did no serious physical injuries resulted, only personal embarrassment. Some times we cheated a bit and jumped where the fence was sagging.

The woods and bushes in the park were central to much of our play and ran alongside the two roadways that contained them. One stretch ran alongside Glanbrydan from near Knoll Avenue to meet the top of Oakwood Road and was quite narrow to start with but opened out into a flat wooded area having a mixture of bushes and trees of different sizes and climbability. Among the trees that grew there were some very tall pines, every year shedding their fir cones which we called 'tistie-tosties', collected for the sake of collecting and sometimes painted to use for Christmas decorations. All the trees and bushes became our friends and we got to know each other very well.

The second area of bushes started at the Rhyddings Terrace entrance gate and ran most of the way alongside Oakwood Road. This stretch of vegetation was more densely wooded with a greater number of trees making it ideal for playing Cowboys and Indians because their layout offered so many hiding places. It wasn't always Cowboys and Indians of course; it could be just the good guys versus the bad guys like cops and robbers. If we were gangsters we would talk out of the side of our mouths like they did in the films and sometimes forgot to stop doing it at home; getting told off for talking silly by exasperated parents who "didn't like the influence the films were having on us."

The number of players in our re-enactments varied considerably, especially if we had made friends with any visitors to our patch. It was usually boys only with just the odd exception for a sister who could make good gun noises. The game would always begin with the ritual of picking sides which could a painful and humiliating self conscious experience for those left till last.

For side leaders it helped to know who could make good sound effects, put up a realistic fight and die well; accepting their fate without argument. It all mattered and with impartiality supposedly being paramount, sides would be picked on the turn of a coin or the spinning of a bottle; the latter being accompanied by some sort of rhyme which ended with the words 'iccle occle out.' No, don't ask; I have no idea of its origins.

Even then of course the game didn't always go according to plan and after battle had commenced disputes about being deceased or only wounded would occur. Holding a hand up with middle and index fingers crossed and yelling "PAX" would bring the whole game to a halt. A "NO PAX" ruling at the start was no guarantee that it would be upheld and really fierce arguments could ensue with an exchange of blows not unheard of, some-times resulting in one or more players exiting through the Rhyddings Crescent gate and out into the sunset.

Playing Cowboys or baddies was a complicated affair and if rule clarification was necessary both sides were invited for a meeting by the universally recognised call of "All in all in a bottle of gin." Once resolved it was usually back into action, or a fresh start if anyone had gone home in a huff. A new cry of, "All out all out a bottle of stout." would announce that a settlement had been reached. Yup! Playing Cowboys and Indians or even goodies and baddies, was kinda' complicated.

FLOSSY, TREES, AND OTHER STUFF

Talking about the rules and rituals of play and how visitors to our patch were handled seems to be the ideal moment for introducing the legend of 'Flossy.' Friendships among schoolboys were was quite naturally always in flux. Some lasted and some were only fleeting. With even regular or strong friendships you didn't live in each other's pockets. One week you might be knocking around with, say Clive and Gregory and the following week it might be just Barry or Mike. You might even go around in a foursome which the labellers would call a gang.

This gang of four, perceived by some adults as threatening, might bump into a couple of their other regular cronies and chatter noisily together for a while and then part company. This meeting of minds could more often than not take place in the park but sometimes it would be on the street. At no time however was any member of the public or the neighbourhood under threat.

It was just a group of noisy schoolboys acting like schoolboys do.

Sometimes if one group met another and not everybody was known to each other there might be a sort of awkward lull in the conversation and it was into this sort of situation that someone might, if he was a seasoned veteran of such encounters, throw in the recovery question, "Anyone seen Flossy?"

Who was Flossy? You may well ask. Well Flossy was a rather unkempt character, unruly hair, slightly overweight and about the same age as us. Other than that his movements always seemed a bit exaggerated and he would often gesticulate wildly and nod his head unnecessarily when talking. Well that was how I imagined him anyway. I was sure I'd met him but not quite sure when and where. We all thought we knew him, and that we'd met him and knew what he looked like but really he was a figment of our imagination. We had no idea who he was, who his friends were, where he lived or where he went to school.

We didn't even know his real name and could only assume that he was called Flossy because of his appearance. We as ordinary schoolboys were naturally scruffy and took a pride in it but Flossy was something else. When the question was asked about his being seen it could draw a number of responses.

"Yeah, I saw him last week in Singleton… Yeah, I saw him by the school two days ago with… You know that other kid he always knocks around with." Or "Nah! Haven't seen 'im but I heard he was…" Then there would be some kind of made up story. Just occasionally a newcomer into one of our little gangs would try to give himself some status by inferring that he knew Flossy from way back and that they had lost contact etc., etc. If we saw him give him a message! Well if he had known Flossy fair enough but we didn't and the likelihood of us meeting up with somebody we weren't sure of and passing on a message which might be taken the wrong way could be a bit risky. By the time this ritual had unfolded we had either found something sensible to say or managed to gracefully extricate ourselves from pointless further conversation and move on. That was the legend of Flossy.

For some reason we always seemed to use Oakwood Road woods for gunplay and the top Glanbrydan woods for medieval stuff like King Arthur and Robin Hood. The reason for this was probably because the bottom end of the Glanbrydan woods was not so thick with vegetation and allowed more room for close quarter battles.

In all our play involving conflict we had to have props. When there were guns involved we used the rather limited choice of non-descript toy weaponry bought from the likes of Woolworth's or British Home Stores on Oxford Street; usually six shooter revolvers or pop gun rifles. It was only occasionally that there were toy automatic type guns for cops and robbers games; none of them of course looking like anything but toys.

Occasionally somebody would show up with something a bit more fancy than normal but nobody ever seemed to have a good holster to put the guns in and they usually fell out when climbing trees. A definite problem if you were planning an ambush. The belts were always a bit floppy and not a bit like the ones we saw in films. The only exception to this I saw was one given to a friend by a visiting uncle from the real land of cowboys: America. I remember borrowing it to practice a quick draw like Hopalong Cassidy. But where I wondered could I get one of my own? Then fate kindly intervened.

While mulling over the problem I got taken to visit

an Aunt in Carmarthen and went to the town centre not far from the cattle market. On walking back to her house we passed a shop window which had something on display that made me stop in my tracks causing my father to almost fall over me and complain about me getting under his feet.

It was a life size cardboard cut-out picture of a cowboy wearing something I just had to have; a twin holster gun belt with two matching pistols. The pistols were so good they even had dummy bullets. Pfwoah! Would I look good wearing that or what?

All the other kids would be jealous. They'd all want to borrow my twin holster gun belt but I wouldn't let them. Maybe I might even get to be sheriff of the Brynmill Cowboys, but how? How could I persuade my parents to buy it? I stated my case offering to wash the dishes for a month. "That's very generous of you," they said, "but it might be too expensive."

When I looked puzzled dad said, "How are you going to pay for all the ones you break?"

"But d-a-d."

"I know the twin guns and holster look a bit swanky," he said, "but you don't really need them. If you're a good sheriff you can catch all the baddies with the gun you've got."

I turned to my mother. A bit awkward for her really. She could see how disappointed I was; half-heartedly trying to back dad up but not succeeding. It was a decision I couldn't accept and walked back to my aunt's house in sombre mood to eat cream cakes and trifle for tea. It was a special treat which alas provided no solace at all. I just kept thinking about that gun belt.

I was still thinking about it days later, day-dreaming wondering if and how I might be able to save enough to buy it when I had a brainwave. It wasn't far off Christmas. I wonder... There was one place I thought where I might get lucky. Father Christmas. Yeah, I know, I know, but I was about eight or nine at the time and things were a lot gentler then. Different times when children then were not as mature at that age as they are today and myths and legends survived far longer. Up until then the man in red hadn't let me down so why not give it a try?

I put my proposal to boy's best friend – my mother. Could she help me write a letter stating my case to Father Christmas? Of course in my innocence I thought I was letting mum and dad off the hook but it was still a gamble. They needn't worry about getting it for me. Father Christmas would supply it. The proposition was one she couldn't refuse and readily agreed to. So mum got a nice clean sheet of white paper and an envelope from her posh writing set in the bureau in the middle room and we both sat down at the dining room table to compose a suitable form of words, emphasising that I had been good for ages and that my mother was in agreement that in addition to all the other stuff applied for, I should be rewarded with a double holster and twin six shooter set, if possible complete with dummy bullets.

To help him identify the exact holster set we even let him know that it was at the toy shop in the main street in Carmarthen, just around the corner from the cattle market, and as an afterthought, where my pillow case would be. A sock would be far too small for the holster set and if he wanted to he could forget about the other stuff, including the usual orange and apple; the holster set and pistols would do just fine.

After taking three attempts to write it without

mistakes or any rubbings out I signed it and then put it into an important looking brown envelope, licking the flap and pressing it down firmly to seal it, adding in bold capital letters on the front: TO FATHER CHRISTMAS. Mum then took it very solemnly in her hand and went over to the fireplace. It was an old fireplace and much to my horror she stuck the hand and arm holding my precious letter up inside the chimney.

For a moment I thought she was trying to burn it. Seeing my anxiety she thought I was concerned that she might burn her arm. In reality I was more concerned about my letter bursting into flames than her arm but I didn't tell her that. Anyway the fire was low and it was done quickly without pain.

"There you are", she said. "It's on a little ledge now so either the Good Fairy or even Father Christmas, if he's got time, will come and collect it." I really was a sucker.

At the age I am now time passes all too quickly, but at eight or nine years of age it just dragged by and Christmas day couldn't come quick enough, Christmas Eve I couldn't get to bed quick enough. Christmas morning I couldn't get up early enough and I never heard a thing in the meantime.

What a rotter! No matter how deep I looked into the pillow case: no twin holster gun belt or twin pistol set with matching dummy bullets. There was just an odinary Woolworth's single holster -I can smell it as I write -one with a new revolver, sheriff's badge and a pair of leg chaps. I was obviously not going to be leader of the Brynmill cowboy pack. Not realy a surprise I supposed. My scheme had been a long-shot of last resort but I was still pretty dang gutted by it.

Apart from that disappointment I couldn't really

complain about the contents of my pillow case which were: the usual assortment of annuals like Superman, Eagle and other adventure books, games, a packet of spangles, a box of Dolly Mixtures, a box of coloured pencils, one or two other things: a pomegranate and an apple. The pomegranate was extremely interesting. I distinctly remembered my mother coming home with some fruit and veg from the Uplands on Christmas Eve and pomegranates were part of the deal.

I forgot how many there were but when I checked the fruit bowl on the dining room sideboard it was a lot emptier than it had been, with only one pomegranate and two pears left in it. I knew Constance hadn't eaten a pomegranate because she always made a big fuss using something to pick the seeds out. There was an apple and pomegranate in her pillow case as well. I smelt a rat. We consulted.

In retrospect of course I realised that being four years older than me she must have been in on the deception; not wanting to spoil the magic. When we tackled mum and asked about the fruit bowl and how the contents got in with our presents do you know what she said? Even at that age how could I have been so gullible...?

She said there were lot of children to visit on one night and perhaps he was running a bit short in his sack and decided to 'borrow' from the fruit bowl as he passed it on his way to our bedrooms upstairs after coming down the chimney.

I could have sworn she was trying not to laugh, and my sister, was looking the other way. I was going to ask about Rudolph waiting on the roof but was so confused by then that I let it pass and went to look at my new Eagle annual.

Life carried on but it was however not the end of the matter. Even good porkies get found out. Sometime after Christmas I was in the in the dining room by myself listening to the a variety show on the radio when for some reason out of the blue I decided to have a look up the chimney.

As it happened the fire had not been lit and sticking my hand up the chimney was no problem. I grubbed around and found the ledge on which my letter to Santa had allegedly been placed. I knew it was that ledge because I felt something. Something - like an envelope. That's funny I thought. I wonder what that is. I retrieved it almost in a trance and examined it very, very closely.

Yes! I recognised this envelope; and when I opened it I recognise my letter to Father Christmas. I was really, really confused. Questions had to be asked and I was going to ask them.

"M-u-u-u-m-m-m-m," I yelled at the top of my voice.

She came running wondering what the emergency was.

"Whatever is the matter Bernard?"

"I just found my letter to Father Christmas." How could it still be there I asked her? Why hadn't the Good Fairy or Santa collected it? This was tricky for her.

"Well," she said, "perhaps he was just too busy this year and had to give you a miss." Then quickly to stifle any more questions, "He might not have had time to collect your letter but he didn't forget to deliver your presents did he? If he had to go around all the children to collect their letters first and then come back to make his deliveries it's an awful lot of work for him. And think of poor old Rudolph. He would be tired out making two journeys."

"Was that why I didn't get my twin holster set? Couldn't the Post Office have collected my letter for him?"

She was losing her patience with me. I could tell when she explained that he would have to pay for their service but he didn't have the money because he spent it all on children's presents. I should be satisfied, she said, and glad that he hadn't missed me altogether.

She was really trying to tell me FINITO! I eventually got the message and just said "Oh," and that was more or less it, finally accepting that I would just have to chase down the baddies with one gun and one holster, albeit new ones. However, with the great pomegranate cover up in mind and now my uncollected letter I was beginning to see serious flaws to this Father Christmas thing.

For medieval battles we made our own swords which usually consisted of two pieces of wood forming a long cross. These were sometimes embellished at the short handle end with a binding of string to give better grip and make it more 'snazzy' or, for the really ambitious swordsman a disk would be used instead of the cross piece with a D shaped attachment over the handgrip.

A lot of work went into equipping yourself as a knight, maybe even with your dad's help if you were lucky. Shields too would be made, usually from the side of a large cardboard box with heavy string or rope poked through to form loops at the back for holding. More ambitious ones of plywood were not unusual and occasionally one appeared that was really artistic even displaying a coat of arms. Some of the work that went in to producing weapons was amazing and could take up a lot of time and thought. Nowadays you can buy the whole plastic kit in a pound shop which in some ways is a pity because lot of the fun was in making it for yourself.

A great deal of time was spent making bow and arrows. We'd scour the woods in Brynmill and Singleton to find the right tree from which to make our Longbow like Robin Hood used and a selection of straight arrows. Some of the results were extremely good but after one boy nearly lost an eye parents stepped in and so did the Parky who kept a sharp vigil for arrows in flight to chase down the archers.

'The Parky' was the unfortunate park keeper whose job it was to keep us kids in order and look after things in general with regard to members of the public. I remember for the first few years after we had moved to Brynmill that the one we had was a Mr John who regularly had to chase us out of the woods and bushes. There was never any chance that he would win the battle. There were far too many of us for him to control but I remember he was always firm but fair. He was never ever unkind or nasty.

When others came after him some were not so kind. One individual who was quite young could be most unpleasant; even nasty at times, with a real sourpuss succeeding him for a number of years. We had been very lucky with Mr John. Singleton park was a much larger proposition so we didn't brush with management there much. The one I do remember was a Mr Chips and he always seemed to have a ready smile on his face for us kids.

When Peter and I played together in the Glanbrydan woods it was either a game of King Arthur and his knights or Robin Hood. More often though it was Robin Hood and we'd come equipped to do battle with our home made swords and shields. It would be Robin and Little John against King John and the Sheriff's men with each of us taking turns at being Robin fighting the imaginary foe.

We had as our headquarters a special tree in Sherwood Forest which was located halfway along the thin part of Glanbrydan woods and stood only about seven feet high. It was a very good tree and easy to climb, with branches that were comfortable to perch on, accessed from the meadow by a handy sort of archway formed by large bushes on either side.

There was one very memorable occasion when Peter, who made a very demanding Robin, drove us so hard rescuing imaginary peasants and maidens that even our imaginary comrade Friar Tuck was beginning to look gaunt. Somehow the idea came up that I should now have a turn at being Robin. I decide that we should change tactics and that our happy band of worn out bandits needed a badly earned holiday.

Battle weary from all the skirmishes with the sheriff's men we endured while Peter had played Robin I quite innocently said that I thought our men, they were him and me – all of us, should have some time off battling and skirmishing, relax for a little while and have a break from it all, have an icecream. Bad idea!

He was aghast and let me know in no uncertain terms that it was an utterly irresponsible idea. What if the sheriff's imaginary men turned up in force while we were languishing in the trees and overrun us. I said, "Couldn't we just cross our fingers, put our hands up and shout PAX," then added quickly before he had a chance to admonish me further, "Let's play cowboys or something else."

Fortunately at that moment three more friends and others of our acquaintance arrived on the scene and hearing the tail end of the exchange put in their two pennyworths, not to play cowboys but join forces and play 'Dying'. Peter was also tired of Robin Hood by now so he was quite amenable to the new game but we needed more body volunteers.

That is to say more participants. So we set out to search for any other of our various friends and acquaintances in the park and by the end of our search had rounded up another seven. This was going to be a massacre.

While we had been going around looking, two other boys who we didn't know had set up a tent on the grass alongside the entrance to Sherwood Forest where we had been playing Robin Hood.

Having completed what they were doing they wandered over to our group which was now in heavy planning discussions and in a short while we had two more potential death victims.

Some more ideas for the scenario were thrown around and it ended up with the tent being used as the headquarters of the defending force. There would be one gunner and depending what he could imitate best it he would use either a rifle or a machine gun. Each candidate was tested for reproduction of authentic sound. Dramatic dying was a serious business.

If you are not familiar with the concept it's quite simple. The gunner lies in wait as the victims take their turn at running past him unsuspecting that he is there. He shoots; they die and it has to be as dramatically as possible. James Cagney and Mickey Rooney could have learnt from our intensive art of dying school. We were the best; and the best of the best was the winner of the game and got to play the deadly assassin next time.

Now you may well think what a potentially blood thirsty lot we were with such an unhealthy sounding game. What you have to remember is that we were only reflecting what we saw portrayed in the cinema: cowboy, gangster and war films together with cinema newsreels showing footage of real bombing and combat from the recent second world war and Korea. We had absolutely no understanding of the reality we were enacting in our play. You may also want to consider that the film industry then was not as gory in their portrayal of injuries as they are today and since actors we saw getting 'killed' were seen again in other films perhaps the finality of real death didn't register. To us kids it was really only a game to copy.

We had picked the gunner, a weedy looking boy of twelve who had that morning had a big bust up with his dad and looked generally miserable. That said he did a tremendous impression of a heavy machine gun so he got the job and was just settling himself in position lying in front of the tent when trouble arrived in the form of a boy who we guessed to be six or seven, a mere toddler to us warriors. We hadn't got a clue who he was or where he had come from. He was very timid and just stood there first just watching and doing nothing. Then he decided to crawl into the tent which was a bad move. The boys who had brought it asked him to leave in quite a reasonable manner but he just point blank refused. They became insistent and he became a bit tearful as he eventually crawled back out and ran off in the direction of the park gate where a rather cross looking woman stood glaring.

Obviously his mother, she bent down to talk to him as he turned around and pointed at the troops waiting to be slaughtered. A look of rage erupted on her face and she went scatty, marching over and shouting what a rotten cruel spiteful lot of boys we were not letting her little Frederick play with us. I remember she had a rather long face and the most severe hair cut I had ever seen. All she needed was a broomstick I thought. Having said her piece she then attacked, walking around the tent pulling out the pegs and guy ropes till it collapsed still with three boys inside. Then with one more throw away about 'nasty kids' she was gone. Later I concluded that they must have been visitors because we never ever saw her or little Fredrick again.

We were stunned. Nobody had done anything only her little precious trying to insert himself into our group. I knew girls could be funny; I had a sister. If they were like that when they grew up, I thought, I'd keep well clear of them. I made a mental note to be nice to Constance when I got home.

Think of the future I told myself. When we had recovered our dignity and things had finally settled down after little Fredrick's departure and Mummy's tantrum, we re-erected the knocked down tent replacing the pegs and proceeded to die on the run without further interruption. By the time the game finished it was worse than Custer's last stand and the afternoon's events became a legend.

It was a few days after being involved in this little skirmish that a number of us who had taken part got invited to our first private showing of some cine films in a very posh house somewhere in upper crust Uplands. The invitation was made by one of the tent boys whose father belonged to a film club. The house where it all took place had a large front garden with wide tiered steps, big flower pots either side, leading up to an equally imposing front entrance and hallway.

The projector room, at the top of the house, was arrived at after climbing a couple of flights of stairs enclosed by ornate bannister rails each side. This wasn't a house, it was a mansion. Simon, the boy whose house it was, called it their attic which was three times as long as our front room. "How the other half lived," dad said to me afterwards.

There were about fifteen of us crammed into their home cinema with other friends of the family, including two giggly girls and an older brother who acted as the projectionist. We -the boys from Brynmill -were all on our best behaviour and since we had told our respective parents about the premiere had been made to dress tidy.

We trooped noisily in, sitting on benches, and without much delay the programme started with a couple of silent cowboy movies, on screen dialogue captions and accompanying music for atmosphere, almost like Saturday morning film club at the Odeon and we were soon cheering and jeering.

The cowboy films were followed by Buster Keaton and Keystone Cops comedies to much laughter, all played onto a roll up screen against the far wall. The show was over all too soon. A very enjoyable and unexpected experience in our young lives. It was Something different, and we talked about it all for several weeks afterwards to other kids whenever we got the opportunity for some one-upmanship.

In some ways it was a rather a strange incident getting invited like that because although Simon was a friendly enough sort of individual he wasn't a regular visitor to our patch in Brynmill, didn't go to our school and didn't really know us at all. After the film show we never saw him down in the park again or anywhere else. I suppose that's how things go when you're very young.

His house had seemed enormous to us but to kids of our age then many things seemed big. In later years when visiting Swansea I have been back to the Uplands to try and locate it, just for curiosity, but to no avail. It was in another time, another place, untraceable and part of childhood history.

The patch of grass on which we had played our macabre game was from time to time also used for more peaceful purposes. Being on the opposite side of the path from the mead-ow on which sport was played, it was the ideal setting for Punch and Judy Shows and for a few years the story of the fun loving family man universally known as Mr Punch would be told on balmy summer evenings to entertain enthusiastic local children.

It was here also on two occasions that brass bands came to entertain the general public. They performed on a bandstand constructed of rectangular timber joists and planks bolted together to form the platform. I don't remember much about the band but I do remember that the man in charge of the stand allowed a couple of us to help unbolt it the next morning. It was fun crawling between the joists and we both decided we wanted to be bandstand engineers.

The trees surrounding the meadow also played an important part in our lives; helping pave our way into manhood by allowing us to demonstrate our ability at climbing. The Robin Hood tree was child's play however, a mere prop in the game and there was no kudos to be gained by saying you could climb it.

Some were obviously more challenging than others and the ones where you had to jump up to reach for the first grip were the best. One such tree was set halfway down in the Oakwood Road woods and was quite tall with a reasonably slender trunk. There were a couple of stumpy bits near to the bottom where a foot could be placed before sort of hugging the trunk and shinning up till you could catch the first outward branch. Once a hand hold was acquired you could pull yourself right up onto a perching point and go on from there. After that it was easy and sometimes because the tree was quite tall and accommodating there could be three or four of us balancing on various branches on the way to the top where there was a good view of the surrounding park.

The only risk was that boys in short trousers didn't look much like leaves and twigs; except perhaps for the grubby legs, and line of sight was reciprocal. When we spotted the Parky things could get tricky. If we had a bead on him, you could bet your bottom dollar that he had a bead on us and it became a race to defoliate the tree, make a run for it and lie low till the next time.

Climbing trees hoping to see where he was didn't always pay dividends; as was proven one day when a couple of us were climbing a large pine standing at the end of Glanbrydan woods. Known as the clock tree it was the tallest one there and stood overlooking the enclosed playground where swings and roundabouts were set out.

It was the one everybody wanted to climb but it had a thick trunk and nothing graspable to start the climb at our limited height. Only one stout branch that stood off at a right angle, far out of reach for most of us unless we had enough spring in our step to jump up and grab a hold with both hands, swing a leg over it and pull ourselves up into a sitting position.

If we couldn't do that we cheated, which meant

getting a leg up, either by one of your mates putting his hands together to form a stirrup, or by sitting on someone's shoulders so that when they stood at full height you could reach the first branch. The first day we were able to climb it unaided was a proud one.

On this particular day, probably a Saturday, a group of us were just generally messing around by it when somebody said they needed to be somewhere else, "What time is it?" Nobody had a watch so Peter volunteered to find out. We were expecting him to go and approach someone walking on the path and ask but he must have been practicing his tree climbing on the quiet because he had another idea. He walked over to the tree, jumped up putting an arm over the bottom branch, swung himself up with a flourish and started to climb.

Not to be out done I decided to follow, having to take several attempts before I was able to haul myself up and go after him. Once at the top Peter would be able to see in the distance the clock tower of the Guild Hall. That's why we called it the clock tree.

He was well ahead of me, having still some way to go, when there was a flurry of activity below and then the gruff commanding tone of the Parky, "Come on you boys. You know you're not supposed to in here or climbing trees." Woops! Where had he come from? Peter by this time was lost among the branches above. How did he know we were in the woods? Had he been lying in wait or had somebody snitched? It didn't matter; we'd been knobbled. As he herded our gang out of the woods he looked up the tree seeing me trying to hide and added another prisoner.

After Mr John had finished wagging his finger at us and laying down the law we huddled together where we played cricket in the middle of the meadow; swapping tales, trying to best each other over the trauma of being chased out of the woods by the parky. As we did we suddenly realised that somebody was missing. Where was Peter? "There he is, "just coming through the gate." And there he was, just nonchalantly strolling over with a big grin on his face and not a care in the world.

He explained that he had just reached the top of the tree when he heard the commotion below. The foliage had done a good job of concealment and rather than risk being seen, by poking his head out to look below, he had leant in over the centre branches and become a twiglet until everybody had gone, climbing back down when the coast was clear. Seeing us in the distance but not knowing if Mr John was still around he had used our emergency escape route, a thick bush with heavy branches lying directly against the bottom railings bordering the corner at Oakwood Road. You can't beat effective planning. Jumping over onto the pavement he'd just walked back along to the gate and made his grand entrance.

Different trees might mean a different climbing technique and for several years I had tried to climb a conker tree out in the meadow which leaned quite heavily to one side. It stood next to another much bigger one which was completely un-climbable; there were no footholds at all. The only way you could make a start on the leaning tree was to take a run at it hoping to get far enough to grab onto something and then pull yourself up between the thick fork where the trunk separated.

Unfortunately the bark was either too slippery through damp or too sticky with sap and it took a long time to overcome these obstacles. Most of us who tried had many slips and slides and urgent jumps back onto the grass before succeeding but we persevered. It was just the challenge and another tree conquered.

Thinking about it now I don't remember ever doing much actual climbing at all in Singleton Park even though the woodland there was much bigger, running all the way down to the bottom entrance off the Mumbles Road. The only tree I can remember specifically was one that had fallen to straddle a freshwater stream we occasionally drank from and dared each other to jump across when we were feeling confident.

I suppose it could have been that the trees all seemed much taller and with being so spread out didn't have the friendliness of Brynmill woods except for when hordes of us came charging through with our mackintosh capes flying after Saturday morning cinema. Other times we just basically messed around in general. The freshwater stream we jumped stretched from the top half of the woodland all the way down almost to the end of the bottom meadow. From the Brynmill gate entrance it would meander at a varying width and depth alongside a rough path from which we would seek out crossing points and try not to fall in. It finally disappeared into a large open mouthed concrete pipe diving at a sharp angle down into the ground behind some railings. We always wondered where it went to but never did find out.

For some reason, I don't know why, although we were in such close walking distance to the beach, we never used to frequent it that much. When we did wander down there in our own little groups we always seemed to end up watching long lines of goods wagons trundling and rumbling behind the various panting steam engines on the LMS line that separated the Mumbles Road from the beach. Standing with our faces pressed through the railings we waved at the engine driver and counted the wagons which seemed to go on forever, giving up well before the last one had rolled past if it was more than fifty.

In the intervening years the secret caves, tunnels and passage ways formed by our imagination in the densely packed bushes and trees that were our Brynmill playground have all now gone. With woodland foliage considerably thinned out the magic places they generated have disappeared forever. Where once they stood now seems lifeless; tidier perhaps but with something missing. Is it just because I am now an adult that the remaining trees no longer beckon to be climbed as they used to and stand alone and uninviting?

I just know that children will not play in them as we did. Each generation is unique and adapts to use their surroundings to what they know in their time. For our childhood it really was a very special place and time and a wonderful world to play in.

THE ART OF FISHING

I first started fishing in Brynmill Lake a few years after we had settled in the area and had played in the park many times before my first foray there with rod and line. I was always drawn to the big pond, having on a few occasions been on the motorboat that chugged around it giving rides to the general public.

Although fishing appealed to me I was not allowed to participate until considered old enough not to fall in, by which time of course I had regularly found my way over the railings or fence that separated the pond from the path without disaster. On one occasion my mother turned up to find both myself and my sister lying face down next to the pond stretching out trying to retrieve a stick that was floating past.

I think we were both grounded for a week after that little episode but things eventually settle down and I started fishing after one of the older boys said that he would keep a wary eye on me.

Before graduating to the big pond in Brynmill I had spent some considerable time at two other smaller ones in Singleton Park. The main and larger one was located towards the Sketty end and set in an open expanse of pasture that fronted the Swiss cottage style residence of the park manager. The second pond was next to the Mumbles Road at the bottom end of the park and was much smaller with the limited attraction of catching just a few sticklebacks in our hands to put in a jam jar and take home.

The one by the Swiss cottage however was covered in lily pads with a few clumps of reed dotted around the edges where it was shallow. It held a lot more interest for us and permitted paddling out to see what we could catch in our fishing nets once shoes and socks had been removed. With younger children this would often be done under the watchful supervision of a mother or older sister on Saturday mornings and afternoons.

I think it was Constance who first took me to see that pond which, although not very large, provided a home for various species of ducks, moorhens, and a few species of fish such as roach, rudd, a few carp, and if you looked in the right place, a lot of tadpoles.

Catching sticklebacks and tadpoles was the most popular pursuit for most of the children who came to visit. These were caught with nets fixed to the end of a bamboo stick but the tadpoles were taken home in a jam jar for transfer to a much larger one begged from local sweet shop owners by busy mothers nagged into visiting them. The display jars were then used as a tadpole habitat in our back gardens where we watched them slowly morph into frogs, only to find they had vacated their property one morning to seek more convivial surroundings.

There was an abundance of creepy crawlies and insect life with colourful dragonflies to inspect al around the pond. I did try my hand at fishing for roach and rudd, casting out into the deeper water with a rod that my father made for me with some square section timber he had in the garage, using picture hook eyes screwed in at intervals for line guides. This hunting stick was completed with a three inch wooden reel from Atkinson's in Oxford Street, then the main fishing tackle shop in Swansea.

Bait was either bread paste or a dough made with flour and water. I could have used worms but didn't really fancy fiddling trying to thread them on my hook, although they might have made some kind of difference to my quest because frustratingly neither paste nor dough succeeded in attracting any fish. Weeds and lily pads I caught regularly, often losing a hook and float in the process. Even so, I still found the experience of just standing there waiting in expectation an enjoyable one and a number of early friendships were forged around that pond with like-minded souls of similar age.

On a number of occasions when I was a few years older, I stayed behind when it got dark as the park ranger carried out his last patrol before closing the gates. There was a large tree that stood beside and overhung the pond which was the ideal cover to hide behind and I would emerge with my rod, by this time a proper one, when I was sure he had gone, and start fishing for carp.

When it came time to leave I would have to find may way in the dark first across the open expanse of grass and then negotiate my way through dense woodland to exit by climbing over the boundary wall along Brynmill Lane. Not as easy as it sounds with all the fishing tackle I had acquired by then.

The business of staying behind after 'closed gates' was always risky and I don't know what would have happened if I had been caught inside after hours. Probably eternal banishment.

One thing I did find out was that hanging around in a pitch black park is really creepy, with strange rustlings and scurryings only making it worse with my over active imagination constantly seeing the park ranger's shadow leaping out at me from the blackness. I did judge it worth the risk for the few occasions I did stay though because my efforts were rewarded with a couple of three or four pounders. But as to regular illicit forays I decided it was just too creepy!

It was not far from this pond and on the same stretch of pasture that, I think it must have been around nineteen fifty five, a heavy fall of snow came which in a couple of days morphed into a thick sheet of ice that lasted for a couple of weeks.

The news soon got around and before long it was a magnet for all who wanted to risk life and limb on the slippery sheet of speed. I joined in the fun first with my sister and then with a number of my long term friends and like everybody else took long runs at it to slide on the smooth surface, ruining a perfectly good set of shoes in the process my father later told me.

Not too far from this sheet of ice was a hilly slope covered in deep snow providing a ready-made toboggan run and crowded with people of all ages having the best snow fun that had been had in Swansea for years. There were a whole host of home made and more professionally built sledges and I also saw the reality of what I had only ever before seen depicted on Christmas cards and cartoons: large rolling snowballs, and I mean LARGE, that could knock you over as they came tumbling down the hill. It was cold but we just didn't care.

There's no fun like snow fun! Eventually and predictably over a couple of weeks it melted away and we just had to hope that it would be the same the next year but it wasn't. Sometimes really good things like that only happen once.

Thinking about it now I remember that it was on this same hillside that a fenced off patch of Foxtail barley grass stood and where Wynford, Alan, and I had occasionally visited on warm days in summertime. The attraction was the sticky buds on top that could be broken off and thrown like darts and we chased each other around like idiots until we were completely exhausted and then collapsed to lie on top of it.

After we had lain there for some time we would roll around crushing the stems beneath us to see how much of the barley heads would cling to our clothes and then spend considerable time trying to get the bits off. It was only later that we would notice the sting of the skin rash we had also collected. OK it was daft but we were kids. What else could you expect?

June the sixteenth was a very important day to many like-minded individuals all over the country. It was a special day because it was the official start to the course fishing season and it was soon apparent that there was a band of brothers from all over Swansea, all ages, shapes, sizes, professions and trades, well turned out, scruffy and somewhere in between, who visited Brynmill lake on a regular basis, and an easy camaraderie of those with common purpose soon developed.

We all had our favourite places with many different nooks and shrubberied crannies creating their own individual ambiance that, we convinced ourselves, were harbouring monster fish waiting in line to get onto our hooks. Some locations would have overhanging trees that induced shadow, some remained calm and undisturbed on the surface in a breeze while other areas would become rippled.

The most popular place was a corner of the pond that had a reed bed and was divided off by a wire fence stretching across to the far bank several yards away. 'The Reeds', as they were known, were a natural habitat for fish anyway but the main attraction was the divided off area called the breeding pond. I never did establish if this was official but everybody called it that because fishing was not permitted on that side of the fence; its popularity was due to the presence of the many large Carp that sought refuge in it and could be seen floating around taunting us on or just below the surface.

Some were so big we wondered how we would cope if we did catch one. It was a very warm sunny day in the middle of summer when we found out. The whole incident was extremely bizarre and lurked in background conversation for months afterwards.

Float fishing for surface carp was a waste of time so we used bread crust instead, fixed directly on to the hook. Three off us had been trying to entice a group basking on the sunlit water between the reeds and the far bank. The wire mesh netting dividing off the breeding pond was close and so was a flotilla of Ruddy ducks that were seemingly intent on disturbing them. After twice having had to remove, renew and recast our floating crusts all seemed well with the world as the feathered galleons eventually set sail for less troubled waters. We should have been looking elsewhere. I should have been paying more attention.

Suddenly my rod, which had been resting on a stand, started to take off across the reeds and I only just managed to get a hold and prevent it being hauled across them and into the water. There was a very strong pull the other end which I started to play.

Was this my giant Carp - my moment of destiny - my moment in Brynmill history?

Yes; but not the kind I was hoping for. Fate had singled me out for humiliation and embarrassment yet again. A sudden commotion on the other side of the fence enclosing the fishing area from the general pathway and a number of people were shouting and pointing. They were all pointing at a large noisy, airborne Ruddy duck. The same one that was tugging away at my rod to which it had become attached via my floating bread crust. Not a Carp then. Too busy watching the receding flotilla on our side of the fence we had failed to notice my crust drift up against it and the airborne protesting mass of feathers had poked its stupid beak through, swallowed the bait and then taken flight.

We were both in a no win situation and after a few minutes of eternity, see sawing back and fore, the line finally snapped and the duck gained its freedom. I knew it was going to be bad when for some time afterwards my comrades in arms greeted me with a verbal quack every time we met up. So if anybody I didn't know asked about the legend of the flying Carp I just kept my head down and played dumb.

Suffice to say that the duck suffered no ill effects, having been caught later in the day and the hook removed from its beak by one of the park keeping staff.

Fishing took up nearly all of my spare time. It was just like an addiction, spending every hour possible standing at the lakeside. The strange thing was that even without catching anything it didn't really matter when you were amongst other like-minded people, they would often be physically spaced out allowing you to meditate in your own solitude alone with your thoughts. I got used to that. It didn't bother me at all, I found it very relaxing to watch the float and just let my mind drift.

Bad weather wasn't really a problem either because hunters of fish always had the necessary positive attitude that something would eventually be caught otherwise they wouldn't be doing it. When rain occasionally hammered down, we almost welcomed it if the fish hadn't been biting, saying that it would re-oxygenate the water and start a feeding frenzy. No it did not. It just made the water wetter and soaked our clothing while the birds started singing with renewed vigour. I wondered what they were saying. Were they tweeting one another?

"Hey there robin. Did that shower ruffle some of your scraggy feathers or what?"

"Oi! You watch your cheeky beak sparrow or I'll get blackbird to knock you off your twig."

In spite of the weather we remained stoic, kept calm and carried on fishing while people said uncomplimentary things about our mental capacity.

THE MAN WHO DRESSED IN TWEED

There was a real mix of characters of all ages but the one that sticks in my mind was Tommy Southport. He was a retired gent of indeterminate age who lived within easy walking distance of the park. Weather permitting would turn up several days of the week fully equipped to do battle with whatever he could catch.

With a sense of deference to the fish he had raided his country wardrobe and put together a uniform of green tweed suit with matching tie and pork pie hat -fly hooks randomly inserted in various places, brown or green woolly socks and a pair of well worn dark brown brogue shoes. It was not what he wore that fascinated us however, it what he brought with him in the way of equipment.

A fold up stool, large knapsack or kit bag, a keep net and landing net, and of course his split cane fishing rod which in common with a lot of other rods was broken down into two or three pieces for carrying in a cloth bag. The contents of the kit bag though never ceased to amuse us. But before I talk about his fishing methods I should perhaps describe a couple things about the pastime and some of the tackle for those not familiar with it.

The basic equipment was a rod made of bamboo

cane, split cane or hollow metal tubing with fibre glass also starting to become popular. Most fishing rods that we used around the lakes and ponds would be two or three piece connected by push-in ferrules. Reels for storing line were made of wood, metal, plastic and the recently introduced Bakelite material with a new revolutionary design that allowed it to spool off without restriction.

For course fishing in a freshwater pond bait could be bread paste, consisting of bread wetted and mixed into a dough, bread flake, which was a piece of bread squeezed around the hook, flour and water mixed into a dough, worms or maggots. Tommy had a large tin of maggots.

Occasionally the fish used to take a fancy to something different. I remember a couple of years when the season opened at the same time as a plague of flying ants occurred. They were all over the place, everywhere and we experimented with securing them around our hooks with cotton or small rubber bands. Hooks were set no more than a foot from transparent plastic bubble floats and cast out from the bank to where carp were basking next to some brown surface weeds that had taken up residence in that part of the lake.

I think one carp of reasonable size was caught the first year but we usually managed to frighten them off as we got too excited, striking early, so that they weren't hooked properly and broke free. The next time the flying ants came we tried again and also experimented with floating bread crust but with limited success, catching only a few small carp while the big ones remained canny.

Whereas a number of us had ambition and were

interested in catching quality fish in the form of big carp Tommy had set his sights on quantity. In this respect he must have been the most successful of us all. If he sat out in open ground next to a pathway a small crowd of both children and adults would soon gather around on the other side of the fence watching his every move. It didn't take him long to start hauling fish in and they would watch agog as he dropped them into his keep-net. This was another piece of equipment which was used to confine the catch until it was time to go home. Although the rules of freshwater fishing then required all fish to be thrown back into the water it was permitted to keep them temporarily while you were at the lakeside. For this a mesh net made of suitable material was mounted around a number of tubular hoops which hung down into the water as a temporary prison.

Tommy's ability to fill the keep-net was down to a particularly sneaky weapon he would deploy as soon as he sat on his stool. It was contained in what we laughingly referred to as his half ton bag. This was his own particular mix of ground bait consisting of already wetted grain, fine crumbs of stale bread and maggots to sweeten it up. As an opening ritual several handfuls of this magic mix would be thrown in while he was setting up his tackle instilling us with a mental picture of the fish grapevine signalling "Grub up – Tommy's free feed."

There was a standing joke that if the lake was ever drained they would find mountains of the stuff in front of wherever he had been sitting. You could almost visualise the sudden underwater disturbance as tiddlers from around the lake raced to get their rations. He never went home without having caught a fish and even if it only weighed a few ounces any unknowing onlooker would always get the impression that it was a monster. This was because the rod he used was a three piece built cane job really designed for fly fishing which didn't take much pull to bend almost double.

Apart from this entertainment value he also served as a trade supply post to schoolboy anglers like myself and others who suddenly found themselves in need of a number sixteen or larger hook in an emergency. The emergency was usually that we had snagged our line in a tree or the reeds, or some other disaster when casting.

It was never, unfortunately, a broken line due to a monster fish that was too much to handle. In one of his l a r g e knapsack compartments he had two largish wallets. In one of them was a selection of hooks of various sizes already attached to a fixed length of gut or nylon of about six inches with a loop at the end. These could be tied to the line which had recently lost the original. The second wallet contained about twenty different quill floats up to about four inches in length, each sporting various coloured bands at the top. Hooks and floats would be sold to us at the drop of a hat and he was a skilled price negotiator.

He didn't over charge but had a memory like an elephant if you were short of cash at the time of purchase. If you didn't turn up for a month after 'borrowing' a hook or float your face would be lodged in his memory till you showed up again. Even at a distance he had eyes like a hawk and would exclaim "Hey! I want to see you." And invariably he did and got his money after a scolding for avoiding him. He was also helpful when he could be. One of life's gentlemen and a real character.

There were of course other places to fish apart from

Brynmill and the occasional jaunt to Singleton. One well known venue was Cockett Pond which was reputed to hold some very large carp. Unfortunately however it also had treacherously sloping sides surrounding it and there had been a few drownings over the years with people falling in from its high banks which made rescue and climbing back out difficult, so it wasn't a realistic option. Whilst wondering where else to go I had one of life's chance encounters in the park and became re-acquainted with an early boyhood friend from Druslyn Road.

Cedric had also moved to the east side of the town and found his way to Brynmill where he too got hooked by the fishing bug. Luckily his father had a car and it wasn't long before we joined forces to go fishing at Llandrindod Wells which at that time was un spoilt by commercial interests and unlike Cockett had flat and level grassy wooded banks surrounding it. So we had a number of enjoyable outings and warm summer days catching decent sized roach and rudd from Llandrindod's reeded waters instead. As things turned out I didn't get to explore any other fishing venues except for two small ponds in an open meadow which I found by chance with two friends. I'll tell you about those later and that's a totally different story.

SAINTS AND SINNERS

Not long after we had landed in Brynmill another call on my valuable time manifested itself. Before we left West Cross I had fleetingly been introduced to the local Sunday School with my sister. I really don't remember much about it except that it was just a corrugated tin shed which was painted a dark shade of green. What denomination the tin shed was I don't know but after we moved to Brynmill we were shanghaied very quickly and directed, much against my will, to a much posher stone built version. To get to the tin shed Sunday school from Druslyn Road used to involve quite a long walk to the bottom of the hill, then along Bellevue Road and up a turning to the far end of a lane.

At our new home it wasn't long before there were whispers of a strange religious sect that wanted to take us into their care. What was a 'sect'? It sounded sinister. Why did they want to take care of us? I thought mum and dad were doing alright but much to my dismay I found out that it was mum and dad who had organised the whole thing with the local chapel. Just a few minutes from where we lived; it was far too close.

No child new to the district was safe.

Within a couple of weeks of our arrival they came

for us. 'THE BAPTISTS'. Even the sound of it scared me half to death. There were two of them. A man and a woman. There was no escape. We didn't stand a chance. Although old enough by now to protest, which I did quite often, my father wanted peace on a Sunday so his word ruled.

We had to go to the services in the morning and Sunday school in the afternoon. A weekly routine which, although I never acquired religion myself, was maintained regularly till I left Swansea in my mid-teens to take up an engineering apprenticeship in another part of the country.

There were numerous and regular social activities associated with the chapel. For the teenagers there was the youth club which provided for table tennis and billiards with a three quarter size table, the latter much fought over by the boys. Snooker was not as popular then as it eventually became but what we had was sufficient and usually played without too many arguments. One of the most enjoyable events for the younger children was the annual Sunday school trip which went to either Port Eynon or Ferryside beach on the Gower coast.

This usually took place on a Saturday when we would all turn up with our sandwich boxes, buckets and spades, cricket bats and balls and other seaside props and stand in line to board the double decker bus hired from South Wales Transport. A real treat with a bus all to ourselves and no bus conductor to ask for our fares. I know for a fact that the adult chapel members who came along enjoyed the outing as much as the kids and took a full part in the beach activities.

It seemed strange to see the chapel minister minus his sombre sermon face and dog collar joining in and having just as much fun as everybody else. Port Eynon was known for its high sand dunes with free running sand which on the steeper ones you could slide down especially when sitting on something like a tray. After the dunes had been slid down to our hearts content and our specially saved pocket money had been spent there was beach cricket, football, rounders and catching the ball to keep us occupied until it was time to leave.

On the homeward journey there was the last Sunday school trip ritual of boisterous singing of anything and everything with an occasional hymn thrown in for good measure. The homecoming was another familiar part of the proceedings with the retelling of many different versions of the day's happenings which was again repeated next morning from the pulpit so that the rest of the congregation did not feel excluded.

They were indeed memorable times with chapel celebrations at any opportunity, including the harvest festival when the local bakers would demonstrate their craft by making loaves of bread in the form of corn sheaves and fruit, and other local traders donated a selection of real fruit and vegetables that together would be made into an attractive eye catching display in front of the pulpit.

For several years in an adjoining hall there would be an annual Operetta performed by children from the Sunday school and a New Year's Eve Special when all chapel members would put on a concert of comedy sketches and musical interludes culminating in the welcoming in of the New Year at midnight with the singing of Auld Lang Syne. It was not very often that children stayed up that late in those far off times so for me especially it was a rare treat. Television however was soon competing for viewers and sadly these volunteer concerts eventually ceased.

When we first joined the chapel it was all new and at first a little confusing as to what was going on. It was a grey stone building, large and imposing and one of the biggest I had ever been in up till then. Inside was a very high ceiling, right up in the roof with all the wooden support trusses visible. Both upstairs and on the ground floor, in a central section and along each side, were rows of wooden benches called pews with two gangways leading down the front to two mysterious doors standing each side of a raised platform. The platform was called the pulpit, facing the people and where a man called the minister stood looking down at them, the congregation, and talked a lot. It was almost terrifying, as were all the grown ups sitting in the pews; people I had never seen before. They had never seen me either and kept looking my way, prompting me to take a lot more interest in my inside suit jacket pocket so that I didn't have to look at them and they hopefully wouldn't be able to see me. After a while, when I had become more familiar with it all, one of the things which began to hold my attention was the ritual performed by the chapel secretary who was a retired elderly gentleman. Each week the minister would make the declaration that the chapel secretary was going to make his weekly announcement of forthcoming events.

At some time in his life the old gent with the title had either received some leg injury or may have been suffering from gout, I don't know which; I was just an observer. Whatever it was the impairment gave him a pronounced limp as he left his pew at the back of the chapel to make his way up the isle and stand in front of the pulpit to address the congregation. They were usually more or less the same announcements every week except for Easter, the harvest festival, Christmas and one or two other specials. He held his notes in front of him as he walked, the important looking pieces of paper on which were written the futures list, shuffling them about before telling us how exciting chapel life was going to be.

He would always finish with a flourish by looking around the congregation to tell us that their "free will offerings would now be taken". At first I used to let what he was saying merge into the background but eventually when I began to take notice of the message it actually took me some time to figure out exactly what he was talking about.

Who was 'Will'? Was he being held captive somewhere nearby? Had he been kidnapped and were they looking for contributions to the ransom demand or maybe volunteers to find him and set him free?

The imagination of a small boy has no limits and for a while it was quite mystifying. When you are new you don't like asking too many questions in case people think you're a bit thick, or as they say in Wales: 'twp'. Eventually I decided that it was just the admission fee because the collection baskets would then be passed around to gather the booty.

The thing I noticed most about the secretary though was his limp. Seen through the eyes of one small boy at that time, anybody with a limp was someone to behold. I had an uncle who had a very stiff limp involving the whole leg and I used to practice copying it whenever I could. The secretary's limp was not as stiff as my uncle's however and therefore not in the same calibre but it did single him out from the rest of the congregation and in my eyes gave him extra status.

Occasionally we would get visiting clergy; either a minister from another chapel or a lay preacher. Some of the full time preachers could be pretty boring and seem to drone on about nothing in particular just to pass the time, but one of them got my attention when he started talking about the rewards in heaven.

The word reward was what did it. I knew about rewards. It meant money and I'd heard announcements on the radio about rewards being paid for information. Just how much money would be paid and what sort of information could I give this minister for him to pass along for my reward? It was very confusing; they just don't explain these things properly, do they?

Lay preachers were usually mature individuals who had been given an opportunity to come from some remote village to attack heathens from the big town and it was not unusual for them to get quite carried away with their own oratory and rip into the congregation with gusto -a practice which sometimes brought unexpected consequences.

I suppose the advantage for any visiting minister or lay preacher was that sermons do not usually include audience participation in the form of debate and vocal opposition to what is being said. The accused, the congregation, are usually pretty docile.

I remember one particular individual who came to spread his own version of 'the word' from somewhere out in the sticks where his kind of fire and brimstone had already terrorised the local population into submission because he obviously believed that he could instill the same fear into us. Physically he was very slight in build and had a pronounced Adam's apple which bounced up and down in his throat as he poured out his venom. He started his sermon by leaving the pulpit so that he could stand and look into the whites of our sinners eyes from ground level. Slowly he built his message into a condemnation of all of us who did not attend chapel every night of the week.

According to him we should have been in the "House Of God" begging forgiveness for our sins whatever they might have been. The culmination of his accusation was that we had instead spent our time "consorting with the devil, propping up the bars in local hostelries while gambling, playing darts, playing skittles and drinkin' alco'l." The men he added, in the company of their women who were "Jezebels dressssed in rrred!" He hissed this last statement at us - emphasising, prolonging and rolling the words for dramatic effect.

Unfortunately although long on rhetoric he was short on vision and hadn't noticed one of the chapel's oldest lady members, a stalwart since time began, sitting in one of the back pews. It was rumoured that she was well into her eighties and now being somewhat infirm did not attend regularly. That particular day was an Easter Sunday and she had arrived dressed to kill wearing a bright red outfit with matching hat and gloves. Her biggest mistake however was to sit in the back row of pews. This is a dangerous thing to do in a Baptist chapel if there is the slightest possibility that you might get a mention. What happens is that absolutely everybody in the chapel will turn to look at you.

Suddenly without warning it must have seemed that a thousand eyes were looking at her, the chapel harlot, from all directions. The poor dear froze and no one could blame her. She endured the stares until at the first opportunity, when the congregation stood for the last hymn; she quietly slid out from where she was sitting and disappeared through the vestibule door and out into the night. I don't think she ever recovered from the attention and was not seen again for some time.

We had quite a few visitors coming to give their versions of the world as time passed and occasionally went to other chapels to see how they spread the message in their particular area; but it was the clergy who came to us that had the greatest impact.

A number of years after the visit of the "'Jezebel" preacher we had a fully-fledged minister come amongst us. He was unlike any that we had been blessed with before. Some of the older ladies were getting quite excited and were heard to say that he was even handsome. I called him the nodding donkey.

From memory I would guess him to have been in his mid-fifties, almost six feet in height, with greyish white hair swept back over what was in polite circles referred to as a high forehead. He stood there ready in the pulpit -ready to deliver unto us his sermon. It was a sermon which was to begin like no other.

Stock still, evaluating, looking at us, a full congregation, first looking to the right side of the pulpit, and then to the left, slowly nodding his head while doing so and displaying his magnificence for all to see. He then began with a question -giving it to us with both barrels so to speak, which in one fell swoop utterly devastated his expectant audience. "Have you?" he said, stopping as though unsure of himself, and then again repeating the question. "Have you ever done anything…really dirty?"

Time stood still. Not a sound was heard except for one strangled slowly expiring gasp from a pew at the back as the rest of the congregation all sucked in their breath at the same time causing a rapid depletion of the chapel's cavernous oxygen supply.

Suddenly everybody was looking down as though a full house had been called at bingo night. It was as profound an exhibition of collective Baptist guilt as you could ever imagine. Nobody dared to look at the person sitting next to them and I had a fleeting mental picture of the red-dressed chapel harlot slowly sliding off her pew and onto the floor in a dead faint. In one sense I thought it was fortunate that she had passed through the pearly gates a year or so previously.

Mr Magnificent stood there, smug and unrepentant, fully aware of the damage he had just inflicted. In retrospect I concluded that he was a twisted wind up merchant and this must be what he was probably known for on the preaching circuit. What were we supposed to think of a question like that? We asked ourselves: What does he know? Who has he been talking to? And most of all, who the hell invited him here? Who on the chapel committee should we burn at the stake?

Some of the chapel elders were beginning to look distinctly hot under the collar by the time he continued his quest for truth but the damage was done.

Things would not be, could not ever be the same but, oblivious, he continued. "What I mean is" he said, no doubt sniggering to himself, "You know, you've done some really filthy dirty chores around the house or garden, or even maybe at work and your hands have become covered in grime but no matter how much soap you use or how hard you scrub it seems impossible to get them clean…" And so he went on to the bitter end, absolutely nobody caring or listening to a word.

Everybody wanted to get out of there and go home. When the service finished there was a subdued stampede out through the doors and almost nobody stayed to mingle as was the normal custom. It was a long time before another minister came to visit and by which time I had moved away.

Unlike many in Wales which either stand derelict, have been converted to other use or demolished completely, the chapel I attended as a boy still remains, open for business and carrying on its mission trying to save sinners and hopefully succeeding.

IMPRESSIONS OF SCHOOL

As well as Sunday chapel attendance there was another more regular call on my time five days a week. This of course was school attendance, the highlight of which was Friday afternoons in both infant and junior schools, each only a ten minute walk from the house.

The infants' school had only female teachers. It was only when we moved up to the juniors, a whole year of us being marched from one school to the other in a long line, that we came under the control of both male and female staff. Before making the move however we were taught the children's anthem under the sheltered part of the school yard when it rained during play time. 'Incy Wincy Spider' was sung with great gusto doing all the actions and conducted by the headmistress.

The reason Friday afternoon sessions were so memorable was because they were set aside for comics and not true education in the sense that we had to sit and listen to the teacher. The logic possibly being that with comics we got familiar with reading because we were more willing to pursue that kind of subject matter than the official curriculum.

Comics were a big part of our life at that age for both boys and girls although of course boys were far more familiar with their reading material than the sissy girls stuff. Cowboy comics ruled the roost with the boys taking along their various and sometimes extensive collections in brown paper carrier bags. Roy Rogers, Kit Carson, Buck Jones, John Wayne, Hopalong Cassidy, Gabby Hayes and many others of that era. There were three that stick in my mind because of their slightly different theme.

These were Lash Larue, the cowboy who would use a bullwhip to disarm his opponents with a flick of the wrist, Batman looking after Gotham City and Superman looking after the world. The Batman and Superman stories were complete rubbish of course but "Superman and the Fighting Cheese" I think took the biscuit!

Presented in black and white they were either around A4 size or slightly larger, especially if they were of American origin, and a smaller but thicker version around half the size; the smaller versions serving less popular heroes like Buck Jones, Kit Carson and War stories. Between both morning and afternoon lessons and lunch break there was playtime which for boys was spent in manly pursuits pretending to be airplanes, tractors, trucks or lorries.

The playground was a hotbed of improvisation for us to drive around, in or on whatever we wanted to be; telling each other exactly what we were driving – "I'm a tipper lorry, I'm a tractor, I'm the bus," and so on, making the appropriate arm and hand movements which in some cases could be fancy interpretations and nothing like the reality.

Almost imperceptibly in the classroom we were indoctrinated into the fact that we were Welsh which was different to being English, although we spoke English and not Welsh. This became even more confusing when our teachers told us that because both English and Welsh people lived on an island called Britain, we were also British, as were Scottish people who lived in another part of Britain called Scotland; somewhere else on the same island. Apparently the men in Scotland regularly wore a sort of heavy skirt called a kilt instead of trousers. We found that very interesting, men wearing skirts. Interesting but funny. Not only were we Welsh and British; we were also known as Celts because of our 'Celtic history' whatever that was, which we shared with the Scottish people: Celts in kilts! As if that were not enough to set our young minds agog, there was even more information for us to digest. Just a few miles away across the sea was another island called Ireland where another Celtic 'race' of Irish people lived. Why was life so complicated?

So we were British Welsh Celts and lived in Wales which had its own language although we didn't speak it, and from what I can remember we were not taught it formally in the infant's school; just a few songs learnt by rote which we didn't understand anyway. It was only when we moved up to Brynmill junior's that were we given a larger helping to get our tongues around although fluency was not the ultimate objective.

Swansea was not a Welsh speaking town and in the Brynmill district there were very few Welsh speaking families if at all. Anybody who did speak the language was looked on in awe. Our understanding of the language difference was helped by sounds.

Welsh towns like Swansea with an English name had their own equivalents like Abertawe although we as children didn't use it normally and had to ponder on it when heard to recognize or remember that both names were used for the town that we lived in. It was the spelling and pronunciation of towns and district names around Swansea that unconsciously helped us to understand how the Welsh language worked and why it sounded different to English names. It had an unfamiliar arrangement of letters that seemed to collide and trip over one another when they became neighbours; before combining to produce un natural sounds compared to normal spoken English. We would occasionally insert typical Welsh Swansea district place names into a conversation just to experiment and roll them around; noting the softer sounds of some compared to the complication and more robust pronunciation of others.

Our Welsh identity was reinforced every year with St David's day on the first day of March when girls would arrive in school dressed in the national costume and boys wearing a daffodil, or a leak for the more avant garde. There was also our own flag which, with its bright red dragon, fired our imagination and impelled us to reproduce the image of the flame breathing beast on paper whenever we felt the urge. To us kids, living in a country called Wales we were told was 'special'. Thus it was that when cousins with heavily accented voices came on weekend visits from predominantly Welsh speaking towns like Carmarthen and played cowboys with us in the park, they were welcomed like a long lost tribe. We had it all worked out. On a Saturday morning they would join us for the Odeon cinema club and in the afternoon they swooped in from distant bushes whoopin' and a hollerin'- sometimes in Welsh -as marauding Carmarthen braves with whom we created magnificent scenes of battle, culminating in victory or defeat with pow-wows of sweeping arms, hand movements and forked fingers pointing first to eyes and then imaginary Brynmill sunsets that eventually led us home to our own tribal wigwams in time for tea.

The war years were not that far in the past and it is only now as I write this that I realise how much it saturated our lives; still very much in the background and having a heavy influence on our play. There were all sorts of war time commando heroes, both British and American, portrayed in the comics doing their stuff and coming through triumphant against overwhelming odds.

Their deeds would be even more dramatically illustrated with the machines of war: airplanes, tanks, grenades, bombs and guns of every conceivable type; spitting fire with their victims taking on the grotesque poses of violent and sudden death.

It was these shinning war heroes which we would become and transfer to the playground perhaps re-enacting cinema newsreel scenes we had seen with the accompanying dramatic throat noises of artillery carving its path through attackers and defenders alike. "pfwoooooar – daka, daka, daka, daka – I'm a spitfire daka, daka, daka, daka. Duduh, duduh, duduh, duduh - I'm a German bomber Pwwchhhhh – I've just dropped a bomb. Daka, daka, daka. -duduh, duduh, duduh."

When starting our airplanes we put our tongues against the roof of our mouths and blew hard from the throat to imitate the engine noise: "thrrrrrrrrr-rrrrrrrr;" whirling an arm in front of us like a propeller. Running forward, taking a small jump into the air we took off; we were airborne. Swinging both arms out either side for wings we ran around the school yard flying, whole groups of us doing dog fights.

It was dangerous out there in the playground. Sometimes of course our airplanes crashed with even more guttural throat noises to simulate the event as we twisted ourselves in a spiral hitting the floor declaring, "I've been shot down. Bail out, bail out." We knew all the right stuff to say. We'd seen it in the latest war films.

Occasionally there'd be another kind of collision as a lonesome cowboy from another part of the yard strayed into our flight path galloping between us; hopping sideways, slapping his hind quarters and with a hand held out in front controlling the imaginary reins. With all the noise however his horse soon bolted galloping away sideway back from whence he had come.

Some boys were exceedingly good at these sound effects lifting them slightly in the pecking order when picking sides, deciding who was going to be a German or a Britisher. At that time in our lives the meaning of these two words was not really understood. What counted was the sound they made. Saying Britisher sounded better than just saying British and seemed to balance out saying the word German.

Sometimes it was the sound of words and not their meaning that attracted us to them. One day dad asked me what I saw "in all that rubbish," referring to the war comics. I was afraid that he would try to stop me reading them and gave what I thought was a pretty intelligent answer. I said' "It's not just about the stories dad, it helps me learn German."

Looking temporarily perplexed and hopeful at the same time he asked incredulously, "How does it teach you German?"

"German words dad, German words."

There was a glint in his eye as he sort of smiled, compressing his lips hard; perhaps more of a grimace than a smile really, as he responded with, "Which words?"

I should have learnt more of them. All I could come up with was "Achtung, dolt, and Englander."

"Almost fluent then," he said slowly, giving his response some thought as he turned to go back to painting a skirting board on the upstairs landing. I had the distinct impression my answer had fallen some way short of what he was hoping for and hadn't impressed him at all.

No matter who was winning in our battleground, goodies or baddies, all fighting would cease when the teacher on yard duty rang the bell to call the end of playtime and we all went back to our classes in one piece to plan our next battle strategy when Miss or Sir wasn't looking.

Just as popular were the mainstream tabloid comics like Dandy and Beano with their zany larger than life cartoon characters enjoyed by children and, I suspect, many adults alike. There was quite a healthy trade in comic swaps on Friday afternoons with frequent bartering as to the value of one character's status against another. If you weren't a skilled negotiator you could easily go home with far less than you brought. Friday afternoon comics also continued in the junior school but only for the first year. After that we had to get down to studies full time.

During the period when this kind of reading material and western comics in particular were really beginning to get a grip and growing in popularity one august body expressed concern that our language and writing skills was becoming contaminated by too much mention of ornery critters, ding blasted outlaws and other phrasing alien to the proper use of the English language.

After a suitable period of reflection they produced a measured response: another cowboy comic -but with a difference. Most, if not all, of the grammar was correctly phrased, cowboys and outlaws were polite to one another and there was no cussing. It failed to hit the spot and soon disappeared. It sure as hell didn't have no effect on me!

At the beginning of the 1950's some new comics emerged having a subtle emphasis on education as well as enjoyment. These were The Eagle and The Lion for boys with Girl and School Friend for young ladies. I can't speak for the content of the girls' comics only the boys which for both Eagle and Lion had a more serious format based on adventure stories instead of zany cartoon characters.

One of the most famous characters was 'Dan Dare Pilot of The Future' and his sidekick Digby, travelling through space together fighting the evil of the Meacons. Yet another notable one with his own short strip was Tommy Walls. This was an unashamed advertising slot for the ice cream brand.

Our schoolboy hero would find himself in some situation where urgent assistance was required, put his hands together to form the letter W with forefingers and thumbs and then go into action to win the day. The final scene was always him and his pals sucking on a Walls ice cream to celebrate. Nobody ever dared to be Tommy in the playground. It was just far too corny.

The most important part of the Eagle comic to the mechanically minded however was the double page spread in the centre which was dedicated to engineering subjects with cutaway drawings revealing the insides of things like: battle tanks, aircraft, ships, trucks, steam engines, tractors and diggers etc.

For schoolboys of that generation when transport and similar new products were being developed and launched regularly it was an essential have to get all the details. Printed in bright colours it quickly became a big hit with boys all over the country and Peter and I would always get together to offer a thoughtful critique on each subject covered.

The Lion was very similar in content having as its main feature another space pilot, Captain Condor, with supporting story lines including a robot, a detective who investigated crime with clues left for the reader and several other characters long forgotten.

I got my own Number 1 edition of the Lion after Peter told me about it. We had become kindred spirits in a number of things not long after I turned up near his doorstep and also good friends, regularly spending time in each other's houses with our dinky toys and Meccano sets which was probably our greatest interest and we would pour over our model instruction books for hours deciding what to build and discussing our various projects. When we weren't looking at the model books it was the Meccano magazine which had all sorts of features and articles mechanical in it especially to grab the imagination of budding young engineers.

The Lion, like the Eagle, gave opportunity to become a member which was very important. If you were a member of something you became part of the brotherhood. A sort of psychological bonding with your unknown contemporaries around the country. You filled in a pre-printed coupon on the members' page, cut it out, and posted it to The Lion with a small fee to get your Lion Birthday Club membership pack and badge.

The best part of the process however was official announcing of your name and where you lived in the next issue so that every other member would know. It would also be announced on your birthday in the members' page making you eligible for a prize draw – always won by somebody in another part of the country.

Peter had sent for his badge previously so I was able to see his credentials announced on the members page only a week or so before I too was accepted into the brotherhood. A cause for great celebration. I wonder if boys of that age now do such things and get the same rush of excitement over something so simple and innocent as we did then.

As well as the regular weekly comics there were also Christmas annuals with additional once a year features and a special feel and smell to them with their colourful hardback covers giving a sharp clean appearance. The Eagle stood out from all of them because of its bright red jacket and it was interesting to see how many boys had received one for Christmas on that first Friday afternoon back at school.

Occasionally American comics of the Beano and Dandy type used to creep into our lives and after I had read a few of them I began to wonder why I had no friends called, Chip, Buzz, Buddy or Clyde. For the life of me I couldn't think of one. The American names had a certain kind of resonance to them that ours didn't.

In addition to Superman and Batman type annuals there was also a more unusual one about a dog. This was Black Bob, the story of a Border Collie built around him and his master Andrew Glenn; a Scottish shepherd. It was a different kind of book with emphasis on adventure in rural surroundings and portraying the various troubles, crimes and hardships of the local farming community.

Sometime after we had moved up to the junior school a number of us got interested in model aircraft and would bring in the various publicity leaflets and listings from model kit makers like Keilcraft and one or two others. After a period of devoted study, during playtime or when the teacher wasn't looking, we would announce grandly to each other what we were going to build; wishful thinking spurred on by the proximity of Fairwood Aerodrome which was only a few miles outside Swansea and running an active private flying club.

Aircraft would be heard and seen overhead particularly at week ends but often mid-week as well. Nothing very exotic, they would usually be high winged Austers or similar doing commercial flights around the bay. Tiger Moth biplanes would also put in an occasional appearance along with De Havilland Dragon Rapides causing much excitement on the ground. The Rapide in particular always looked graceful; the distinctive tone of its two piston engines running in unison usually heralding arrival well before coming in to view.

The problem with schoolboys of our age then was that we had too much imagination. An imagination that fuelled by the model kit leaflets we were ogling turned us into experts in aircraft identification. Anything that flew overhead we could identify at a glance. Leaving aside the visitors from Fairwood we could immediately identify the many official RAF Spitfires, Hurricanes,

Wellington and Mosquito bombers and others that we were sure flew over the Brynmill district in general. Well that was what several ten and eleven year old experts earnestly proclaimed them to be; so who were the shopkeepers and tradesmen to argue?

I think even a Messerschmitt 109 and Focke Wulf 190 were identified on a couple of occasions but thankfully, as far as I am aware, no claims were ever made about Stukas or we might have caused a real panic. What we really did observe up high on rare occasions during those years were genuine Lancasters; an absolutely beautiful thing to see in flight as well as one other very rare aircraft. It was rare because only one was ever produced and I was lucky enough to see it during the brief period it was allowed to fly before being scrapped. The Bristol Brabazon was something even my mother recognised and pointed out to me one day as it flew over Swansea on a one off flight in that direction. The only thing I can remember from such a long time ago now was that it was very noisy and very large. Gradually as jet aircraft took over from piston engined types we would look up into the sky to see things like the de Havilland Vampire with its twin tail booms or a Gloster Meteor, and read about others which were not so familiar. Along with the glamour of the aircraft came the names of famous test pilots like Neville Duke and Peter Twiss who fired our ambition to do what they did when we grew up. It was an age of progress and things were changing and being developed as each day passed.

Less exciting was stamp collecting; far more mundane but quite popular and encouraged as being educational and we filled our albums full of them from continental countries and other more exotic locations like China, India, Africa, Ceylon and numerous other places whose names have long disappeared off the map into history. Cigarette cards depicting all kinds of subjects were also collected with the most popular being anything to do with aircraft, ships, forms of transport and football players.

Two footballer and film star card series came along with Dollar bubble gum and could be stuck into an album which had to be sent for with the payment of a number of the gum wrappers. The special wrapping was printed in the form of an American dollar note which we cut out and bundled together to use as currency in our play as American gangsters. If you wanna be a gangster you gotta have the right props OK? We actually had to pay for them with our precious Dollars. What a Swizz! The wait till the album came back by post was torture. Yeah! They took us for schmucks and made patsies out of all of us.

Several of us also decided to collect cigarette packets. Smoking was very common then. Mum and dad both smoked as well as aunts and uncles. Everywhere you went people smoked. In the street, on the buses, in the shops, on trains, in the cinema, in cafes, everywhere. You would even hear people lighting up in plays broadcast on radio. In films we had noticed heroes and villains alike would take time to casually light up in a manner that was intended to portray the persona of the character they were playing.

After lighting up they would hold the cigarette either between just the index and middle fingers or between index and middle finger together and thumb, each method designed to complete the mood of the scene. A lady or upper class toff, or twit, would often be shown using a cigarette holder. It was the way gangsters held their cigarettes that impressed us most however and since sweets looking like cigarettes could sometimes be had in the local tuck shop we used to buy them to use when playing cops and robbers dragging on them as menacingly as we could to frighten the good guys.

Cigarettes were seductive, and we saw them as a rite of passage to manhood albeit a little early for us to indulge in then. But they would collide with us very soon. Not yet but very soon…. sooon! How they impacted into our lives I will reveal in due course but until that happened we did the next best thing and collected the packets that held the cigarette and there were a lot of them to collect with both ten and twenty pack boxes along with any other special derivatives. So how many were there? Well to start with the ones we knew about were: Players Navy Cut, Capstan Navy Cut, Piccadilly, Kensitas, Pall Mall, Park Drive, Express 555, Dunhill, Senior Service, Gold Flake, Woodbines, Craven A, Black Cat, Churchman's No 1, du Maurier, Passing Cloud and Three Castles. And that was before we even began to think about imports like Camel, Marlboro and the many others on the market.

Those of us who collected split between the two easiest choices that would save space otherwise we could just imagine irate mothers finding fag packets lying around in our rooms and accusing us of clandestine smoking. Some collectors just took out the trays and kept the outer parts in a shoe box or similar while after much dithering I elected to go one better by just saving the fronts of the outer box and sticking them in a scrap book. Anything and everything new in cigarette packets would be kept to add to our collections and like the cowboy comics there would be regular swapping and trading. At the time of course we never appreciated that in the years to come our collections would become the prized memorabilia of a forgotten age; so when the craze faded as we got older they all ended up in the dustbin.

There were periodic crazes for everything. Fivestones, also known as dandies, was played from time to time with some of us using the irregularly shaped brown and yellowish coloured stones acquired by stealth from the bowling green border in Brynmill Park. As long as the stones could be picked up easily and quickly however they could be from any source. Conkers though was a more exciting game played every year when the Chestnut trees in both Brynmill and Singleton started to drop their tree grown ammunition on the ground. With a wary eye out for the Parky, only the odd one or two of whom were spoilers, weekends and evenings would be spent hurling heavy sticks high up into the branches to help dislodge the spikey green balls and their much sought after contents for us to do battle with.

Supermarkets were yet to arrive so milk was delivered fresh every morning to the doorstep in glass bottles by local dairies which were often a small independent family run business. At first it was by horse and cart and then by three or four wheel electric milk 'floats'. Why they were called 'floats' I have never discovered. When no longer required the cardboard discs that sealed the bottles were used to play bottletops; each player throwing down a disc with the following player try to cover it with his own. There were various rules but put simply a player who threw down and covered one or more to form a continuous unbroken spread of tops won the game and the tops.

More energetic games occasionally replaced the more mundane ones as when somebody had the really bright idea of playing jousting knights after seeing a film about King Arthur and the Round Table. Several teams of two players were formed with one member giving the other a piggy back; each team charging each other pair trying to either dismount the rider or knock both off balance. It was great fun but soon banned after one of the horses fell and suffered a broken fetlock.

Although the junior school had mixed classes the building itself featured separate boys' and girls' entrances and playgrounds on opposite sides of the school. The boys could thus play their rough and tumble games in their yard without knocking the girls over and the girls got on with whatever they did which as far as I was able to work out was skipping, playing hopscotch and doing hand stands against the school wall flashing their knickers.

We were given this last piece of information by some of the boys who stayed for school dinner. After they had finished eating they would slowly make their way down to the tuck shop opposite the infants' school and on the way back detour around to the girls' entrance to watch and make ribald comments until shooed away by the mistress on yard duty. Eventually the school management declared that both tuck food and knicker spotting were un healthy pursuits and lunch time visits to the tuck shop were also put under a restricted notice for the foreseeable future.

Walking to and from school was not without many distractions. Marbles, also called allies, was the one which dominated, accounting for most of the late arrivals as we slowly made our way along the Marlborough Road and Bernard Street gutters, chasing our little glass balls with occasional cries of "ups and outs" or maybe if things were a bit more tricky "double ups and outs" as we stepped out from the kerb to get a better shot. The marbles themselves came in a variety of sizes and patterns with the ones involved in winning games becoming treasured objects sorely missed when lost to an opponent. Very large marbles were sometimes introduced at times together with ball bearings which were more popular because of their appearance and weight. Personally I couldn't understand the logic of the really big marble. It just made a bigger target but there were all sorts of personal reasons why some became favourites. The most important thing of course was the outcome of the game. When you lost all your marbles you were 'scumped'.

The gutters had many drains along the way and we became very familiar with each and every one of them; particularly those that had claimed one of our treasured glass orbs. But there was also another reason for our familiarity, which was the drain lorries that cleaned them.

Although the modern day version called gully cleaners are much bigger and more technical than the ones we used to follow, there do not seem to be many around where I now live. I wonder where they all are. In the 1940's and 50's schoolboys would crowd around and watch in fascination as they dipped their necks into one drain after another all along the school route. The drain lorry had a driver and a drain man who would do all the labouring; first dragging the heavy grill out with a long hook before swinging the sucker nozzle out from its parking bracket and dropping it into the murky drain hole. Once submerged the engine note would wind up as it was shuffled around; sucking the contents into a large sludge tank on the back of the lorry. The nozzle would then be put back in its keep, the grill replaced and the operation moved on to the next drain which was never very far away. A group of spectators would follow, watching intently until we had to run to school to avoid being late. We were often late.

A more unusual kind of school bound distraction was in the very early years when still attending the infants. At the top end of Bernard Street just around the corner from the school was a large house standing in its own plot of ground. Its garden was seriously overgrow and the property was derelict with boarded up windows. Set into a porchway between two side panels the front door and its surround had originally featured decorative stained glass. Much of it was missing while the unsecured door stood partially open allowing a glimpse of broken floorboards and the dank blackness beyond.

On dark winter mornings it appeared particularly sinister and we, the children, adopted it and declared it haunted. Depending on the latest scare stories dreamed up by over imaginative and fertile minds we would either give it a wide berth, run past it, or dare each other to walk up its forbidding path and take a look inside. Although we had already terrified ourselves beforehand it was still too inviting and occasionally a reckless child would slowly creep up the pathway to look inside. The girls could be real drama queens and would turn suddenly and run screeching back down the pathway after seeing a skeleton pointing a bony finger or a veiled figure glowering from the shadows. In time of course the house was reclaimed by civilisation and has now been lived in for many years. I wonder if its present day occupants realise that it was once haunted and ever wake in the middle of the night to the ghostly echoes of children screaming and laughing long ago as they ran down the front pathway to escape bony fingered shadows.

THIS OLD HOUSE

When we first moved into the new house it was sorely in need of decoration everywhere. In his mind I'm sure dad must have regarded it not only as a new home but also a major project to be attacked with gusto for the foreseeable future and beyond.

Over the years it was transformed with gallons of gloss paint and thousands of brush strokes, the latter being applied with great care and precision, more of a loving caress really, onto every square inch of wood that could stand it. The first thing attacked were the doorways into every room and closet. But before the new paint could be applied the old had to be removed and it was done with his favourite weapon; the paraffin blow lamp.

Direct the flame onto the old paint till it turns brown and bubbles and then extinguish said flame before everything catches fire. Lovingly apply the triangular blade of a paint scraper to door framework and remove burnt debris with long smooth strokes. If paint proves stubborn and resists removal utter Anglo Saxon incantation and repeat procedure until wood is clear of all paint.

This usually took considerable time because

previous occupants had, since the house was built in the early nineteen hundreds, just plastered on layer over layer t h u s making it even more difficult. Now if it had been me doing all this, once the scraping was completed I would have started slapping on new paint right then as the next step. But it wasn't me it was dad and he was meticulous and spent a few more hours rubbing it down with sandpaper; first with rough or medium grain and then fine.

By the time it was finished the wood was almost back to a tree. It was only when the surface reached this level of reincarnation that paint was applied. Firstly there was the main undercoat, and when that was dry another sanding down with very fine sand paper before another primer and final coat of best quality top gloss. It really was a first class job with only expert brush strokes being allowed so my assistance was not required. To say that he was pains taking would be an understatement. Myself I avoid painting like the plague and when I have to decorate it just gets slapped on as-is.

Over time all the downstairs doors were also changed from solid to half or full glass panel with mortise lock door handles being converted to spring keeps. Just push the door into the frame and listen to it whisper, "I'm closed."

One by one the down stair fireplaces were also changed from the original cast iron grate and hob style of original to being replaced by a modern tile finished unit with special draught arrangements permitting easy resurrection the next morning. This of course begat the night time ritual of stoking and planning out each lump of coal just before bedtime. It worked splendidly however saving my mother the grubby chore of laying a new fire every morning with sticks and newspaper. I did on occasion lay the fire myself as I got older but fortunately for the insurance policy the new grate superseded my efforts before I managed to set the house aflame.

I should mention as well that all the walls also received special treatment with either paper or something he called Distemper. I thought that was what dogs used to catch but dad said no you buy it in cans and paint it on the wall. Painting was usually a weekend job but he knew when to quit when it came to hanging paper. This was when men came to the house. Usually it was two or three of them. A father and son outfit with an assistant and they came on and off for years whenever there was paper hanging to be done. Told to keep out of the way while they went about their business I would still always manage to get into whichever room they were working and watch with fascination as they mixed the porridge looking wallpaper paste in a bucket and slap it onto the wallpaper laid in folds on a purpose built table. The art was in the hanging of it, particularly if it was onto a ceiling, which sagged surprisingly towards the centre; demonstrated dramatically as it progressed along its length.

When lunch break arrived my mother would always give then a welcome cup of tea and a fry up of bacon egg and chips which was eaten sitting on the floor amongst their decorating detritus.

While dad took a great pride in decorating the house it was mum who kept it all spick and span and spoilt us rotten. In particular I remember wash days which were always on a Monday. All the laundry would go into a big galvanised boiler that had a hinged copper lid. This she would fill with boiling water and soap powder and then pummel and stir the contents until the water had discoloured sufficiently to indicate they were ready for rinsing.

The clothes then came out one by one to be rinsed in the sink before winding each garment through a hand mangle. It was hard work which we never appreciated. The clothes would then be taken out the back to be hung on the line which was suspended between the gable end wall and the garage.

Some of the pegs used to hold them in place would have been purchased from gipsy women who called from time to time and give her some sort of hand made good luck charm for her custom. It often seemed to rain on wash days and if Constance and I had been bored by not being able to go out and play she would tell us to go and see if we could make the rain stop. So we did. We would go in the front downstairs room, look out at the rain swept street and endlessly repeated the magic incantation. "Rain, rain, go away. Come another washing day. Rain, rain, go away, come another washing day."

I don't remember how long we would keep this up but it never seemed to work and if we went to complain she would just say, "Never mind. It will stop some time." And she was right. It eventually did …..at some time.

When we had had enough of chanting we would go upstairs, find an old eiderdown and some blankets and make a tent. The upper floor of the house had two landings. A long one leading from the top of the main stairs to the back bedrooms and a much shorter one leading up a smaller flight to the two front bedrooms. The short landing was the ideal place to set it up and we could in our imagination easily transform it into a jungle encampment with the rest of the floor full of imaginary animals or anything else we could think of to help pass the time.

OLD SMOKEY

After Smokey our cat had been with us for a while he would often go walkabout around the house sometimes prompting mum to have a one sided conversation and chide him for getting under her feet wandering around like a lost soul. Occasionally he would have a mad half hour, as we called it, and tear around the house running up and down the stairs till he exhausted himself and found a place to flop. It was one of these episodes that led to his confrontation with my father. But before I tell you about that I need to tell you more about 'Old Smokey.'

I have always had a soft spot for cats and from an early age would try to befriend anything that came within talking distance. A few years after we moved to Brynmill I started badgering my parents for one of our own. Dogs were of no interest. Maybe it was because of the bite from the neighbour's wire haired terrier I had received at West Cross. I definitely didn't want a dog. I wanted a cat and was so determined to have one, started bringing home anything judged to be lost or stray back home for adoption.

This went on for quite some time until I eventually wore them down after constantly having to find out where the latest moggy on four legs came from with human retrievers turning up on the doorstep every other week to recover their lost family pet. Mum made it known around her friends that they had been persuaded and eventually this ball of fluff arrived on our doorstep; hand delivered by somebody in search of homes for recent offspring from their own cat.

From the very start it was obvious that it was a definite head case, slightly nervous and easily startled but extremely good natured. A male, it was some kind of Persian mix having mostly black fur with distinctive wide brown stripes and a small grey white patch on his upper chest. We christened him Smokey and I had to vow that I would look after him through thick and thin.

A day or so after he arrived he went completely crackers, stiffly jumping up and down springing from place to place and then running around the house from one room to the next. We all thought it was quite funny at the time but in retrospect realised that of course he was still only a kitten, very young, wrenched from the protection of his mother and now in surroundings that were entirely strange to him. This panic behavior was repeated a couple of times in the ensuing weeks but he eventually calmed down as we did our best to be gentle and spoil him and it was not too long before he accepted his new situation and us as his new family.

As he grew older he proved to be a very playful buddy, and very amenable to being dressed up in a woolly hat and waistcoat at Christmas. Over time he also impressed my friends by running to me from down the street when called, jumping up onto my forearm and climbing up around my shoulder. It wasn't only me he played with however. He had a neighbour, Tibby, who lived next door.

Tibby was black all over except for a bright white patch on his chest like Smokey and the two of them would play for hours together chasing each other around the two back gardens. When they had exhausted themselves they would take it in turns to wash each other down or act as a pillow for the other to rest his weary head on.

The most amusing thing to watch however was when they had access to mum's wicker shopping basket which had rounded sides and would easily tip over. They would frequently climb into it together for a snooze whenever they were having a hard day, or if they wanted a bit of fun, they took it in turns to run from the end of the garden, dive into it and roll around to get thrown out because of the curved sides.

I swear I could hear them laughing at times. I had never ever seen two cats play together like that so good naturedly for so long and don't think they were ever on bad terms with each other. It was a friendship which seemed to endure throughout their lifetime. I said Smokey was a head case and he was. His problem was that he liked to climb but did so just for the sake of it without thinking where it might lead to or if he could get back down. The silly animal didn't climb trees where claws could be used in descent, he climbed houses. If there was a ladder leaning against a wall he would climb it. Even if it ended up in a cloud he would have climbed it. But claws were no good going down ladder rungs so if he went wandering around the district and got stuck somewhere I guess somebody must have rescued him because he always seemed to find his way home.

The real trouble came when he decided to climb the neighbour's house the other side of us from Tibby's.

The old gent living there, well he seemed old to me at the time, did odd jobs and on this occasion was sorting out some loose roof tiles.

I wouldn't normally have cared but at the time was sleeping in the smaller of the back bedrooms at the side of the house with the neighbouring house wall located about six feet directly opposite. It was a Saturday morning and a lie in, peacefully slumbering when my reverie was interrupted by a fearful yowl from outside the window. As bleary eyed as I was I definitely recognised that little voice but how was it coming from high up and outside the window?

They were deep houses and they were tall; about twenty feet to the roof guttering. I left my warm and comfortable bed taking a glance at the alarm clock. Twenty past nine. Who gets up at that time on a Saturday morning? I asked myself, opening the curtains. Directly opposite was the neighbour's chimney and standing next to it on the roof apex howling in my direction was my four legged buddy. He was trying to tell me something, and as soon as he saw me started walking back along the roof line to where a ladder was sticking up at the end. Then he walked back again and let me know in no uncertain terms that he was stuck, stuck, stuck. Stupid cat!

Mum heard the commotion and got up to my room as I finished dressing. There was only one thing to be done and that was to knock next door and tell Mr Beynon the situation. After some while he removed the ladder from his gable end wall, passed it over the garden wall and then came around through our garage to set it up again on our side, leaning against the wall by their chimney.

In the meantime Smokey had crossed over to our

roof by the connecting span and was beginning to panic. Smokey, I thought, your days are numbered. Mr Beynon was not too keen to put himself at risk for our mad cat so after managing to persuade mum that I would not do anything stupid, she let me climb the ladder where it had been put against the wall leaning just under the guttering.

Smokey continued to howl from our roof until he realised that if he wanted rescuing he was going to have to come to me. He eventually did but just to be awkward kept himself just out of reach until I succeeded in catching him by the nape of his neck, whereupon he went rigid.

I didn't know if he'd suddenly become scared of heights, but being in a bit of a precarious position myself, no longer cared. So if he didn't like it too bad. Very gingerly climbing back down the ladder using one hand and reaching terra firma without incident I presented him to my mother who gave him a good scolding. Unfortunately it was not the only time he got onto the roof and had to be rescued on a number of other occasions as well. But that was Smokey, our furry bundle of fun who came to incur my father's wrath one Saturday lunch time with 'The incident at the foot of the stairs'.

Sometimes dad would go on the prowl, walking around the house looking for extraneous pieces of fluff or other microscopic particles which had no business being there, picking them up off the floor to dispose of in a more suitable location. It must be in the genes. I find I've started doing it now. How sad is that? What really used to tick him off however, was a carpet being rumpled or kicked out of place and being left in disarray.

On one of his tours of inspection he found the carpet in the hallway by the front door had been displaced and I had been accused of the offence which I had allegedly committed while running up the stairs straight off the street.

This was strictly FORBIDDEN! Constance was earnestly trying to defend me, telling him that Smokey was the real culprit and she had just heard him run up the stairs like something demented. Even so, dad was having none of it. But this was when fate intervened, for once on my side.

By some freak of chance the three of us had while, discussing the matter, set up the ideal tableau for pussy to make his grand entrance. Dad had elected to continue his solid case for my prosecution while standing in the open doorway immediately to the left of the front door, grandly referred to as 'the lounge'. Constance was facing the stairs standing on the door mat and I was in the hallway next to the study door. Cue stage left. A noise coming from the direction of the dining room caught our attention.

The door was unsecured. It's "whisper I'm closed" technology had failed and a little black tipped paw was trying to pull it further open. Smokey's head appeared, joining his paw, with an innocent looking expression on his face that said "is somebody talking about moi?" He surveyed the scene, the rumpled carpet and then me and realised that we were indeed talking about him and he was culpable. Astutely he must also have realised that his young master was up the creek without a paddle. With memories of rooftop rescues perhaps still vivid in his mind that cat realised he owed me big-time and now it was "PAYBACK."

Suddenly he accelerated from a standing start to the

speed of light, shot up the hall, and passing me on the way, leapt onto exhibit one, the carpet at the foot of the stairs. It was a leap like none before it. Twisting in the air he landed tail end facing the front door with all paws engaged, flailing like windmills scrabbling for grip. As they found carpet it was thrown out behind him even more into a heap with the under felt following. Claws eventually digging into bare wood beneath he shot forward up the stairs and kept on running along the landing till we heard a thud as he hit the secured back bedroom door; unfortunately for him still fitted with original mortise lock door closing technology: attached knob needing very positive turning either way to allow closing and releasing. If it had been dad's special "whisper shut" it would have probably given way and "whispered open" on contact reducing Smokey's impact.

I had never known dad lost for words but before he could say anything in response to what we had just witnessed monsieur le cat unfazed, amazingly undazed, and none the worse for his instant deceleration, swaggered slowly back to the top of the stairs displaying what I can only describe as a self-satisfied pussy smirk on his face while fixing me with a look that said "chew the bones out of that pal -now we're quits." He then sat and smugly began preening himself. The three of us burst out laughing but at that moment Smokey's life was hanging by a thread. If dad could have got hold of him he'd have strangled him there and then. He was in need of a safe house and a new identity.

Sometime later that day I had a man to man talk with him. Not with dad, with Smokey. He had disappeared and I went looking and eventually found him seeking refuge under my bed. He was obviously a bit worried about his future so I coaxed him out from his hiding place, picked him up and sat down on the bed.

Turning him on his back in my lap and poking him gently in the white spot on his chest with my right forefinger I told him that while I appreciated his little high speed demonstration of how to rumple a carpet I wanted to know why he thought we were even.

"Listen Moosh," I said, using the schoolboy phrase to indicate authority. "How many times have I pulled you off that roof?" No response. I asked again. "How many times?"

Then I relented remembering how good he made me look in front of my friends, showing off jumping up my arm and onto my shoulder. Looking good with your cat in front of one's peers was important. "I'll make a deal with you," I said. "No more rooftop walkabouts and you're off the hook. How about it?" He just fixed me with a dewy-eyed stare, licked my finger with his sandpaper tongue and content that he had suckered me yet again closed his eyes and drifted off to sleep. Typical Smokey.

Whatever! I had been exonerated and later in the day after acknowledging his wrongful prosecution of his only begotten son my father had another chuckle about it promising that he would not be seeking retribution on my buddy.

They lived in relative harmony together, each only slightly wary of the other, until Smokey expired peacefully in his Oxo box sleeping quarters under the scullery table several years later. I had left home and was working away by then and by chance the works summer holiday trip fortnight had begun the day of the evening he died. You'd have thought he could have hung on for one more day. Anyway when I arrived home the next day I said goodbye to my erstwhile friend and buried him in the ground under the garage almost thirteen years after he had arrived in our house. I knew my mother would miss him. I was sure that Tibby next door would miss him terribly.

THAT'S ENTERTAINMENT

The house not only provided us a place to shelter, eat, and sleep. It was also a provider of entertainment, firstly in the form of radio and eventually television. There were so many new radio programmes that it is of course impossible to mention them all but I hope that at least I can conjure up a flavour of the time. Even when at Druslyn Road I can remember from a very early age being awakened to the sound of Bow Bells, the time check pips at the breakfast table, and then hearing, but not understanding, the radio announcements. In my first few years of life it was just background sound which slowly developed over time into recognition as I began to appreciate language; taking more notice of the strange incantations and mysterious messages that began the rhythm of the day with the proclamation that you were listening to the BBC Home Service and they were going to give you the news, both good and bad.

When the new bulletin had finished there would be information to impart such as a weather forecast and maybe 'A gale warning for all shipping issued by the Met Office,' with all kinds of coded information about wind speed, from which direction it was coming, who was going to receive it, and at what time. I especially liked the way that rain was declared. Instead of simply saying it was expected soon and you wouldn't be able to see much through the gloom, the news reader would grandly tell you visibility was poor, becoming moderate and precipitation or rain was in sight. A list of place names followed saying where it was going to be, way out in the sea: Sole, Fastnet, Rockall, Tyne, Dogger, German Bight, Shannon, Heligoland, and numerous others as it progressed. What, I wondered, did dogs have to do with the weather? And that word German. It was often in the news but what made them want to bite and who? There was so much to learn. Sometimes at the very end there would be more dramatic announcements with requests for a relative to get in touch with a particular office telephone number and obtain information on a dangerously ill family member who had been out of contact for some time. A more sinister invitation might also be made for the public to provide information on the whereabouts of certain individuals to The Home Office or Scotland Yard by ringing Whitehall 12 12. Was that something like ringing 999 but worse?

I didn't really have a clue what it all meant but found the sound of the words and the metre in which they were spoken almost hypnotic. It was BBC pronounced English and as time progressed the announcers, who were apparently dressed in full penguin suit and bow tie, were permitted to tell you their names which helped to erase some of their mystery Instead of disembodied voices they became people. The two most regular readers were Frank Phillips and Alvar Liddell who both looked nothing like their voices when they eventually had their photographs published in the Radio Times magazine.

There were many different programmes that provided both for information and amusement. Typically there was a morning serial for housewives like Mrs Dale's Diary which portrayed the trials and tribulations of her family life while being married to a doctor whose name was Jim. "I'm worried about Jim," was often the lead-in phrase to what Mrs Dale wrote about in her diary. Music While You Work, broadcast twice a day on weekdays, was a programme of continuous live popular music. While for lunch time three days a week there was Workers Playtime; a travelling variety show visiting factories around the country introducing many of the well known artists of the time: comedians, singers, harmonica players, general musicians and impressionists who imitated everything from other people's voices to birdsong and steam engines clattering over railway lines.

In the evenings for children there was Uncle Mac and Children's Hour with Larry the Lamb and stories of Toytown and other content to keep us amused. At weekends serials for children were a bit more adventurous like Norman and Henry Bones the boy detectives. One children's hour adventure broadcast by Scottish radio told the story of a fictional planet called Hesikos, a yarn later adapted for a very much over acted television version with one of the actors lying face down on a blackened couch to give the impression of floating in space. Unfortunately its outline wasn't quite invisible and totally destroyed the illusion as it was pulled along from the side of the stage.

Science fiction was starting to become a popular programme theme, attracting adults as well as children. Journey in to Space was one of the first to get us hooked, along with its weird mood music, and it was a sad day when the series finished. Heavily dramatic accompaniment was also used in Counterspy, a story set in mid Wales with the centre of the action taking place around the town of Rhayader.

Dick Barton Special Agent, a morning broadcast, and Paul Temple on Saturday nights was often followed by Saturday Night Theatre, with both detective adventures also accompanied by pacey music. Dick Barton music really ripped along with a fast galloping theme while the Paul Temple accompaniment imbued the listener with the sense of a railway train running through countryside.

Remembered from very early childhood, Dick Barton, with its whirlwind style introduction, always made me hide under the dining room table whenever it came on the radio. Compared to present day productions the dialogue and sound effects were really primitive. Barton had two sidekicks: Snowy and Jock with another lead character being Inspector Burke. Whenever they got into a fist fight the verbal knockabout between opponents would always include; "take that, oh no you don't – oh yes I do, you take that, I'm warning you" and a number of similar declarations. When one of them fell, even if it was onto soft ground or gravel it always had the hollow sound of contact with floorboards. It was wonderful stuff. But why, when they took the bad men off to jail, I wondered, did they always put them in custard? It would only make them all sticky.

Typically Saturday lunchtime would have a regular selection of programmes such as Variety Bandbox with music hall stars like Arthur Askey, and Have A Go with Wilfred Pickles which was an audience participation type event having a quiz at the end for contestants culminating in a cash prize; a meagre amount usually, presented by a member of the cast with the catch phrase 'Give her/him the money Barney,' from Wilfred Pickles. Other radio lunchtime Saturday shows featured the early careers of many well-known names like Ray's A Laugh with Ted Ray, Take It From Here with Jimmy Edwards and many more.

On Saturdays in the afternoon football would be broadcast, the commentary very often undertaken by Raymond Glendenning, a gentleman known just as much for his enormous handlebar moustache as his voice. I wasn't really a football fan but some times you just couldn't avoid listening and wondering how it was that such a detailed commentary could be kept up at the same time as identifying all the players and their field positions.

After Children's Hour with Uncle Mac would usually bring one of the thrillers and another variety programme with a regular host comedian like Jimmy Jewell and Ben Worris. The Archers – An everyday story of country folk -was a regular contributor to our entertainment during the week and also the catch-up omnibus edition broadcast over the weekend. The last meal of the day was supper and sometimes as a special treat mum would mash and fry up some potatoes left over from lunch and spread it over fried bread. It was the perfect ending to a Saturday.

Next day was Sunday and the usual chapel programme except for specials. Chapel celebrations like Easter and Whitsun were preceded by the inevitable requirement of a new costume for Sister Constance and a new suit for her poor brother; everything brand new, stiff and uncomfortable with sharp creases. Constance always loved her new costume, but I always hated my new torture suit. I was not alone. All my mates in the chapel felt the same way about it, entailing as it did the same sadistic fitting ritual every time. We could never understand why girls always seemed to enjoy the experience when it was applied to them. Not quite so bad came footwear because we went to SAXONE's shoe shop. This was in High Street just down the road from the station and almost next door to Lewis Lewis the department store which had something unusual.

What they had was a fancy vacuum system for their billing and accounts recording. It was unique in Swansea. Payment for goods would be made to a sales assistant who would then put it into a barrel like canister attached to an overhead cable system. Pulling on a handle made it whiz to an office in another part of the store. A little while later there would be a rattle and thud from a nearby vacuum pipe hatch as the canister was returned with change and receipt. At any one time these containers could be seen flying from different sales counters from one end of the store to the other.

SAXONE had something different. It was an x-ray machine for feet and we kids always used to make a beeline for it when we went there. You could stand with your toes in the bottom of it and look through the display screen on top as you wiggled them and watched your bones moving. It was fascinating. I think it is commonplace now but they were the first shop to introduce it; certainly in Swansea anyway. We always ended up getting my shoes there whenever we went but the machine still didn't stop dad prodding and poking my feet through the leather though. He was determined that his authority would not be undermined by a mere x-ray machine.

It all ended of course having to attend chapel at Easter or whatever the occasion was, standing amongst a group peers, trouser creases sharp enough to cut and shinning like a new pin, to be inspected after the service by well meaning chapel elders, a total menace, commenting on the elegance of it all as. Life could be tough.

Sunday radio was a little more subdued than other days with programmes like Down Your Way with the presenter named Franklin Engelmann interviewing people and asking what they did in locations all over the country, followed later by Palm Court Hotel which was an orchestral programme featuring violins and other posh instruments with strings.

We didn't get television in our house until I was about thirteen because it was considered that it would not be beneficial to my education, more of a hindrance or distraction. Yeah! Great!

Sometimes I needed a distraction. Schoolwork was interfering with my enjoyment. One of the first TV series that we watched regularly starred Lloyd Bridges as Mike Nelson, a sort of detective frogman. It was a completely different theme from the usual type detective stories and got me hooked right away. There were many others series to follow but of course one of the most interesting things about the new television age was that the stars of radio were now coming on the box and we could put faces to names and voices. Sometimes seeing the faces of radio personalities whose pictures had never been published came as quite a surprise.

The uptake of television around where we lived was not rapid and although there was a growing number of fancy shaped TV aerials sprouting from surrounding rooftops a lot of families were still waiting for the moving pictures to come in to their living rooms. Fortunately an elderly neighbour living a few doors up had one well before we did and I got invited to see it on a Saturday evening quite regularly for the children's programme Whirligig and a few other variety shows as well as television news.

This was in time for the then big event of the century which was the Coronation of Queen Elizabeth II after her father King George IV had died early the previous year. On the day there were so many friends, neighbours and family in the room we were like sardines crammed in to a tin. It was almost standing room only.

A while after seeing the black and white version on TV all the schools took a trip to see it in colour at a local cinema, different schools going to different cinemas in their locality. For us it was the good old Odeon again in Sketty. The coronation also spawned a colour feature film called John And Julie which was a popular draw telling the story of two children who ran away to see the coronation for themselves because their parents wouldn't take them.

The small television screen still had a way to go however before it could compete with public cinemas which, while still showing a lot of black and white movies, had an increasing proportion of colour films along with developing projector technology. Major stories, often with a biblical theme, were used to introduce new wide Cinemascope screens and ever improving sound and colour quality. Films like The Robe featuring leading actors including Wales's Richard Burton and Ben Hur with Charlton Heston were heavily promoted and drew large audiences when they were shown at The Plaza cinema in the Kingsway which, compared to some of the other picture houses, was dead posh.

There were several cinemas in and around the Swansea town centre then, quite a number of which have now closed. The main ones were the Plaza, Carlton in Oxford Street and the Albert Hall in Page Street. If there was a good film showing we would go as a family on a Saturday afternoon or evening and perhaps stand in a queue, slowly shuffling forward as the seats became available.

Sometimes the commissioner in a full uniform coat and cap would come out and announce a few singles or pairs of seats available in different parts of the auditorium and there would be a dignified but authorised scramble to jump ahead of the line.

Once inside some families would treat the whole thing like a picnic, passing sandwiches around regardless as the cinema activity and programme carried on around them.

If the film was popular things could get pretty crowded and long queues would form sometimes three or four people abreast snaking around the corner of the building which is what used to happen at the Albert Hall. The queue would start from its head in Page Street, slowly growing until it turned the corner into Mansel Street where on hot sunny afternoons and evenings the projection room doors would be open and the technicians would pose technically for the public.

Unlike now, where the programme consists of one feature film preceded by adverts and trailers for future presentations, in the 1940s and 50's a B movie was shown first to support the title film. Often they were very good and sometimes better and if you had been queuing for some time you could miss the start of the B movie. It didn't matter though because the whole programme was continuous and you could stay and watch until things rolled back around to "where you came in" and as long as you wanted afterwards; sometimes even swapping to a better seat when the theatre started to empty and the new audience started flowing in. When the films were good the place would get jammed really full and if the plot was complicated it was a good reason to stay for the re-run and see if you could understand the bits you didn't get the first time.

Next door to the Carlton Cinema was the Empire Theatre which we would visit at Christmas for the pantomime or the Grand Theatre, next to the National Welsh bus station a short distance away around the corner, the choice depending on who was the guest artist and supporting players. These would usually be radio and later the television personalities like Harry Secombe, Stan Stennett, Gladys Morgan and Wynn Calvin with a female lead playing prince to another female playing the hard done by princess. A well-known male comedian usually dressed as the dame or Baron Hardup. Along with most of the other kids I just couldn't understand why they had to have a girl play the principal boy and then marry the princess or whatever at the end. Dad understood though. Well that's what mum said anyway.

There were plenty of topical jokes and references to locality and events with children from the audience going on to the stage at some time to join in the fun. It was not unusual to arrange for one child to be left stranded on stage and consoled with a special prize.

Occasionally fruit or vegetables such oranges or cabbages were thrown into the audience which, at a time when food rationing was still on, resulted in quite a scramble. In one pantomime there was a character filling in at the interval whose stage name was something like Billy Bluebottle. Dressed head to toe in blue with even brighter blue lace up shoes to complete the outfit, he was supposed to do his routine and then finish off with a song as comedians often did. The intention was then to exit stage left as he gave a farewell wave, leaning and almost falling over in that direction before recovering balance at the last moment in good enough time to pirouette and turn on his right foot while stepping away with his left. It was sad. Ooooh! Sooo sad.

That particular night his left shoe lace had come undone, was trailing on the floor and he hadn't noticed that his right foot was standing on it. You can guess the rest. He fell away to his left and kept on falling because his left foot couldn't move away. There was an almighty 'thwack' as he hit the floor. Everybody thought it was part of the act and fell about laughing, many children almost hysterical.

He got up, dazed and confused, doing his best to exit as nonchalantly as he could but hobbled shakily off instead of the hop skip and jump he normally performed; probably getting the best exit applause he'd ever had that night, before or since.

Membership of the library in Alexander Road came along at nine years of age. It was right alongside where the fire station was then located and I remember being taken on several occasions to see if my legs would reach the pedals or were long enough to climb the ladders with smiling encouragement from firemen.

The first library book I borrowed was called Tenderfoot, about a young cowboy. I borrowed many and over time was introduced to Enid Blyton's Famous

Five and Secret Seven series as well as Just William by Richard Crompton, both of them I found to be thoroughly enjoyable. The William series was particularly funny and my parents would often find me convulsed with laughter in any room I was sitting in as I read about his exploits.

The word computer was completely unknown to our generation when we grew up and I think we were blessed by its absence and all that it now entails. We stretched our imaginations to their limits with radio, books and play and benefited greatly from it.

YOUNG GENTLEMEN

At around nine, going on ten years of age I took up with a couple of regular friends named Alan Aplebie and Wynford Lawson. Alan was a rather thick set individual having a square shaped face, heavy jaw line, jet black curly hair and blue eyes. His habitual dress seemed to be an old school shirt and blazer, sometimes a jumper and short dark grey corduroy trousers when not in school uniform. Grey socks and some well scuffed dark brown shoes completed his outfit. Elegantly dressed he was not but then neither of us were. His voice was also deeper than most boys of our age and when he chose to he could really put a bit of rasp into it.

Wynford was lighter in build and a little shorter compared to Alan, or me for that matter. He had wavy light brown hair worn in a regimental parting to one side unlike Alan's which completely refused to be trained anyway. His face was rounder with a broad nose and brown eyes set beneath an almost permanent frown as they gazed out on the world.

It was not unusual for him to wear Wellington boots instead of shoes and when he did wear shoes they were well worn school cast offs topped by the usual pair of school socks. We all wore short trousers then and for Wynford they served to display a pair of very stick like legs which we occasionally ribbed him about.

Don't worry about them we told him; one day you'll be big and strong and grow into them. To keep himself warm he always wore a thick jumper over an ever changing shirt with a jerkin sort of thing which I was quite jealous of.

Myself I had one very distinct feature which was a considerable disadvantage when ringing doorbells and then making a run for it before they were answered: a mop of fall anywhere fair hair that had once been likened to the colour of burnt corn by one of the chapel elders. A lady of mature years I could quite happily have strangled on the spot as she described it thus while I stood, stopped in the street by her, with a group of my friends looking on sniggering. Whenever they wanted to put me down after that they referred to me as 'corn head' which I greatly appreciated.

I wasn't spindly or heavy set; just average with a sort of oblong face that always seemed darker because of my hair and a wide forehead that unfortunately accentuated a longer nose than I was happy with. I usually liked to wear an old school blazer with shoes that were almost has-beens, used for everything, but also had a fondness for jumpers; worn most of the time like Wynford. None of us wore ties if we could avoid it. They just got in the way.

We must have looked a motley crew but we got along fine and had been knocking around together for some time when we decided that pretend cigarettes from toy shops and sweet ones you could eat did not project the image of masculinity that we believed we were entitled to. Seduced by the heady scent of real tobacco from our cigarette pack collections we decided that smoking with real ones was the more sophisticated and manly thing to do and we needed to change our image by forming our own smoking club. The decision made our first hurdle was to get hold of some tobacco filled ciggies. Unfortunately unless we could acquire them by surreptitious means, like sneaking one from our various parent's supplies, the only option was to buy or roll your own. In practice however going into local tobacconists nonchalantly trying to buy a packet of five Woodbines was not very successful no matter how deep we tried to make our voices. Skinny white legs and short trousers were a dead giveaway. Saying you were buying for your dad could sometimes work if you could brazen it out but that ploy only really worked if you were buying a ten or twenty pack.

One of our respective parents, which was usually dad, had of course already been into the local newsagent or tobacconist so the vendor was already familiar with him and his errant son who sometimes accompanied him. Dad regularly buying ten or twenty Senior Service somehow didn't gel with junior trying to buy five Woodbine on his behalf. A fact which also took a while to register with junior who had not yet acquired the sneaky mind of the hardened criminal.

I actually remember us on one occasion cadging some cigarettes off an unsuspecting watchman who was guarding roadworks. Every so often the highways department would repair or resurface the roads in our area. Sometimes it would just be in small patches undertaken by a gang of two or three workmen using picks and shovels with a tipper truck. If it involved re-laying a whole road with tarmacadam and gravel a full crew would move in, often with a steam roller which were still seen around on the odd occasionally into the mid 1950's.

Occasionally there would be a tarmac spreader attached to a Sentinel road locomotive used to heat and melt the road surface and that was something really interesting. Luckily for us they seemed to like parking up outside Brynmill Park and if there was no night watchman's trailer on tow they would set up a canvas tent mounted across a form of tubular knockdown framework open to the elements on one or two sides. There would usually be a wooden bench inside and a coal fired brazier outside.

There was nothing better than having 'the craic' with a watchie man to talk about worldly things and guide the conversation onto cigarette brands and which ones were preferred by him and us. The trick was to try and get him to take pity because we didn't actually have any to smoke during the conversation. If we played our cards right and the watchie caught on, occasionally he would surrender one for sharing. Night watchmen were usually getting on in years and rather weather beaten after having spent a lifetime at the roadside. They were not that well paid for their services and couldn't really afford to give their smokes away willy-nilly but at that time we hadn't developed social awareness and were only looking out for ourselves.

We were nearly caught out one night just after we had extorted a ciggie from another unsuspecting victim. I was just lighting up when who should walk past with his girlfriend but my art master Mr Bowen. Alan and Wynford, who I was with, were not that concerned because they went to different schools. It was my bad fortune to be seen not theirs. I don't know who saw who first but he raised an eyebrow as he saw me give a pained double take as I clocked him. It was lucky that he found the incident amusing otherwise he could have caused trouble.

I could have sworn I heard him and his girlfriend giggling as they carried on walking, not quite out of earshot. My next art class was attended with much trepidation but when he saw me he just gave an amused half smile and carried on with the lesson. He went up a notch in my estimation and probably had some fun telling the tale to his fellow teachers in the staff room. I know for a week or so afterwards I got some funny looks and smirks from a number of them.

Taking all things into consideration meant that we had no option other than to perform the ultimate sacrifice by clubbing pocket money together to fund a more deceptive purchase.

Success with a packet of ten meant three ciggies each and shared puffs on the last one. There were other methods of getting cigarettes. I mentioned rolling your own. Buying just the tobacco in a tin or packet was a lot smoother in operation and didn't bring forth so many searching questions particularly when you got the roll papers somewhere else.

If we went to a shop on a side street they were usually not so particular in selling to aspiring gentlemen of leisure like us and we found we could bribe them with money in exchange for a packet of five almost every time. It was during our ongoing investigation of how to acquire cheap tobacco that I had a stroke of luck.

The middle room of our house, as we called it, was my father's office come study which he used occasionally for writing railway correspondence or letters. It was also the room in which both my sister and

I in later years would study for school exams, she successfully, me not. It was furnished with a couple of arm chairs and also had a magnificent oak desk made especially for him by one of his business acquaintances. In addition there was a very fine oak bureau and book case with fold down flap for writing.

This particularly fascinated me because as you opened the flap which revealed small draws and compartments at the rear, two wooden arms slid out for it to rest on. The whole thing was topped by a glass cabinet which was used to store a variety of books. Under the desk were four deep pull out drawers in which were stored several jigsaw puzzles and games like snakes and ladders, Ludo, Monopoly and drafts. This was where I got lucky.

Occasionally when bored or just being nosey seeing what he had collected I would have a rummage in all of the drawers. The only things I would find worthy of interest though were a railway identity and pass card for the docks during wartime, some un used food ration books and a solidly constructed cardboard box containing a gasmask. On this lucky day however I found a tin of mouldy cigarettes which I had missed previously. They were too far gone to consider but were concealing another tin underneath.

That tin contained gold dust or to be more precise: tobacco. It too was a bit musty, heaven knows how old, pre-war perhaps but a better proposition than the ciggies. There were also some papers for rolling, along with – I couldn't believe my luck -a rolling machine. Just lick the edge of the paper, put it in the machine, lay in a suitable amount of brown weed and turn the handle. Hey presto! One perfectly formed rather thin cigarette that tasted absolutely foul. But hey! Why complain. One small step towards manhood. As soon as possible, I took my new found manufacturing centre along to a specially convened meeting.

The find was received with much joy until the weed had been rolled and sampled after which it was concluded that it was definitely too vintage to be healthy. What we needed was a more mature brand like St Bruno if and when we could acquire some. In the meantime another potential source of sucking delight was discovered.

One of my more responsible hobbies was basket-work, which used pliable cane to weave with.

The cane was naturally porous and why I did it I don't know but I decide to see what it burnt like. It burnt slowly and if you sucked on it the lit end glowed. Fortunately neither of us knew how to smoke properly so we didn't take any fumes down into our lungs. It was of course no substitute for the real thing so we had to struggle gamely on in our pursuit of manhood and to this end we found one last unexpected source of supply which echoed the strategy of sneaking the odd ciggy from an unsuspecting parent.

The new found treasure trove was more plentiful however. Alan's father was an engineer for an oil company travelling all over the world and would regularly return with all kinds of exotic smokes from foreign lands. The resulting collection had built up to the point where the odd packet would not be missed over a period of time and the son of the unsuspecting parent managed to wangle it so that some of the contents found their way to us.

The fact that the odd cigar also followed was just incidental and we must have looked a strange sight on a Sunday evening after chapel strolling down Swansea

Bay promenade, three ten year olds, going on eleven, in short trousers, chugging away at three rather large cigars in full view.

But we were oblivious. There were a few sniggers and raised eyebrows from people that we passed but nobody of authority challenged us. We were young gentlemen out enjoying the evening air. We were going places.

The place where we went however was not actually what we had in mind. Our downfall came when we started to look around for suitable premises to set up our smoking lounge. Obviously we could not use any of our houses or an adjoining garage. Even if no parent wandered out to see what we were doing the evidence of cigarette smoke would hang around for some time so that option was out of the question.

The three of us lived in different streets but not too far away from each other in a district with all the houses having a lane at the rear giving mostly both garage and back door access. What we needed was a detached and deserted garage which was not being used and we spent some time doing a survey around quite a number of the local lanes and there were plenty of them.

Eventually we found a separate group of eight in a side lane set out in the form of a rectangle. Four in the middle and a pair at each end at right angles to the others. I tell you this because it will help you understand the ambush.

One of the middle cluster at one end was unsecured, obviously not in use. It had a long multi hinged folding door which had to be pushed from one end to park it against the opposite inside wall to open. When we found it the door was partly open so we just swung back the first section, stuck our heads in and all unanimously decided that we had found our young gentleman's club. The garage was empty but for floor rubbish and completely devoid of any furnishings, windows or lighting. What a surprise. It was consequently pitch black when the door was closed so we had to grope our way around by the light of a match or fag end.

Yes this would be ideal we decided so we immediately lit up and christened the place. It lasted as our smoking headquarters for about three weeks until one fateful Saturday afternoon when we were slowly emerging after fuming up the place till it started to make us dizzy. I slowly swung the door open to my right standing behind it to see if the coast was clear. No problem. Wynford followed with Alan still inside having a last puff.

We were facing each other talking not paying attention to our surroundings so the voice made us jump. We turned to look and there casually standing in the corner between the two garage rows was a young bluebottle – all six foot of him.

"Hello boys", he said with a smug predatory grin on his face. "It's nooo good running," he said. "I can run faster than you do."

I know for a fact that my jaw dropped as I did a double take with cigarette smoke slowly wafting out from the garage over our heads. We were stuffed!

"I was wonderin' when you'd be payin' another visit. Where's your other friend? Is he still chuffin' away inside?"

I said "Er" then "Aah" and then Alan emerged with a puzzled look on his face which soon turned to one of abject dismay.

PC Bluebottle strolled over to us still smiling as though he'd cracked his first big case and poked his head inside the garage.

"Oh my my," he said, "what a fug. Is this your smoking room? Not very healthy is it?"

"Are we under arrest?" Wynford suddenly asked rather nervously. "Will we go to jail?"

What a pratt I thought. Alan looked aghast. PC Bluebottle stifled a laugh, looked down at him and giving a slow conspiratorial wink said, "I'll put in a word in and see what I can do for you but I think mummy and daddy should to know about this don't you?"

Wynford looked as though he might faint. PC Bluebottle was becoming annoying. Alan tried to brazen it out.

"No not really", he said airily," they'll only make a fuss."

"Yes," the bluebottle replied, "Possibly so. But you do look a little young to be smoking. Where did you get the ciggies from?"

Now this was a leading question which we really didn't want to answer. It could be real incriminating, so we pretended we didn't understand. Could we plead the Fifth Amendment like they did in gangster films? No we couldn't. That was only in American gangster films.

The three of us responded. "Ah, oh, ummm."

"Yes I thought so," he said.

He was quite pleasant really in an irritating sort of way and I though he must be rooting for sergeant.

"How old are you?" he asked." I have a good idea so no fibbin'."

We told him. I said "Twelve." He looked at me with pity and said, "Rather small for your age aren't you?" I said, "Ten."

"Right! I think I had better have your names and address. I'll be along to see mummy and daddy later this afternoon." It was the way he kept referring to mummy and daddy that I found most annoying. If he had said parents that would have been OK. But mummy and daddy? It was humiliating. He was beginning to get on my wick. We were ten dammit; almost men. But we were still filled with dread knowing only too well the sort of grilling we would get. Prison was a better option. The three of us departed our separate ways to an unknown fate wondering if we would ever meet again; bidding a fond farewell to our smoking lounge and au revoir to the man in blue. I did not head for home and directly to jail however. I most definitely did not want to suffer the humiliation of a grilling from dad with the law looking on smirking so I played it crafty, stretching out the afternoon by wandering around the fairground that was blaring out music on the recreation ground alongside the Mumbles road. This only served to delay confrontation and retribution though and father dear father was already lurking in the hallway as I arrived.

"You've had a visitor," he said, getting directly down to business.

"But of course you knew that didn't you?"

He made this statement looking at me rather pointedly. I tried to put on my very best blank look.

"The policeman Bernard, the policeman who caught you and your friends smoking." I surrendered.

To my surprise and relief things didn't go at all badly after that. I had expected him to be incandescent and foaming at the mouth with rage but instead he was perfectly reasonable. Had I got him all wrong? He told me I was a chump for smoking. It was too late for him to give it up. He'd smoked all his life knowing no better but I should stop before I got the habit. It was so unnecessary he said and gave me a lecture on the risk to my health. I tried to debate the point by informing him that we only smoked filter tips and not straight unfiltered Players like he did, totally of course leaving out any mention of our failed attempts at rolling his old cigarette tobacco, but it went down like a lead balloon.

He just looked exasperated. Unimpressed by any effort at debate and in a desperate attempt to convince me of my foolhardiness he gave me a demonstration of the muck you take into your lungs from cigarettes by lighting up, taking a deep drag and then blowing the smoke out through a clean white handkerchief to deposit a thick brown tar stain. Now that did impress me. Not for long but it did impress me. I later used it as a trick to demonstrate to some of my other friends.

I was still surprised at his overall reaction. I had expected thunder and lightning which is exactly what poor old Alan got from his father, being grounded for about three weeks. Wynford fared a little better however but the whole episode seemed to herald the beginning of the end of our regular threesome unfortunately.

"Ones parents" saw to that with the usual knee jerk response of "Keep away from them. They are a bad influence on you." Mum and dad said it about Alan and Wynford, Alan's mum and dad said the same about me and Wynford, and Wynford's mum and dad said the same about me and Alan. Well I certainly didn't agree that I was a bad influence on anybody and we did keep meeting up but it always seemed that we were looking over our shoulder. During all this time of course we did have other friends and acquaintances that we mixed with and over the ensuing weeks and months our individual allegiances and interests did inevitably change so that we saw less of each other than before although we still remained friends.

The local police substation was more or less central to the district where the three of us lived and no doubt a record of our crime and apprehension would have been entered into their incident book. Unfortunately my house was sandwiched between the domestic arrangements of a senior police constable a couple of doors up and a sergeant several doors down. They both always acknowledged me if we met in the street and for some time after that fateful day whenever our paths crossed it was always with a knowing half smile on their lips or a stifled smirk but they never ever mentioned PC Bluebottle's bust.

WHEELS AND THE COAL HOUSE DOOR

Alan had previously mentioned his ambition to build a soap box or trolley as we called it, sometimes also known as a gambo, depending on where you were living. Soap boxes were more sophisticated than trolleys, perhaps even posh. Instead of just open planks of wood with wheels bolted to them they were enclosed all around with some sort of styling and brightly decorated with numbers.

They were occasionally seen on cinema newsreel being raced down hilly streets in front of cheering supporters which was what inspired him to try and build one of his own. We had loosely kept in touch since our encounter with PC Plod and about six months later we just started knocking around together again.

We really wanted bicycles but realised fairly early on that one's guardians would not be providing funds so we did the next best thing and occupied cuckoo land for a while, ogling them in a shop window that we knew. Everybody now has heard of James Bond; well we knew him before anybody else did.

He had a bicycle shop in St Helens Road not far from the hospital and we started to spend a good part of our Saturday mornings in front of his window; looking at the display and deciding which one we were - someday in the near future -going to buy. Fat chance! All the ones we fancied were sporty drop handlebar or butterfly types with ten speed derailleur gear change. Sturmey Archer three speed did not match the image we had of ourselves riding down to Langland or Caswell Bay.

As well as complete bicycles, from sit up and beg granddads to racers, the window was littered with other bikey bits and pieces like fancy handlebars, lightweight pedals, wheels, pumps, bolt on change gears, boxes of other mysterious looking stuff, and even a couple of lightweight catch me if you can speed frames; one of then painted a shade of grey that really took my fancy and I pictured myself putting it all together and racing away to exotic places like Fairwood Common. Yeah! That was the one bit I'd fit all the other bits to I thought, along with the really cool looking extended drop handlebars on the shelf next to it; me, Alan, and Wynford. We'd make 'em all jealous.

I thought about boys a few years older, now wearing their long trousers tucked into their socks, who would ride their bikes deliberately into us when we were standing together, forcing us to move apart, just to show off. Casually pulling up on their drop handlebar steeds, their brakes biting and nodding them to a halt, they would stand straddling them, one foot on the ground the other on a pedal. To complete the pose they then leaned with one hand on the saddle the other in the middle of the handlebars.

Most of them were just showing off without malice but a few were inclined to bully. After forcing us apart they would gaze at us underlings around them with disdain, making sneering and unnecessary threats or critical remarks to assert their superiority before moving off to make a nuisance of themselves elsewhere.

They could really get under your skin sometimes and made us feel like rushing at them with a hard shove to push them over. Very tempting at times but they were generally bigger than we were but one day… perhaps one day?

We pored over the collection of Raleigh leaflets we had amassed between us and dreamed. Alan had found a pedal at the back of his garage. If we could only find something else bikey to attach it to with another pedal and then a few more bits after that perhaps we could build one of our own.

We would call it 'MARK ONE'. Well that was what we understood you always did when making the first something on wheels. Once completed and road tested we would start on an improved version we would call 'MARK TWO'. We were, as I said, living in cloud cuckoo land. We needed wheels, chain, frame, handlebars, saddle and everything else and buying them from 007's bike shop was not an option. We couldn't afford a tire pump let alone the rest. Our ambitions were totally out of touch with reality. We would just have to develop a 'MARK ONE' trolley instead.

In the meantime even during our distraction with window gazing Alan had had the foresight to put it about on the grapevine that he wanted some pram wheels because they were the right size for a trolley. He'd forgotten all about it until a messenger of the unexpectedly kind arrived at his garage door through the back lane one Saturday morning, shortly after we had abandoned our bike project. It was Wynford –

riding his bike. Woh? Since when did Wynford have a bike?

Apparently he'd just got lucky. One of his dad's work colleagues had a son who had outgrown it and flogged it to him cheap and Wynford was the beneficiary. We were jealous. I was jealous but it didn't help. We asked him why he had come. Not that we weren't pleased to see him; it had been a while, and he also brought us some good news.

One of his cousins had a pram he was about to sling out. The message had reached his ears just in time. Our friendship had stalled since the encounter at the Young Gentleman's Club but now he was welcomed back with open arms and became our facilitator and bosom buddy again, taking us to retrieve the abandoned vehicle from his cousin's back yard in Catherine Street the following week.

The pram body was certainly clapped out but the wheels were good and perfectly retrievable together with the axles. We didn't want to push the thing all the way back to the garage so his cousin gave us a hand taking the axles off the body with two side springs, just in case, and said he'd put the rest out for the rag and bone man. The three of us then carried our trophies back to Alan's place to our metaphorical drawing board; the garage floor.

There was an old wooden sideboard set along one wall of the garage and fortunately Alan's engineer father had made a bit of a tool store out of it with the draws and cupboards containing an assortment of nuts, bolts, wood screws, washers, other bits of mechanical thingies and a selection of hand tools consisting of pliers, hammer, screwdriver, hacksaw and several different sized spanners.

Leaning against another wall, a gift from the gods, was the old coal house door which had become redundant when his dad had extended their kitchen just before his latest trip abroad. Dead handy was Alan's dad, who fortunately at the time was still away somewhere on the other side of the world or he could have put a spoke in the wheels so to speak. Funny huh! I could almost hear Alan's mind working, thinking that perhaps his dad could be quite useful after all.

After due deliberation about possible consequences and a cover story for the future we set to work. The first thing we did was dismantle the door and make a long chassis board with cross piece on the back to mount the rear axle. Cutting the bits to length looked like being a problem until Wynford our facilitator noticed a very sharp wood saw hanging on a piece of string in one corner of the garage. He was proving almost as useful as Alan's dad we told him.

With a bit more fiddling and jiggery-pokery we fixed the second axle to another sawn down plank with some heavy duty U form nails, like we had done with the back axle, and attached the assembly to the front with a bolt using two large flat washers and lock nuts so that it was free to turn in either direction. Only two things then remained to be done. The first was to acquire a piece of rope and attach it each side of the front cross plank for steering. Wynford thought we could steer with our feet but if one slipped off, we said, it would turn to one side, probably roll over and throw the rider off. No; we needed a rope. We didn't have one and couldn't find any so Alan, at great risk to his personal relationship with his mother, used the cord of his dressing gown; after he grubbied it up on our workshop floor to disguise it.

'MARK ONE' was now almost ready for its first road trial but before opening the doors the second thing to do was sorted when Alan found an old wooden crate from somewhere and mounted it upside down on the chassis board to sit on. Apart from several delays to allow for injury time where the hammer missed the sweet spot and the saw blade sliced through skin instead of cutting wood, a couple of weeks after starting the project we were ready to take it on its first test run.

We opened the garage doors and wheeled Speedy MARK ONE into the waiting world. Not far from the garage was a long gentle sloping lane that went on for a couple of hundred yards, around a bend and then down a much steeper slope.

It was the ideal christening ground and since it was his project and his garage Alan became the test driver. He sat on the crate, got hold of his dressing gown cord and we gave him a shove and watched him slowly accelerate away. It took him a while to get used to the steering and almost hit one of the lane walls but by the time he got to the bend he had just about mastered it...but not quite.

We had been chasing down the lane and lost sight of him as he went around the bend and only heard the crash. When we got to him he was just lying there in the middle of the lane on his back, appearing to be comatose, but laughing like an idiot. There was a pothole just around the corner that couldn't be seen until it was too late and a front wheel had caught it, pulling the whole thing violently to one side, slewing it around and throwing him off with the trolley half rolling after him ending up on its side.

We were pleased he wasn't hurt, and even more pleased that the trolley hadn't suffered any damage because we hadn't yet had a go on it. So we pushed it back up the lane for a way and took several turns riding back down before calling it a day. Over the next few weeks we took it out for a run in different and riskier, steeper locations whenever we could, falling off many times and not caring a bit. Not always the three of us but we played fair, made our contribution to running repairs and had an equal share of the fun.

After an unintended tip-off from Alan's sister that his mother was looking for a certain dressing gown cord, part of the repairs included a steering modification. A short piece of much stronger clothes line was slyly requisitioned from the existing wind drying service arrangements and substituted while the two ladies of the house were out shopping together.

Although a great success and lots of fun the trolley project had become a major distraction from our original objective though and soon Alan and I, still without bikes, started to think about them again with Wynford still keen to get involved even though he now had a steed of his own. Since we had first asked months ago, where rag and bone men took all the dead bits that they collected, the answer had gradually trickled back through a friend of a friend of a friend of an even more distant cousin whose dad actually was a rag and bone man with a horse and cart whose immediate family, we also heard, had disowned him. Just how lucky could three collectors of scrap bicycle bits get?

There were scrap dealers, they said, on the town's west bank at the end of Quay Parade; down by the docks and along from the swing bridge; a part of the town now been completely rebuilt with new bridges crossing the river and an old anti-aircraft gun standing as a monument to the wartime defence of Swansea.

Where now lies New Cut Road in our school days was a cobbled street next to the river with the remains of bombed out houses each side serving as scrap bays for the bone men and dealers. Now we knew where to go and we started to make plans.

I can't remember exactly what time of the year it was but I do remember that it was dry, sunny and quite warm so it may well have been one of our summer school holidays. Now Wynford had a bicycle and Alan had the trolley things might actually be easier for carrying our bits back. It was a fair distance from where we all lived and would take a while to get to, but each of us had at some time walked the round trip to the town centre by different routes a number of times so we weren't worried about how far it was.

Walking to the river wouldn't present much more of a challenge so we were rearing to go. Whatever day it was, we set off fairly early; Alan and me taking turns to pull the trolley which he had temporarily modified with a bigger box for carrying stuff, and Wynford pushing and then riding his bike when he felt like. Daft really but he said if we had anything big to carry we could tie it to the bike and push it along. Privately I thought it was more likely he was planning to push off home when he'd had enough of scratching around in the scrap yard but I didn't tell him that or Alan for that matter. So we made our way in a zig-zag diagonal line for the Mumbles Road, passing the hospital on the way and then cutting through back streets, aiming to come out by the Mumble Tram terminus at Rutland Street. From there we continued our way along Quay Parade passed Hancock's brewery and then Easton Brothers crap yard. Easton Brothers was a heavy industrial scrap yard; not what we were looking for but still interesting.

A couple of years hence I was to become very familiar with both them and Weavers Basin, a bit further along on the other side of the road.

I suppose it took just over an hour. The trolley was proving more of a drag than expected but by the time we realised it time was getting on. If we gave up we would never even start building our racing bikes. We were hungry. I think I'd only brought an apple and a little bit of my pocket money with Alan and Wynford just sharing a bar of chocolate and couple of biscuits that Wynford had scrounged. We hadn't planned very well and it turned out the cobbled street at our destination wasn't paved with bicycle bits either. When we arrived there were a couple of bone men standing in a doorway at the top end of it where a partially damaged house had been converted into a reception office.

They were in discussion with somebody at the window and we made our way up to it as they turned away to start offloading stuff from their carts. We approached the window and formally stated our business across an improvised hatch to the man inside.

He was wearing an old bowler hat and the remains of what had once been a nice silk scarf around his neck with the ends tucked into a waistcoat buttoned most of the way… but no shirt. Bowler hats were still worn in some quarters then as the symbol of authority. I didn't know it was fashionable in scrap yards though.

We wanted, we said, to have a rummage amongst their rubbish, we didn't quite put it like that. We actually said bits and pieces for anything we could use to make a bicycle.

"Oh yes," he said smiling pleasantly with an amused expression on his face.

"So you're going to build yourselves a bike are you? I don't think there'll be much stuff suitable for that here but have a look around if you like. But!" he added with emphasis," be careful what you're doing. There's lots of things poking up and sharp corners all over the place – OK? And when you're done be sure to come and see me before you go. I need to know what you're taking."

We nodded in agreement and started to wander around the bombed out remains; slowly making our way down the street through the ruins of what had once been people's homes. We wondered briefly if anybody had been killed there and how horrible it must have been but soon put such morbid thought aside and continued with our endeavours.

We were not there rummaging long when we were distracted by the sound of two old steam cranes rattling, clanking and chuffing away back and fore on railway lines right alongside the river bank.

They were busy hooking up and lifting much bigger lumps of what looked like old machinery. So we made way over to get a closer look for a while and watched them loading onto rail wagons before we went back to doing what we had come for.

After just under an hour of wandering around, crossing and re-crossing the bombed out street, we had found a set of drop handlebars, saddle frame with mounting tube less actual saddle, a chain-wheel complete with pedal cranks and spindle, two bent and distorted wheels without tyres and a pair of slightly askew front forks with lamp bracket attached. Totally brilliant! We could already visualise the finished racer. The wheels might not be a hundred percent aligned but we knew you could get spare spokes and a special spanner to reset the tension. Huh! We were specialist quality bike builders weren't we?

As we contemplated our treasure I looked up to see another rag and bone man arrive and make his way to the office, recognising him from an encounter a couple of years previously. If he recognised me he didn't show it, although I would obviously had changed a bit since that day riding on his cart. He'd diddled my dad over an old boiler but I wasn't going to remind him. He didn't look in a good mood and might have taken it out on poor Dobbin his horse who was looking decidedly weary that morning.

We'd put what we could into the trolley box but there wasn't room for all of it so it looked like we would have to carry some bits separately. If we could scrounge some string from the man in the office perhaps we could tie the wheels to Wynford's bike. As we were weighing up the options I suddenly noticed a pram lying on its side in one of the doorways underneath an upturned kitchen table and some broken drawers which had once been part of it. We dragged it out from underneath and took a closer look. It was a bit battered with just the main box of the pram and wheels around the same size as on Alan's trolley. My brain went into overdrive.

Why didn't we take this as well? We could use it to carry the remaining bits including the wheels and also make a second trolley called MARK TWO! -for me. Only snag was I didn't think dad would let me put it in the garage at the moment. He'd temporarily hired out the space to a neighbour for parking his car and there wasn't any room to put a pram as well. I discussed the problem with Alan but as far as he was concerned, he said, there was no problem.

We could store it in his dad's garage, as recovered from the scrap yard, and if necessary keep the wheels and axles and dump the rest. In the meantime we would use it to carry the rest of our pickings. So I wheeled the pram with my bits in, Alan dragged the trolley with his bits in and Wynford pushed his bike back to the office building and we wondered what the man in the bowler hat would say about the pram.

What he said was, he'd swap all the bits we had collected and the pram for Wynford's bike. Alan and I didn't think he was serious; Wynford did and shook his head in horror. He didn't know what to say in reply. Mr Bowler hat looked at him in mock surprise at his reluctance like it was a good deal he'd offered. Then he looked at me an Alan straight faced and winked.

"You've got a lot of treasure there", he said. "Are you sure you'll be able to afford it?"

Silly really but it was only when he said that we realised that it wouldn't be for free. It was scrap wasn't it? Why would you have to pay for scrap?

He shook his head bemusedly. "You thought you could just take what you wanted because it was in a scrap yard did you?" he said, reading our minds. Then chuckling again to himself, "Sorry boys it doesn't quite work like that, but don't worry you won't have to get a bank loan." Oh this guy was funny.

"How much money have you got?" We made a big show of looking through our pockets and after pooling our resources, with Wynford finding some small change, showed him two shillings and nine pence; twenty nine pence in today's money.

"Oh dear me", he said seeing our plight; "times really are tough aren't they? By rights I should charge you at least sixpence for the pram."

Our hearts sank and Wynford and Alan also began to look glum. At that rate we were going to have to put most of the stuff back where we had found it.

"But," he continued, "today is your lucky day. That's what I should charge you; but it's my birthday. I'm in a good mood and you seem nice enough kids so how about we settle for two bob for the lot?"

Great! Two shillings; we'd have some change. What a nice man. What a very, very nice man.

We had become businessmen and just done our first deal. We handed over the dosh: a shilling, a sixpence, a thrupenny bit and three pennies, wished our new friend in the bowler hat a happy birthday and set off down the cobbled street to start our long trek back to civilization as we knew it. Alan was once again pulling his newly laden trolley, I was pushing the pram with the bent wheels and other bits and Wynford who had stayed uncomplaining throughout was once again just wheeling his bike.

The cobbles made the bits in the pram rattle and vibrate and until we got to the end of the street the wheels kept falling out. Once we turned the corner into Quay Parade things settled down and we just kept slogging back home taking turns and swapping the trolley, pram and bike around. Pulling the trolley was hard work.

We were tired and looking forward to something to eat. My apple had long since been eaten and the bar of chocolate and biscuits had been shared between the other two. Alan also seemed preoccupied and deep in thought and I asked him what was on his mind. He'd had news his dad would be home in the next couple of days and was worried about what he'd say about the coal house door we'd destroyed and converted into a trolley. I didn't blame him. I'd be worried as well, but I didn't tell him that.

Apart from that things were uneventful until we were going through one of the back streets someway past The Vetch football ground. We must have looked a motley sight and along the way had already drawn a few funny looks. We were looking decidedly scruffier than when we had set out that morning. Not surprising really after having climbed over the junk-pile for an hour or more. I knew I was going to catch it off my mum because I'd torn my pullover and put a deep gash in one of my shoes.

Rounding a corner we saw a group of four rough looking boys, around our age, fifty yards away walking towards us on the same side of the street. We were outnumbered and our sixth sense immediately told us they were predators and saw us as prey. They were spoiling for a fight; we were not.

The three of us looked at each other, our past lives flashing down through the ages bringing us to the present encounter. Were we destined to die here, savaged by a gang of Swansea's back street boys? It was so unfair. We had only recently had our smoking lounge closed down by the law and now this! What would I give for a last chug on a Woodbine?

In between our two gangs two women were chatting away on a doorstep and had immediately began to look wary as soon as our grubby little threesome had entered the street. We had a quickly muttered consultation, still walking, trying to act casual.

"Oh 'eck," Wynford said, "Look tough." "Yeah," Alan agreed, also looking worried, "look tough." So we did our best to brazen it out looking sullen and glaring at everybody. Then a really funny thing happened.

"Roger!" One of the women who obviously knew the boys and seemed at the time to be looking at me in particular said, and then again more sharply for a second time. "Roger, stay clear of them. They're trouble; they're Didicoy boys." What was a Didicoy boy? We wondered, and glared harder as the group of boys slowly crossed to the other side of the street. We kept looking tough and sullen and then Wynford, the idiot, decided to almost ruin our escape with a spontaneous attack of bravado, turning and staring in a brief threatening last look at them and then back to me as though he was saying something.

The doorstep woman repeated the warning to her friend, then again nodding her head emphatically, "Yes they're trouble alright; especially that one with the bicycle." Irony, pure irony.

We kept walking to the end of the street, like we didn't have a care in the world and after turning the next corner, out of sight; I said what we had all been thinking for some time. "Quick! Run like hell in case they change their minds and come after us," and as one we accelerated to full pelt and ran to the end of that street and halfway down the next until we had to stop and catch our breath.

Heaven only knows what people thought as we ran past; me pushing the pram trying not to lose the contents, Alan running and dragging a very noisy trolley, slewing all over the pavement, and Wynford shoving his bike ahead of him instead of riding it. When we judged we were safe we slowed down, laughing like idiots and continued on back to Alan's garage.

Wynford parted company with us at the bottom of

Ryddings hill glad to still be alive. In fact he pedalled away so quickly he almost burned rubber. He'd been wanting to slip away for some time but hung on valiantly till he could wait no more. Alan went in through the lane door, opened up the garage and we dragged the trolley and pram inside where we gave our bits and pieces a last once over before I left him, arranging to meet up again tomorrow... but the tomorrow we planned never came.

It was well past lunch time by then and unfortunately dear father was not in a good mood and thwarted my plans for the next day by detaining me against my will for my various misdemeanours. Namely: A bad tear in one good jumper, a deep cut in a good pair of school shoes, and late; very late; too late for lunch.

So I didn't see Alan until the day after we had planned and in the meantime his father had arrived home by train early that same morning. Not knowing all this I called around some time before mid-day. I was on the way back from walking to have my hair cut at Harry Wheelers in St Helens Road, just a little way along from Eddershaw's furniture shop. I don't know why but he always called me "Shooks;" ever since I first started going there with dad when we first move to Brynmill. Funny name that – Shooks?

Thinking Alan would be in the garage I went the back way through the lane and knocked on the door shouting "It's me, Bernard."

A gruff voice I wasn't expecting and hadn't heard for some time answered, "Come on through the back door Bernard. It's not bolted." It was Alan's dad and I heard muffled protests and a bump against the garage door. Was he was pushing him around?

He must be giving him a heck of a telling off and now he's going to have a go at me.

Standing outside in the lane somewhat apprehensively I did as instructed, went in through the door, putting it on the latch behind me and walked up the path alongside the garage, which was quite large. Things were not as bad as they sounded. In fact they were considerably better as I saw when I entered. The natural gloom, only relieved by daylight coming through a side window, allowed me to see what was going on. His father, dressed in a pair of knockabout dark grey trousers and dark blue heavy cotton shirt was wearing a pair of good quality black leather brogues.

Of leaner build than Alan, but a powerful looking figure none the less, he stood a couple of inches over five and a half feet in height with short cropped graying hair and bushy eyebrows over a set of blue eyes like his son's. His facial features made it easy to recognise that he was Alan's dad and he had hold of him, bent double, in a playful headlock talking to him with a big grin across his face.

Alan was both laughing and protesting repeating his plea to daddy to "g-e-r-r-o-f-f" while being slowly walked around the garage clamped under his arm. I think his dad was hoping that he would eventually follow in his footsteps and take up an engineering career and it was quite honestly a bit surprising that he was being so playful.

Normally he was like a bear with a sore head but they hadn't seen each other for two months so in one way I suppose it was his version of a joyful reunion.

He was addressing Alan. "I said what happened to my coal house door you little horror? I had plans for that door and you and your mate here have destroyed it

– haven't you Bernard?" he said, emphasising my name and whipping his head around suddenly and looking in my direction asking, "Are you the one who's been helping my wayward son?" I gulped, wondering what was going to happen next.

"But we needed it dad. It was just leaning against the wall." He'd forgotten all about our pre-arranged cover story and was still trying to stop laughing.

"Yes it was leaning against the wall where I parked it -till I came back to re acquaint myself with it and decide what I was going to do with it." As daddy bear said this he gave Alan another little shake bringing further laughter and protest before he finally letting him go.

"Alright then," he said. "I was probably going to throw it out anyway but you seem to have made good use of it. Let's have a look at this trolley you've made."

The look on Alan's face was utter enjoyment at the masochistic banter they had just shared and I stood to one side and only commented sparingly as Alan told how the three of us had put it together, the finer points of its design and the tribulations we had endured. I could have sworn that his dad wanted to have a go but couldn't quite bring himself to submit to the possible sacrifice of personal dignity.

Eventually he turned to the far corner of the garage where the pram containing our bicycle bits was standing. It must have been nagging away at his peripheral vision for some time and he finally got around to asking why we had a pram parked in there and where it had come from.

So we both explained the bicycle and trolley projects including Wynford's help in getting some of the bits and wheeling it all the way home from the scrap yard. He seemed both amused and aghast. I suppose we should have mentioned our encounter in the back streets and asked him what a Didicoy boy was but it might have taken the shine off his mood so we didn't.

"Well, you and your two friends have been busy haven't you?" he said as he went over to inspect the junk we had salvaged. Then, shaking his head and sighing in a show of disappointment he added, looking at me again and winking, "It's a pity really."

Alan was puzzled. So was I for that matter. "How d'you mean dad?" he said.

"Well If I'd been able to sell the door instead of you cutting it up the money could have gone towards that bicycle you've been chasing me for. It's a real pity." He was really winding him up.

Alan's expression became contorted. I wasn't sure whether it was disappointment or anguish; probably both and I thought," you jammy sod." First Wynford gets a bike and now it looked like Alan could be going to get one. Then as he stood there trying to work it out daddy bear confirmed my fears, took him in another headlock and finally put him out of his misery.

"Alright," he said, "You'll get your bike. You'll have to wait a few weeks yet but you'll get your bike. How's that?"

Alan responded with a grin from one ear to the other but things were getting embarrassing and I decided it was time to make my excuses and leave them to finish bonding. It was also getting exasperating and I reviewed my own situation yet again.

Wynford had just turned up on a new bike, albeit second hand, but still a bike; and now it looked like Alan was going to get one. Could this be a good negotiating strategy with ones parents for a bike of my own? I could see our bicycle factory venture turning to dust. That evening after tea I tried to make my parents feel guilty. I was bereft of my own transport I told them. I would lose friends and wander alone in the wilderness.

No dice! Adapt, expand your horizons, seek out and make friends with pedestrians they said. But as I sought them out to befriend I found more and more ex-pedestrians had seen the light and converted to cyclists trying not to knock down pedestrians still striving to fulfill their own ambition to breeze along on speedier rubber tires.

I didn't see Alan again till the end of the following week because of his dad being home and also the fact that we were back at school. The three of us went to different ones so there wasn't any chance to hook up again till then. When we did it was just to potter around to clean off the bits and pieces from the scrap yard and dismantle the pram so that we could throw out the body. Ostensibly we were saving the axles for my trolley but in truth I knew it was never going to happen…just like the bike.

The project, like a lot of other fleeting and fanciful schoolboy schemes, died a natural death over the next few weeks and apart from the axles kept for spare trolley parts, the pram body and the rest of the collection eventually found its way, presumably on a horse and cart, back to the bombed out cobbled street on the west bank of the river Tawe. I wondered briefly if they had been booked in and recognised by the elegant old gent in the bowler hat and if he was now wearing a shirt under his waistcoat with the weather turning cooler.

THE LAUGHING CAVALIERS

It was a very busy period in my life and as well as messing around with the trolley and things, other interests like fishing and model aircraft were constantly overlapping and disrupting continuity. My busy timetable was also making it extremely difficult to fit in compulsory school attendance but somehow I made the sacrifice. So if this record of my boyhood doesn't always fit chronological order please bear with me. It was a long time ago and the elastic around that part of my brain that holds memory of yore grows weaker by the day.

With such a heavy schedule it should not come as a surprise therefore that despite all my endeavors I had still not actually mastered a very important skill. I still couldn't ride a flippin' bike. I had tried but not having one of my own had rather limited opportunities to learn. On a number of occasions friends had lent me theirs for short periods around the lanes and streets but balance had eluded me; that is, until one late Saturday afternoon when a group of us had gone to watch some older boys flying their model control line airplanes in Singleton Park.

The flying area they used had a tarmac strip for

playing cricket and was at the far end, where the University College now stands alongside Mumbles Road. At that time it was still very much open pasture where one of the first agricultural type shows had been held and where I had my first personal encounters with tractors and other farming machinery.

For any mechanically minded young boys of the time it was quite exciting. Also on show was and old Dakota airplane. Having never been that close to any real aircraft before it topped off the visit; although I did wonder how they had got it into the display area.

Fly it in, or bring it in pieces and assemble on site.

On this particular afternoon the modellers were using the tarmac strip as a take off point for their diesel powered stunt models. While we were waiting around for things to happen I got talking to a builder who had arrived late on his bicycle but without a model. I knew him vaguely because we had chatted before. He said that his name was Paul and he had witnessing my recent failed attempts at riding and offered to let me try again on his bike while he ran alongside to keep me steady. So off we went with him keeping hold of the back of the saddle to stop me falling over.

It seemed we had only just started riding and running when I suddenly heard him shout "Oy! Bring my bicycle back." Without thinking I turned around in the saddle and there he was about a hundred and fifty yards back laughing and watching me ride metaphorically into the sunset.

I could ride. FANTASTIC! I pedaled back to him feeling the big grin on my face. He was also grinning and seemed quite pleased that with his little bit of assistance I could now ride without a problem. Balancing on a bike is a very strange thing; it becomes instinctive. Chuffed to bits and riding around for another ten minutes to practice my new found skill it was easy to become over confident and unprepared for disaster. A couple of years into the future, at the Tech school by the docks, I would be trying to grapple with the laws of physics. It was right there and then though that mass, inertia and kinetic energy became embedded into my psyche. The three wheeled tricycle ridden as a much smaller, lighter child at our Druslyn Road house had been closer to the ground with much smaller wheels. Slamming the brakes on with impunity was no problem, but now, older, heavier and much higher off the ground on a bigger bike it was.

On a two wheel bicycle the rear brake should always be applied before the front one. I didn't know that. I thought I would just test the front brake to see how good it was and it was very good. The bicycle slithered to an abrupt halt on the dry edge of a long muddy puddle. Initially it started to pivot around the front wheel with the back end lifting off the ground. My rear end though was merely resting on the saddle and not physically anchored to it so we soon parted company and the back wheel fell back down to mother earth. Now at critical mass, I had kinetic energy and inertia took over.

Look down - see the grass, look up – see the sky in front. Look down -see the saddle and the back wheel, look up – see the sky behind. Look down – see the grass in front, look up see the sky in front while airborne. Four feet or so off the ground in a slowly unfolding sitting position flying without wings - till gravity said hello. Splat! My bum kissed terra firma the opposite end of the muddy puddle I had just taken off from. Fortunately the ground was not hard and it was a relatively soft but messy, very messy, landing and very embarrassing. Howls of laughter all around.

The bicycle owner commiserated with me leaning on his now recovered steed while trying not fall over laughing himself. I thanked him sincerely for his patience and, trying to hide my embarrassment, hung around hoping that the part of the puddle collected on my rear end would dry off a bit and also that it would soon get dark enough that nobody would see me waddling home like a duck. I just didn't want to be seen in daylight and my rear view misunderstood.

The following week Paul was walking through Brynmill and he started laughing again as soon as he saw me. In the exchange that followed he said that all those who had witnessed my slow-motion somersault thought it was the best they'd ever seen and would be remembered for a long time. To me however it would always be the day I learnt to ride a bike.

Because I didn't own one at the time and my ambition to build one had come to an abrupt halt, if any of my friends who did have a bike went out for a spin I was stuck. This was how I came to meet Clifford, who lived a few streets away, and how the three former members of our smoking club came to have another run in with authority a couple of months or so later; although it wasn't as traumatic as our first encounter.

The world of work can seem far more glamorous and exciting to a schoolboy than the tedium of reality for an adult and it was because of this perceived glamour that I happened to befriend him, borrow his bike and start down the road to my second brush with the law. We met by accident in the back lane of the Uplands shopping area where we had found an electricity substation.

Behind the substation was an open yard used to store wooden pallets and large packing crates and cardboard boxes. When the comings and goings of delivery vehicles ceased for the night and when it was also unattended on Saturday afternoons, we would move in and experiment making various dens and hides either high up on the top levels of stacked boxes or underneath where we busied ourselves making connecting passages from one den to another.

It was amazing the fun we had messing around there. Potentially it could have been dangerous if one of the stacks collapsed when we were underneath or we could have fallen from a reasonable height but we were just kids with very little sense having some innocent fun. I expect the operators arrived some mornings and wondered just what had been happening after they had gone home. "Huh! Flippin' kids again."

It turned out that Clifford actually lived not far from me but we had never met until one Saturday when I was coming home from a mooch around the town centre with Alan and Wynford. It might have been a mile or so from where we lived but at that age we didn't feel the distance. We would walk for miles everywhere, something we used to do all the time. Few households had cars then and parental chauffeurs were yet to be invented. It was around lunchtime on this particular day while making our way through the Uplands lane that we discovered his uncle's tea warehouse. What actually happened was that Clifford emerged heavily laden with boxes walking towards a van parked outside with its rear doors open.

Unfortunately the boxes were too big for him to see over so when he collided with Wynford he lost his grip and dropped them on the floor. It was all rather good humoured with no talk of suing anybody, human rights issues or permanent damage done to either party. He was about the same age as us so we had a good laugh and helped him stuff the boxes in the van. When we stuck our noses in and asked what was in the boxes he told us they contained packets of tea, which by then we had got a whiff of, and took us inside explaining that it was a wholesale storage warehouse run by his uncle and a business partner.

Although they sold some instant coffees, he said, it was mostly tea that they dealt in. They catered for quite a few brands and on the various storage racks we could see all the colourful labels announcing Brooke Bond, Typhoo, Tetley, Glengettie, PG Tips, and several other exotic brands on the boxes. They were of course loose leaf and not the tea bags that are sold everywhere today. It wasn't a large warehouse, more of a garage, stretching back about thirty feet by fifteen feet wide with a small office taking up half the back wall and a small kitchen galley alongside to sit and brew up.

The main floor was taken up with several racks set at right angles from the right side wall with one long rack running half the length of the other. His uncle was there in the back office but didn't seem to mind our presence. Things were much easier then, with the focus on getting things done so we had an interesting half hour swapping tea bag boxes around and chatting and said we would come back and help again just for something to do.

The outcome was that for a period of a few weeks we went to help out on Saturday mornings for a bit of fun during which time we got to appreciate Clifford's easy going friendship a lot more. We wondered why we hadn't seen him in school and it was then that we found out he was actually a year older than us and had left Brynmill juniors the previous year to go to Oxford Street School in town. When he told me that he had an interest in machinery and had acquired a number of the I Spy books and a collection of tractor catalogues I knew I had found myself another kindred spirit.

A couple of weeks after our informal meeting Alan was talking about going for a bike ride down to Clyne Valley set half way around Swansea Bay and two miles from where we lived. The four of us had become bosom buddies by then and when Clifford learnt that I didn't have a bike he very kindly volunteered to lend me his. I was tickled pink at this offer. Lending somebody your bike was unheard of in our circles but he was quite adamant that he was not bothered about going to Clyne so with my new riding skill now under my belt I took advantage of his generous spirit and immediately accepted the offer.

He said he usually rode to the warehouse on a Saturday and suggested I collect his bike from there at around nine o'clock. It wasn't a piece of junk either. Very swish actually, bright orange in colour with butterfly handlebars and a ten speed derailleur gear change. As long as I returned it to his house by tea time it would be OK because he was due to visit his aunt and uncle over in Sketty. So come the Saturday the three of us set off as planned along the main mumbles road to Clyne Valley.

Not a very exciting or eventful outing really. We probably had a bit of a picnic but did nothing special except following the river to see if we could spot any of the rumoured trout. We decided it was just a rumour.

On the way back we had plenty of time and decided to go home through Derwyn Fawr where we had been told there was a large field with a couple of ponds that were good for fishing. We eventually found it hiding at the top of a long hill which had some expensive looking housing either side.

The ponds also looked promising, one of them being rather shallow containing only roach and the second one, according to someone fishing there, much deeper but having roach and some reasonable sized carp as well. I vowed to come back but Alan and Wynford weren't into fishing that much so it looked like I would be on my own and would maybe have to borrow Clifford's bike again.

But that could be pushing my luck and his good nature. He had been generous enough already. I didn't mind walking there I thought but it was probably about three miles each way so it wasn't really a practical proposition. Then mulling my options over as we left the ponds and headed back home I almost missed the solution. It was called a bus stop and I had just gone sailing past one at the bottom of the long hill.

As I looked back up to the top I could see another stop. All I needed to do now was to find out which bus service it was and then start planning my first expedition. I returned Clifford's wheels but we didn't have time to stop and chat. He needed to set off for Sketty and if I didn't get a move on was possibly going to be late for tea again.

So I walked back home and thought about the boring non-events of the next day which was Sunday. Sunday was a day with no chance of going anywhere but Chapel in the morning and Sunday school in the afternoon. Times were tough for an eleven year old getting on for twelve.

There was a new young bluebottle on the beat and

when we first saw him Alan, Wynford and I were on foot stood talking outside my house and he was on a bike. Not a sleek multi-geared creation like bobbies ride today but a sit up and beg bone shaker with a large ding-a-ling bell to ring when he was in hot pursuit and a small, ever so small really, leather saddle bag swinging behind him. Perhaps, we wondered, it was where he kept his hand-cuffs.

He was built like a beanpole and his grip on the old style handle bars only served to accentuate his awkward looking posture as he pedaled. When we saw him we just sort of fell about laughing, to his obvious embarrassment.

We could see he was not amused although he didn't make any comment by way of response, just a cursory glance as he slowly sailed past. The expression on his face as he clocked us however said it all. "You are mine and retribution shall be come," and it did and not long afterwards.

The following two Saturdays we went along to the warehouse intending to help out for a couple of hours. We were enjoying ourselves so much in the working world that we stayed there a bit longer than planned and our efforts were rewarded by Clifford's uncle with chocolate biscuits and cups of tea from the pirated stock of damaged boxes. He told us that splits, as he called them, were replaced by new packets and used to top up their kitchen galley reserves.

It must have been in the following week that there was a school holiday at half term or something because Alan and Wynford decided to go for another ride but this time a bit further afield to Oystermouth where Wynford had an older sister living. Clifford again lent me his bicycle without fuss and we set off on another sunny morning full of promise. We had forgotten that sometime previously PC Swinging Saddle had made himself a promise and he was about to keep it that very morning.

We were riding in line down the road alongside the bottom end of Brynmill Park when a long familiar shadow dressed in dark clothing, helmet and shiny buttons waved us down. It was our good friend in blue himself but this time minus his trusty steed. Things did not look good.

"Wellwellwell!" He said, as though it was all one word. "Bless my soul. If it isn't the three laughing cavaliers. Do you know I was thinking about you as I came on duty just an hour ago?"

We returned his greeting. "Oh! Er hello. Yeah hello. Uhh."

"I see," he said, "that today our situation is reversed." We looked at him blankly.

With a seriously smug smile on his face he said, "Today you are riding your bicycles and I am on foot. Last time when you were on foot and I was riding my bicycle you thought it was funny. Today we are all going to have a laugh as I examine your bicycles and see what I can find wrong with them. What do you reckon? Does that sound like fun, huh?"

"Sounds hilarious," Alan commented.

"Oh it will be." he said with a really wildly exaggerated grin. "It will be. Now let's have a look starting with yours first." He said turning to me.

He inspected Clifford's bicycle, then Wynford's and finally Alan's. He was reasonably thorough but not overzealous. It was lucky really that he did them in that order and inspected Clifford's borrowed bike first. He was so pleased with himself and his wit that he didn't look closely enough at the tyres which, I had by now become aware, didn't have a lot of air in them as we set off on our pilgrimage.

Really he was quite good natured about the whole thing. I don't think he really wanted to find problems. Just to send us on our way with a flea in our ear for laughing at him. He wasn't stupid. Instead of making enemies he made three new friends – sort of.

The moral to the story is if you are going to laugh at policemen don't do it when they can see you. They never forgive, never forget and always lie in wait!

Before proceeding any further on our journey I decided that it would be prudent to sort out the problem of the soft tyres. None of us had a pump so we started to have a look around, once our new friend was out of sight, to see if any other bikers were about.

We were in luck. Just down from where we had been stopped and opposite the park entrance was a café which was just then serving the needs of a group of swankily dressed drop handlebar dudes.

Fortunately they were all equipped with pumps and weren't in the least bit snooty so I was able to firm up the tyre pressures and we were on our way. Oystermouth was a bit further than we normally went and of course I wasn't that used to riding a bike because I didn't have my own so by the time we got there we were glad of a rest and the refreshments made ready for us by Wynford's married sister and husband who ran a small motor vehicle repair business.

I wasn't to know it then and neither did Wynford but six months later his father decided to move down to the Mumbles district with Wynford and his mother so that he could join his son-in-law in the business. Ironic really. Me moving from there to Brynmill and him moving from Brynmill to there. It was a bitter blow when he eventually moved but I did of course have other friends and interests so it wasn't the end of the world. I always remember him now as one of the laughing cavaliers.

After we had rested and eaten our fill we wondered if we should press further on to the Mumbles Pier and have a look at the lifeboat station. Our journey however had taken longer than expected and I was concerned that Clifford's bike was returned in good time. It was now one o'clock and a long ride back. Someone suggested that we look at the ruins of Oystermouth castle. That didn't sound very exciting. "Just a pile of rubble," Wynford said. Alan asked "Why do they always build old castles out of rubble?" What were we going to do? Going straight back seemed a bit of a waste really and then I had a brainwave.

Both Alan and Wynford knew that I had lived in the area and had been born there so I suggested that we headed back taking a detour past my old house on the way.

They were agreeable and curious to see from whence I had come so off we set. Wynford's sister lived in one of the streets running parallel and behind the main Newton Road so we made our way, first cycling down the lane between the school and Doctor Kyle's old residence, up through the village into Belvue and eventually turning left into Druslyn Road. It was a long steep hill so we decided to dismount our steeds and push instead of pedaling ourselves into oblivion.

The house where I was born was still standing but it was just a house. I don't know what I really expected. My days there had retained no vivid memories to come flooding back. I was now getting on for twelve years of age and, apart from a neighbour's dog biting me when I was about three, the seven years which had passed since we left West Cross had mostly erased my memories of the place. It was over a lifetime away that I had lived there and on a day which had now become overcast, the piece of ground opposite looked desolate and Mr Collier's field which had been our childhood paradise just looked forlorn.

The transient magic of my precious early childhood was lost in the history of those moments. No dog daisies, buttercups or bluebell clusters. No dragonflies to chase and no cows. I don't know if I had been expecting to see children playing in the field as we had played but there were no children anywhere. Time like some of the people I suppose, had moved on and speculators had moved in and were announcing on a large hoarding that this valuable building land was up for sale and tenders were invited.

My appetite for nostalgia somewhat chastened I left my former homestead together with Alan and Wynford and we set off on our return journey, pushing our steeds up to the top of Druslyn Road and then freewheeling down West Cross Lane. It had been a long climb pushing and riding up the hill and we were glad of the opportunity to give our legs a rest and coast. Reaching the dip at the bottom we then pedalled up the hill and out through the Mayals onto the Mumbles Road to make our way homeward.

Eventually we got back in time to return Clifford's steed shortly after four o'clock, confirming that we would see him at the warehouse on Saturday morning in a couple of days' time. When Saturday arrived one of us was missing. Alan had been roped in by his mother to go to the Saturday morning cinema club with his sister at the Odeon in Sketty so it was just me and Wynford who were helping out. In truth of course we were not really helping. We were still just kids hanging around trying to out tell each other's tall stories of life and adventure while we occasionally shifted a few boxes around to look important. But it made us feel more grown up than our contemporaries and we were harming no one, so why not? We didn't really know why Clifford spent so much time there. I don't think he was obliged to be there really. Perhaps it was just that he enjoyed the atmosphere of being at the family firm. Some kids were like that.

In some ways he was a strange sort of boy. Physically he was of average height for his age with a rectangular shaped face and jet black hair parted formally to one side like Wynford's. His uncle had also fixed him up with a grey warehouse coat which made him look more the part. Almost studious in manner he had a natural presence and demeanour that without deliberate intent seemed to project an air of expectation as if waiting to fulfil some kind of destiny. My destiny at that moment though was to go with Wynford who was restless and said that he couldn't stay long that Saturday. I suspected the novelty of tea boxes was beginning to wear off.

Anyway when he left, we went together, but not before we told Clifford about the encounter with our policeman friend a couple of days previously. He found it highly amusing but also seemed anxious about having his bicycle inspected.

Having been the one riding it I assured him that his ownership had not been mentioned so there was no need worry about a policeman knocking on his door any time soon. It was just as well that we couldn't foretell the future. Just before we left I arranged to meet up at his house the following Thursday to look over the tractor catalogues he had collected. Thus organised we parted company leaving him to his tea boxes.

On the way out of the lane we passed the back of Andrews Garage which held an agency for Morris Cars. It was a deep building stretching from the lane right through to the frontage on Uplands Crescent. At the open end where we stood looking in could be heard the fascinating sound of a compressor blowing a safety valve with a loud clatter and swish every few minutes and there was a car on the raised repair ramp so we could see the workings underneath.

A mechanic standing at a bench nearby grinned at us and asked what we wanted so we asked a couple of quick schoolboy techie car questions which he had started to answer before he was interrupted and had to leave in response to a disembodied voice calling from an office above.

It all looked really grubby and greasy; our kind of paradise. We both decided we wanted to be mechanics. There was a dividing partition between the service bay and the showroom which was partially open allowing us to see through to where a dandily dressed white haired sales executive was showing a couple of potential customers a gleaming new Morris Minor saloon. It was a fascinating glimpse into another world and we left the back of Andrews Garage to make our way home, parting company by Thomas's the Newsagent. It was the last time we ever saw Clifford.

It was back to school that week so there was less free time for us all. It was also the year of the eleven plus exam. I hated exams, tests, whatever you wanted to call them. I was not mouldable academic material.

Thursday evening eventually came and after tea I trekked across to see Clifford.

The long rows of terraced houses on both sides of his street where he lived were unusually quiet and deserted. Normally it was milling with children of all ages in and out of each other's houses with parents yelling various domestic scoldings, everyone generally busy and going about their evening activities. But not that evening. All the front doors were closed just like Clifford's.

I felt decidedly uneasy but I didn't know why. Perhaps it was instinct. When I rang the doorbell it took a while for it to be answered and it was his uncle who came. He looked strained and then surprised to see me and asked why I had come. I explained that I had made the arrangement with Clifford the previous Saturday and he just looked at me vacantly and shook his head.

"Oh God!" he said, sighing heavily as he tried to break the bad news to me as gently as he could, "I'm sorry son." He hesitated again, trying to find the right words. "You obviously haven't heard. Our Clifford had a bad accident yesterday on the way home from school. I'm sorry Bernard – he's dead."

It didn't register. My brain stalled; refusing to accept the terrible information. I was confused. I had come to see Clifford and it sounded like he was telling me that I couldn't.

"No, no, it's alright. He is expecting me," I said. "He is in isn't he? Can I see him?"

His uncle looked at me aghast not sure how to respond and then said very gently, looking even more anguished than before.

"No Bernard... he's not here... I'm sorry. Did you hear what I said? Do you understand what I'm saying?

He's dead son. He's not in this world anymore and we'll never be able talk to him or see him again."

He was now looking very concerned at how I was behaving.

"Are you alright Bernard?" he said, "I can see it's been a shock for you."

I just looked at him stunned; suddenly understanding only too well as the enormity of the information slowly dissolved into my consciousness. Clifford was dead? No! It wasn't true… Clifford dead! It couldn't be true… but it was. Clifford was dead and I would never see him again. My body went numb, my mind totally blank, my head fuzzy. All I could feel was the pulsating emptiness of a throbbing void.

I think I must have nearly passed out, but shakily managing to stay upright, unable to speak, turned around and walked home in a trance. When I got there my parents could both see something was badly wrong and that I had suffered some kind of shock because of my complete inability to say anything intelligible.

I was even too shocked to cry. "What's wrong?" they kept asking, but I couldn't tell them, except to shake my head at them and repeat "Clifford," several times over. I had told them earlier that I was going to his house while we were having tea.

Having themselves gone through the wartime experience of impact and aftershock of sudden death they immediately guessed that his life had somehow been abruptly extinguished; confirming it when they opened the evening paper which had been delivered some time earlier. The brief story was at the bottom of the front page. No details were given except to say his name, where he lived and that he had been knocked off his bicycle by a heavy goods vehicle and died instantly at the scene.

Alan, Wynford and I met up a day or so later. It was a terrible blow for the three of us. They had both heard and were also having problems coming to terms with it. I know I was unsettled for weeks afterwards. Until then I don't suppose we had ever considered death applying to kids of our age. The odd accident to other people somewhere else yes. Old people and relatives we knew died from time to time. We had seen funerals pass by.

But that kind of thing didn't happen to kids like us. Not friends of ours, people we knew and mucked about with. It was horrible. We of course didn't go to his funeral. We didn't really know anything about funerals at that time and as far as I knew kids didn't go to funerals anyway. I don't think I had ever met his mother or father so I never found out how they fared but it must have been hell for them. He was such a pleasant individual.

It was too young to have to learn that kind of lesson but it made me realise that life can turn around and bite you hard when you least expect it.

We didn't find out the details till a couple of weeks afterwards. He had been on his bike, the one he used to lend me, riding home along the Mumbles road. His front wheel had gone into a pothole and he got thrown off into the path of an eight wheel Foden lorry. You couldn't have got a much heavier vehicle than that.

It was overtaking at the time and struck him a glancing blow on the side of his head killing him instantly. The only fortunate thing about it all was that he had, mercifully for his parents, not been physically damaged. The collision had knocked him back into the side of the road and he had not fallen under the wheels and been crushed. His bike had fared less well with its front portion having been flattened by the Foden's back wheels. I shuddered as I thought of my recent journey on it the previous week. The thing was that he didn't normally use that way to get home. Whatever induced him to use it that day, we would never know. It was a stupid silly accident that should never have happened and although I hadn't got to know him well I still mourned his loss and the friendship that might have been some time afterwards. It wasn't destiny that had claimed him. It was the fickle finger of malicious, cruel fate.

A few years later I was to meet up with our friendly bobby once again. He was on duty in Swansea town centre and I grinned at him with recognition as we almost collided on a shop corner. He returned my look with a questioning frown until I said, "You don't remember 'The Laughing Cavaliers' then?"

I could see his mind slowly scrolling back searching till it finally clicked. "Yes," he said, smiling whimsically, nodding confirmation with folded hands resting on his hips looking at me.

Although pleasant enough I could sense that he wasn't the same individual we had met a few years previously. He was older and wiser with a physique that had filled out considerably, now giving him a considerable presence; certainly no longer the beanpole on a bicycle. The boyish innocence had also gone and under the façade of friendliness there was a professional hardness that had not been there before.

"I remember 'The Laughing Cavaliers" he said. "What are you up to these days?"

So we swapped pleasantries for a couple of minutes during which time I told him about the flat tyre he had missed that day on Clifford's bike and sadly what had since happened to Clifford. And then we went our separate ways. He actually wished me luck but I never did see him again. I wonder what became of him.

POND LIFE AND AN ANGRY COW

The time had come to take a proper look at the ponds found with Alan and Wynford in the pastureland behind Derwyn Fawr. The field of course no longer exists today. The whole area was built up a long time ago so it must have been around nineteen fifty five or fifty six that I actually went to fish it for the first time on my recently acquired Hercules three speed bicycle, giving that its first good road test as well.

The field was located a short distance from where the hill crested the incline and either side of the road were rows of houses which ended with clumps of wild bramble bushes separating them from open pastureland. With a wrought iron fence spanning the gap between the rows of houses a gate was set into it in such a way that bicycles could not be wheeled through but had to be lifted over instead.

The thing that really attracted me was that in the smaller and shallower pond you could actually see the fish trying to take the bait. The water must have been fed from natural springs because it was crystal clear. The middle of the pond was not that far out, with some sort of plant life growing there, and bait suspended six inches from the float cast alongside it could actually be seen hanging in the water. Immediately it was cast and the float settled swarms of fish would start attacking, dragging it around the pond as I stood and watched in amazed amusement.

Nearly every time the float went under a responding strike would come up empty with nothing left on the hook. They were masters at it. They were taking the mickey. A few succumbed to really rapid strikes but far more escaped than were caught. It was frustrating as well as challenging. The other strange thing was that even though the water was so clear if you walked around the pond looking for activity elsewhere it looked to be completely empty. It was only when a line was cast that aquatic life seemed to materialise and although nothing worthy of note, one or two fish did actually manage to find their way on to my hook when I made the effort.

The second pond some distance away was completely different. Standing alongside a large overhanging oak tree it appeared to be much deeper and darker with a reed bed on one side and a gathering of various forms of plant life on the other. Also fed by a natural spring it was reputed to have some reasonable Carp and Perch but it might just have been a rumour. It wasn't transparent like the other pond and no trace of fish could actually be seen anywhere.

On the few occasions I visited the field there were usually one or two boys or adults trying their luck by the oak tree but the shallow pond always seemed to be deserted for no apparent reason. There was a vague rumour casually mentioned about it once, but nothing more which was puzzling; that is until the last occasion I cast my line there, when I thought I might have found out why.

Sometimes the odd cow could be seen grazing in the distance but they had not taken any notice of me and I had not taken that much notice of them. So cows were not on my mind and nobody had ever to my knowledge directly brought the subject into any kind of conversation for discussion.

On that particular day it was overcast with rain threatening and not very encouraging. Arriving alone with nobody else in the field there were just one or two cows grazing some way off from the pond which I ignored; in hindsight, a bad mistake. It didn't take long to set up my tackle, but sensing almost immediately that something was amiss I took a casual look around and noticed a few more had gathered, all standing nearer than they had been, just minding their own business doing what cows do and chewing the cud. But there was menace in the air. I could feel it.

I carried on in the usual style, watching the fish surround the bait beneath my float and push it around the pond. There was an extra presence. Three more cows had sneaked up directly behind. I looked up again and they were all staring at me directly. I was not imagining it. Where the hell had they come from? They were slowly but surely encircling me. I looked back across to the ones in front just as their leader walked very deliberately into the middle of the pond, stopped, and glared with pure malevolence. There was no other word for it.

The herd was surrounding me. Until then I had always believed that cows were docile but right then there was no doubt that I was wanted off the premises. The meadow had been reclaimed.

Collecting everything together but without bothering to break down my rod I made a rapid but controlled departure, wheeling my bike between two cows to the fence and hoisted it and my tackle and then myself over and thought "stuff your pond." Packing it all away and taking one last fond glance back at my paradise lost I high-tailed it for home never to return until over fifty years had passed to find the field, ponds and cows had all gone. In their place now stands a very large housing estate. Only the long faded memories of forgotten pasture and its bovine guardians remained.

SPLISH SPLASH

I had been dropping heavy hints that my ambitions and skill at angling needed a better rod than the twelve foot bamboo one I was using. Serious carp hunters used only the built cane type of rod because they could stand up to the duty of playing even the biggest fish. Oh yeah! But nothing was happening.

Then completely out of the blue, dad came home one night clutching a long green cloth bag. Handing it to me he asked "Will this help you to catch some of those big carp that you keep gabbing on about?"

It was a rod bag; quite heavy, not split cane. Inside was a three piece aerial rod that screwed together making it around eleven feet long. Brownish in colour it also had agate eye line guides, the latest thing in carp handling technology, and a long cork handle with a portion set into it for a reel that could be secured by two screwed collars.

"Pfwoar!" It was a real beaut'. I was so stunned that I almost forgot to thank him. "Gee!" (all American like) "Thanks dad." I couldn't wait to try it out and flash it around. Having a rod with a long cork handle would make me look real serious about catching carp. I'd have to practice the haunted look I'd been reading about.

That's what all real carp hunters had because it was such a mental strain lying in wait playing mind games with them. I had come to recognise that there were three types of fishermen that came to Brynmill. The casual type with the minimum of kit, there just to pass time, treating it like a social occasion, seemingly unconcerned whether he has caught any fish, how many or what size they were if he did. Next was the enthusiast who has all the kit, knew the names of all the fish species and was almost a walking encyclopaedia of angling. I wanted to be the recognised as a member of the third category, which was as a hunter of carp.

According to an article I read in the angling press and which I could only assume was meant to be a bit tongue in cheek: carp fishermen were different because they considered themselves on a mission. Their haunted intense manner usually turned away enquiries before they were uttered. But If by chance the question passed the inquisitors lips to ask "What are you hoping to catch?" the answer was always carp; the sacred name that is whispered in hushed tones with the reverence bestowed on it by all that had been touched by a swirling vortex of water and a broken line. Those who proclaimed it with such solemnity were treated with appropriate dignity and understanding and then left well alone.

On second thoughts I decided the article was more sarcastic than tongue in cheek. I didn't think we were that far gone in Brynmill. Other articles in similar angling journals inferred that serious carp hunters didn't fish in places like Brynmill Park because they were too close to civilisation. No. They found remote locations out in the wilds with plenty of grassy banks littered with reed beds and overhanging trees near the water's edge that they could merge into.

Real carp hunters wore only rustic green and brown coloured clothing, rubbed mud over their face and painted rods green, unless they were naturally brown split cane which could easily be mistaken for a twig if spotted by a sharp eyed carp. I couldn't imagine that happening at Brynmill either. For one thing there were far too many human beings around and secondly there were no grassy banks with overhanging trees.

The lake was paved all the way around with just the one small reed bed mentioned earlier. The most serious strategy that we engaged in was climbing over the gate a couple of hours before the park was due to open like Don, an aquaintance of mine, who caught an early five pounder once. I tried this myself a couple of times, expecting to arrive well ahead of anybody else and secure the best position but to my dismay was thwarted every time by the same two individuals who were already in place.

One of them I had fished alongside several times before and the other a tug man working a late shift just grunting to acknowledge my presence, not pleased to see a twelve year old at that time in the morning even if he did have a fishing rod that had a long cork handle. No. None of the early morning visits produced anything and 'Tug', if he was there, was usually grumpy. A further setback to my ambitions came one evening when the new carp rod suffered an unusual misfortune.

I was fishing with Cedric, who had now become a Brynmill regular, and we were on the bank at the deepest part of the lake packing up to go home. Having already detached the reel I decided to demonstrate the rod's flexibility. It would bend around quite a bit with even just a reasonable size roach on the end so I started whipping it up and down quite vigorously; unfortunately over the water. I had replayed that moment in my mind countless times afterwards in the following few weeks because it was a disaster.

One second the rod tip was whizzing up and down in a blur in front of my eyes and a split second later it wasn't. I heard a slight splishing sound and saw a small, ever so small, ripple on the water and the rod was a couple of feet shorter. I looked at Cedric aghast. He looked at me with his mouth hanging open but he remained much calmer than me. It wasn't his rod. He suggested we get some weights tied together with a couple of hooks that could be cast out and dragged back along the bottom and maybe catch the broken piece.

I was beginning to panic. How was I going to explain my shorter rod to dad? I put it out of my mind and Cedric got his rod fixed with the dragline set up, casting it out and dragging it back in. No contact. After about fifteen minutes I realised that unless 'One Eye' or the 'Parky' granted a request to drain the lake the end of my rod was gone forever. Resigned to my fate with dad if he found out I set off home with Cedric parting company at the park gate. I had on the way formulated a plan.

I would simply act all nonchalant and not even mention my little mishap. So I didn't. "How's the new rod?" dad asked a few night later. "Oh great", I said. "Haven't caught any carp yet but they are a bit elusive – you know."

"Oh I see," he replied and left it at that. I was going to have to be very careful.

Fortunately the point where the rod had broken off still left the possibility of adding a new line guide eye at the top and one in between the remaining guide just above the screwed joint; so it more or less at least looked the same – if you didn't look too closely. So when the coast was clear I managed to carry out the necessary modifications and fortunately it seemed to suffer no ill effects apart from now being stiffer.

Fate intervened a couple of weeks later when dad unexpected turned up alongside at the water's edge on a balmy summer evening. He could do that – sneak up on me. Nearly caught me smoking again once. I just saw him in the nick of time and flicked my fag into the bushes. We chatted for a couple of minutes and I could see him glancing at the rod frowning and obviously trying to reconcile a distant memory. The light suddenly went on and, concentrating fully on my reply, he asked what's technically known as a rhetorical question, "I thought your rod... Didn't it used to be longer than that?"

"Ah, Err, Um, Yeah." The game was up.

"It got caught in the fork of a tree trunk as I was hurrying to move to a different pitch ahead of someone else."

Just like the carp in its quest for survival I was becoming devious. Further interrogation followed as I described in imagined and hopefully convincing detail just how ….."Blah, Blah, Blah."

Unsurprisingly he didn't really believe a word and must have been wondering what the real explanation was. I couldn't blame him I suppose and he only got more exasperated as I mumbled, "I'm sorry I meant to tell you," by way of an apology.

Conversation sort of fizzled out after that and he finally just said, "Don't be late home," and left me wondering if there would be any further questions at headquarters.

Fortunately there weren't but just to be on the safe side, and put him off the scent, next day diversionary tactics were instigated and fishing ditched for a while to get on with some more model building that had been abandoned at the start of the season.

The doorbell rang one Saturday morning some two weeks later. It was a messenger and my attention was re directed to recent activities at Brynmill Lake. The messenger was my old friend Cedric and he was obviously excited and dying to give me some hot news. Had I heard about Tommy Southport? "No," I said. "I haven't been fishing for a couple of weeks. What's happened? What about him?"

Cedric explained. In the Brynmill brotherhood of fishermen our Tommy had become an overnight sensation. A couple of days previously at about 7.30 PM on another balmy evening he had inexplicably hooked, played and landed a four and a half pound carp. My eyes were wide in disbelief as I asked "How the heck did he do that? He only ever catches tiddlers."

Cedric was apparently fishing nearby and saw the whole thing unfold in front of him on the opposite side of the lake by an old feeder pipe lying just below the surface.

"I know," he said. "He was fishing by the pipe and just had an ordinary little nibble, setting his float twitching and nothing else. It had been going on for about ten minutes and he decided to give it a half-hearted strike to see what was tickling his hook and it pulled back.

"Anyway," he said, continuing to relate the story, "the carp shot out from the pipe and took him by complete surprise. Looked like it was going to pull him in the drink for a minute. You should have seen his rod.

It was bent right in half.

Never been bent around that much before but he played it like he had a salmon on the end. He knew what he was doing. Took him fifty yards down the bank and he had to get off his stool to follow it. Then it went out towards the middle before heading back to the pipe. But old Tommy stood his ground and played it back to where he was standing and close enough to land.

Lucky for him I suppose, the tug man, happened to be passing by with his wife out for a walk without his rod. He saw Tommy needed a hand and went in through the gate and took the landing net to slip it under, nice and calm like, and picked it out of the water for him. He was really pleased for him. Shook his hand he did. You should see old Tommy. He's had a grin on him from ear to ear ever since. Can't stop smiling He can't really believe it happened because he was only using a tiddler hook."

Stone the crows! Tommy caught a carp. It was a four and a half pounder. They don't get caught as big as that in Brynmill very often. Tommy would be a legend for years. His prowess as a fighter of big carp soon spread around the lake and his hook and float sales shot up exponentially as anglers of all ages picked his brains to see if he would impart his secrets. It was a double edged sword however and until things calmed down enough for him to concentrate on what he did best there were more vacant spaces in his keep net than usual.

Although the season officially lasted for around nine months, depending on the weather and how cold it was, enthusiasm and the number of those fishing usually began to dwindle at the end of October or the beginning of November. Not long after that the reed bed would die and together with surrounding trees losing their foliage the lake began to look dead and desolate. If it occasionally took my fancy when I was bored I might go out in December or maybe the first couple of months of the New Year.

During the main season a look into the breeding pond would reward you with the sight of one or two carp grubbing about on the bottom at the water's edge. After November – nothing. I suppose I thought the fish would be starving and easily attracted to the odd bit of grub even if it was on the end of a hook. But no. The place was dead and disappointment would prevail until June. Perhaps this was why some of the angling fraternity went sea fishing when leaves started falling off trees as autumn began to approach. Little did I know it but I was soon going to join them and all because of Royston.

Sadly at the end of the nineteen eighties fishing at Brynmill ceased. They didn't drain the lake but the fishing club lease ran out so they netted all the fish and transferred over fifty thousand of them to a new location on the outskirts of the town where the club has now lived for another two and a half decades. Remembering the happy days I spent there, at Brynmill lake, gazing into the water waiting for bites, the number of boys who were given an interest and the many friendships that were forged there over those years, I cannot help but wonder if the Brynmill generation of today ever realise what they are missing.

Unbelievable! Fifty thousand fish had been hiding in that flippin' lake and I'd hardly met any of them. I wonder if I had perhaps tried a different bait…

ROYSTON MY MENTOR

It was after Tommy Southport caught his carp and just as things were beginning to settle down again that Royston came on the scene and disrupted my tranquil existence. We were both around the same age, eleven or twelve as I recall. My memory may not be a hundred percent correct. It was a long time ago. I'm not very good at describing how people look either so instead I will say he looked like a young Mickey Rooney but with a squarer set face, around the same height as me, about five feet, and he wore wire rimmed glasses that made him look rather serious.

He was also another individual with self-confidence albeit not the kind of commanding but humble presence that I later came to see in Clifford. He wasn't bossy and he wasn't unpleasant but his father allegedly owned a transport fleet consisting of a van and a motor coach. The van was used for general purposes and the coach took day trippers around the South Wales coast and beyond. In his mind this gave him status. More to the point was that the coach regularly took parties of sea fishermen.

How he managed to bunk off school I don't know but according to Royston he often went along with them on trips which might last several days. It was thus influenced by the habits, discussions and mannerisms of older men that he came to believe that even if not one of them he was at least their equal and it showed in the way he carried himself and in what he told me he had said to them during their manly discussions.

"Oh I told them this and I told them that. I said I didn't agree. I said they were doing it the wrong way." He was obviously a touch deluded about this relationship and oblivious that his senior companions were probably amusing themselves winding him up.

Even so, if I wasn't careful I could easily have believed him. He was quite convinced by his own utterances.

In time I came to suspect that a lot of his outings were really just a figment of his imagination. Apart from his tall tales however he was good company and started me off sea fishing.

We met purely by chance one evening at the reed bed. He'd managed to get there ahead of everyone and was just setting up for his first cast. In the course of introductions I mentioned that I hadn't seen him there before and was informed that he didn't do much lake fishing. "No, no," He said. He was more into sea fishing.

Then with the authoritative air of the worldly wise he started regaling me about various pitched battles from the beaches he had fought with bass and tope in foaming Welsh surf. All by courtesy of the family coach.

It was utter piffle of course but having known him for only a few minutes, and being a sucker for a good fishing story, he led me by the nose like a donkey. Having drawn me in he made me an offer I couldn't refuse. He would teach me all he knew about the art of sea fishing.

During the ensuing conversation on the subject he told me that he lived in one of the myriad streets behind the hospital and suggested we could meet up on Saturday at the end of the following week. Our first outing would be to explore the contents of the sea on the foreshore between the jail and The Slip. He was "too busy to do anything before then." It was a Tuesday when he said that and any eleven year old knows that ten days or more is a lifetime away. It was far too vague an arrangement and I suspected that ten days was going to be too great a leap in time for him to remember any plan we made.

He then backtracked on his "too busy before then" statement when I asked if he would be back in Brynmill anytime sooner than that. To which he replied, nodding his head sagely, "Yes, well as a matter of fact I was thinking about coming next Thursday."

We had been fishing in each other's company by then for a couple of hours conversing on and off and he had his back to me starting to put his tackle away. I was watching my float and sort of half turned in his direction to query his self-contradiction saying "I thought you said…" and stopped. Never mind I thought to myself, just keep an open mind. Instead I said, "Oh that's even better then," smiling as I did so. "We can firm things up then." If he had noticed his slip he didn't show it but completely unabashed replied, "Yes that would be easier for us but you never know though. I might have to change that arrangement again at short notice if I'm too busy."

I thought how very important he sounded and dug a scrap of paper and a pen out of my tackle bag to make a note of his address before he left to catch a bus home. "Where are you getting the bus?" I asked, and when he replied "From the top of Rhyddings Park Road," I immediately thought of the little cake shop opposite the bus stop which sold iced tarts for tuppence each and it made me feel hungry. Too late for cakes I thought, but what about chips?

There was a chip shop in Bernard Street half way to the stop. "What about a bag of chips on the way?" I said, and his face lit up and then dimmed in disappointment when he realised he didn't have sufficient funding for both bus fare and the chips. "We'll club funds," I said, "and buy a bag between us then we can share them on the way to the stop. It's not far from where I live so I don't mind walking back."

He seemed genuinely pleased by the suggestion so that's what we did. Walking and talking companionably between munching vinegar drenched chips. He was just in time to get the 8.30 bus and waved a farewell hand as it pulled away. We would meet up again the following week.

In some ways the time passed quickly, like time to go to school while the event itself dragged by until home-time, and the time till the following Thursday also seemed to drag. Royston turned up as planned after tea having caught the bus to speed him on his way. It was a miserable evening however with a constant drizzle enveloping the lake in gloom and discouraging the fish from biting. Our efforts were half hearted and most of the time we concentrated on making plans for Saturday morning.

I had not really considered the practicalities of sea fishing before but he explained that our activities would all be governed by the times of the tide. Swansea Bay was known to have a very long tidal distance with a five mile sweep. If you looked out towards the flats of the exposed sand any day of the week you would see groups of men making sand mounds in numerous places around the bay as they dug for bait. Oh I thought. So that's what they were doing then. I'd often wondered what it was.

The bait was lugworm. Yuck! I never used garden worms for bait in Brynmill. I just didn't like worms, particularly when there were a number of them together in a tin, and I didn't like the idea of delving amongst them to pick one of the wriggly things out and stick a hook through it in several places. OK maybe I was a bit sissy about it but if you don't like worms you just don't like them. Lugworms though, they were something else, two or three times as long and at least twice as thick.

Royston didn't know about my dislike for worms and dropped his bombshell. "What we'll do," he said, "is meet up by the hospital corner on St Helen's Road at 10 o'clock and walk down to the beach from there. It's not that far. There's a reasonable spot for lugworm straight in front of the railway arch. The tide should be well out by then and we can spend an hour or so digging. By the time we've got enough it'll be getting on for lunch. If we walk back to our house my mum said you can have some dinner with us. Then we can collect the tackle and go down to the same bit of beach to catch the tide coming in."

He had it all planned out. I especially liked his invite to dinner which was totally unexpected. When I reminded him that I didn't have a rod or any tackle for sea fishing, there was definitely some hesitation in his response, if only for a second before he quickly offered to lend me one of his spare ones from their garage storeroom and I left it at that.

As we parted company in anticipation of Saturday morning he said, "by the way don't forget to bring a garden fork for digging."

"Yeah," I said, "I'll borrow my dad's." So that was it. We would meet up on Saturday morning and go down to the beach first for bait. Yes -I was really looking forward to that part of the outing.

Saturday morning I arrived to meet Royston outside the hospital, on time, equipped ready with borrowed garden fork. I had to threaten dad that he wouldn't get any of the bass that I was going to catch if he didn't lend it to me and by way of reply he then threatened me that I would catch it if I lost his garden fork and didn't bring him any bass.

I had also remembered to wear my Wellingtons boots. They were not the most comfortable things to walk in and mum suggested, since they were going to be on my feet for some time, I should put on an extra pair of socks and travelled to meet Royston by bus. She had also given me a couple of biscuits and haute-cuisine Spam sandwiches "just in case" although I had already explained that I would be dining out. On her insistence I also took an old raincoat that had seen better days. Unless the great Swansea monsoon season started though I had no intention of wearing it and put it in my tackle bag along with the survival rations.

I refused point blank to wear my peaked school cap. No self respecting schoolboy wears his school cap on a Saturday morning. If it rained it rained. My hair would survive, I said.

Royston also had a fork slung over his shoulders ready and a large empty paint can in which to store the lugworm delicacy. So we set off with the day overcast and not looking very promising. The walk was long, turning left and right and right and left till I thought we would never get there.

It was much further than I bargained for and Royston seemed worried that I might quit before reaching our destination. As it happened I would be grateful for the familiarity I was to gain with these back streets to and from the beach over the coming weeks. On an autumn night two years into the future I would use them to flee from a terrifying situation.

As we approached the main road we could hear a lot of activity on both the Mumbles tramway line and the mainline LMS steam railway on the other side of the stone wall that separated them. When we rounded the last corner we could see why. A duplex tram set had just passed and was clattering its way back to the Rutland Street terminus while an LMS heavy goods train was rumbling along in the opposite direction trailing perhaps eighty wagons and headed by a steam locomotive billowing clouds of heavy smoke from its chimney.

We crossed the road and the tram line and then walked under the railway bridge to the beach beyond with the noise of the rolling wagon wheels overhead reverberating in our ears as we went through to the other side to enter lugworm-land.

The sea was well on the way out and on the freshly exposed tide washed sand there were already a number of fishermen looking for lengths of wriggly buried treasure. The beach sloped down for about 150 yards and then levelled off before chasing a receding tide which was now some considerable distance away. Trudging to the area where others were already digging we cast our eyes around to look for a good spot.

"Where do we start?" I asked. "It all looks the same to me."

"Anywhere," Royston replied, "but keep a watch out for any worm-casts." I looked at him enquiringly.

"If you watch the sand," he said, you will occasionally see shapes like worms form on the surface. I don't know how or why they do it but what it indicates is that there's a worm lying somewhere underneath. That's a good place to start."

I thought to myself, I'm not going to just hang around waiting for a worm to wave at me. Stone the crows! We'll be here all day.

So I started to dig. I had just finished my sixth forkfull when a couple of yards in front of me a worm-cast formed. We moved nearer and started digging together. Just over a foot deep later we spied one of our quarry; a big thick reddish brown thing with one end sticking out of the sand.

I looked at Royston and he looked at me.

Was he expecting me to pick it up? It was no good grabbing it then anyway. It was still half buried in the sand. We had to dig away some more and there was plenty more of it to uncover. About twelve inches of it. When it was clear of the sand and ripe for picking I said "Your worm Royston."

Fair play to the boy he grabbed it without hesitation and it didn't even try to fight back. It was very lethargic. The worm can was nearby and after first throwing some wet sand on the bottom he dropped in the first tenant. We just carried on digging after that. Each of us slowly adding to the growing wormery. I re affirmed my dislike of both handling and looking at them as we progressed. Especially after I had cut at least one in half and speared another with a fork prong releasing a squirt of lugworm blood everywhere.

By the time we had a couple of dozen I just couldn't look at them in the can anymore. Every time I did I felt the back of my throat meet the front. I thought we had more than enough by then and said so to Royston. Agreeing with my observation he threw some more wet sand on top of the pulsating contents and loosely secured the lid. Then with me carrying the fish feed we set off back to his house.

It had been tiring work which I was certainly not used to and I wondered if I'd have the energy to walk back. My Wellington clad feet were killing me. I seriously began to doubt that I even wanted to return to the beach and fish. Plumb tuckered out as the saying goes and Royston's condition wasn't much better, although he was trying to pretend otherwise. Also hungry by now, but with blood on my hands, lugworm blood, there was no way I was going to start my sandwiches and decided to wait until we got to his place so I could wash it off.

On the way home I asked him about the rod that he said he was going to lend me. I hadn't meant to but it was obviously on my mind if not his so it just sort of jumped out of my mouth and caught us both completely off guard.

"What's this rod you're going to lend me then?" I said. His jaw dropped as he momentarily lost his air of authority

"Oh, Ah, Err, I…"

"You haven't really got a spare one have you?" I said, and his face sunk at having been found out, although I hadn't meant to sound malicious or triumphant.

Before he could respond I added "I thought we were friends? Why did you make it up about a spare rod? I'd still have come fishing with you – you flippin' head case."

"Oh would you?" he said, sounding relieved.

"Of course," I said, "But if I'd known I wasn't going to have a rod to use I'd have left it for a couple of weeks 'till I could have shortened my old cane one."

He just said "I'm sorry. I didn't mean to. I just sort of said it so that you'd come."

"Give me another couple of weeks to organise my old rod," I said "and we'll arrange another outing." "What about this afternoon?" he said. "You don't want to go now I suppose? "

"Listen," I said, laughing. "I promised my father some fresh bass. Are you listening? If I don't deliver you might never see me again. I'm going to the beach with you to help you land one."

He was obviously relieved that I wasn't ditching him and it was about then that we reached the back lane entrance to his house and let ourselves in. I don't think his mum would have approved of him bringing a large can of lugworm through the front door and dining room into the kitchen so he was under instruction to come in that way. He parked them outside the scullery door after first lifting the lid to check that they were OK. Unfortunately I was looking when he did and caught a glance at the moving mass which made me start to gag. I just hoped I could put them out of my mind while I was eating.

Royston's mother came to meet us as we entered with Royston in the lead. "You must be Bernard then," she said with a big smile. "I hope you're both hungry."

She was obviously on the same wavelength as my

mother. Lunch was fried Spam pieces and fried egg served with a drizzle of chips, all washed down with a good cup of tea. Fortunately I was able to avoid thinking about what was parked outside their back door and tucked in. Royston had the presence of mind not to mention the subject either. I think his mum was pleased that he'd brought someone his own age home instead of being brainwashed by a busload of scruffy old men in fishing gear. By the time we were finished and ready to set out again the weather outside was looking even less encouraging, but no raindrops so far.

Having dug the bait though we weren't about to waste the effort and Royston collected his tackle from the hallway behind their front door as we departed. His rod was tied to a couple of longish thick wood strips the purpose of which would be revealed later in the afternoon. I retrieved my kit bag with rain coat inside squashing the uneaten sandwiches and with deference to his mother volunteered to fetch the bait tin and meet up at the front of the house. Everything ship shape we set off once more.

Our second journey to the beach was not as enthusiastic as the first even though we were actually going to fish this time albeit with only one rod. I was also getting uncomfortable as a blister was growing on the back of my ankle on one foot and under a big toe on the other. On the way I made a mental note to collect dad's garden fork on the way home. We crossed the main road and the tram railway and then passed under the LMS railway bridge without incident with both lines devoid of traffic.

Arriving back on the beach we walked to a spot just before the line of the incoming tide and surveyed our prospects. An ocean full of fish and we only wanted a few. Royston slid his two piece rod from its cloth bag, fitted it together and then mounted a six inch centre pin reel from the large ex-army kit bag he used to hold the rest of his kit.

The saltwater tackle was different from fresh water equipment. To start with there was no float and number sixteen hooks were definitely not required. Sea fish have much bigger mouths than the ones we caught in Brynmill. Hooks were accordingly much bigger. I say hooks because Royston actually had three spaced out at intervals on a wire framework called a paternoster.

At the bottom of the framework was a large lead weight with four prongs sticking out of it which I presumed were to help it stay in place on the sand as it got buffeted by the tide. It was Royston's tackle so when he finished setting it all up I let him have the honour of threading three large lugworms onto the three large hooks. Yuk!

There were only a couple of other people in the area where we elected to fish. Some of the groups we had seen digging in the morning were obviously trying their luck elsewhere, either around the bay or off one of the piers: the Mumbles Pier at the west end or the old West Pier at the east end forming one side of the entrance to the docks.

Royston's rod was sturdier and stiffer than his freshwater one and only about eight feet in length. Quite long enough for him to handle. Casting was also much more demanding and physical because the lead weight was used to take the bait out into the tide. I was quite impressed when he took his first cast.

Standing just where the water was reaching us on the flat he stood sideways on with his legs braced apart. Holding the rod out sideways parallel to the ground facing away from the sea, one hand at the butt end of the rod and the other at the forward end of the long cork handle.

When he was ready he swung it in a rapid arc throwing the baited and weighted paternoster up over his head and out into the wild blue yonder. Then maintaining a firm grip on the rod with his right hand he steadied it with the left one at the same time keeping the forefinger of that hand on the edge of the spinning reel to keep the line taught.

I suppose he must have cast that weight around seventy yards. No mean feat for someone standing an inch or so under five feet in height. Declaring himself satisfied with his performance I'm sure he was also relieved that he hadn't made a mess of it in front of his pupil. What he said was that the distance didn't really matter much then because the incoming tide would bring in the flat fish. After it started to climb the sloping beach it didn't work so much in our favour and would only have a short distance to go before turning. That was the down side of the equation.

The up side was that the rising tide would get deeper and bring in the bigger fish. If in the meantime he had to retrieve his line for any reason then he would have to make sure to recast it further out to keep amongst them.

I presumed that he meant after he had landed his first bass but it didn't quite work out that way. We stood and waited slowly walking back up the beach as the sea stretched as far as it could to reach its ultimate destination.

The stand which his rod had been tied to for carrying consisted simply of two strips of wood about five feet long and screwed together six inches from the top so that they could be opened out to form a V in which to rest the rod. A small bell mounted to a cloths peg looking thing was also clipped to the top of the rod to indicate when the bait was being interfered with.

Unfortunately crabs and eels also came in with the tide so there was no real point in getting excited about a bite until the line had been wound in and you could see what was hanging on the end of it. The first strike came after we had been standing in patient anticipation for about half an hour.

Royston had noticed the top of the rod give a sudden lurch after vibrating for a few minutes and finally rang his bell. Hands to the rod and a swift strike. Then slowly haul on the rod and wind in the line. By the effort he was having to put in it looked like it could be good. Not necessarily a bass but perhaps a dab or some other kind of succulent sea morsel. Behold! A green crab.

"They can be a real nuisance." Royston said with the air of a world weary fishing boat skipper. It wasn't a very big crab. Not one that could be taken home so he threw it as far as he could back into the water. The lug worms left on the hooks were looking very sorry for themselves by now and very much 'got at'. So with a look of resigned disgust Royston opened the bait store, selected the juiciest looking candidates, replaced their predecessors and made ready to cast out again.

Before doing so he suddenly turned to me and said, "Do you want a go at casting?" I considered. It didn't look too hard but on second thoughts I decided to decline on that occasion. "Perhaps," I said, "when I've had some practice with my own tackle. If I mess up I could end up snapping your line and losing your weight."

My comment seemed to satisfy him so he took another swing and putting in a bit of extra effort managed cast some way further than before, hopefully to where there were some bass looking for lugworm I thought. He then propped the rest under his rod again and attached the bell.

All the while we were there the sky above had been getting slowly darker and black edged clouds were forming. I could have sworn I felt a couple of rain spots and it also seemed to be getting a bit colder. I was ever so slowly getting a little disenchanted with the afternoon and decided to drop a gentle hint, opening my kit bag to put my raincoat on. We both looked out to sea wondering how much of its content we would diminish in the next hour.

There wasn't much we could do while we stood there waiting. Alongside Brynmill lake there was always something happening and usually some other people to exchange pleasantries with or talk about the latest fishing news. We had exhausted however our intellectual conversation and now stood making just the odd comment or observation and as we did we looked out into the overcast and darkening bay.

Way in the distance lying at anchor waiting for the tide were two large ships. One of them by its profile looked to be some kind of tanker while the other of similar size could be anything that carried cargo. Much nearer working close to the dock entrance was a bucket dredger. Swansea was a very busy tidal port having a number of docks and even its own small fishing fleet. It was an interesting view but for two schoolboys it soon got boring.

Where was the bass I had promised dad? The nearest people to us were the other fishermen at two separate pitches further down near to The Slip railway crossing and road bridge. They didn't seem very active either. I didn't appreciate it at the time but sometime later, on a couple of brighter days with clear blue skies, I came to fish with a proper rod of my own. It was only then when looking at the same view as now that I noticed how green and pure the water looked as the waves foamed and crashed onto the beach. But that was then – in the future.

Royston suddenly came to life and took a few steps forward reaching up to grip the line, pulling it down slightly he held it in his palm canting his head over to one side as if in deep thought. He muttered to himself, almost inaudible to me, "Something's nibbling again but I can't tell what."

The move was very impressive. He really looked like he knew what he was doing. Turning to me he said, "Come and see what you think. I can actually feel something playing with the bait. It's not really tugging at it like a fish though."

So, trying to identify the culprit from all else that was in the sea, I took the line from him -and yes he was right. Something was actually fiddling on the end and then there was a very definite tug. Without thinking about it I let go of the line. Pupil became master and I gave the command. " Strike! You've got something."

He wasn't expecting that and his jaw momentarily dropped in surprise before he reacted, grabbing the rod and quickly pulling it back. An open jawed smile lit up his face and he exclaimed, "Yeah, you're right. It's not a flippin' crab this time either."

Just then it started to drizzle. Royston started to haul in whatever it was on the other end. We waited in anticipation.

While he hauled in he said, "It's definitely not a bass."

Oh! I thought. Dad will be tickled pink. And as I held that thought a crescendo of wriggling eel broke the surface.

Royston gave a loud groan. "Oh no," he said, "I thought it was a dab."' The thing was about eighteen inches long and writhing like mad, wrapped tightly around the paternoster. But Royston knew exactly what to do. I hadn't a clue. What I was really concerned about was teeth. Some eels had very nasty teeth. Was this a nasty toothed eel?

Royston said "Here, hold the rod." and I took it off him while he grappled with his catch. The weight was clear of entanglement sufficiently that Royston managed to get hold of it in one hand while doing his best to hold the eel just behind its wriggling head in the other. Two quick blows to the head and it writhed no more.

It wasn't a conger eel. They were dark grey in colour and much bigger, sporting the sort of teeth that I was worried about. Royston's had a green back and was white on its belly. Just a common beach eel, I thought.

"What are you going to do with it?" I asked. "Oh, I'll take it home," he said. "You can eat these. Just cut them up into slices and fry them."

My stomach wondered about the lugworm it had swallowed and gave an involuntary shudder.

"Eels are a nuisance as well," he added," but at least you can still eat them."

We were starting to get wet as the drizzle seemed to be changing into heavier droplets and we both arrived at the same conclusion. It was time to go. We packed up his kit, dropping the eel's body into a mesh pouch on the side of his bag.

"What about the lugworms -are you going to fry them for tea as well?" I asked laughing. He didn't seem to see the humour in that remark but just responded by telling me that he knew someone in the next street who went out regularly and would be able to use them. "Unless," he added, "you want to come out again tomorrow afternoon and give it another try?"

Not keen to repeat such a disappointing experience, especially without a rod, his invitation was politely declined, citing the reasonable but truthful excuse that it would be Sunday and I had to go to chapel in the morning and also in the evening. Clomping down to the beach again would not be practical due to time constraints. He nodded his understanding and I responded by asking if the lugworms would get a little "high" overnight.

"No! As long as they are kept moist they will be alright for a couple of days," he said. So I put the image of lugworms out of my mind, picked up the can and we both set off back to his house.

The only thing he was wearing to give him some respite from the rain was a semi-waterproof jerkin. It would have to suffice. We arrived to a warm welcome from his mother who seemed quite amused by his trophy and the prospect of frying it. I thought, just you wait till you come to slicing it!

When I told him that I had to go to chapel on Sundays I never thought to ask him if he was under the same sort of commitment. Thinking about it afterwards I concluded that with all the week end fishing trips he said he'd been on he obviously wasn't.

Remembering to collect dad's fork I reminded him that I wouldn't be going sea fishing again for a couple of weeks because I had to shorten and modify my existing bamboo cane rod. Some sea tackle also had to be purchased somehow, like paternoster, hooks and a couple of casting weights not to mention extra strong sea line. Things like that cost and my funds were not looking good so it might take a bit longer.

Anyway I said I'd probably see him over at Brynmill before then since we was still both trying to make friends with the fish there. I also explained how to get to the house where I lived and that it was in the street next to where he walked to get the bus home.

If he didn't see me at the lake he should call in, or if I wasn't there, he should make himself known to my parents so that we kept in touch. Then, although having had no physical contact with the lugworm since before lunch, I washed my hands again and departed to catch the bus home; quietly starving and tucking in to two of mums four sandwiches on the way, hoping she would fry the other two for tea.

On arrival, and while I related the day's events to them both and commiserated with dad on his culinary disappointment over the bass, she did just that. Saturday we normally had some kind of a fry up for lunch anyway so she also added what I had missed earlier. Fried mash potato, egg, and tomatoes. From famished to feast. Not the end of a perfect day but not bad either.

Forgiven for the lack of bass after I had related the sad tale of our beach exploits, and the fact that I couldn't really join in, dad took pity on me and said he would see if he could help out with the tackle if I looked after altering my existing cane rod to suit the sea. He never mentioned the new aerial rod he'd bought me or my unintentional modification of it. I'm sure it crossed his mind. It sure as heck crossed mine.

I cut the bamboo cane rod back to make it about six feet in length. Anything longer than that and it just wouldn't be stiff enough for swinging the lead weight when casting. I also had to consider the position of the ferrules where they connected the two halves and make sure there was sufficient length left in the top section to make it a practical proposition. When that was sorted all that was left to do was fit a new line guide at the top by binding it tightly in position with strong twine and then waterproof with appropriate varnishing treatment.

On the second weekend following our fishing trip dad and I went down to Atkinson's sports and tackle shop in Oxford Street to buy hooks, weights, strong sea line and a paternoster. I was ready to take on shark but for one thing; another reel. I only had one and it was on my other rod and wouldn't be able to hold enough of the heavy duty line needed to fight bass with. Dad had one of his occasionally favourable brainwaves.

The hedge needed cutting and so did the grass; back and front. We had a deal. I hoped it would rain and thought that since he was being so unusually accommodating I would be real clever and try a little blackmail. I said tongue in cheek "Can you afford my fees then?"

"I expect so," he said, "especially after you've paid my invoice for hiring the mower and shears for your local gardening services."

Ah! Oh! That was below the belt!

He gave a half smile and knew he had me. Once again I was stuffed. He coughed up for a three inch free spinning wooden reel that was just about capable of storing the newly acquired hundred and fifty yards of Cuttyunk line. A bigger one would probably have been too big on the cane rod anyway. I went home pleased as punch.

I hadn't seen or heard from Royston since our day out on the beach and two busy weeks passed. I was still fiddling about building my model aircraft, an 'SE5' kit I think it was, and other things as well as the abomination of homework which was now becoming more onerous as the weeks progressed. I was also disappointed that he hadn't been to Brynmill or rung our door bell. He knew where I lived but hadn't called and I'd been fishing in the park a couple of times without seeing him.

Surprisingly I did see Bryn Lucas the tug-man which was unusual. He was not normally about in late season and was in good mood explaining that he had a few days off while his boat was in dry dock undergoing repair. He'd come down on spec to see what the place looked like at that time of year and try ledgering on the bottom out from the reeds where we had both been drawn to. It was definitely a mistake.

In season a rich green colour standing proudly at attention they were now a jaded, dark brown colour, drooping and mostly struggling to poke above the surface. No self-respecting fish would want to be seen near them. So while we looked at the dead reeds standing in the dead water we got chatting and after mentioning my ambition to try out sea fishing he suggested trying the West Pier at the opening of the docks channel.

"You can get to it from off the beach," he said, "or by going down through the fish market where their boats are moored. But if you go onto the top deck of the pier be careful of the floor timbers because they are a bit rotten in some places -and," he added with emphasis, "be particularly careful of the railings where you lean your rod. Some of them are not as secure as they look."

He wasn't into sea fishing himself he told me. Saw enough salt water from the tugs. He was not as grumpy as I thought then, or perhaps he was just having a good day. Anyway I thanked him for his advice and we both more or less decided to call it quits as far as the lake was concerned, packed our tackle and headed our separate ways. As I walked home I decided that I was going to have to call on Royston to find out why he hadn't been in touch.

I gave him another week and then made my move on the third Saturday. It was a fine dry day so I decided to walk to his house. It was one of several terraced houses standing at the centre of the row and typical of the area. On arriving I walked up the short pathway to his front door and rang the bell. There was no answer the first time so I rang again. Then I heard the muffled sound of somebody moving around before a shadow interrupted the light coming from the back of the house as his mother came to open the door.

"Oh! Hello Bernard," she said," I'm surprised to see you. I thought you and Royston had a falling out," adding that he was not at home having gone out earlier. I never thought to ask where, just assuming he was off with another weekend fishing party. She saw my puzzlement and I responded by telling her that I had only called because I had been expecting to see him at Brynmill or for him to call on me.

Sensing things were not as clear cut as she had been led to believe she invited me in, leading me to through the house to the kitchen. "Now,' she said, "sit down and tell me exactly what the arrangement was that you made because he seems to think that after your visit to the beach a few weeks ago that you didn't want to bother with him again."

So I went right through what I had told Royston and how there was no point in me going fishing without a rod and that I would have to modify one of my existing rods, and so on. She listened and shook her head sadly. "Oh dear!" she said," I'm afraid he's so wrapped up in himself sometimes that he doesn't listen to what people tell him. He tries to act older than he is and assumes things. He's not as confident as he appears and thinks people don't like him. He can be very silly at times. What shall I tell him?"

"I think you can tell him that my rod is ready," I said, "and a friend of mine told me that a good place to fish is off the old West Pier.

If he wants to give it a try we can do that but we'll have to meet up to make arrangements and sort out bait again. He's gone on a coach fishing trip with his dad has he?"

She responded by looking very puzzled and, frowning deeply, just shook her head and said that no he wasn't on any fishing trip but had gone to visit his gran and granddad in Morriston. I mulled this over for a couple of seconds wondering what to say next when she broke the silence asking, "Do you like the pictures?" completely changing the subject and catching me off guard. "Uh yeah," I said by way of intelligent reply.

"Cowboy films I suppose?" she replied. "All you boys like cowboy films don't you?"

"Yes," I said again, this time with proper diction, wondering what was coming next. "I'll tell you what, "she said, "why don't you come to dinner next Saturday around midday and I'll treat you and Royston to a John Wayne cowboy film I know he wants to see.

It's in the Plaza, and you can walk up there afterwards. I'm sure he'll be pleased that you still want to be friends. You can make arrangements to dig your bait and go fishing then. Will your mum and dad be OK with that?"

I didn't know about mum and dad but it was certainly OK with me and said so. I would of course check with the parents. "Er, how will I know that Royston's OK with the arrangement?" I asked.

"Jungle drums," she said and explained, "Royal Mail Post." Back then you could post a letter in Swansea in the morning and it would be delivered in the afternoon. Oh for those halcyon days of long ago. Royston's mum was alright. She was cool! "He'll send you a postcard confirming spam egg, chips and the flicks by the middle of next week. I'll stand over him while he writes it." she said, smiling.

"Great," I replied, grinning back.

"Before you go," she added, "you better let me write down our address as well for you just in case you need it. It would be nice to have a telephone but we'll have to wait a while yet I'm afraid" So she wrote it out on a piece of paper torn from a used envelope giving it to me and showing me back to the front door. On the way home I thought what a twerp Royston was and how much easier life would be with a telephone. I was beginning to wonder really why I was a bothering with him. None of my other friends were this complicated. I was still in touch with Cedric and had occasionally caught the bus to visit where he lived in Cockett although we hadn't been fishing together for a while.

Cedric was only interested in freshwater fishing

though and in particular for carp. Could it be I wondered that like me he also didn't like worms and was afraid to declare it in case I called him sissy? I decided the reason I was bothering with Royston was because Royston went sea fishing and didn't mind handling the cold and lifeless 'orrible looking things.

ALL LIT UP

The following Wednesday a post card arrived from him. Very curt and to the point; it simply said, "Thanks for calling in. See you on Saturday as arranged with my mum." So that was our Saturday sorted out. I had explained the situation to my parents and they saw no problems although mum insisted on giving me ticket money "just in case." Secretly I think she was afraid that Royston's mother might think we were poor. I suppose that's what mums are like. Always worried about what other kids' mums think of them.

The rest of the week passed without anything exciting happening and I set off on foot again for Royston's arriving around just after midday. This time I was wearing my best school raincoat, short trousers as per usual, Sunday tie at parental insistence but no cap. How I yearned for long trousers. My skinny legs were becoming an embarrassment.

When I arrived Royston greeted me at the door as if he'd seen me only the day before still carrying his worldly poise. "Glad you could make it," he said, "Dinner won't be long." He then launched into a number of questions about my new rod and tackle, passing the time till his mother called out instructions to go and wash our grubby hands.

Lunch was served and proved to be a super fry up of Spam, tomatoes, egg and chips. Bacon I think was still on ration then so no one gave it away without careful thought. Royston's mother had also gone to the trouble of making a jelly and blancmange for pudding so we tucked in to a veritable feast, which we washed down with some Tizer pop. Yeah! I thought. His mother was cool.

After we finished we sat down for five minutes or so to make some preliminary plans while she went into the kitchen to wash up. Then as we were about to set out she gave Royston money for tickets and was about to add something for ice cream when I told her that my mum had also given us some dosh and we could get it with that.

Everything sorted we left for our appointment with the John Wayne and moseyed down to the Plaza corral, on the way discussing Bryn Lucas's suggestion to fish off of the old West Pier. Once again he took the opportunity to regale me with stories of fishing trips he'd been on with the boys to far off shores like Oxwich, Rhossili and Llangennech. He didn't seem to have much in the way of interests outside of fishing. It was all he ever talked about.

We arrived in good time and had to stand in a fairly long queue with a lot of other cowboy fans but it wasn't too long before we were watching our tickets slide out of the narrow slit in the counter as we paid our dues at the booth. We were led to our cheap seating somewhere in the middle and far too close to the screen for my liking. We couldn't do anything about it then because the Pearl & Dean adverts hadn't started and the lights were still up.

I'll try and do something about that when the main

film came on I thought. Like sneak back to the seats a few rows behind and hope the usherettes didn't notice. I forget what the B film was but when the John Wayne film began we made our move. We were really sneaky. I had it all planned out and led Royston astray, taking him with me to the farthest front corner to buy a couple of ice-cream tubs off the Lions Maid girl and then returning to better more expensive seats in the flickering gloom. He was not a happy bunny. He looked around nervously waiting to be carted off to jail; tempting fate and fate answered the call. It was not a successful mission.

We had only been sitting smugly in our newly acquired position for about ten second when we suddenly found ourselves lit up by the beams of two torches cutting through the darkness and disturbing everybody around us. Others had tried that move before and one of the usherettes was on to it and us in an instant.

"I think you've lost your way boys. The seats you were sitting in before you got your ice creams are six rows in front of you. Come on. Let me show you the way back to them."

I sighed heavily and Royston groaned in dismay. His so-called friend who actually went to chapel had led him into temptation. Complete and utter humiliation. Everybody was guffawing and tittering. The really annoying part of it was that some of those who doing most of the snickering were our contemporaries; two of them from my school!

The whole cinema was watching as we were hoiked out of our seats and led back to where we had been before. To make matters worse somebody else was now in our original places and there was an even greater disturbance as the usherette sought out other seats to replant us. Poor Royston didn't know where to look. I had led him into a life of crime. He would never be able to hold his head up again.

I think he had assumed that because I went to chapel I was gooder than good and could do no wrong. Huh! Welcome to the real world Royston. Us chapel goers could be real hypocrites when we felt like. Maybe right now I was on a one way ticket to the fire and brimstone club. But things would be different when we got long trousers. People would show us a lot more respect.

So it was that we had to sit craning our neck upwards as Big John stopped a range war, cleaned up the town and saloon and put the ever-slick Lyle Bettger behind bars where he belonged.

When the programme finished we decided to catch the bus home and went down through the arcade to get the number seventy-five to Tycoch just outside Oxford Street School. Royston was not in a talking mood, looking very morose. He was sitting across the aisle from me and I kept looking at him until I just couldn't stop myself laughing. Eventually he began to see the funny side of it and started laughing as well when I explained that it was a regular game played with 'the management'. Most of the boys who were pointing the finger and enjoying our discomfort did the self-same thing on a regular basis. That particular afternoon they hadn't been caught.

At last, when he'd settled down, I was able to steer him on to some proper planning for our next fishing expedition and we'd only just finished sorting the details before it was time for him to get off at his hospital bus stop. We arranged to try the West Pier the following Wednesday, which was a half term week with no school. Different arrangements from our previous expedition: this time we'd dig the bait, catch the Mumbles Train to Rutland Street and walk down the back streets through the docks.

I hadn't been very optimistic setting out that afternoon but disembarking from the bus at the top of Rhyddings Park Road I was already looking forward to the following Wednesday. In the meantime we would both check the tide times in the South Wales Evening Post.

There wasn't really anything more I could do to prepare my new sea fishing tackle; it was all there ready waiting to be christened. Whereas my rod used to be about ten feet in length it was now six and sufficiently stiff to withstand the new casting stresses that were going to be imposed on it. Before meeting up again with Royston I had been down to the beach the previous week at Brynmill to practice my new weight casting technique. The park would have been more convenient but with football and other play activities going on it was safer on the beach with no people around. Messing around with a model aircraft project to fill in time before Wednesday, I'd spent fruitless time trying to unstick some pieces I shouldn't have stuck together in the first place. Some days you do things like that.

We had judged it right with the tide. I called for him as arranged mid-morning on the Wednesday and we made our way straight down to the beach where the tide had just turned, digging as before but this time there was nobody else about.

Working steadily we harvested roughly the same number of worms until the tide had crept so far up the beach that we were hitting drier sand and had to call a halt. This time we organised ourselves a bit better and washed our hands in the sea using some old towelling and rags to dry them off.

I still wasn't comfortable with lugworms but I thought they would be a lot more uncomfortable than me when my hooks were poked through them. Wearing my Wellingtons again but with two pairs of socks this time to help ward off blisters; I also had on an extra jersey under my old raincoat. Royston was also wearing a heavier jacket and his Wellies and apart from the fishing tackle both our mums had organised flasks of tea and sandwiches.

We walked back up the beach and under the LMS line to the nearest stop for the Mumbles train and only had to wait around ten minutes before one arrived going the right way. The tandem tramcar units stood ticking over, humming and mumbling loudly waiting for us to climb aboard. The concertina doors slapped shut and the train pulled away clattering and lurching on its journey to the east end of the line.

Stowing our tackle alongside us on the lower deck near the front of the second car we placed the bait can on the floor by our feet. A number of the passengers watching seemed decidedly amused by our antics and in particular the contents of the can. This also attracted the conductor's attention and I made the mistake of asking quite innocently if he'd like a look at our lugworms.

No he certainly would not he said and would I make very sure none of them escaped. I'd never thought of lugworms escaping from anything before. Snakes might escape from somewhere I thought but not lugworms. Just then we passed the jail and I tried to imagine them forcing the lid off the can, dropping onto the floor and making a determined mass wriggle for the door. When I mentioned these thoughts to my fishing companion he started giggling and we were both still laughing about it when we reached the Rutland Street terminus.

We climbed down from the train and made our way towards the road behind the railway viaduct, reaching the junction to turn to our right and walk down to the swing bridge spanning the fish market and the South Dock. Fortunately we caught it at the right time when it was closed to shipping so it took less time than we thought it would to reach the beginning of the wooden part of the pier. Instead of going on to its upper deck as originally planned though we elected to stay on the concreted causeway which had a wall on the landward side against which we could leave our kit and shelter if it rained. Making sure that we didn't fall into the oncoming tide was a robust horizontal corrugated steel fence standing at chest height. There were a few souls already scattered about with their lines in the water. Just a half dozen or so on the causeway and a few more seen in the distance dotted along the top deck.

We were definitely the youngest there but nobody was making fun. We were all brothers. We set up out tackle and Royston watched with interest as I took my first cast after successfully persuading three lugworms to swallow my hooks through the side. I put all of my effort into it and succeeded in chucking it out a fair enough distance to be happy with the result and then leaned my rod against the rail, tightened the line and clipped on my peg-bell. The tide at that time had about three hours to go before full flood so it had quite a way to rise up the sides yet.

A NEW FRIEND

Although I had cast out a reasonable distance the angle of my line, when everything settled on the bottom, was still quite steep and nowhere near midstream where I needed to be to get the best flatfish or whiting. That was what the man twenty feet away to our side told us a while later but neither of us had a hope in Hades of casting that far. We'd just have to get lucky with some strays.

Royston finished baiting up, took his stance and swung his rod overhead in a broad sweep. If it had been a golfing swing he could have ended up with an ace but sods law turned it into disaster. At some time previously when he had been winding in the line a loop had formed and concealed itself beneath the following turns.

As the reel now spun the line out behind the weight and the paternoster the loop somehow managed to hook itself around one of its projecting handles. The mechanics of such a thing happening were completely illogical, but it happened.

The line straightened out until it could go no more and the casting weight on the end waved goodbye as it parted company with the paternoster, landing with a delicate little splash at the exact target spot but, alas, without the bait. Normally the sort of thing that happens with line on a spinning reel is a bird's nest on the inside between the reel and mounting bracket. Fortunately such a tangle had not occurred this time.

Royston looked on with jaw sagging disbelief; his worldly façade looking like it might crumble at any moment. All that effort preparing for our expedition and he had stuffed himself on his first cast. Now what was he going to do? I didn't think he had a spare weight but fortunately I did and was more than happy to let him borrow it. Then kind fate intervened. The man fishing next to us had observed the whole thing and now approached to commiserate. "Wind your line in young un" he said, "before the tide tangles it with the others further up." Personally I didn't think the line would have tangled because it hadn't gone that far out and now devoid of weight it was more likely to be carried into the side and get caught up that way. It was an expected angling courtesy nonetheless.

"Oh uh yeah," Royston muttered almost to himself as he complied with the stranger's instruction rather dejectedly.

"That was a piece of bad luck," the man said. "What happened?"

We explained the cause of the entanglement as Royston swung the paternoster back over the rail for inspection showing that it was the swivel link at the bottom which had failed. While he held the rod up I pulled off the line from the reel to untangle the loop that had caused the problem.

"You were unlucky," the man said and then by way of introduction with a smile added "My name is Conroy by the way. Let's have a look and see what we can do to save the day. Get rid of the bait, take your paternoster off and put it back in your bag. I've got a couple of spares I always carry which will be more than strong enough for a young fella' like you. What are your names then?"

We both responded with our identities and when introductions were complete he went to his kitbag leaning against the wall opposite to where his rod was resting and brought it over to us. It was then that I noticed his left hand which was like a claw. He had lost three fingers and only a thumb and forefinger remained. With oriental looks and a weathered face that had seen hard times he was stocky in build and looked fit. I was to learn some months later that he was originally from Hong Kong and had come to Britain shortly after the war.

Opening up the bag he rummaged around and lifted out a very robust looking paternoster with weight and two hooks already attached. "Now let's have a look at the end of your line," he said. Royston looked on rather bewildered by all this attention from a complete stranger and was, I suspected, like me, wondering what this was going to cost him and how he was going to pay.

Conroy must have read our minds because the next thing he said was "Now don't go worrying about payment Royston. These spares have been in my bag for a while and I've also got another one wrapped up in there somewhere."

It was quite a large bag I noticed. "Everybody has some bad luck sometime and us fishermen," he said grinning and winking, "have got to stick together."

We were both impressed with his genuine kindness. Royston was absolutely thrilled. Conroy then did a very fancy new double loop knot on the end of the line attaching it to the paternoster with a kind of safety clip that I hadn't seen before. His nimbleness with the thumb and forefinger was surprising and he explained the reason for only two hooks by saying that more would make things get too crowded and the fish would end up fighting each other instead of taking the bait. I didn't know if he was joking or serious and had to stop myself laughing. Royston sucked up his every word. He was Father Christmas come early.

"Righto," he said, "bait up and have another go with that."

Royston was nervous this time but held himself together and did a really nice cast. Didn't reach the whiting but it was a good cast and he placed the rod against the rail heaving a sigh of relief. Just then Conroy's kindness was rewarded with a very loud ring on his own rod bell. In fact the end of the rod was jerking quite violently and he rushed back to strike. There was something there alright, something that fought back.

The water level had risen quite a bit by now and as he wound the fish in we saw a large silvery white head break the surface; a magnificent cod. He wound it in gently and lifted it, still flapping and kicking, over the rail and laid it on a piece of sack cloth he had ready; giving it a sharp clout on the back of the head with a short piece of metal pipe he carried. It was almost eighteen inches in length. I think if Royston or I had hooked it we might have been pulled over the rails.

"Nice fish Conroy," we both said together congratulating him. This time it was his turn to be pleased.

Nothing further of significance happened during the

remaining time we were there. Conroy caught another smaller cod and a whiting and after thinking he had a bite and pulling in twice Royston caught a dab. Not very big but sufficient to warrant the use of his mother's frying pan when he got home he later told me.

Conroy's success was obviously down to his ability, in spite of handicap, to cast a considerable distance beyond where we could put our bait which was well short of where the best fish were feeding. With my rod measuring only six feet I was even worse off but thankfully after a few false alarms also managed to catch a small, very small, blin which was also taken home for tea. It was so small that my mother laughed and said it was wearing short trousers and still in the infants' school. It was only later in the evening that I appreciated her quick wit.

We visited the West Pier on several occasions over the next few months trying the old wooden upper deck as well. More often than not Conroy would be there with one or two others we got to know and become friendly with. Sad to say our catches didn't improve that much; mine certainly didn't.

The problem was my rod being so short didn't allow me to cast out far enough, particularly when fishing from the top deck. Royston felt more at home on the causeway so that was where we ended up most of the time. I also think that Royston liked talking to Conroy who pulled his leg something rotten.

Considering the whole thing in retrospect I don't think I really minded not catching many fish. If I did it was a bonus. It was the anticipation of going there and being there with the atmosphere and smell of the place where, although essentially next to an industrial environment, there was fresh air and the camaraderie of it all. Although I would often go home tired I would do so with a feeling of exhilaration.

We were chatting in general one day with a few of 'the guys' while standing watch over our rods when the subject of bass came up and in particular our lack of them. It wasn't as if we had been catching much of anything but we were out to impress.

"Oh yes!" said a middle aged smiling and weather beaten face.

"You have ambitions to get into battle with bass do you?"

Royston's phantom experiences were notably absent during the ensuing discussion but the general conclusion was that the place to be for bass was at the far end of the pier. Nothing much was happening that morning with our bait. The fish were obviously looking elsewhere so we left our tackle with Conroy and went for an exploratory visit to see for ourselves where some hardy souls braved the turbulent wind in search for the kings of the sea, although none had been caught so far that morning.

It was very exposed with the sea looking quite rough at the end and I wondered what would happen if someone fell in. The thought crossed my mind as to what both our mothers would think if they could have seen their precious sons standing so close to paradise. I concluded they'd probably both have had the screaming habdabs.

The water level was far enough below where we were standing to have made any rescue very difficult if not impossible. There was no barrier and falling in would be very easy to do. I certainly didn't feel comfortable. Royston was also standing well back so after a brief exchange of polite questions and answers with the bass fishermen we made our way back. It wasn't an easy walk in either direction. The only way to get to the end was on the lower level which didn't have a proper walkway for most of its length. It was just timber balks and bracing struts laid over some fairly large foundation stones that had to be climbed over most of the way.

Sometime later on a particularly biteless morning we found where it was possible to get directly on to the beach. Here the concrete causeway finished and became original heavy timbered construction.

So we again left our tackle with Conroy and walked along the sand to where it became a raised bank supported by a heavily built stone wall as its steepest point. The first hundred yards or so of sand that we passed was fenced off by the MOD with danger signs warning that the area was still a possibly uncleared minefield, the residue of war. Our imaginations ran riot. Beyond the raised portion of ground the wall ran some way till it terminated at another tunnel leading from the beach beneath the LMS railway line and out onto the Mumbles road.

At the back of the elevated stretch of ground running the length of the wall on the landward side were a number of ram shackled workshops and assorted building that backed onto the South Dock. We had heard that 'The Sea Wall' was also a legendary place to catch bass because the tide came right up to it for some depth, remorselessly crashing against it and soaking all those who stood at the edge with their rods. Standing too close even with a normal tidal swell looked dangerous; too reminiscent of the end of the pier. On that particular day we were just exploring and having general mooch around and happened to come across what some people might have called the seamy side of life.

It was as I recall a Saturday lunch time and a bunch of workers, dressed in well-worn work attire of varying fashion, were just finished for the day and anxious to risk their freshly paid, hard earned, wages on the spin of a coin. Some of them were even wearing wooden work clogs on their feet which I had never seen before except in pictures of Dutch people. Another discovery.

It had been raining earlier in the morning and there were a number of large puddles scattered on the pathway which was laid over the sand with a mix of crushed bricks and hardcore, worn flat over time by the passage of many work boots. Not far from the entrance to the tunnel a group of men had formed into a lively jostling, noisy circle in the one dry spot there that would accommodate them.

We were both curious. Was it a fight we wondered and should we take a look? Somewhat apprehensively we sidled up to the crowd to see what was causing the ruckus. As we did so they seemed to subconsciously part to let us through. This both surprised and pleased us when we saw that fighting was not the attraction.

We looked on with excited interest and stood for some time completely absorbed as first one man and then another together flicked half-crown pieces into the air with both hands, watching as they spun and dropped onto the barren ground. The circle of men closing in crushed together as they craned to see which way up the coins had landed: heads or tails.

They were all betting on the drop of the coins with shouts of frustration, groans and complaints from the losers -joy from the winners. Dismay and delight. "You didn't throw them right. You didn't spin them properly," the losers complained.

I didn't know about Royston but I had never really seen a pay packet before. Never seen men rip a new rough brown envelope open to reveal green blue pounds, brown ten shilling notes and silver half crowns. It was enthralling. Not for the men ripping the packets open though. They were the ones who had lost the bet and in one sense even as a young schoolboy it was sad to see the hard earned currency handed to somebody else on something as frivolous as the toss of a few coins.

Just how much had been lost we wondered? Would the same people risk another toss of the coin only to lose more money or would they be winners the next time and would the winners keep on winning or would they lose. The permutations of chance were endless.

There was one sudden scuffle with a number of raised voices which could have got serious but common sense prevailed and it blew over as soon as it started; which was when a firm but friendly hand was placed on each of our shoulders, an equally firm voice saying, "Come on now you boys. This is no place for you young'uns to be."

We turned to see a tall grey haired individual in a working smock who had the definite air of authority about him as all present seemed to demur to his comment and stood aside as he led us away from the gathering.

"Where have you come from then boys?" he asked. "You're not from around here are you?"

"No", we told him and related how we'd walked down from the pier to have a look because we had been told it was a good spot to catch bass from the wall.

"Fishermen are you?" he said. "Where's your tack

then? I don't see any rods."

He obviously thought we were lying; he must be the foreman.

When we explained that our tackle was being looked after by our friend, he suggested we should get back to it, or we would miss the last of the incoming tide when the fish would be biting.

Then as a parting shot he said," If you're thinking of fishing off the wall I would advise against it. I don't think your parents would approve if they knew you intended coming here."

He went on to explain that he himself sometimes fished there and it could get very rough and dangerous especially with a wind. A few months back somebody had lost their balance and fallen over the edge. It was only because the tide was relatively calm and shallow at the time that he was able to wade to the end of the wall and get out.

"Very lucky he didn't fall in at full tide otherwise it would have been a different story," he said, concluding," I don't want to spoil your fun but it's far too risky for you -do you understand?"

We both nodded our understanding and walked on to the tunnel telling him we were just going to check were it came out onto the road. It wasn't the same one we used to go through when digging for lugworm. That one must have been much closer to The Slip and as we made our way back to the pier I wondered if we walked home along the beach which of them might save us the most time. The gamblers had disappeared by then either to go home with their winnings or drown their sorrows in the nearest pub and concoct a good excuse for their wives about how they seem to be short on their wages – again?

Conroy was waiting to show us a very aggressive looking conger eel he had caught while we were away but that was about the only thing of any size landed that morning by anyone so we hadn't really missed much. We told him what we had seen and the story about the chap falling off the wall and he said he'd heard about it a while ago, and yes it was true and the fella who got the soaking was very lucky; echoing the foreman's advice not to go fishing there. He was also interested in the story about the gamblers and asked us what we thought about it. I think it pleased him that we both declared that it was a very foolish and easy way to lose your money. "There's hope for you yet then," he said with a smile on his face.

Our visit to the gamblers' circle was still some time in the future then and on our return from the end of the pier we found a few of our comrades preparing to pack up since the tide was due to turn. With our own efforts that morning producing nothing we decided to do the same thing, going home the way we had come by the Mumbles Train. We were really too tired to contemplate a long walk along the beach. When we did try it however we would use what we would by then have christened 'Gamblers Arch' but that would be for the future.

During some pre departure conversation the subject of ragworm was mentioned. Oh no I thought -not more worms. "Oh yes!" said Royston. Some of his fantasy fishing friends swore by them for bass he told me. Further discussion on them ensued in which the few fishermen remaining at their posts passed their opinions giving much anecdotal evidence to back up the various claims.

Apparently they were not as docile or fat as the

lugworms we were using. They were a lot livelier and wriggled more which supposedly attracted the fish more. Bass were particularly partial to them which was certainly worth considering. Unfortunately they did have a small extra feature that lugworms didn't which I found most disconcerting. This was a set of pincers on their head which could give you a nasty nip. They also had what looked like furry legs along their entire length which reminded me of a centipede. Conroy was still there and nodded in agreement so it was inevitable that Royston would ask where they could be found, bless him, and the answer was unfortunately "Not far away."

We were in fact within a couple of hundred yards or so of a very good source. On the way to the causeway where we were fishing there was an L shaped pier jutting out into the river. It was quite old and slowly withering away in parts with the short leg of the L providing a pathway to the long section which had both a stair way and a side ladder leading down to the contained portion of the river bed. This enclosed area featured a number of rotting wooden hulks lying forlornly on silty, sucking clay, which to the wrecks was a graveyard but to ragworm was a home. My mighty mentor enthusiastically made plans for us both. Oh no!

CLAY IS A GRAY AREA

It was probably on the following weekend I suppose. It's a little hazy now. Suffice to say that we arrived with our fishing gear and forks ready to do battle with the clay. We had to get there either before the tide was fully out or just before the turn. Although where we were going to dig was on a higher level than the bed of the main river, once the tide did turn it wouldn't take long to reach us.

Unlike lugworm there were no casts to indicate where ragworms might be lying. You just have to find a spot and dig there, we were informed. So we arrived at the rotting L shaped pier and made our way, me to clamber carefully down the ladder and Royston a bit further along the walkway, down the steps to the bottom and onto the sucking clay bed.

Oh boy did it suck! We were both soon in trouble. Some parts were firmer than others and unfortunately the few ragworms that we did find were in the softer parts. We had to dig down about a foot, like with lugworm, but once you had turned a lump over you had to prise it apart by hand to get at the worm.

Twice I got bitten by their pincers. I was getting covered in slimy clay and it stuck where it touched. My mentor was having the same kind of fun. Staying upright was also a problem. If you kept moving around it wasn't so bad but if you remained in the same place for any length of time you just sank deeper and it was difficult to extricate your feet from the stuff.

It was almost frightening at times. I was first to inadvertently step out of my Wellingtons and tread directly into the clay with one of my feet. A really slippery spot where there was nothing to hold onto. The only thing I could do was jam the digging fork into the ground for support while replacing my now clay covered foot back in the Welly. Royston didn't step out of his; he just fell over flat on his face with a squelch. I didn't see it happen because my back was turned to him at the time as I tried yet again to extricate my other Wellington from the abominable, cloying, sucking morass.

His day was not going well. Mentoring a pupil from Brynmill was proving to be a tough project. I had a sudden mental image of him being slowly upturned and disappearing head first, only his empty Wellies left, pointing skyward. His quarry beneath had mounted a counter attack, surrounding him in a mass pincer movement, dragging him below to their larder. Royston was roughage for wrigglies. The great ragworm dig had backfired spectacularly. I shook the aberration from my mind as he give a strangled yell.

Two passing seagulls joined him in chorus but their harmonising was suddenly interrupted by the sound of heavy slapping rubber clad footsteps descended the stairway as a voice in humour proclaimed "It's no good diving on them young'un. You'll never catch rag worms like that." I was only half extricated and part turned in time to see Conroy making his way to our clay swimmer who was lying fifteen feet out from the steps face down and trying to prize himself off the sucking grey mass.

Where the devil had Conroy come from I asked myself as Royston's hands sunk deeper, getting him nowhere. His rescuer taking several squelchy sucking footsteps allowed him no dignity as he arrived to pull him off the clay bed and upright by the armpits, suspending him thus to carry across the great divide to dry land. I knew Royston was a Superman fan; I had seen his comics lying around. He surely must have thought he was being rescued by none other for a few brief seconds as he looked bewilderedly about him from the steps, clearly shaken at his closer than expected encounter with the colour grey.

His glasses had fallen off and looking across to where he had been floundering I could see them lying next to his bait can as he explained his predicament. I pointed them out and once more unto the breach Conroy squelched his way back to where my mighty mentor had fallen and retrieved glasses, fork and worms.

I had had enough myself by then so picking up my own can of worms I made my way slowly, suckingly, to the pier ladder and climbed back up to meet them both at the top. We were both puzzled by Conroy's unexpected appearance and also grateful.

How we asked had he come to be there? "Well," he said a little self-consciously, "I finished my shift early to dig for bait and I remembered you saying you were going to try for some ragworm in this old docking area. There was an incident a few years ago when somebody nearly got trapped in clay with the tide coming in and I thought I'd just come over and give you a hand in case you got stuck yourselves. Good job I did huh?" Who was he kidding I thought.

We weren't in any danger -were we? The tide was nowhere near us -was it? On the other hand, Royston poor dab, had been floundering and I looked at Conroy in awe. A virtual stranger out of concern for the safety of a couple of kids he hardly knew had gone out of his way and made a lame excuse to protect them from their own folly.

I eventually spoke to thank him and said "You're a real friend Conroy, and we both appreciate your concern." We solemnly each shook his hand. It was an "Aw shucks it weren't nothing," kind of moment and he looked decidedly embarrassed but then said. "I think you to two need to get cleaned up. You can't go home looking like that let alone stand in front of your rods like it for the fish to laugh at."

We both grinned sheepishly wondering how we were going to get tidy but again Conroy saved the day. As we came off the jetty carrying our gear another of the regular west pier crew named Phil arrived asking, "Everything alright Con?"

"Yes," he replied smiling. "OK now. They just got suckered into digging for ragworm, didn't you?" he said, turning to us and making a joke out of it and adding, "I'm just going to take them to the fish market to get cleaned up."

There was clay everywhere. Royston was in a really awful mess and just as we were about to set off I suddenly had a thought and asked him, "Is your mother working today?"

"Er yes," he said, "She's going in at lunch time, working this afternoon, why?"

"Well," I replied, "If she's working this afternoon

and you go home straight after we get cleaned up you'll be there before she gets back and she won't see you in that state will she? Not if you get changed before she gets home. I dare say if she saw the state of your clothes she wouldn't be very pleased – even if you do get the worst off."

"Er no. I see what you mean," he said. Then I asked him if he could get in the house. There wasn't much point going home if he couldn't get in.

"Yes. My neighbour will be in and she always has a spare key in case of emergencies."

Then Conroy chipped in and said that sounded a better plan than carrying on fishing. By this time anyway I wasn't really looking forward to standing around in a Wellington boot now sodden on the inside with sticky clay, and apart from how he looked I'm sure

Royston wasn't that comfortable either. We rearranged our plans accordingly and instead of leaving our tackle with Phil to look after we took it all with us. Having to undergo a few amused comments from arriving fishermen on the way, we followed Conroy to a washroom facility adjacent to the fish market which was alongside the trawler moorings. Swansea didn't have a large fishing fleet but it was enough to warrant a dedicated dock for the boats to offload directly onto and sell their catch to the various fishmongers and other trade establishments.

When we got there Conroy fetched us some old rags and towels from a friend he had working there and left us to it, wishing us well and saying that he would probably see us again in the next couple of weeks. We hadn't realised it but we were both quite tired with all the activity and when we were as presentable to the world as we could manage walked back across the swing bridge to Rutland Street to catch the Mumbles Train.

There was a duplex set just emerging from the train shed as we rounded the corner into the street and we watched as it crossed the road onto the main line to wait, humming and murmuring as passengers clambered aboard. We would have liked to have had a look inside the tram shed but apart from not being very convenient at that moment, as schoolboys we didn't think we would be allowed; not realizing that if we asked in the right place we could probably get shown around if accompanied by an adult.

The mechanical and industrial world was starting to beckon but the possibilities would have to wait for another day.

Looking for somewhere to stow our gear we headed for the front car to put it all under the alcove under the stairway to the upper deck. We were far too grubby to sit down so we stood next to it trying to look as inconspicuous as possible as the train accelerated away from the terminus.

Our visit to the washroom had allowed us to emerge looking tidier but evidential splatter still remained; especially on my mate who had been face down in the clay and up to his elbows trying to lift himself out. I had only got my Wellingtons covered in clay and one foot when it pulled out and trod in the darn stuff.

They had cleaned up alright but my foot was still soggy and the whole front of Royston's jerkin, knees and trousers were stained grey and drew a lot of amused attention as passengers got on at our end of the tram. If he had walked out of a fog you wouldn't have seen him coming.

I don't know why he hadn't bothered to clean his knees off. I think he was completely thrown by the whole episode no matter how casual he tried to act. The conductor had also noticed our lacking in sartorial elegance and was intent on having a bit of fun as soon as he had collected the fares.

"Aha!" he said, "the worm hunters are back with us again. Have you got any worms you want to show me today? Where's your can? Have you lost it?

It suddenly clicked. This was the same one that had bantered with us a couple of months ago and it was the first time since then that we were travelling once more on the same train journey.

"No not today," I said' trying not to get involved in a prolonged conversation. I didn't know where this was leading.

"Where've you been then? I don't see any fish. Have you not caught anything worth talking about?"

He was asking the questions in a friendly enough manner as opposed to being sarcastic so we explained what sort of a day we had been having and why we were looking rather the worse for wear. A number of passengers were listening to our tale of woe by now and he was obviously waiting for the right moment to make a wisecrack and it wasn't long coming.

"It looks to me," he said, "from the state you're in that the worms turned and fought back and you lost the fight."

Laughter from the passengers.

"So," he said looking at Royston and asking me, "Did they take him hostage?"

Even I had to laugh at that. Royston giggled all embarrassed at the attention he was getting and I had a funny feeling that he was about to become a living legend.

"Off home now then is it," the conductor said, "to face the music from Mam."

Royston nodded his head sheepishly amidst more laughter from some passengers and sympathy from others as just then we reached our stop. With a broad grin across his face the conductor wished Royston the best of luck and we both climbed off the train with our bits and pieces.

OVER THE GARDEN WALL

We walked unhurriedly up through the back streets to his house, both hoping that his emergency arrangement with the neighbour's spare key would work out. On the way I told him of my own backup plan to gain entry to our house when there was nobody at home and how it had come into being. The best laid plans can and do go wrong as he was now only too well aware and I explained that if my mother was out of the house when I was out with my friends or fishing in the park I didn't always have a key to get in.

Sometimes a chap might have to answer an urgent call of nature or get fed up with fish that didn't bite and have a reason to go home, but my parents didn't leave the front door key with a neighbour as a matter of course. If I thought I might need it then it was done by arrangement. Dad would always be in his High Street office in the morning and came home for lunch by bus. It was very convenient for him. Sometimes I wished that it wasn't!

The lack of a key used to be a source of great annoyance to me at times until I discovered a way of getting in the house without one. My dilemma was solved when I made the simple observation that the small pantry window in the kitchen was not always closed. Hinged from the topmost edge it was held open by a swinging arm having a series of holes along its length to engage on a window frame peg. Being of slim build I thought I would be able to slide through and when there was nobody about did a test run. Yes, I was small enough to be a cat burglar. MEEEOW!

The second part of the equation was the garage which gave me access but only with some difficulty.

Our house had no back lane entry like a garden gate or door. It had a garage that filled the whole width of the property. With a corrugated sheet for one side wall and roof, and a stone wall on the other, it had folding wooden doors, normally bolted, that swung back inside to open. On the corrugated sheet side of the garage the neighbour's garden wall ran just below floor level. It was the only garage in the block, all the others having access through back doors set into a fairly high wall that ran the length of the lane.

Anyway – with all the practice climbing trees in the park scaling the lane wall was easy peasy, and with my back to the garage's corrugated side, I was able to inch along the top of the garden wall until I could drop down into our side. Hurdle one. Next was the tricky bit. If the pantry window was unsecured the back lawn would be crossed to step over the pathway below and on to the window ledge. From there the arm holding the window open could be unhooked allowing me to slither through and drop down onto the cold slab inside.

I had used this method only about four times in total but was now too big to use it anymore; a fact which seemed to mollify Royston's growing concern. He still seemed to me however to be mentally reliving our seat swapping activities at the cinema and wondering just what sort of criminal he was associating with.

When I asked him if his house had a pantry window he actually gave a sharp intake of breath. It was such an opportunity to pull his leg some more that I couldn't resist winding him up and said earnestly, "You will come and visit me when I'm in prison won't you?" and his face froze. He was obviously for some reason unsettled by my kind of humour so I gave him a playful nudge just to calm him and added "Only joking Royston." Oh dear. Me and my big mouth!

Actually, the emergency plan had backfired on one occasion because I went home in a hurry once without checking that mum was out when she said she would be. Going up over the wall, across the garden and through the pantry window, I was just emerging into the kitchen when she came through the dinning room door. I don't know who had the biggest fright. She had heard my noisy entrance and come to investigate.

Explanations were in order which I duly gave but she was quite understandably not too happy and recalled that on a couple of occasions she had come home with a feeling that things were not quite the same as when she had left the house. Oops!

My usual exit was to go out the front door and slam it shut after me and that apparently answered another question for her. A neighbour had casually mentioned seeing me leave the house some time previously when she wasn't in and I was supposed to have been elsewhere. It had obviously been something she had been trying to reconcile in her mind and I got a right good telling off.

Was she going to tell dad? Not this time she said but don't do it again, and I got a key a week later. I hadn't originally intended to go out by the front door but climb back out through the window. Unfortunately it wasn't as easy as entry, almost slipping out upside down and landing on my head. Pity about that neighbour. I didn't tell Royston all this of course. He didn't need to know all my secrets did he?

We got to his neighbours house, which was actually a couple more doors up and I waited by the gateway with our tackle. At first nobody came to answer the knocker so he had to really give it a hard bang the second time. The door eventually opened and a rather tall lady with a long pointy nose and straggly grey hair came out onto the porch way exclaiming loudly at his disheveled appearance.

"Oh goodness gracious Royston. What on earth have you fallen into? What have you been doing to yourself?"

"Ah, oh" he said, "I fell over in some mud and came home to change. Has mum given you the spare key?"

"Yes, lucky for you Royston. I suppose you're going to do a quick change act now are you?" she answered, smiling.

"I hope so." he said, and she nodded, disappearing inside for a minute before returning with her arm outstretched at shoulder height with the key held between forefinger and thumb.

"Better make it quick then." She said chuckling to herself as she handed it to him and then with a parting smile turned and retreated back into the house closing the door behind her. I left him to his fate and went to catch the bus. The next time I saw him he hardly said much about it except that his mother hadn't given him too much agro over it because he had already washed and changed by the time she got home.

After the 'Clay Incident' we just went back to using lugworm for bait, although for some time afterwards we were the butt of cryptic comments about ragworm until things finally settled down and the episode eventually passed into West Pier folklore.

THE SECRET

My friendship with Royston endured for about nine or ten months and only ended I suppose because events overtook us.

During this time I had become painfully aware that with regard to his fishing exploits without my presence he didn't always tell the truth. His exaggerations were sometimes so obvious that even at age eleven going on twelve the word deluded came to mind.

For the life of me I couldn't understand why. When you've known somebody that long in the normal run of things such pretence usually disappears. He was still telling his fishy stories about trips with the boys on his dad's coach however. Nobody got that lucky.

I knew from a comment that his mother made that he often went to see his gran and granddad in Morriston on Sundays but he seemed to be unaware that I knew this.

I didn't really want to have to tell him and imply that he was lying because underneath I felt that there was a reason for it and that something was very wrong if he had to keep up the deception. He was not only trying to fool me; he was fooling himself. The other thing was that we had on a number of occasions arranged to meet at his house to go digging for bait before going on to the pier fishing, and twice to go to the cinema. I had arrived as arranged and he hadn't been there; no one in. When we had reconnected afterwards he was dead casual about it. Very dismissive, no apology, and no explanation.

I was really being far too good-natured about it but his attitude was beginning to annoy me. Things came to a head one Saturday morning the last time I called for him and he wasn't there when he should have been. His mother answered the door in her nurse's uniform and I remembered her telling me on a previous occasion that she was a nursing sister at the hospital nearby. I asked if Royston was in because we were supposed to be going fishing again. When she said no he would be out for the day I said, I suppose out of sheer exasperation, "Oh, I suppose he's doing another fishing trip on his dad's coach?"

Fair play to her, she frowned, squinted and opened her mouth, letting her jaw drop all at the same time; obviously puzzled. Then her demeanour changed, like her facial expression, to one of sad acknowledgement of something she would rather not have to deal with.

"I think," she said, "you had better come in. I think I need to have a little talk with you, Bernard."

I shook my head momentarily. "What about?"

"Just come in a minute Bernard please. It is Bernard isn't it?"

"Yes," I replied, both puzzled and worried. She must be really distracted if she couldn't remember my name I thought as she led me through to their kitchen.

"Would you like a cup of tea?" she asked.

Never refuse a cup of tea. "Er, yes I wouldn't mind thank you," I said, thinking I was going to need one the way she was acting. I just sat there and waited till she sorted things and put a few biscuits on a plate. She didn't talk while making the tea. I guessed she had something to say and was working out the best way to say it.

Now you would think wouldn't you that after I had been knocking around with Royston all that time that I would have prised some of his secrets out of him. Well wouldn't you? We've all got little secrets at that age but you usually give some of them up over time -eventually -to people you think you can trust. I thought I had earned his trust by that time even though I knew he liked to keep things close to his chest. But boy! Did he have a secret?

It was so blindingly obvious I should have known. The evidence, in one sense, had been staring me in the face for yonks. Or rather the thing which was so glaringly absent should have given me a clue but it never registered. And now suddenly without warning his mother slapped me in the face with it. After she served the tea she drew in a deep breath and looked me squarely in the eyes.

"Bernard," she said, "I am going to have to trust you. Can – can I trust you? I am going to have to ask you to be very discreet. Do you know what discreet means?"

I was flummoxed to say the least. What the hell had the boy done?

"Er yes," I said pensively, "I think I understand what discreet means. Keeping something secret and yes you can trust me." I paused and then said, rather indiscreetly, "Why, what's he done?"

She almost smiled at that but then said, "Oh no, no Bernard. Royston hasn't done anything." She shook her head then, adding as she sighed, "I hadn't realised it had affected him so much. Tell me. What's he been saying about his dad?"

I still didn't know what the problem was and it must have shown because out of the blue she suddenly blurted it out, "Royston's father is in prison."

I hadn't seen that coming. The world stopped turning. I sat in front of her, stunned and speechless, my stomach turning over as I remembered my comments to him some time previously. I nearly fell off my chair. I know my mouth must have been gaping and my eyes went wide open.

Prison then was a much harsher regime with no human rights laws to exploit by slick lawyers and suing a prison was unheard of. Little about inside conditions was really known by the general public and certainly not by children. Newspaper information was sparse and television was not then available to the masses with gritty prison dramas. For kids like me prison meant total terror. I couldn't begin to imagine the horror for my friend having a father locked away in one.

Shaking my head slowly and then nodding I sighed and almost talking to myself said, "Aaah – so that's what it's all about."

"How do you mean Bernard?" And what, she asked again, had he been saying about his father? I had no option. So I told her about the fishing trips he said he'd been with on his dad's coach with 'the guys' and all the stories he had been telling.

"Oh dear," she said, "the poor boy. He's just trying to cope. I suppose that's his way of dealing with it. He's obviously created a fantasy world for himself. It's been two years now and I thought he was alright, but obviously he's not. Unfortunately his father did something very silly and got found out and we are both suffering for it, especially Royston it seems."

She continued. "First of all Bernard his father doesn't own and never has owned a coach. His uncle drives a coach for a company in Morriston and I know that they do occasionally take parties of fishermen. He has been able to take Royston along on a couple of occasions but it's difficult because he's only the driver. That's where he must have got his fishing stories from and made them up as some sort of comfort. He loves his dad and not having him around is really hurting him. They don't allow children in the prison very often so he doesn't see him very much."

The obvious had been staring me in the face for so long that I hadn't seen it. Subconsciously I had been wondering why I had never seen his dad at home, never even thought to ask where he was. In retrospect it was probably a good job that I hadn't.

Heaven knows what might have been his response but it had never really registered until that moment; the van also being a figment of his imagination.

She carried on giving me some more details about his troubled life and said, "I'm afraid Royston doesn't make many friends in school because they found out about his dad and some of the children were very cruel to him. You're one of the few friends that he does have Bernard and I know he values your friendship. Can I ask you not to tell him that you know about his dad? He'd be very upset if you did."

I nodded my head vigorously. "Of course," I said. What else could I do? Poor sod, I thought remembering how some of his worldly demeanour disappeared whenever we were fishing near Conroy.

He'd really taken a shine to him and didn't give

him any of his man of the world routine. He'd tried it once and Conroy had just taken the mickey out of him for doing it. There had been a number of us close by when this happened and everybody had burst out laughing including me. Far from him being embarrassed or upset Royston had taken it in his stride and laughed along with them, a big fat grin across his chops. He was one of the boys after all wasn't he? I was almost proud of him.

Then his mother came out with another bombshell. "Has he told you we are moving?" That also took me off guard and for a moment. I couldn't reply, sort of wondering how I felt about it, so I just said, "Ooh no - he hasn't told me. Where are you going?"

It turned out that they were moving to Morriston where she was going to be a senior nursing sister at the hospital. It would also give an opportunity for Royston to have a fresh start in a new school where the family history wasn't known and his gran and granddad would be close by to look after him sometimes when his mum was at work.

Considering his problems it sounded quite sensible really. I did wonder how he would cope with being so much further from the beach. Perhaps he'd lose interest but his mum didn't mention it so neither did I, wondering if he'd miss the real fishing crew we'd got to know at the Pier. Maybe a new start would do him good. I knew I would to some extent miss his company but in all honesty I didn't really want the complications of his troubled life impinging on mine; so I suppose I was somewhat ambivalent about the whole thing.

Some new interests like scouting were beginning to surface in my life and some other new friends as well. Perhaps it was all for the best. I was still disappointed that he had never mentioned he was moving and wondered if he would have let me find out only after he was gone. He really was a strange one but then again in the circumstances I suppose it was understandable.

I also wondered when his father would get out of jail but it wasn't the sort of question a twelve year old would ask then so it was left unsaid. I made up my mind however that I would call to see him before he went and told his mother that was what I wanted to do.

I think she was pleased about my attitude and said she would just tell him that I had called in on spec and had been told about the move. So we left it at that. I said I'd pop in the following Saturday morning and she said she would make sure he was there.

The week passed in its usual way and delivered me to Royston's front doorstep as arranged. This time he was there to greet me and for once seemed a little more relaxed saying, "Hi, I'm glad you came. I wondered that you might not after last week. I'm sorry. I really forgot."

Well if that was an apology it would have to do. I wasn't about to complain and merely replied, "Ah that's OK. It happens."

While at the same time thinking perhaps a little vindictively, it's happened too many flippin' times, but said nothing. He invited me in saying his mother had got some iced custard slices for us. I was a sucker for custard slices so there was no turning back.

I had expected the occasion to be rather awkward considering that it would probably be the last time we would meet but his mother's presence and a cup of tea seemed to ease things and we fell into talking about some of the fishing exploits we had shared while we sampled the treats. When it came to the parting of the ways I said goodbye to his mother and a bit self-consciously shook hands with him outside the front door. I wished him the best of luck and reminded him that he had my address so he could send a postcard when he got settled and maybe we could arrange to meet up at the West Pier sometime. I think it was politeness more than anything. In hindsight I don't think our parting really bothered him that much either. I never really expected to get a card from him. I bade him farewell and that was the last I ever saw of him.

I continued fishing down the pier by myself but never once saw him there again. I did see Conroy though and when he asked about him I explained that they had moved to Morriston because of his mother's new job at the hospital and he probably wouldn't be coming any more.

"Oh that's a pity," he said, "I think I'll miss seeing him down here. He was a good laugh." Yes," I said, nodding my head by way of reply. Then, picking up my already baited rod I cast the line out as far as I could. And that was how Royston my sea fishing mentor passed out of my life.

It's a funny thing but it is only now, as I write these words and recall the past, that I wonder how he fared in life; if he eventually got his head together, and I suppose, where he ended up. I also wonder when his father got out of prison and if he too got his life together but I know I'll never find the answer to either question. I never did find out why he went to prison in the first place.

On our journeys to the pier by Wellington clad feet and tram I had become painfully aware that a bicycle would be a much better and more amenable mode of transport. So not long after I had said goodbye to

Royston and tired of trying to make friends with ex-pedestrians who rode past me, I started a campaign of concentrated attrition directed at the family's chief executive: my father.

Maybe it was in the mistaken belief that he would perhaps someday taste fresh caught sea bass that he eventually caved in and coughed up, and I became the proud owner of a bright new shiny Sturmey Archer three speed Hercules bicycle with white wall tyres.

Over the next few years, before I left home, I gradually acquired a proper sea fishing rod and tackle which I used many times off the West Pier and various places from all along the beach as far as Blackpill and even the Mumble Pier. Occasionally I would bump in to Conroy and would fish alongside him for the duration of the tide, swapping yarns and recalling the days. He was still doing it when I eventually left Swansea; inconsiderately without telling him that I was leaving or bothering to say goodbye. I hope he fared well. He was a genuine and generous individual.

Reminiscing about it after all these years and remembering all the times I cast into the sea and time spent fishing from all those places, it is strange to realize that I never caught a single bass or one decent sized fish but enjoyed every minute of it. Spending time with rod and line can do that to you.

AERONAUTICAL ENGINEER

Fishing of course was not the only thing that schoolboys then did in their spare time. There are crazes and phases as in all hobbies and at the time the other thing that was engaging my interest was model aircraft. Probably the first type everyone starts with is the glider giving us all hours of fun. Built of balsa wood it was the simplest of models; usually bought in an easy self-assembled kit, with the main wing and tail plane pushed through two slots in a flat fuselage. Sometimes there would be printed details on the kit to make it more realistic for the young pilots of the future. These would be thrown into the wind and chased all over the place. Not usually very far because the wingspan was usually no more than a foot or thirty centimetres in metric measurement and if not trimmed correctly would nose dive into the ground.

Fortunately with these small gliders the impact was usually not sufficient to cause any damage so appropriate adjustments could be made till straight and level flight was attained. The next step was a bigger version which usually had to be built, either from simple plans purchased from a plan service company, or by using your imagination to design your own. The

MAP plans service, run by a model magazine, had literally hundreds of plans to choose from. Not only simple gliders but rubber powered and miniature diesel powered aircraft as well.

It was a wonderful hobby to get involved in because useful skills were learnt as well as patience and many friends made with like-minded individuals from around the area and elsewhere. It usually didn't take long for regular groups to form and bring their models to Brynmill in the evenings and weekends. With bigger gliders came the practice of catapult launching and sending the model higher for longer flight duration; mostly done with strong elastic held in the hand but occasionally with a stake driven into the ground to provide a more solid anchor point. The elastic would then be hooked into a notch in the fuselage and pulled as far back as wisdom would allow before letting go.

This method could come at a price however depending on the trim of the model. A heavy launch would sometimes caused it to perform a perfect loop resulting in the flight path taking it into the back of the launchers head. OUCH! These were the simplest models to make. They had to be made because unlike today there were no other semi-finished models to buy apart from the simple glider.

More complicated glide or rubber powered models with three dimensional wings and fuselage were available from model shops that sold a large variety of kits with encouraging pictures of the finished project on the box cover. Alas the pictures were often deceiving. Few models ever flew as depicted and I never smiled like the boy on the box because I knew damn well that when I launched mine it was going to nose dive into the ground as soon as it was released.

At any one time there could be several of us working on different kits comparing notes as we either progressed or failed in the attempt. From memory the average kit price was around three shillings and nine pence for a rubber powered Auster, Chipmunk, Fury, Spitfire, or similar aircraft of the day, all with an average wingspan of around twenty inches.

The first kit I chose to build was a Globe Swift, which was really far too ambitious. Fuselage and wing formers were all printed on balsa wood and had to be cut out with a sharp blade. A sharp blade to me was one of dad's razor blades, which didn't really have the right shape but sufficed to split a lot of the cut out forms in places where they shouldn't have been. By the time all the bits had been cut, after a couple of weeks of bad tempered effort, quite a few had been repaired using the special balsa wood cement. The kits were always stingy with cement, which meant buying at least one extra-large tube, which was a real strain on limited schoolboy pocket money and there would be other extras we needed as well.

This meant looking for ways to earn extra model building funds like paper rounds or similar part time jobs. Since most building went on in the summer months I persuaded dad to lend me his lawn mower and shears to cut grass and trim hedges around the neighbourhood, which was a very useful and flexible way to earn a few bob and I only ever got diddled once. My customer had obviously been watching through his window till he saw me cutting the last blades of some very long grass with the garden shears. Suddenly he burst through his front door, walked across to say, "Thank you very much young man," and then thrusting sixpence into my hand he swiftly turned and disappeared back inside closing the drawbridge between us very firmly, leaving me speechless. What a tight fisted…! When I told dad he was livid.

There were two things that we found out about balsa cement. One was that it stuck to your fingers like no other glue and went off so quickly that we were forever peeling it off like a second skin. A more serious property was its subtle noxious fumes which were harmless until you caught a whiff. That was the danger. The aroma was sweet, heady and attractive making you want to inhale it more deeply. Although the risks were not then understood we were able to recognise that it would probably pickle our brains and didn't succumb to temptation or hear of anybody else who had.

There was however another smelly hurdle to overcome. When assembly of the model was complete and the fuselage and wing surfaces covered with tissue it was necessary to first shrink the paper to make it taut and then seal it with a liquid called dope which had similar properties. Fortunately dope and glue sniffing was unheard of by schoolboy aviators. Our main objective was to fly the model airplane and not get high as a kite ourselves and since we didn't realise that was what would happen we never gave it a thought.

With the kits came a set of plans and once all the wing, tail plane and fuselage formers had been cut out and repaired they were ready to assemble. The plans had to be laid flat on a board and pinned down so that the individual pieces could be set in place and glued together with spars and stringers to make up the sub-assemblies. All had to be held in place using round colour headed pins while the glue was setting.

It was only when trying to remove them from the plan after setting that you wished somebody had told you to grease the parts of the plan where glue was used because by that time everything had stuck together and you ended up tearing the plan apart and perhaps destroying freshly dried joints which was very frustrating. I had assembled a few slide together gliders and boxy looking rubber powered models by the time my first major kit project was completed and had literally agonised over the Globe Swift for weeks before deciding to build it. This was a major schoolboy executive decision that required much discussion among my contemporaries.

A low wing aircraft of twenty-inch wingspan it looked to me to be half Spitfire and half Hurricane. As usual the picture on the kit box showed its short-trousered, skinny legged young builder standing well back as his just completed project took off after a short taxi run along the ground. Dad as ever was standing in the background, hands on hips smiling proudly at his young son, the aeronautical engineer of the future. As usual the picture was a complete con.

I was proud of my Globe Swift. It looked like the model on the box. It was painted dark green with about four extra coats of coloured dope to make it withstand any impact. Launch day came and down to Brynmill I went to meet a couple of my aviation buddies who had come along for this momentous occasion. I decided that as on the box Mr Swift would taxi along the ground and then gracefully take off and probably do a circuit before coming in for a soft landing on the grass. Dad would not be standing in the background however. He was at work and would not share this proud moment. I had also forgotten to inform the local press, which was a pity. There would be no pictures of my triumph in the South Wales Evening Post.

My engineering colleagues would be there however and if they met dad later would no doubt report back on the maiden flight. Came the moment I put plenty of turns on the rubber motor. In all the pictures I had seen in Aeromodeller Magazine the chap winding on the turns did it with a hand drill adapted for the job. I had no such luxury. That would come later with my soon to be acquired reputation as a model builder of note. For now it was hold the thing in one hand and wind the propeller with the forefinger of the other. A few extra turns than advised but at moments like this etc.

I placed Mr Swift on the path pointing into the wind and let go. It almost shot from my hand, but not quite, and proceeded to run along the path. It kept on taxiing and just kept on taxiing, refusing to take off. It was all very embarrassing for the engineering support team. I was glad that I had had the foresight not to invite the press.

When asked by the South Wales Post to comment on the failure of the Globe Swift's maiden flight senior aviation engineer and constructor Bernard Andrew said, "I think that possibly I didn't put enough turns on the propeller and may have to resort to using stronger elastic.'" Yeah! That would have looked good. Dad wouldn't have been able to live with the shame and not come home for a week.

The support team tried not to look embarrassed for me when a few minutes later I tried doing a hand launch and it actually flew with the flight characteristics of a brick. Wonderful!

"Er, I think it must be the trim." I had remembered at least one technical phrase to use on days like this. When you have to bluff your way out of a situation do it technically. With luck maybe the uninformed onlookers will not understand anyway and take your word for it. Then when they are not looking you can sneak away and hide somewhere for a week.

The reason it flew like a brick was probably a combination of, trim like I tried to bluff, and all the extra coats of dope. But since it hardly flew any distance at all I concluded in my defence that it was a rubbish model to start with. I decided anyway that I would try a bigger propeller but the next trial flight would be held 'in camera'. A posh phrase used for secret. I also used much heavier rubber in it, putting even more turns on the propeller. In fact -if I had wound any more on I'm sure the fuselage would have imploded nose to tail.

Even with these modifications though the cotton pickin' thing still wouldn't take off like on the box. It only flew when hand launched and then only for about fifty yards in a constantly descending flight path. My Globe Swift pointedly refused to even try to gain height which was a crushing blow to my ego. It was also a constant story in my attempts to build model aircraft. My particular path to glory would have to be in another direction. It was only in retrospect that I could see my failures so carried on regardless of continual wreckage.

I was helped enormously in my constant quest by the enthusiasm of the various building groups and individuals I came into contact with around Swansea. There were a number of teenage and older builders in the area who would meet at weekends in both Brynmill and Singleton Park to fly models powered by miniature two stroke diesel engines. Unfortunately there were a number of sensitive souls living directly outside Brynmill who objected to the 'too loud, too loud' noise that they made if even for just a short duration so most of the time the groups went to fly down the bottom end of Singleton where the university now stands. Brynmill was relegated to gliders, rubber power and testing short distance diesel powered free flight models.

Miniature diesel engines were used because of their durability. As long as they didn't develop any mechanical faults they would keep running until the fuel ran out. That was all very well but for one major disadvantage. Just how far would they fly and if they flew out of sight, what then? What it usually meant was giving chase in or on some form of transport to see exactly where it landed for recovery or using some method to limit the distance.

This was already done with some of the Wakefield design rubber powered duration models of the era, which would often have a cunningly contrived device called a de-thermaliser fitted to the hinge mounted tail plane assembly; a time delay arrangement allowing it to swing up at the back causing loss of lift so that the model floated back down to earth before it had completely disappeared.

Because of the distance factor the nearest sort of places that could be used and partially cope were an airfield or abandoned wartime aerodrome of which there quite a few country wide but only Fairwood near Swansea. Even then unless the fuel was limited the models could still fly out of sight and make recovery a problem. It was for this reason that the free flight models, as they were termed, usually had the builders contact details stuck prominently somewhere on the fuselage in the hope that some honest soul might eventually find it and 'do the right thing'.

The powered models flown in Singleton Park were all for use in what was known as tethered flight, made in a continuous circle and attached by wire lines to a control handle held by the pilot standing in the middle. As the aircraft flew around and around the dude hanging on the control handle end would endeavour to walk a circular path instead of just turning in one spot to avoid becoming dizzy.

One group of senior builders in their late teens, early twenties, made some wonderful stunt and combat aircraft with names like Blue Pants and Kittyhawk that had wingspans ranging from three to four feet and sometimes even larger. Many years later I was to build my own Blue Pants from the same set of plans. Even bought a new engine to fit it but it never got started and Blue Pants never flew. For some reason I just never got around to it and the model languished for years up in the loft before the engine was eventually removed and the rest of it cremated.

Several of us followed the senior group around as their building and flying skills developed over a number of years, and without realizing it, treated them as our role models. We were probably a nuisance really but still aspired to emulate, build and fly models just like them; one of whom was in the years ahead to become a successful industrialist. With weekends being the only really feasible time to fly they would set off for the Singleton tarmac pitch with a small posse of kids gradually growing behind them. I wouldn't say we were a nuisance, more of an embarrassment, but we tried not to get in the way too often.

Along with the models would come all the kit: bottles of diesel fuel (with its overpowering smell), spanners, spare propellers, batteries, rags etc., all carried in an assortment of boxes. We would stand as close as possible watching every move as they unwound the control lines onto the grass and attached them to the wire connections sticking out of the wings that directed the flight pattern.

When everything was ready the squeezy fuel bottles would be connected up to fill the tanks, elevator controls checked again and then came the moment everybody was waiting for: starting the engine or engines if there was going to be two of them in flight. There was no mechanical assistance. It was an operation that had to be conducted manually; turning the propellers over by hand, flicking them over repeatedly until the engine suddenly screamed into life. The thing I suppose that amazed me most was that nobody ever lost a finger. The propellers were usually made of plastic, fairly large and quite sharp, whizzing around at several thousand revs a minute.

Occasionally they would backfire or kick back while being turned in this manner and they could certainly give you a nasty knock. I found that out later when I had my own models to play with.

"Try more compression, too much fuel, you're flooding it, not enough fuel, try givin' it a bit more fuel; de-compress, yeah! de-compress, watch what you're doing, don't tread on the lines you idiot!" would usually come from one or more of the flyers keeping desperate vigil that in our enthusiasm to get closer, we the watchers, didn't spoil their day.

We learnt all the buzz words and phrases and occasionally had a go at appropriate suggestions to the pilots as they struggled to start their engines. Our advice was not appreciated and drew some very cryptic instructions to us by way of reply.

Once the engines had fired up it was time to launch which would be done either from the strip if the model had an undercarriage or otherwise by hand. Then the fun began as we watched them perform the various stunts that they were capable of: loops, bunts – which were reverse loops starting nose down -and wing-overs, performed by climbing the aircraft vertically right over the pilot's head to bisect the flying circle and then leveling off again on the opposite side.

The most fun for both flyers and onlookers would be had when two models were 'in combat' trailing coloured streamers behind them. Each airplane would try to get behind the other using wingovers, loops and bunts in order to cut its streamer with the propeller. Inevitably there were collisions resulting in much wreckage but fortunately for the builders this was not a frequent event. They were usually highly skilled pilots as well.

Standing and continuously turning on one spot without getting dizzy is not easy. Some people like dancers know how to do it because they have been trained to cope and compensate accordingly. How pilots of model control line aircraft do it is a mystery.

Some of them make it look really casual without a care in the world apart from that required to keep the aircraft under control.

The giddy barrier was experienced on my own first control line project which flew fine for a few laps and then, as things became progressively more blurred, seemed to fly in ever decreasing circles until it crash landed into the long grass which was our airfield. The inward flight characteristic was probably caused by some misalignment in construction but dizziness was definitely a problem.

Several weeks later an even more dramatic example was to occur, this time unfortunately not with my own model but somebody else's just completed project.

New friends come and go when you're young and two that I got to know through model building were nicknamed Klondike and Kipper. Klondike lived up on Beechwood Road and Kipper on one of the streets not far from the entrance to Singleton. Klondike's given name was Roger. I knew that because it was me who actually christened him Klondike due to his footwear and general appearance. Wearing shoes that were more akin to hiking boots he was the first one of my friends to get long trousers: add to that a longish face, crew-cut style dark brown hair and gangly build and you just couldn't call him anything else. He was all arms and legs.

Kipper on the other hand was completely the opposite. More conventionally dressed, he was stubby, rounded in appearance with unkempt jet black hair mounted on a face that always seemed to host an expression of amusement. It certainly didn't take much to make him laugh and with an almost permanent grin on Klondike's face they made an ideal couple of chums.

It was a while though before I found out why Kipper had been christened thus. I asked him one day and the answer made me laugh it was so simple. His dad he said was a fishmonger and had a stall in Swansea market. When he told me that, things sort of 'fell into plaice!' Heh heh! Sorry! Sorry!

Klondike got me into the model club not long after we met one Saturday afternoon when things were not going according to expectations. There were regular little groups who used the tarmac flying pitch but sometimes when there were quite a few waiting to fly it got over crowded, particularly when the seniors had arrived first at the take off strip.

In that situation another site was sometimes used which was how I had come to meet up with him when one of the older boys who I knew only as Dawnay was causing a few problems. On that particular day he had arrived with a whiz looking stunt model powered by something called a glow plug engine.

The only thing different about it that I could see was that it had a small plug thing on top of the engine that needed connecting to battery leads while the propeller was flicked over. Something like a spark plug somebody said; supposed to make starting easier but it wasn't working. Dawnay was a solid looking youth of about seventeen with a mess of straggly fair hair and a bad tempered mouth from which came periodic explosions of Anglo Saxon; giving vent to his frustration while onlookers including myself were impatiently hanging around waiting for some action.

Apart from the immediate problem the situation did have one benefit -for model groupies if no one else - because of all the exciting buzz words being mentioned to go with a glow plug engine. Any technical terms and references to engine procedures, we the few who stood around, observed and waited, sucked up and memorised for the next suitable opportunity to insert them into conversation and let people know that we too had aviation brains to be reckoned with.

It was while all this was going on that we heard in the distance the Doppler buzzing of another engine rising and falling in the manner of a circling control line model. Somebody said it must be coming from the other field and we asked "What other field?" One of the seniors hearing the question explained that we would find it at the top end of the park further along the path that led out to Sketty Lane. Not many people knew about it so it didn't get so crowded he said. So with Dawnay still swearing at his engine three of us set off to find the other field which we did ten minutes later.

It took us a while to locate because on our way there the engine ran out of fuel and we had no sound to latch onto. It was also well hidden and surrounded by trees but just before we arrived the model began flying again and gave us the final direction. Standing in the middle of the field controlling a small stunt aircraft was Roger -soon to be known as Klondike -and outside the flying circle acting as his mechanic was Kipper. I don't think Kipper ever built any models himself; he seemed to be content just to act as mechanic and general assistant.

Although he was a little older Roger was naturally affable and easy to talk to so a friendship was soon in the making as I admired his model building skills and questioned him about its construction. At that time I wasn't actually a member of any club; a fact which emerged during subsequent conversation. That was no good at all he said and he would take steps to rectify the situation by taking me along to the first meeting of his club's winter season in September. A kindness I soon repaid by almost destroying his next aircraft project not long after he completed it several weeks later.

CRASH LANDING

On the day before that disaster he called around the house after tea to ask if I wanted to come with him and Kipper the next evening when they were going down to the tarmac strip to christen his new combat model. I was pleased to have been asked and accordingly went up to his house in Beechwood the following day to give him a hand to carry all the kit. We walked down to the Singleton entrance where Kipper was waiting and then into the park intending to cut across the large meadow and then down the path leading to the tarmac strip.

On the way we passed close to the top pond which I fished occasionally and a copse of large trees standing not far from it. Between the trees and the path we were heading for was a cricket pitch which had a game going on in full swing. It was a warm summer evening just made for cricket and we could easily have walked around it without disturbing anybody but Kipper had a better idea.

Apart from the cricket match there was nobody else about on the meadow and there was plenty of meadow. Enough he thought that we could fly well away from the match without disturbing them or anyone else. What a good idea I said. Well it wasn't. Let me qualify that. At first it was because Klondike was flying the thing but he then insisted that I had a go.

On the first flight I did a hand launch for him and he took it from me with no bother: looping, bunting, wing-overs, figure eights, the lot. He was just showing off really and who could blame him, it was a delight. I told him I'd not had a lot of experience flying myself and he just said, "You don't have to do anything fancy. Just keep it level and if you feel up to it just do a wing over." So I gave it a go with Kipper this time launching it for me while Klondike looked on to offer any advice.

While he had been flying I had looked over to the cricket pitch and noticed a number of the players watching, or was it glaring, in our direction obviously distracted by the noise of the ED Racer engine. It was a big engine, definitely a bit noisy if you were in reasonable proximity which was why we always flew off the tarmac strip away from housing. The loud buzzing they were hearing in their ears was no bumble bee. I had been flying without any problems for about three minutes performing a few wing overs and even a couple of loops when disaster struck. I was starting to get a bit giddy and afterwards both Kipper and Klondike said that I had been mistaken when I thought that the aircraft had started to turn in on me. But that was what caused it. I started to retreat trying to compensate and tipped over backwards as one of my feet stepped into a dip in the ground. Already disoriented I completely lost my balance and fell over backwards letting go of the control handle. On a number of occasions I had wondered out of curiosity what would happen if somebody let go of the control handle when flying a control line model and had assumed that no longer being under pilot command it would nose dive immediately into the ground. It was an incorrect assumption. The model kept on flying around and around in a circle with the handle maintaining an equal, opposite and level flight path at the other end of the control lines. How interesting!

It did two other things; it kept gaining height and also moving closer to the cricket pitch. Klondike looked on in dismay wondering about the kind of inevitable crash landing Kipper stared, holding his head grimacing and I got back on my feet watching the cricketers occasionally looking up at the big angry bee that was getting ever closer to them. As they watched we started apprehensively walking towards them.

The flight lasted for almost another minute and finished just as the bowler was commencing his run up to deliver a howler down the pitch towards the batsman, poised to give it his all. We never knew what decision the umpire made about that ball; it must have been an interesting debating point because directly over the wicket the engine cut out and as the aircraft stalled the handle, losing its equal and opposite impetus, swung down with the model nose diving a split second later.

Really the bowler should have waited for the inevitable but on the other hand perhaps he was deliberately taking advantage of the situation. Completely distracted by the sudden silence, the batsman, wicket keeper and the rest of the fielders instinctively looked up and then scattered to the four winds as the aircraft plunged into the ground where only seconds before had stood the batsman. As they ran the bright red leather spinning sphere bounced once in front of the crease before colliding with the offside stump to take it clean out of the ground and send the bails flying!

We were not a popular trio but surprisingly there were no angry repercussions. The returning batsman and wicket keeper each picked up different ends of the offending wreckage and trailing control lines to carry over to us as though contaminated with the plague. Neither of them spoke; each just sort of grunted, nodding at us with raised eyebrow expressions. Nobody actually said a word except Klondike and me, trying to mumble our apologies.

Fortunately they did seem to consider it a freak accident but with the players just standing around saying nothing to us and the onlookers sitting outside the nissen hut style pavilion glaring in stony silence it was spooky.

We retreated to where we had parked our kit as swiftly as we could without actually running. Briefly looking back I saw both the batsman and wicket keeper trying to repair the pitch and beating it flat with the bat. Woops! I was frankly gutted to think that I had wrecked Klondike's model on its first outing and tried to apologise and sort of negotiate with him wondering if we were still friends.

"Er I'm really sorry Roger." It wasn't the right time to use his nickname. "I don't know what to say. Can you repair it…?"

I trailed off not really knowing what to say next but to my astonishment he just burst out laughing and told me not to worry about it. Yes it was a pity about the model which he thought he could fix anyway but it was, he said, the best laugh he'd had in a long time. "Did you see them scatter? Boy it was brilliant wasn't it?"

"Oh," I said, "we're still friends then?"

He looked at me mildly insulted and scoffed,

"You're a pratt Bernard. Of course we're still friends. You told me you got giddy anyway. It was just bad luck you stumbled in that dip. I can't wait to tell the guys at the club about it. They'll fall about laughing and take the mickey out of you something rotten, won't they Kipper?"

Kipper nodded his head vigorously saying, "Oh yeah! Definitely," while Roger added, "I'll get my own back on you that way," chuckling as he did so. I decided I had two good mates.

THE EXHIBITIONIST

Belonging to a club was considered to be more respectable than allegiance to a gang which always seemed to have a stigma attached to it. Say the word gang and immediately anyone who was associated with one was a potential delinquent even when three or four of us were walking down the street with models in our hands and obviously doing something constructive with our time. When you were indoors you were club members; out in the street you were gang members.

The model club we joined was located in the gymnasium of a school somewhere in the back streets of the town between Mumbles Road and Oxford Street. Starting at about half past six in the evening it lasted for a couple of hours finishing around eight thirty or occasionally nine o'clock. Most of our age group had to finish early because we walked there and back and in the winter months of course it meant walking home in the dark. Two or three of us lived not far from each other so we walked home together as a potentially dangerous gang of delinquent club members!

The meetings were usually held mid-week during the winter months, from what I can remember, so that the longer summer nights could be devoted to flying.

The older more experienced builders were always available to give advice and also organise the evening in a pretty relaxed manner. They were so relaxed in fact that they even let us use their Christian names. A small point maybe but the protocol of the day was for schoolboys, especially those of us still in short trousers, to address seniors with the prefix of Mr before their surname.

To do otherwise was considered to show disrespect. The granting of this privilege was sometimes misread and overvalued however and although harmless in itself, made us metaphorically puff out our chests kidding ourselves that we were one of the guys, on a par with them and commanding similar respect. Huh! I don't think so. But we kidded ourselves just the same.

As well as discussing and advising on various aspects of model construction, senior members would sometimes bring old issues of Aeromodeller magazine, which we would pore through avidly in the hope of finding inspiration for future projects. These would have plans and written descriptions for many possibilities, most of which were far too complicated and advanced for us to build but it didn't matter. We had dreams. Occasionally small rubber models suitable for the confines of a school gymnasium would be flown. Most of these would be of ultra-light material with the objective of flight duration which was a relatively new aspect of the hobby. All conversation containing technical terms and know-how was listened to intently and memorised.

Sometime after I had joined the club the secretary announced that it would have the centre display area slap bang in the middle of a forthcoming exhibition being held in the Patti Pavilion. All members were encouraged to find something to put on show. I hadn't been to many exhibitions of any sort up till then and had always had to pay to get in. Members of an exhibiting club however would have an exhibitor's pass and full access to wander around freely.

The downside was that I had absolutely nothing I was building then; nothing even worth putting on our sideboard let alone showing in public. The quality of display models need not, the secretary said, be competition standard. A reasonable visual standard would suffice in order to encourage others to at least start building so that they could improve as time progressed.

Mulling things over inspired a brainwave. An old school friend of mine had a control line model that had not been flown for a while and which might, if he was willing to lend it, make a good substitute. It was a semi-scale low winged job called a PHANTOM; bright red in colour and bound to catch attention. When approached he was eager to help and it was agreed there would be a note alongside to let the general public know it was his model and there by his kind permission. Thus having made the arrangements it was duly collected and carried it to the exhibition on the set-up evening.

There was a wonderful array of models of all types: gliders, rubber powered, engine powered control line, free flight and a couple of big radio controlled jobs. Radio control was only just beginning to develop and the Rudder Bug display model being rather larger than anything else and built by a senior member drew a lot of attention. The whole show was very popular with quite a number of other hobby and semi commercial stands to keep things interesting. At various times in the evening and on the Saturday the club also mounted displays of around the pole flying with rubber powered models designed specifically for the purpose.

Throughout the exhibition I made the most of my Exhibitor status, walking around continually, from time to time making a nuisance of myself crawling under the display tables to the inside to fiddle with the Phantom trying to look important. I was no longer just a paying spectator on the outside looking in; I was a non-paying exhibitor standing on the inside looking out. I had arrived.

While wandering around, a couple of stands in particular had caught my attention; one showing basket weaving and raffia work and the other displaying various rope knots on loan from a retired sea captain. I was interested in the basket and raffia work having taken up both of these handiworks some time previously although other interests had by now superseded them. The basket-work had been particularly useful because it enabled the making of a number of cheap Christmas presents for various aunts over a period of two years or so. There were a number of craft shops in the town centre that carried instruction booklets and stocked the cane and pre shaped and drilled wooden bases on which to weave the various projects. It also incidentally happened to be the source of the cane used in our group project for alternative smoking which you may recall I mentioned earlier.

Raffia work was less interesting because my sister did it and I therefore considered it was more girly. It was also essentially only two-dimensional whereas basket-work was 3D and there-fore more… macho?

It was getting towards the end of the last day of the exhibition as I was having a look at the display of knots when a gruff but friendly voice behind me made me jump. "You like my knots then do you?"

It was the old sea dog himself, a white haired old gent smartly dressed as usual in a navy three-piece blue pin striped suit. I turned around to see a smile on his weather beaten face which I learnt had seen no less than eighty two years of life; a good proportion of them on the high seas.

I knew his face and he knew mine. Hard not to really because he lived with his black Scotty dog less than a hundred yards away in the next block of houses from where I did. He always said hello when out walking the dog but we had never really had much of a conversation before, other than to make polite comments as we passed in our respective directions. That was about to change.

We had a brief chat there and then about some of the knots he had on display, culminating in an invitation for me to pop in and see him in the next few days when he would tell me more about them and, more importantly, how to tie them.

So it came to pass that over the next few months I paid him a number of visits when, using heavy duty cord, he very patiently showed me how to tie some very simple and other not so simple knots, how to weave rope, how to three and four strand plait rope and how to splice it; topping the demonstration off with the making of a very simple net. I regret to say that the skills he taught me in those far off schoolboy days have long since been forgotten.

He was a very accomplished sailor of the old school with truly impressive skills and it was no surprise as I learnt more about his life on the sea: one of the last of a breed of men that had actually served an apprenticeship aboard merchant clippers sailing the world and astonishingly had himself been a cabin boy on board the Cutty Sark when it made its last voyage around the Cape Horn.

While relating this part of his life to me he went to an old chest of drawers standing in one corner of his parlour and from its depths withdrew a package of photographs. I assumed before he had unfolded the covering paper that they might be of some of his shipmates of the time. I was however dumbfounded to see that they were in fact pictures of the ocean in full storm, waves so high that you would not believe any ship could sail on them.

Some of them he said had been taken from a position high up in the rigging in the crow's nest; an amazing feat considering the way the ship must have been thrown around in the wind and tumultuous sea. I had not realised till then that photography had developed to such a stage before the turn of the century. It was a real eye opener.

I had been talking with him for some time and the exhibition was drawing to a close. He had come down, he said, to have a quick look around and oversee the packing away of his display so that it could be returned by whatever means to his home sometime later. The model club was also busy sorting out the dismantling of our display stands, packing things away while owners of guest models were removing their individual showpieces.

So I watched for a few more minutes; enjoying the atmosphere of having been a participant, albeit by the proxy of a borrowed aircraft, and then crawled under the display tables for the last time to retrieve it. Klondike had also put a model on show so after he had collected it we walked companionably together on a reasonably mild evening, clutching our models and making plans for future projects as we wended our way homeward.

I never did find out why but for some reason the club was evicted from the school gymnasium before the end of the winter period.

I think in retrospect it was council politics but that is only my supposition. They did eventually find another venue but some how I didn't bother to find my way to it. I can't even remember where it was now. Over the next twelve months I still kept up my model building and also in touch with Klondike, Kipper and a few of the other boys as well as going down to the tarmac strip occasionally. Time was moving on however and in the following year I began life as a teenager and started my final stint of education at the Secondary Technical School down by the docks.

DOWN BY THE DOCKS

My move to the new school of course started some time before the actual event because it involved a new school uniform which was always embarrassing. With dad leading the way followed by mum, Constance for moral support and a reluctant son acting as tail end Charlie, our team trudged along to the Uplands one Saturday afternoon after lunch and caught the number seventy four down to the Walter Road stop opposite Sidney Heath. Dad got all his gear from Sid's and always bought our school uniforms there as well. The place always had that musty smell of cloth and everywhere there were display stands, glass cases and hundreds of drawers in stacks around the walls. The same musty staff had, it seemed, been there since the place was built and recognised us from previous visits, greeting us like long lost friends

Having been appraised by management I was taken away from family protection, mum and big sis', to the other end of the store for attention by the 'Sidney Heath tactile fitting team' where, skillfully directed by dad, I was pushed, pulled, poked and squeezed into numerous sets of green blazers and sharply creased grey trousers, still annoyingly short ones, and paraded in each ensemble until I fitted. Shirt and penguin cap finished the shopping list, shoes already having been acquired elsewhere; probably SAXONE's. All the time this was going on of course other boys being kitted out for other educational academies were also undergoing the same kind of ritual humiliation. We would all though, I thought, soon take the shine off our new uniforms in the rough and tumble of getting acquainted in our new schools.

Getting to the new school presented a new challenge. It was a lot further to go than Brynmill juniors and meant that for the first time I would regularly have to catch a bus. But would the buying of bus fares every day be a practical proposition? Not only for the many pupils but also the conductor who would no doubt have his patience sorely tested at times with those who had either lost or forgotten to bring the fare. There was a simple answer called a season ticket which nipped the potential problem in the bud. Only the occasional pupil would forget to bring his season ticket…surely? Yes.

The stop at the top of Rhyddings Park Road where I caught the No 75 had a wonderful view of the bay where vessels of various types and tonnage could be see either inbound for the docks to discharge cargo or starting their outward journey to other lands far away. On foggy mornings in the winter when you couldn't see them the sound of their fog horns could be heard blaring out from the early hours announcing their presence, not only to commercial seafarers, but also the landlubber community in general over their breakfast tables.

Winter foggy mornings were not the best mornings to go and catch a bus but it was part of my domestic contract. If I went to school I got fed when I came home at lunch time, so it was a duty borne of necessity rather than desire and seemed to work quite well. By the time the bright red 8:20 AM double decker arrived at the top of Rhyddings hill there were already quite a number of pupils on board picked up along the way as far afield as the Tycoch and Sketty districts.

We would always try to sit upstairs out of sight if we could because it was less busy than being on the lower deck. As we gradually awoke to the day ahead there was always a lot of banter and on some buses the conductors would join in and take the mickey. Others were not so cheery and would direct a stony glare to any pupil who just mumbled "season" instead of showing their pass promptly when requested. The fleet was run by South Wales Transport and before they started to renew them there was an aisle between the seats on both decks.

The newer buses had only one narrow aisle on the right hand side of the top deck with bench seats mounted on a floor at slightly higher level, each seat just managing to squeeze six schoolboys onto it. At times it could get quite rowdy and the conductor would have to come up the stairs and tell us to belt up or get off and walk. He did of course say it in more moderate language. We were fare paying passengers after all.

My memory is a bit hazy now but I think our dinner break was from 12 o'clock till 1:30 PM which gave sufficient time to catch the bus home for lunch and get back again in reasonable time. The double decker featured something more or less unique to Britain. It had the open to the weather standing platform at the back end with a vertical pole handle at the rear corner. All macho males of the era, of all ages, loved to perform on this platform and as it pulled up to the stop at the top of Rhyddings hill I performed; standing on the back edge holding onto the pole handle, timing it just right, and letting go to drop off on the run while the bus was still in motion. A very British thing learnt very early in a schoolboy's life.

I don't know what the interiors of grammar and other secondary schools looked like but by comparison The Swansea Secondary Technical School, or 'Tech' as it was more commonly known, must have been sheer opulence. A magnificent former Guild Hall of the town originally built in 1884 it had been cleverly adapted to perform the requirements of a school; full of character with corridors, alcoves leading to hidden rooms and even a small spiral stairway you could almost walk past without noticing.

It also featured behind its main entrance doors a wide marble staircase leading in right angled tiers up to the main floor. It is unfortunate that it was destroyed during reconstruction work for a tribute museum to the Welsh poet Dylan Thomas.

For those of us who read the LION comic it was like Sandy Dean's Schooldays or Billy Bunter at Greyfriars who featured in another publication. Masters wore mortarboard and gown and hurried down draughty corridors to their various classes with black capes billowing out behind them like educational supermen.

The Headmaster was a wonderful gent given to utter some very interesting phrases like "I am very disappointed in you," when a pupil had caught his attention and committed some unforgivable misdemeanor, or "You – yes you. Come here boy." When guilty pupils tried to look innocent, some of the masters would try an extended more aggressive version of his phraseology with "Who sir? Me sir? Yes sir, you sir." It was almost poetic.

It was a school designed for pupils with more vocational aptitude than academic and endeavoured to support the town's industrial and commercial needs by offering appropriate course subjects for both boys and girls to fulfil those needs. At the end of the term before I took my place, the female part of the school was moved to another location. I was unworried by this development. I remembered the scatty woman who had attacked us in the park and concluded if that was what girls turned into when they grew up I wanted nothing to do with them.

Former court rooms and council chambers had been adapted to function as main assembly hall and both physics and chemistry laboratories, giving an air of grandeur that was totally lost on the unruly lot who were now let loose within its labyrinthine interior.

Morning assembly was celebrated in the former criminal assize court. The headmaster was a tall individual with a slightly bent nose on a long patrician face which for most of the time managed to hide a dry wit and sense of humour. Procedure was for the boys to enter first and remain standing, followed by the general staff in their superman regalia who would also stand. After first quelling any noisy talk from pupils the stage was set for the grand entrance and the headmaster swept into the hall like a high court judge through a pair of large swing doors, walking with each hand on a lapel of his gown as he took long loping strides to the lectern at the front. At the lectern he formally bid the school good morning and then we all burst into the first hymn. I think from memory that two or three hymns were sung, interspersed perhaps with a reading, and then any announcements to do with school business we should know about.

If any misdemeanors had been committed by pupils affecting the reputation of the school he would make his feelings about the miscreants very plain and if any names were known the boys bearing those names would be invited to his study for further discussion. When this happened my imagination ran riot and I pictured him in red robe and wig sternly sitting in his office being presented by the deputy head with his mortar board on a black cushion. Placing it on his head like the infamous black cap used for the judicial death penalty he would then pronounce sentence on some wayward pupil.

After all assembly business was complete the last hymn would be sung, the head would leave followed by most of the staff and then us; set free to harass whoever was unfortunate enough to take the first sessions of the morning.

On one particular occasion the headmaster entered the hall in his usual manner when the staff had failed to subdue a particularly noisy gathering. He was not best pleased and on reaching the lectern sternly addressed the school with the immortal words: "Upon my soul, what is this hubbub of conversation I perceive upon my ears?" A phrase forever embedded into the annals of school history and the psyche of everybody present for repeating and inserting into any conversation when deemed appropriate.

Being a school in Wales meant of course that there were plenty of good voices to sing well known Welsh hymns like: Calon Lan, I Bo un Sydd Ffyddlon, and both the Welsh and English version of Bread of Heaven. Another favourite was the classic Jerusalem;

on one occasion sung with such gusto by a group of senior boys in the gallery at the back of the hall that the headmaster asked for the last verse to be repeated, not by the whole group but by one boy in particular who had crowned the end of the piece with a resounding tenor note.

He had been sitting, avidly listening and stood to address the group in the gallery and thank them for their rendition saying "That was most enjoyable boys. I wonder if Mr Dorman would mind giving us his personal rendition of the last verse again. Would you mind, Mr Dorman?"

Taken off guard by the request Mr Dorman was now regretting his original enthusiasm but couldn't really refuse the headmaster.

He was trapped and just mumbled that he would be pleased to do so. With noisy encouragement coming from pupils next to the increasingly nervous soloist, the head turned to the music master Mr Samuel Dawson to give him his cue. Unfortunately for the school wit, the background noise wasn't loud enough to mask his impromptu interjection, so when the head said "Would you mind playing it again Mr Dawson?" the wit's gruff impression of film star Humphrey Bogart saying "Yeah – Play it again Sham," came out loud and very clear.

Amidst howls of delight from the boys and suppressed laughter from the staff even the head master smiled. It did however pose a dilemma for Sam the pianist. It was a potentially awkward situation. One of the boys had taken the mickey out of him in public and in front of the headmaster.

How should he respond? He looked somewhat aghast in the direction of the pupil concerned not quite sure what to do. Fortunately, while he was deciding how to recover his authority, the head saved the day and ever the gentleman apologised to him in a very oblique manner saying, "Oh dear Mr Dawson I'm so sorry. I'm afraid I did rather set you up for that didn't I? I do apologise. Perhaps we can re arrange the request and ask Mr Dorman to sing the first verse and then let the whole school join in. Would that be alright for you Mr Dorman?" Dorman smiled apprehensively back saying, "Yes sir - er thank you sir."

Then just before signalling the first few bars the headmaster turned very pointedly in the direction of the impressionist who was smugly sitting in the gallery and said, "Mr Bogart can see Mr Dawson in my study afterwards and apologise to him directly for his impishness." Not impudence but impishness. Wonderful. Just when he thought he'd got away with it. The headmaster had completely disarmed a potentially uncomfortable confrontation and saved face for the music master. The resulting chorus of Jerusalem all but raised the roof and assembly finished with everyone departing in good humour. The episode also gave us another gem to wrap our tongues around and we used "impishness" like all the other classic utterances whenever we could quote it for weeks afterwards.

Although the main function of the hall was for morning assembly it was of course used for occasional concerts at Christmas and what might be called emergency gatherings of the school when something untoward had happened which fortunately in the latter case was not very often. Sometimes such gatherings took unexpected turns like the time one of the senior boys brought along his guitar to sing about the legend of Davy Crocket the American backwoodsman who was in the public eye at the time.

His rendition of the recording went down well enough but even better was his own surprise composition featuring members of the staff; in particular the metalwork master. He had apparently built a bicycle, which comprised part of the mickey take, and also owned a car resembling a Model T Ford; allegedly mistaken for scrap by a passing rag and bone man in one of the verses. It was as well perhaps that the composer did his craftwork as a member of the carpentry class.

Very occasionally The Tech did school trips and I was fortunate enough to go on two of them. We had both cricket and football teams in the appropriate seasons and were lucky enough to have a star player who was picked to represent Wales in a schoolboy cup final played at Wembley Stadium. Unfortunately we didn't win, but for us it wasn't so much the match we looked forward to as the trip itself. We all gathered in good time in the assembly hall on the morning of departure and then made our way to the railway station by a bus hired for the occasion.

I don't remember anything about the match, only the gathering of the spivs and souvenir sellers outside the grounds. It was a really exciting atmosphere. I think about five members of the staff accompanied us with the headmaster also tagging along keeping a very low profile. After the football game it had been arranged for us to see an ice hockey match which we had never seen before. During the intervals we were fascinated by an army of sweepers who came out and removed surplus ice from the rink; three or four of them marching both sides with their brush movements in unison. Who would have thought they would have bothered to regiment anything as mundane as that?

All too soon the ice hockey was over and it was time to catch the train home. I think there must have been about twenty of us on the trip and we all piled onto the steam train into two styles of carriage. One had tables set between pairs of seats and the other had corridors and individual compartments. Tired we may have been but we were all fizzing like bottles of pop. Indeed some of the older boys had managed to dodge the watchful eyes of the masters and smuggled samples of the alcoholic kind on board just out of curiosity they told us.

Even without that stimulus however it was a heady atmosphere and there was quite a bit of hijinks on the way home. When one of the boys went temporarily missing the alarm was raised only to be quelled soon afterwards when he was discovered in one of the corridor compartments blissfully asleep tangled up in the netting of a wall mounted luggage rack where he had been dumped by some of the older boys.

The wee small hours seemed to drag. None of us could sleep or wanted to sleep. Every minute of the event had to be savoured so that we could repeat the experience afterwards ad nauseam to those who had not been there. Inevitably however some of us did succumb, to be reluctantly awakened at 5 o'clock in the morning as we steamed into Swansea High Street Station.

How to get home? Dad was not driving the office car then and it was too early for buses. I remember distinctly it was a fine morning so it was Shank's Pony. In other words – a walk home. It didn't matter; walking that distance was no problem. We walked everywhere then, so I set off at a keen pace anxious to get home, have some breakfast and a good kip. Funny how things work out. I had just crossed the road from The Albert Hall cinema and passed the number 74 Sketty stop on Mansel Street when this big red shiny new bus drew alongside and slowed up with the driver leaning out of the cab window. "Where are you going this time of the morning then young'un? Been out on the tiles all night?"

I laughed at his cheek and said, "Home," briefly explaining where I had been. When he asked me where I wanted dropping off I told him I didn't have enough bus fare. Good habits die hard.

"Don't worry about that," he said, "this bus isn't official yet." So I said "The top of Bernard Street," and hopped on. I was tickled pink. A free bus ride on a brand new bus.

The driver dropped me off at the top of the street as arranged and I was home in no time at all. A very early fry up for breakfast and then my waiting bed where I slept dead to the world for ten hours much to the amusement of mum, dad and Constance who said I had been loudly snoring for quite a bit of the time.

The other trip arranged was much more ambitious and was to 'La Continong' the other side of the English Channel where all the foreign people lived. This time it was a coach trip lasting about ten days and visiting seven or eight countries. Once again we all met at the school and excitedly climbed aboard, not knowing what to expect really but looking forward to it anyway. Four masters and two of their wives accompanied us and the tour was happily a great success -although one of the masters got sick and we had to leave him behind when we came home...

It is so long ago now though that many of the details are lost in the mists of time, except that is for some small ones. My first memory is of a lunch at an Autobahn restaurant. It had been quite a tramp to the cross channel ferry on the road network that existed then. A road system like the Autobahn would have cut the journey considerably but Britain's first motorway was still a year or more away so we were all highly impressed, especially with their catering arrangements.

The restaurant was first class serving steak and something like mashed potatoes with gravy for lunch. If we had been on our own road system it would probably have been bacon egg and chips in a transport café. It would take a few more years yet for them to get up to Autobahn standards. We chattered and bantered noisily away enjoying the experience but all too soon the masters were chivvying everybody to get back on the bus and we were on the move once more to new places.

One of the towns we visited was Innsbruck. My memory of that is waking up at six o'clock on a bright sunny morning and looking out of the bedroom window at clear blue skies forming the backdrop to snow-capped mountains. I had only ever seen such scenery before in photographs. To see the reality was truly breath-taking. After breakfast we had a little free time and a group of either Austrian or German boys of about the same age had gathered in the courtyard in front of the hotel kicking a football around. It wasn't long before we joined them in a game and although we couldn't speak each other's language we had a good half hour of fun before we had to make ourselves ready and get our things loaded on to the bus for the next journey to Switzerland.

Departure was made all the more memorable because of the comment made by the hotel manager as we exited the door. He had obviously enjoyed having us stay and as we departed bade us a very cheery "Good Riddance." An English phrase he'd heard somewhere and thought was a compliment. Well we assumed he meant it as a compliment, wouldn't you? It was a wonderful trip and enjoyed immensely by all the boys. We were singing and telling jokes till we got back home to the school yard where our parents were waiting to greet us. It took a long time for the memories to fade and even longer for us to stop talking about them.

Life at The Tech was not all play and good times however. There was a reasonable amount of serious homework that we had to contend with and although we never consciously acknowledged it our time there was a serious part of our lives where our educational outcome would be the stepping stone into the big wide world of work and the rest of our lives. There were new subjects available for us to learn like chemistry and physics which we had never experienced before, and more complicated forms of what in an earlier life we called sums. Henceforth manipulation of figures would be known as mathematics, a subject we would hopefully extend into something called algebra, and maybe beyond, into infinity with calculus.

The Welsh language was catered for as well as both French and German and a few of us had used the opportunity to mangle the latter two when we visited their respective countries of origin on the aforementioned continental school bus trip.

There was art and biology and a more intensive study of the English language along with British history and culture to get to grips with. The latter subject was enthused over by our English master who, noble in his mind, tried to impose his will and improve our cultural awareness with the linguistic challenges of an apparently well-known playwright named Shakespeare. But alas, it was not to be; it was out of the question. We did not see eye to eye with Will, were less than euphoric about Yorick, and after a number of futile attempts to understand his meanderings concluded it was all much ado about nothing. He had absolutely no influence on us whatsoever.

Practical work for both carpentry and metalwork was taught in sizeable workshops fully equipped to give pupils as broad an experience possible, learning most of the basic skills required in the relatively short time available. Just like we didn't get along with Shakespeare a number of us were found wanting with wood.

We had no love for each other. Compared to metal wood is soft and we usually managed to remove too much of it when planing. Instead we tried to make friends with metal, a task, which was enabled with the help of the well-endowed metalwork centre and a master determined to salvage something from the boisterous bunch of fumble-fingered boys in his charge.

There were plenty of workbenches, two or three centre lathes, a mechanical hacksaw, a forge and plenty of ancillary tooling and other equipment to help us get the job done. I remember some very sweaty times during practical tests but not too many cut fingers. In recent years over zealous health and safety dogma with its attendant insurance culture has deprived many potential young engineers of this kind of practical experience and it is with a real appreciation that I look back to my days at The Tech considering myself extremely fortunate to have been there.

Chemistry was one step too far. Carried out in a

laboratory with jars of this and that, and substances locked up in cabinets in every available space, it had been converted from another former assize court, which provided a very imposing interior as I remember. It was a subject where so much had to be remembered about different chemicals and their behaviour when mixed with others or subjected to numerous forms of treatments that many of us just could not get a grip on it.

It was totally beyond me and I gave it up as soon as I had any say in the matter, much to the chagrin of the chemistry master who was wont to throw a wooden board duster or a piece of chalk at you from across the laboratory on a whim if you offended him. This was a skill which a number of masters had acquired but it was only he who also wandered menacingly around the class with the leg of a stool in his hand ready to take a swipe. Oh happy days!

The subject of physics was more appealing and something could relate more easily to everyday practicalities. Although there were complicated calculations involved to do with things like latent heat, calorimeters, Bunsen burners, light prisms and other experimental apparatus more than made up for it. Bunsen burners were of particular interest.

We had used them for experiments in the chemistry laboratory quite successfully although sometimes the actual experiments had ended with unexpected results. I hated it when the Chem' master singled me out for ridicule. It was humiliating but did help me acquire some more friends; other boys grateful that I had taken the flack instead of them.

In the physics lab one of the boys sort of accidentally found out how to use the burners in a very original way. Well that's not quite true. What he actually found was a way to manipulate the pressure of the gas being supplied to the one the physics master was using to demonstrate with on his bench in front of the class.

All the lab benches had gas taps with rubber hose connections to supply gas to the burners. What this boy, Atkins, did for some inexplicable reason was put his mouth over an unconnected gas tap outlet and blow into it when he turned the tap on. Why did he do that? Who would think of doing that? It is how great inventions are invented isn't it? Well -yeah! Nobody else but Atkins. None of us saw him doing this at first. What we did notice, because we were all dedicated students, was the Bunsen flame in front of the master grow slowly weaker and smaller and then suddenly spring back to full blast. After it had done this a few times we heard the sucking and blowing behind us just as the physics master suddenly realised that "someone was mucking about" and said so in no uncertain manner. Atkins subtly broke his connection with the tap as we stifled our sniggers.

All that the physics master could see was attentive pupils bent on learning. So once again he returned his attention to his bubbling calorimeter and Bunsen. When he was fully engrossed a few of us sort of sidled around in a group against the bench in front of Atkins to give him cover as he again blew down the gas tap.

Once again the burner 'neath the physics master's calorimeter started to fade and this time almost died altogether to such a point that he removed the calorimeter from the stand that it was sitting on to inspect the flame below more closely. Mr Atkins's timing was immaculate. When the physics master's nose got close enough to the flame Atkins stopped blowing, shut off the tap and resumed a look of concentrated intelligence behind our shield. It was the right thing to do. The joke was in serious danger of back firing on us.

The physics master jumped back with a start as the flame tried to lick his nose and left him in absolutely no doubt that someone was indeed mucking about, but doing what and how, he knew not -because I'm almost sure in my mind that we also had a couple of other burners going that were unaffected by Atkins's totally irresponsible antics.

I still don't understand why his blowing down the gas tap did what it did, and this being so I don't suppose it even crossed the mind of the physics master but understandably his instincts must have told him that somehow there was a culprit. Normally not given to threats we had this time tried him too far and he made it plain that if we didn't settle down he would send for the headmaster and get us an extra-long detention. Couldn't say we blamed him really. I think he had singed his nose. For the rest of the lesson he kept rubbing it and wincing.

There was a lot of fun but while recognising that we were not academic material who would become professors of medicine or doctors or science, we the happy few, the irresponsible happy band of brothers who were privileged to be part of this particular educational establishment, were expected to learn. Some of us were slower than others. Some much slower and thus always anticipated our end of term school reports with trepidation at the various remarks written by subject masters. 'Tries' was one of their favourites. Dad used to see that quite a lot on mine. I could tell he was expecting more by the way he sighed as he read it, slowly shaking his head.

As well as general class time performance the school reports also took into account assessment tests given at the end of each term which, although worrying, were not as terrifying as the official education board exams. For these our desks were spaced out to prevent peeking at the next boy's answers and instilled an air of distrust over the proceedings from the start. Tension was slowly built up as the question papers – sometimes referred to as booklets – were placed face down one by one on each pupil's desk by the master in charge and when everybody was suitably wound up he would give the instruction, "you may now turn your exam papers over."

This was when we found out, despite previous denials, who the swots and clever clogs were. Some would begin writing furiously straight away; others took their time trying to understand the questions. One or two like me made sure our names was spelt correctly on the first page.

There was always a choice of questions and I usually managed to continue writing for the whole of the allotted time even though one or two boys would put down their pens early. This meant that they either knew much more than anybody else and were fast writers or knew even less than me. When the results were eventually announced however they usually confirmed what I already knew: I had been writing drivel. I was never any good at exams. Dad was no doubt hoping that his only begotten son would become what he called a late developer. You were right dad; I have now arrived in my seventies and I'm still trying to friggin' DEVELOP!

NAILED

Though I struggled with some subjects there were others that came more naturally. One of these was technical drawing which I considered to be the knitty-gritty of engineering without which nothing could be designed or made, and it was taught in the technical drawing office we called a classroom.

The main entry point for pupils was through heavy double doors at the end of a corridor running behind the main assembly hall, but there was also another doorway at the front end of the drawing office leading directly into a top corner of the assembly hall. It was this doorway through which the masters would enter directly adjacent to an extra-large wall mounted blackboard.

On this blackboard numerous geometric forms were described, subtended, extrapolated, extended and bisected by the technical drawing master with the aid of a large wooden compass. Having felt the weight of it I had to admire the skill he used in creating all the forms that he did. They were hard enough to do with pencil and paper in our books on the desk. To do it all with clarity standing against a wall using a piece of chalk stuck in the end of a heavy 12 inch wooden compass was amazing.

We had two masters take us in tech' drawing but the one I can remember in particular was a middle aged upright gent in his fifties. Of military bearing he had a roundish face on which was mounted a bristling moustache. He would often begin the class drawing session with the strangled voice instruction to "Stand up straight -no slouching. Stomachs in, chest out."

I thought he must have been at least a major; he just looked the part and I'm sure he could control men. We christened him The Major, or Major Bob. I think his first name was actually Robert but we liked Bob better and stuck to it. Not out of disrespect. It just seemed to fit his character.

Controlling men must have seemed a doddle compared to controlling an unruly bunch of schoolboys however and we must surely have presented him with a real challenge. On the whole I would say that he did well having a natural authority that was fair, firm and pleasant enough with it. He was nobody's fool though and didn't miss much, but we did get one over on him that I recall which must really have puzzled him for some time.

There were about ten rows of desks in the class and it was in row six or seven that the grand vanishing act took place. While our tutor had his back to us, carefully drawing some complicated arrangement, two of our seekers of truth and knowledge had discovered a couple of loose floorboards, both about four feet long lying alongside each other lengthways towards the front of the class. They had surreptitiously removed them from the joists on which they were resting to reveal a substantial space below, as wide as the room and about four feet deep.

One of the boys, Paul Johnson, volunteered to

inspect the space more closely and dropped down into to the void beneath to hide while the boards above were replaced. Hearing some sort of mild disturbance behind him the major turned to see an innocent bunch of pupils hard at work diligently copying what he had just drawn on the board. The atmosphere was tense though. He could sense it in the air. The picture of dedicated study was too contrived. Something was not right – but what?

"Ah, where has Johnson gone, Jenkins?" he asked. Jenkins was now sitting alongside where Johnson's seat had been vacated. Stifled sniggers from other boys. "He's gone to the toilet sir."

"Oh – I see." But Major Bob didn't see and didn't believe it. Something was wrong. You could hear the wheels turning over in his head and was that just the merest ghost of a smile trying not to break through? I knew what he was thinking. The main doors through which Johnson would have gone were heavy and hung on pre-loaded torque hinges to make them swing shut; quite a noisy operation because they usually swung back and fore couple of times before coming to rest. In fact you almost had to fight them open and there had been no swinging shut sound to indicate that anybody had left the class. The major slowly said "I see," again and turned back to the blackboard. Was he playing games with us or were we playing games with him?

While his back was still turned to us the two floorboards slid aside and Johnson's head appeared followed by the rest of him as he climbed back out from the darkness and resumed his position, quickly copying the drawing from the wall mounted blackboard out in front.

The major returned his gaze to the class, noted the reappearance of Johnson, looked pointedly in his direction compressing his lips and raising his eyebrows. His gaze then wandered to the back of the class where a large deep cupboard stood against the side wall.

Was it deep enough to hide behind? We read his mind. The only thing he said was "Hmm." Again that ghost of a smile trying not to break through. He knew we were up to something but of what he wasn't sure and he wasn't biting.

I was actually sitting in the row behind Jenkins and Johnson and wondered just how far their prank was going to go because as soon as the Major's back was turned again Jenkins started his disappearing act through the floorboards. Johnson had only just finished replacing them and resumed his pose of intelligent concentration when the major suddenly sighed heavily. A few of us afterwards agreed that it was one of sheer exasperation.

Did he have eyes in the back of his head or what? He picked up a duster, methodically wiped everything he had just drawn off the board and then turned to face the class yet again. My instincts said he had metaphorically just drawn a line in the sand. Noting the re appearance of Johnson and now the absence of Jenkins he pursed his lips once again and then said very deliberately,

"Now listen. I enjoy a good joke now and then. I even occasionally like conjuring tricks. I especially enjoy a good vanishing trick… For my" – and he emphasised the word my – "next trick, I want to show you all" – emphasis on all – "how to draw a nut and bolt correctly. I shall do it facing the board as before and when I have finished I will turn around and expect to see a full" – he again placed emphasis – "class. Anybody missing will not be allowed to re-join the class for the rest of the term."

Pressing his lips firmly together and raising his eyebrows he pointedly scanned the room, turned his back on us, and once again recommenced drawing. The threat was implicit and very real, announced with a quiet firmness which left no one in doubt. It was the iron fist in a velvet glove. This was the major issuing a command; disobey at our peril. It was 'Battle Stations'. A full class was thus accomplished as long as it took for Jenkins to reappear and reset the flooring and it was with quiet satisfaction that Major Bob was able to walk around checking our attempts at drawing a nut and bolt sometime later.

Throughout the whole episode not one harsh word was uttered or show of temper demonstrated by the major. But he was subtle. Oh was anybody ever so subtle? His full mettle was shown when we returned the following week for the next class. Normally he would be there when we arrived to meet and greet us and establish what state of apathy we were in. If he thought we were in need of encouragement he would subject us to a few minutes of deep breathing to wake us up and then various arm stretching exercises with our stomachs in and chests out to make us alert and help our brains to function.

That morning he was absent -but he had left a message. Slap bang in the middle of the blackboard about a foot high was a perfectly drawn pan head nail. We were all puzzled by its lonely presence at first and wondered why it was there but as I sat at my desk the solution revealed itself and I started to chuckle. Looking to the row in front, where Johnson and Jenkins had literally gone through the floor the week before, I observed that six rather large nails, as per the drawing, had been driven through each of the two floor boards. That man was something else. He arrived only a couple of minutes later. Looking very chipper and rearing to go, he casually wiped the nail off the board without comment and proceeded to mark out the next lesson. The rest of the term went by without incident. I just wondered why he didn't take our gym lessons.

AN AFTERNOON AT MARKS & SPENCERS

We had a good fully equipped gymnasium located on the ground floor of what must have been a more recent two story addition to the original building, providing extra classes on both the lower level and a veranda above. In addition to gymnasium facilities, for the benefit of our physical well being, arrangements had also been made for us to visit the Bishop Gore Grammar School swimming baths in Sketty; an extra privilege we all made good use of.

I think it was one afternoon every other week that we all caught a particular bus to get there; the number seventy five to Tycoch.

The bus stop was located at the bottom of Wind Street and alongside a shop that sold delicious pasties which mum said I wasn't supposed to buy on my way home in case I couldn't eat her dinner. I bought them just the same and still ate what I was supposed to. Well I was still growing wasn't I?

As well as catching a bus to go to swimming classes in Sketty we also had to get a single decker to take us to our games field at the top of Town Hill. If I remember correctly this was at Dynevor Place just around the corner from Dynevor Boys Grammar school. Across the way from the bus stop was where a sixty foot long whale came to visit the town lying on the back of a trailer. It was on display for several days to the public and drew queues longer than outside some of the cinemas. I think the site it was parked on was where the Dragon Hotel was eventually built. At the time it caused quite a stir and brought some fleeting excitement to the town.

The sports field we used was on the top level of Townhill and had both soccer and cricket pitches as well as a rough running circuit around its perimeter. I didn't enjoy playing football or rugby that much. Cricket was far less physically demanding with less running around and more static time. I was useless at running, usually getting a stitch after only a short distance, but I totally deny being a wimp; instead I got my exercise by borrowing a bike off another boy to practice my riding skills.

Getting to the Townhill bus stop was a reasonable walk from the school, taking us up Wind Street, through Caer Street and passing the end of Oxford Street on the way. It was in Caer Street for several months that a major distraction occurred because Mr Sidney Heath, of school uniform fame, had decided to move there, lock, stock and schoolboy apparel from Walter Road and build a new store in mock Tudor style. The resulting construction work caused a large hole in the ground running from one end of the site to the other with two diggers making it grow bigger by the day. They were smallish machines with brown and white painted wooden cabs. Chugg-chugging and putt-puttering away, it was an irresistible sight to watch, as they dug the foundations ever deeper making me ever later for school.

Going to games on one occasion we never reached the bus stop at all because of a more unusual event. As we made our way to Oxford Street we could see a pall of smoke hanging over it as we approached and in Oxford Street itself crowds were starting to form. Marks and Spencer's was on fire. Wow!

We thought we had better take a look. So we did; for the rest of the afternoon. As far as excitement went it was a disappointment really. When they said fire we were expecting flames shooting skywards and ladders with firemen running up and down them spraying water everywhere. But there were no flames and only two ladders with both police and firemen were running around looking flustered. Hoses were trailing up through the various windows pouring water in endlessly one way while smoke poured out of others and the brigade in general tried to establish 'the seat of the fire'. We hadn't heard that phrase before and it proved to be another quotable to be brought into conversation whenever possible. Although there were no flames there was a considerable amount of water damage and the shop was closed until such time that the mess had been cleaned up and the building refurbished where necessary, the water having caused more problems than the actual fire.

The really strange thing about the event was that although four or five of us never showed up for games that afternoon, because we were doing important investigative work in Oxford Street, no questions were ever asked by the school busybodies. Normally there would be at least one master who would want an enquiry but not that day. So, grateful for the lack of prosecution we kept our absence from games on what is now known as a "need to know" basis and let sleeping dogs lie.

STANDING BEHIND THE LEVERS

I mentioned biology earlier. This was a subject which you really had to have an aptitude for if you wanted to get anywhere with it. Like chemistry a lot of it seemed to rely on facts to memorise rather than working things out. Art was far less complicated. You either had some kind of aptitude for it or you didn't. Whilst most pupils managed to just sort of get by with it, others displayed talent that surprised not only themselves but a lot of other people as well including the art master. I liked art though more because of the location of the classroom which looked out on to an engineering yard with all sorts of machinery lying around, either under repair or awaiting attention.

For me the location of the school was everything. It was right in the heart of industry next to the docks. At the front corner of the engineering yard was a pile of sand, which would regularly be attacked by a tractor with a shovel bucket mounted in front. The tractor would line up, drop the bucket arm to the floor and then charge at the sand to fill the bucket, which would then be hoisted in the air by a winch mounted at the rear.

You could see the wire rope going down behind the cab where the driver was sitting. It would then do a reverse turn and drive forward to dump the load into a waiting lorry and I would watch intently for the moment when the driver pulled a rope from inside the cab to trip a latch allowing the bucket to rotate on its pivot and tip the sand out.

As I watched it working the art master would invariably notice and draw my attention to what I was supposed to be doing. If he was in a good mood he might occasionally tip me off about its activities and the whole class would watch it charge across the yard for one load before settling back down to continue their allotted drawing project. Thinking about it now I'm wondering if he was also a secret loader fan and used me as an excuse to watch it himself.

There were all sorts of yards like that in the area. On the same street were a coal merchant and a small ship repair works where at lunch time some of us would wander along to observe what was happening. Directly between these and the engineering yard was a sand and gravel business, which had an electric grab crane running on a short railway line raised a few feet above ground level. This was particularly good to watch in action, sorting stockpiles and filling sand hoppers from the various heaps that were surrounding it. Suspended by a single chain, the grab was like a giant mittened hand reaching out to snatch each fistful and dump it only after first landing on the discharge area. How did it do that? Mechanisms like this were becoming increasingly more interesting and after telling Peter about both the grab and the tractor we made a special journey down to the yard one Saturday morning to watch them at work.

By that time I had acquired a bicycle of my own. I remembered telling Peter about the tractor sometime previously because there was a model just like it in his No 10 Meccano book. So after our visit we both had new projects to get on with. It's such a pity that Meccano is not implanted into the schoolboy psyche any more.

Although I was mechanically aware like a lot of other boys from a relatively early age, it was not until these years at secondary school that I was able to get really absorbed in the world of engineering; visiting industrial yards and workshops nearby. The workmen in all these places were always pleased to answer questions from boys who were interested in what they were doing and as long as you were sensible nobody ever got officious and sent you on your way. This was helpful to those who wished to help themselves by getting early unofficial experience in a working environment. I know for a fact that a couple of boys in my class were interested in tugs and used to go out on them at weekends through word of mouth by uncles or friends of the family who knew someone who knew somebody who could whisper in the right ear.

With railways being a big potential employer for the future, some boys visited depots and sheds in the area. Train spotting drew a lot of railway enthusiasts of all ages to the main station and other locations from where engine numbers could be taken but I never got into that. Although drawn by their mechanical presence jotting down numbers was something I just couldn't see the point of especially after trying it once on a Saturday afternoon down at High Street station when only one train came in. It was not a good time to pick with hardly anything moving except for a solitary passenger diesel locomotive. These were completely foreign to me, not then really knowing what a diesel engine was.

I remembered years earlier when I was very young my father pointing out a diesel standing alongside one of the less busy side platforms. Only identifying with the last part of the word I had wondered where the weasel was and had looked everywhere without seeing one. I don't think dad realised my confusion because I didn't know I was confused; too intent looking for a small long furry rodent like I had seen in my animal picture book.

Attempts at train spotting were repeated on a couple of other occasions but to no avail. I had just one interest mechanically by then and that was diggers and cranes. Later, when the time was approaching for me to leave school and try for an engineering apprenticeship dad was convinced that it would be relatively easy to get one at Swindon locomotive works because of his job connection in the railway world. Travel to and from the works would also be funded by railway passes so that I could be home for weekends. Although undoubtedly a well respected world class training establishment it just wasn't for me. My engineering ambitions were elsewhere.

Whereas the side adjacent to the art class hosted a number of engineering and other concerns, on the other side of the school was a location known as Weavers Basin after the large flour mill which was built there just after the turn of the century in 1906.

Originally this small dock was part of the larger north dock now filled in. Heavily laden grain boats from faraway places would regularly just squeeze through the lock gates to moor alongside for their cargo to be sucked up by dropping large vacuum heads into the holds. As the contents were transferred from ship to mill for eventual conversion into bread and cookies it was interesting to see the vessel rise higher in the water. How many fields had been harvested, we wondered, to make it ride so low when it had first arrived?

Weaver's Basin had another feature, which for me was of far greater interest. On the side opposite to the mill and directly outside the technical drawing room was the stockyard belonging to the South Wales Sand & Gravel Co. Even better was the fact that directly outside the class windows stood a sand hopper and several piles of sand.

When the yard was busy, pulsating through closed classroom windows would drift the wonderful sound of a labouring six cylinder AEC diesel engine powering a grab crane, either feeding the hopper from existing stock or renewing the piles from a moored sand dredger which had been sucking it up from the sea bed out in the bay. Like the art room the grab crane supplied an encouraging source of distraction but only for me. The major was not impressed by it and only complained about "that noisy crane making a nuisance of itself again."

In time I eventually got to know the operator whose name was Stan and his sole task was to keep on driving that crane and offload the sand dredgers at whatever tide they came in on, day or night. The men working there were a friendly bunch and if they were working during the dinner hour a couple of us would occasionally wander around the corner from school to watch. On one occasion in the winter we were not so friendly when for a bit of fun several of us formed a platoon and went on the attack with snow balls. They must have come under fire before because they soon beat us off with deadly aim and an uncanny knowledge of the best cover points.

When I went around on my own to see Stan he would always invite me on board to stand behind him as he worked all the levers to open and close the grab with two steel cables and swing the machine around from loading to discharging points. It was enthralling, watching the machinery and winding drums turning; the band clutches engaging and releasing and then listening to the brakes squealing in protest as the rope drums spun out their coils, dropping the open grab back down ready for the next snatch of sand.

Little did I know it then but less than ten years into the future I would drive that same model of machine at a sand pit near Romford in the county of Essex.

Another thing I was beginning to take notice of when I got closer to machinery was the information plates attached to the sides of lorries and other things on wheels and crawler tracks. During the course of our studies we had been learning about the imperial system of weights and measures which existed then, before the present day metric one, when things like tons and cwts were used to define how heavy big things were.

Well I knew what a coot was, they were feathery things that swam around getting tangled up in your fishing line, but what was a cwt? It could, I supposed, be Welsh for coot but unlikely if attached to an information plate on the side of a lorry, digger or crane.

On a lorry it helped define the tare or unladen weight and on a crane it was part of the information telling you how much the crane could lift before it tipped over; the latter being particularly useful if you were standing anywhere near it when the load left the ground. The term cwt of course was an imperial measurement abbreviation for a hundredweight; twenty hundredweight making up a ton. But how big was a ton?

It seemed enormous when you looked at the size of a vehicle which might weigh several tons but how big would it be we wondered if it was a lump of metal weighing a ton, a container of water or a block of sand? Although we now use the European metric system I think it is a decidedly less colourful terminology than our original system. Speaking for myself, pounds, tons and hundredweights seemed to add more impact to a statement of heaviness than a mere kilo or bland metric ton.

Another question that exercised us in class for some time was asked by the math's master. It was a tough one. Which was heavier, a ton of lead or a ton of feathers? That one really concentrated our minds; not only wondering if it was a trick question but reminding us of the chemistry master who asked us, completely straight faced, to devise an experiment to decide which water was wetter and why: the stuff coming out of a tap or water running in a stream. Once we had found the answer we had to determine a coefficient of wetness? If they had asked us where cuckoos lived it would have been easier. We'd seen those in clocks when we went to Switzerland on the school trip. All these questions we had to find the answers for and I thought I knew where I could find at least one of them.

At the top end of Weavers basin used to be lock gates allowing access to the North Dock which by this time had been defunct for a number of years. They had long since been removed and the void filled in with a heavy wall blocking the top end. A new railway line had been laid and a small engineering workshop erected on the land between the basin and main roadway known as Quay Parade. One day I found the engineering workshop. I remember it was a very dirty brown corrugated affair which gave me my first real view of machinery engaged in making things with a centre lathe and milling and drilling machines. The first thing I ever saw being turned on the lathe was the vee groove for a rope pulley. It was where an engineer very kindly tried to explain what a strange looking thing called a micrometer was as well as a host of other 'obje de engineerin' equipment.

It was all extremely mind stretching to an inquisitive schoolboy 'engineer wannabe'. Many years later Weaver's Basin was filled in to provide the site on which Sainsbury's Supermarket now stands and where the sand silo stood outside our technical drawing class window being fed by Stan's NCK grab crane is now their boiler room. What a bland end to an interesting place.

The landscape was gradually changing in that part of Swansea and at the time although the lock-gates had been removed and everything filled in there was still remaining some kind of road girder-bridge at ground level. It must have been not long after I started at the Tech that this was dismantled and removed by a gang of men with burning torches and a green painted Neal's crane mounted on crawler tracks. A number of large pipes which had formerly been part of a water hydraulic system had been uncovered during the preparations and these too were being cleared.

At one stage of the operation I can recall the crane manoeuvering a really large piece suspended from its hook and balancing on tippy toes whilst loading it onto a trailer. It was a breath-taking experience, not only for several schoolboy onlookers beginning to brush shoulders with the working world, but also quite a number of older spectators holding their collective breath adding to the anticipation of impending disaster.

The crane's back end had lifted well off the ground; obviously operating beyond its limits and in danger of tipping over. Will it? Won't it? No one breathed and by doing so averted an unhappy ending as the lump of ex-hydraulic pipe was finally placed on the bed of the trailer.

As the changing landscape evolved the character and ambiance of this part of Swansea became increasingly interesting with its dockland and pockets of commerce and industry located beneath stone built arches supporting the railway viaduct. At one time the railway ran from the Danygraig side of the River Tawe, over the river to run past Quay Parade, then crossed the bottom end of Wind Street, on to Victoria Station at Mumbles Road; from there to continue alongside the bay and eventually curve away to Mid Wales and beyond at Blackpill.

Lying alongside the viaduct almost opposite Weaver's Basin was Barney Easton's scrap yard and Barney had a yard crane. It was the ideal place to find the answer to questions about how big a ton of metal was. They had plenty of scrap metal laying around but alas no feathers.

Unfortunately it also stood next to the town mortuary which struck terror into me whenever I passed it; especially if there was a black vehicle stood in attendance outside. But despite this drawback my quest for knowledge prevailed. Many snatched moments were spent there before school, both in the mornings and at lunch times, and if the crane was not immediately in sight one of the Easton brothers or the foreman would very quickly inform me that it was "down the yard," which usually meant at the far end. You could always hear it wherever it was, because it had a diesel engine with a very staccato bark to the exhaust.

Whatever the load, whatever it was doing, it always went "putt putt, putt putt," as it stood marking time as various bits and pieces of scrap were loaded into a sort of spoon shaped metal pallet suspended by three chains from the crane hook. I always remember this Neal crane because it was mounted on large diameter road wheels and was operated while standing at the controls even when driving along the highway. After I had been calling in at the yard for some time Bryn the crane driver invited me up onto his platform. Up there was a different world. Directly behind him was the engine ticking over loudly with the sickly smell of diesel fuel and alongside that on the inside of the crane an assortment of spinning cogs wheels and other important looking things.

Below floor level lurked a mysterious winding drum with coils of dirty wire rope around it leading up into the roof. It was this winding drum, he said, that moved the crane's long lifting arm, called the jib, up and down. I was on his crane platform standing in paradise. With a load just ready to lift he turned to me suddenly and said, "Righto, stand by there and pull that lever back gently."

So I did as bidden and it was amazing. It's hard to explain in one sense -but I could actually feel the load as the crane responded under my feet and through my hand on the lever.

You could say I was well and truly hooked on cranes by the experience and from that moment never wanted to be involved in any future job unless it was with oil, grease, gears and grime. In due course I was able to learn that Easton Brothers also did a bit of contracting with demolition and land clearance and with several bombed out sites still scattered around Swansea there was steady work for them. What else could I do but talk to the Easton yard crew and investigate further?

Perhaps a mile or so away from the yard by road was High Street railway station and leading away from it was Alexandra Road on which stood the fire station with its bright red fire engines inside. A little further along from the fire station however and around a corner was an even greater attraction, at the former Trinity Place Orthopaedic clinic which was now being demolished. It was an address I had attended some years previously after sustaining leg injuries as a child. Now it was defunct and one of sites Easton Brothers had been contracted to clear, and where once again Bryn the crane driver invited me to stand behind him as this time he attacked the rubble from the demolished building and loaded it into a steady stream of tipper lorries.

The machine he was driving now was a mechanical shovel built by the company of Ransomes & Rapier of Ipswich and it must surely have been one of the noisiest excavators I have ever been on, then or since.

On the plus side however it had a very interesting array of levers and rods to marvel at. Observation of these levers engaging and disengaging the various motions of the machine only served to blur the noise and add to the excitement. I can picture it now with Bryn bouncing around on the tractor type seat fighting the levers as he tore into the rubble, while yours truly, with teeth rattling, clung for dear life to the main 'A' frame from which the digging apparatus was suspended. I didn't dare let go but it was absolutely thrilling. There was no other experience like it.

To paraphrase a song title of the coming rock and roll era: "There was a whole lotta' shakin' goin' on." Another song title also springs to mind – "Magic Moments!" for me then these really were magic moments and a portend of the future direction my life was destined to take.

By contrast and as an example of different worlds colliding in close proximity: at the same time the mechanical digger was working on one side of the road, on the opposite side was a forge with a farrier busy re-shoeing a pair of dray horses quite possibly for Hancock's Brewery situated at the bottom of Wind Street. A pair would often be seen hauling a load of beer barrels from their premises in that part of town.

The kind of hands-on contact with machinery that I was lucky enough to experience would unfortunately never be allowed for schoolboys today except maybe in very rare circumstances.

Overzealous officialdom and emphasis on health and safety seems to have taken things well over the top and only inhibits interest in things mechanical. It has become an ever growing bureaucracy and an industry in itself producing volumes of paper work and 'courses'. The experiences I had taught me a lot and not only assisted my understanding and respect for machinery, they also confirmed my eventual choice of career and helped me secure an apprenticeship with a large engineering company that specialised in the manufacture of such equipment.

On my various site visits I had noted that cranes

and diggers were not all built by the same company and on a visit to the South Dock offices I was made aware that the various manufacturers produced technical brochures with photographs, dimensions and specifications of machinery layouts. One of my school pals had a brother who worked for a coal company there as a diesel fitter. How wonderful that title sounded. So I decided to go and visit him one day where he worked next to the coal tipplers and hydraulic cranes on the quayside. He wasn't expecting me and was out on a breakdown so I ended up on the opposite side of the dock watching another crane working. To cut a long story short I made friends with the operator who took me into their works office to look at some of their brochures and get a few addresses to write to.

One of them was Blackwood Hodge located in Cardiff, a well known agent for American manufactured equipment and that was how I started the catalogue collection which still clutters my office as I write. Within a few days of my first begging letters I received very encouraging packages by return with exactly the information I was looking for to help me better understand how things worked and talk with the men driving them and others working alongside.

Through my childhood years visiting the town on visits to shops, cinemas and theatres I became very familiar from a very early age with the many bombed out sites that lay both in the centre and its outlying districts. I remember one visit made with my mother and sister when we must have been still living in West Cross. We gazed down in astonishment from where Castle Street overlooked the lower level of Oxford Street to the maze of broken buildings and the scars of bombing before us. Constance and I did not really understand what we were seeing but my mother understood only too well. A bomb had landed in the street where she and dad used to live near the town centre not long after they moved to West Cross.

When I got old enough to wander independently I would go with one or two friends and we would notice the gradual changes taking place as the town was rebuilt in the new styling of the post-war years. It was exciting to see modernity replacing the old but with the new also came regret as familiar landmarks and streets disappeared, including the workshops and businesses located in archways beneath the many railway viaducts in the industrial and commercial neighbourhood.

All these lent character to the town and I was pleased that some of them did manage to remain for a number of years afterwards until they too got absorbed into the new geography. The up side to all this of course was more cranes and diggers about the place and by the time I had been attending the Tech for a year or more I literally knew where every building site worth visiting was located, inside or outside the town. Spotting a heavy haulage vehicle carrying a crane or digger on the back from WNNS or PICKFORDS was a bonus sighting and to be followed up whenever possible on my bike.

The real key to my industrial activities however was the arrival of my bike. From the moment I had wheels I was in touch with the town's happenings almost every day and had intimate contact with many of its big new stores any spare minute I could salvage from lunch break. Unfortunately this very often meant getting back late for the first class of the afternoon and a telling off from the master taking it. When they built the new Marks & Spencer's in Oxford Street I stood behind a crane driver as he pushed a row of bright red control levers, placing girders high up in the sky, aligning them with the others for bolting to the steadily growing skeleton of steelwork supplied by a well known engineering company on the east side of town. Previously, as the groundworks were prepared, I had watched with jealousy as a blonde headed youth, who couldn't have been more than aged twenty, drove a brand new bright blue Priestman digger, dipping and diving to dig the foundations, filling up with earth and rubble to discharge it all into a waiting Foden tipper lorry. Seeing the transformation from bomb site to finished store was inspiring.

The new Boots building at the bottom of Princess Way also made me late for school, and I can still remember the distinct aroma of hot molten tar as I sheltered from the rain next to the boiler of a steam powered derricking crane. With gears ringing, it hoisted a huge bucket of tar onto the roof at the end of a hundred foot jib! WOW! – that was huge. Cranes and diggers were taking over my life and I think it must have been around this period that I mislaid Gordon, another one of my friends. Perhaps mislaid is not the right word. What happened was that he just sort of disappeared without trace. It was just after he, Trevor and I had been messing around one night on the beach in the dark trying to signal ships in the bay.

One day he was there and a couple of days later he wasn't. Nobody saw or heard from him again. The thing was his parents went along with him. It was really weird. I'll tell you more about that a bit later. Anyway – I just thought I'd mention it in passing. It was disturbing. Losing my friends seemed to be coming a habit.

Weekends on my bicycle took me further afield; surprisingly in one instance to the very heart of dock land which was not that easy to penetrate. I had tried on a few occasions to get into the Kings Dock; always busy with the hazard of steam locomotives shunting around the place requiring constant awareness. The problem for schoolboys, or anybody wanting to get in for that matter, was the police box at the entrance. Dock Police and schoolboys were not meant to see eye to eye so how I got through without the expected hostilities on that occasion is lost in the mysteries of time.

I think it was probably more of a holiday weekend than a normal one when the box was unmanned and the police had taken time off to make sand castles on the beach. Anyway I got past the entrance and much further than anticipated, eventually wheeling my steed across a set of lock gates that brought me to the new Duke of Edinburgh dry dock; very much in the early stages of construction with another one alongside being upgraded.

Fortunately the tide level at the lock gates was right up at the time and I was unfazed by any differences in the water levels either side of the gangway crossing to get to it. On a few other occasions when I visited the difference was considerable and very discouraging. The narrow wooden walkway became no man's land and there seemed no way I could have wheeled my bike across it without falling over the side and into the black sullen depths below.

It was a cracking new discovery and I made the most of it visiting on sunny days and also when it was raining. There were two dragline excavators at work on the project: one manufactured by Ruston Bucyrus, a company whose name I was beginning to notice more and more; and the other an NCK like my friend Stan drove at Weavers Basin. NCK cranes I learnt were manufactured in Sheffield. That was another word enquiring schoolboys were beginning to use more often. To the uninformed, things were 'made' but to those with a knowledge of engineering type stuff they were 'manufactured.'

I made friends of both drivers and when the rain came took turns on each machine, standing behind them as the holes in front of them grew ever larger. For hours at a time I watched as the winding drum clutches slammed in and out of engagement and coiled and uncoiled ropes to drag in bucket loads of earth that were emptied into trucks and taken away to fill other hungry holes on some other building site.

Although my bicycle took me around any places I wanted to go, in my quest to find excavators or cranes, one of my most treasured memories is a site visit made because of my father's occupation.

Casting my mind back nearly sixty years it is not that easy to remember things in chronological order but that particular event does stick in my mind and occurred in 1957 when I had my first encounter with a machine of American manufacture.

Dad was employed as a property inspector and occasionally when I was on holiday I used to accompany him on some of his visits which could entail car journeys covering a substantial part of South Wales. He visited all sorts of places in his job, driving only two vehicles that I can remember.

The first one was a Wolesley 1500 and the second, later, car was an Austin Somerset. All these years later I can still remember the registration number of the Austin; NXN10. Memory is a strange thing. All life's experiences are stored there somewhere. I don't know how many miles my father covered all together in his job but he certainly got to know a lot of cafés on his various trips visiting towns and villages within the Welsh borders.

One of his favourites was an Italian café on the outskirts of Port Talbot which is still open to this day although the original family have long since departed. I myself got to know it well in later years when I sought refreshment during my own travels working on earthmoving equipment in the area. On the day when we made our discovery our destination was the village of Pyle which before the 'Beeching Axe' still had a railway running through it and its own station.

Travelling out of Swansea was a very different road experience in the 1950s to what it is today. Dual carriageways were yet to come in a lot of places and the Jersey Marine road was still single carriageway with high banks and fencing dispersed at intervals on either side leading out of the east end industrial area. To get to Pyle you had to pass through the steel works town of Port Talbot which meant driving over the new Briton Ferry Bridge, completed a year or so earlier, to cross the River Neath.

The bridge was a very welcome development for dad as it meant considerably shortened journeys on his way to inspect housing and other buildings owned and maintained by the Great Western Railway Company. On the Swansea side entry to the bridge span was accessed by turning right at a traffic roundabout with the road from Swansea rising up to meet it. You had to turn right at this point because the road ahead did not then exist. It was just a blank wall of rock.

On a previous trip we had discovered a side road

leading off the bottom of the hill after we noticed two long arms sticking up heavenward above the level of the main road. Investigation led us to a couple of large Ruston Bucyrus mechanical shovels parked there which I inspected with great delight.

They were the biggest I had seen with enough gear wheels, clutches and chains to get any mechanically mined schoolboy excited. I think it fair to say that although dad was not what you would call mechanically inclined he was also impressed. It was a good day. I would have loved to have seen them working but it was not to be. The question was -where had they come from? There was a name painted on the side of their cabs which I remember was Cowman and dad later found out that they had been parked up awaiting their fate after the company had gone bankrupt attempting to dig away the solid rock wall at the top of the hill. It was going to be the gateway of a new trunk road to Carmarthen.

THE PERFECT DAY

Digging away the rock had obviously been a tougher and more costly job than had been appreciated and that was their bad luck and my good fortune because not long after we had discovered the two lay-by shovels we were again on our way to crossing the Briton Ferry bridge when we found that the rock wall on the other side of the roundabout had finally been breached and thrusting its magnificent black digging arm into the air from below ground level was an even bigger digger than the two Ruston Bucyrus machines.

Unfortunately we could not stop for an inspection then and I had to endure several hours on the other side of the bridge before our return journey allowed first hand examination of our latest discovery. We parked the car a little way off and scrambled over some rocky ground to where we could look down on it. But I had to get closer.

It was huge with an enormous bucket at the front end, even bigger than dad, and had obviously not been idle very long; still ticking and creaking as the machinery cooled and wafting the wonderful smell of hot clutch and brake linings and diesel oil through the air.

Painted in a two tone silver and red colour scheme, the rotating machinery deck was mounted on a heavy, solid looking under frame set between very wide crawler tracks each side. With its digging arms also painted black it was the meanest looking digger I had ever seen. The surrounding rocks seemed to cower as it stood menacingly waiting to attack them again; all ninety eight tons of it, I was later to learn.

The manufacturer's diamond-shaped name plate proclaimed the name Lima. It was of American origin and I was in awe and couldn't wait to see it working. By the size of the thing I guessed that I couldn't leave it too long or it would have eaten a lot more rock and be even further away from the road. Our visit that day was a mid-week one because of holiday. On the Saturday I was on my way back there, pedalling my bike like fury. It was a fair distance to go but an opportunity not to be missed. Arriving mid-morning which was later than intended I just wished I had owned a camera to record the scene.

When dad and I had first set foot on site for a few days before the Lima shovel was the only piece of plant there, standing at rest awaiting its next day's tussle with the tough terrain. Now, as I found a place to park my bike, I looked around at a far more interesting scene with the Lima now fully engaged loading a fleet of distinctive green dump trucks as the biggest bulldozer I had ever witnessed was busy having an argument with several large boulders in the background.

I stood for some time watching the activity, listening to the engine note of the digger as it alternated between an insistent labouring drone of power, moving everything aside in its path while filling the bucket, and a near stalling surrender as the ancient ground fought back. It was doing what a big American digger had to do and I was once again standing in my own vision of paradise. I thought things couldn't have been better, but they improved steadily as the morning progressed.

I had been watching for around ten minutes without anybody on site taking any notice of me when a freshly loaded truck came toward where I was standing, off to one side, a little higher than site floor level. As it drew next to me I noticed the Euclid legend on the cab door and as I did so it came to a halt, the driver wound down the window, poked his head out and said the magic words, "Wanna ride?" I remember nodding my head so enthusiastically that I felt it might fall off. I was alongside the driver and in his cab like a shot.

With the hiss of released air brakes and one quick rev of its monstrous diesel engine, we were away down the site road. He was a cheery sort of individual who told me to call him Roddy and that the rocks in the back of the truck were going to help make the road up further along, filling in holes and bringing it up to level so that it could eventually be topped up with smaller stones and gravel in preparation for the final finish. It only took about five minutes to get to the dumping point, bumping along, changing up and down gears as we went, before finally arriving to reverse the vehicle into position ready do discharge its load.

The engine had been noisy enough in the cab as we were driving there but now as Roddy put his foot to the floor to lift the body it screamed in protest as he wound it right up and a big three stage hydraulic ram expanded, punching it into the air. I watched in wonder through the back window as it lifted from its resting place, pivoting on its back end to throw the rocky load out in a cascade behind us. When we had done tipping he released the auxiliary drive and quite quickly the body dropped back onto the chassis with a satisfying little jolt and we started on our way back to collect another helping. I took two more round trips with Roddy and after returning from the second one he pulled into position under the digger again, leaned out through the cab window catching the operator's eye and pointed to me, sitting grinning alongside.

The rather dour looking operator, whose name was Russell, nodded back to Roddy and I found myself scrambling out of the twenty five ton capacity Euc to walk around the front of the Lima while he waited for me to climb onto the tracks and up into the cab behind him.

I had been on quite few construction sites by now, starting as I did from about age nine or ten, so was quite familiar with plant machinery and site protocols. There were no Hi-Visibility vests then so I made sure of always keeping a wary eye out for potential danger and that I could always be seen. The other thing I did was to always ask before going near any machines. It must have paid dividends because I never fell out with any of the drivers or site foremen and never had any accidents.

Being on board the Lima was an experience like no other. As well as being several times bigger than the one that Bryn drove at Trinity Place it was much, much noisier. One reason for this was the three sets of heavy duty roller chains used as part of the digging machinery, one of them winding halfway up the main digging arm and back. As the machinery turned they made the most glorious cacophony of banging and clattering as they drove the bucket teeth into the wall of ancient resisting rock.

The Lima also had another feature I had not seen before. This was air controlled operation of the clutches and brakes. Instead of long mechanical hand levers connecting everything through yet more levers and bell cranks there were short easily operated stubby ones working air valves for the clutches with air assisted cylinders for the foot operated brake pedals.

I may have been just a fourteen year old schoolboy but I was learning about this kind of machinery and terminology fast. It was not the usual schoolboy pursuit to chase mechanical diggers or even an interest that was engaged in by ordinary members of the public, unless it was work associated. Nevertheless I was making the most of my opportunities when they came. Even Dad could see in which direction my future was going to lie.

It's hard to say how my particular interest in cranes started but I do remember that when I was about three I was given a toy crane mounted on rubber wheels. It had a fixed jib with a winding handle, green string and a red hook. I can also remember that it had cut out windows in the sides and was bright red in colour. One of my favourite toys; maybe this was the seed that sowed the interest which has lasted a lifetime.

Because of its size the Lima digger also had a walkway around the outside of its upper works, the machinery deck enabling me to swap position several times and stand either alongside Russell outside the cab or behind him inside. It was exciting to watch the machinery turning; to see and feel the clutches expand and contract; alternating and combining duty with the brakes as both utilities squealed their protest, radiating heat and the smell of hot linings. There was nothing like it.

A well-known advertising hoarding in the Swansea

town centre and around the country at the time was proclaiming the virtues and aroma of a well-known gravy ingredient with the portrayal of two young urchins sniffing as it wafted under their noses with the slogan: Ah! BISTO. At that moment, to fit the occasion, I could think of another one: Mmm! – FERRODO – Hot linings! A very distinctive aroma. It wasn't only exciting, it was exhilarating, just to be there and be part of the operation, feeling the machine responding to the challenge as it dug hard into the bank of rock, straining and overcoming resistance to fill the bucket and hoist it away, turning in a half circle to discharge the winnings into a waiting truck.

Like the latch on a garden gate, a latch on the back door of the bucket was operated by an air cylinder mechanism mounted on the digging arm, allowing the hinged door to swing open and discharge the contents. As Russell turned the machine back to take another bite the weight of the bucket door pivoting on these two enormous half circular hinges automatically reset the latch in its keep and digging began as before.

Compared to Bryn's digger at Trinity Place the noise was more solid with less rattling and not so high-pitched an assault on the ear drums. It was altogether deeper, an all-enveloping staccato sound brought on in part by those heavy duty roller chains as they rattled slack and then banged and clattered tight over their sprocket gears with the back end of the machine regularly lifting off the ground when 'getting stuck in' and then just as quickly sitting back down with a jolt as the rock surrendered to the biggest set of teeth I had ever seen.

The experience was of course in some ways exaggerated because of my age and the fact that it was all new, different and dynamic unlike school. It was also greasy and dirty and it all smelled wonderful. To Russell and the other site workers of course it was all just work.

Not long after I elected to stand on the side platform a workman suddenly emerged through a side door around the back of the machine where he had been hidden from view doing a bit of mechanical tinkering. This, I learned, was Dai. He was dressed in a well-worn and elegantly torn boiler suit, professionally stained with overzealous use of oil and grease and held together, more by chance than design, by a wide leather belt around his waist.

Complementing the boiler suit was a black beret pulled down tightly around his forehead. What I noticed most though was his footwear. Instead of Wellingtons like the other men he wore wooden soled clogs with leather uppers. Very comfortable and durable he told me. "Just the job for working on the Lima," he said. "The soles aren't affected by oil so they last a long time."

When I innocently queried this statement he told me that he was the official greaser and travelled with the machine wherever it was sent. He looked very much the part and I did wonder if he actually slept on board. It was not unheard of on some sites and it did of course save on lodging money especially if there was on-site catering.

I don't think he was that old, probably in his twenties, but he had so much oil and grease about him that his facial features were obscured and it was difficult to tell without asking. I was very aware that I was still just a schoolboy in a grown up world so I didn't. I was having too good a time and in the course of our ensuing conversation I also found out that he could drive the machine if necessary and almost asked if he wanted to swap places with me. The time passed far too quickly and suddenly everything on the site went quiet and came to a halt. I hoped it was nothing to do with me but no. It was my first really personal industrial experience. Tea break!

They were a friendly bunch and I was invited to sit with them and have a cuppa. I followed Dai to what today would be called a Porta-Cabin, although 'Porta' it definitely was not. More like a temporary shed on wheels. Nevertheless I joined them inside and was very kindly given a mug of tea of my own to sup while I sat with him and the other workers on that first phase of the new road all the way to Carmarthen.

It's funny how even so long ago I can remember so many details of that day. Oh, what a day it was. There was Russell and Dai on the Lima, three dump truck drivers, the fellow driving the yellow bulldozer, a couple of general labourers and the foreman. Nine in all and later on a mobile fitter and the greaser service van would turn up.

As we all sat, supped and chatted I got questioned about my interests in general and excavators in particular and it was during some leg pulling banter that I got introduced to Billy who drove the big yellow bulldozer, or as he called it 'The Cat'. To those in the know it was 'The Machine' to drive: A D8, which in future years would become a bulldozing legend surpassing all others. To cut a long story short Billy had a word with the site foreman and fixed it for me to sit alongside him on the dozer. I was really going to be able to brag about this experience when I went back to school.

With tea break over everybody trooped out of the canteen and made their way back to what they were doing and I followed Billy up onto the machine. Unlike later practice it had no cab, just a bench seat with the operator sitting out in the open enjoying whatever weather was happening at the time. Billy gave me a hand as I climbed up alongside in great anticipation. "Hang on tight kid," was his only instruction before he started the engine with a mighty roar. In front of him were two angled pull levers and with two brake pedals - worked together to steer, and a manual gear box with several forward and reverse speeds as well as a throttle lever. The bulldozer was parked a little way from the canteen so the first job was to travel to where rocks needed pushing somewhere else so that's what we did, leaping forward over rough ground as we went.

To an onlooker our journey would have looked relatively smooth but this was a deception. Now I understood Billy's instruction to hang on tight. I was bouncing all over the place even though I had one hand gripping the side of the seat and the other thrown over the back as best I could to stop myself sliding off onto the floor. When we actually made contact with rocks it got even rougher. Billy was doing fine, changing gear speeds, reversing a distance, braking and disengaging clutches to steer and then going forward again in a different direction lifting. Or dropping the blade as needed, occasionally turning to grin at me 'hanging in there' and ready to grab and stop me falling off if necessary. It was so much fun I couldn't stop laughing. Today such activity would give the health and safety brigade a heart attack. Well hard luck chaps; I'm glad you weren't around.

After about ten minutes or so I had to call a halt.

Both arms and legs were weak and aching from bracing and holding and my rear end was also suffering from cushion bounce. It was by no means a soft seat. It was still a fantastic ride though and I gratefully thanked Billy for the experience as I reluctantly and somewhat sorely clambered off to see if I could get one last stint at watching the Lima working. I was only just in time to see it finish loading the last truck before Russell climbed down and everybody else, as if by telepathic command, also stopped what they were doing and made their way to where their own transport was parked further down next to the site office. It was time to go home and enjoy the remains of the day at leisure. Some of them made their way slowly on foot and the remainder cadged a lift in the Eucs or by sitting however they could on the D8.

I got a lift on the Lima along with one of the labourers and my bike while Dai sat at the controls to move it out of the cut, winding a big wheel next to the operating levers to steer the tracks and then drive it down to where the fitter and his mate had set up a temporary service area not far from the office. The Lima Caterpillar bulldozer and the three Euclid trucks would be inspected, greased and adjusted during the rest of the afternoon.

Next to the site office was an exit lane leading onto the main road by Llandarcy oil refinery. I would go back home using that road because it lead through Jersey Marine village and onto the main route back to Swansea. But there was a bonus. A short distance to one side of the lane was another area which was being utilised for the supply of additional rubble and hardcore filler for the construction site. The material seemed to have been dumped there years previously and now another shovel was digging and loading it into a second fleet of smaller commercial tipper lorries.

The cab was painted a sort of grey blue colour with a white roof and the name Ruston Bucyrus prominent on the side announcing that it was a 22-RB; a name which I became even more familiar with and which would eventually play a major part in my life in the years to come. It was about the same size machine that Bryn had driven for Easton Brothers but more modern in design.

Swansea council had over the years acquired a few of the smaller machine they produced for utility work and the 10-RBs, as they were designated, could be seen digging roads and trenches all over the place. The duty these smaller machines seemed to be used for mostly was digging up roads with what was called a skimmer scoop; a boxy sort of thing with teeth, mounted on wheels and pulled along the digging arm by a cable when set horizontal with the road. Lifted clear on reaching the end of its travel the whole machine then slewed around to drop the rubble into a waiting lorry. This was the most interesting part because to discharge the contents the driver pulled a rope from the cab and the floor of the box swung open.

We, the spectators, watched this action time and time again, hypnotised by the pulleys constantly turning first one way and then the other as the digging arm was lifted up and down and the box floor flipped open. The closing of the box was even more dynamic and was accomplished with a final flourish as the bucket, as it was officially called, was allowed to run un-braked down the lifted digging arm a short distance before sudden application of the brake caused the floor to swing into the bucket latch and snap shut. With appropriate adjustment to the front equipment this very popular machine could also excavate trenches and were the grandfathers of today's modern JCB diggers.

I was late and the morning's activities were coming to an end with the 22-RB also shutting down, so getting acquainted with it would have to wait until my next appointment with the Lima. When I did arrive on site the following weekend it was to some disappointment. The Euclid trucks had gone, Billy and his big yellow Caterpillar were noisily busy bulldozing prehistoric rubble further along the site but of Russell and Dai there was no sign. The Lima had completed its work, eaten all there was on offer and was now standing idle while awaiting movement to a new location. Its digging arm and bucket had both been detached from the front and were lying on the ground alongside. I thought it looked hungry and dejected, just standing there, dismembered with nothing left to chew on. Someone from the office later told me that its next site was near Cardiff and completely beyond a bicycle ride so I never saw it or the crew again.

The 22-RB was hard at work however and it had, for me, one big advantage over the smaller skimmer scoop. There was enough room to accommodate a schoolboy standing behind the operator and I soon got friendly with him and did just that. His name was Jimmy; a dark haired heavily tanned individual in his early thirties and wearing a dark blue boiler suit which looked like it had been tailored especially for him - Unlike Dai's outfit. There were no wooden clogs on his feet. Instead he was wearing a pair of black leather brogues. I'm sure if it had been raining he would have had an umbrella. A gentleman driver and he made driving look so easy that I longed to ask him if I could have a go. Good drivers always made it look easy though, and although I yearned to sit in the seat that he was occupying I wisely refrained from asking.

It had been a good sunny day when I first visited the site the weekend before and this occasion was also blessed with a clear blue sky, luckily as it also was on the two or three remaining visits I made in the following weeks. The last visit was nearly my last visit to anywhere and was a stark reminder of the cruelty of coincidence and spiteful vindictiveness of fate.

I had left the site after a full morning standing on the platform of Jimmy's digger, watching the clutches spinning and the digging arm dipping and diving into the spoil heap and then being swung out over an ever changing line of lorries to dump the rubble into to each one in turn. The spoil tip had almost been dug out by this time and I would not be coming back.

I was cycling through Jersey Marine village when it happened. Would you believe - an eight wheeler Foden tipper lorry came shooting past, leaving hardly any room, just as I was drawing level with an open piece of ground on my near side. The vehicle didn't physically touch me but punched a slab of air out of the way as it drew level, knocking me hard sideways, sending me sprawling and badly gashing both hands on the ground as I put them out to break my fall. I was exceedingly lucky not to suffer serious injury.

It was a painful reminder physically and mentally. Whether the driver saw me I don't know but the lorry never slowed and I was quite shaken by the incident, remembering all too vividly how my friend Clifford had perished some years before in similar manner by the same make and type of vehicle. It was too much of a coincidence and I never cycled along that stretch of road again. As it happened there wasn't any need to, because things started getting a lot busier around the town.

LOOKING TO THE FUTURE

As our teenage school years progressed we became more aware of what was going on around us as the world of work beckoned. But there were also a new kind of distraction. With the advent of Radio Luxembourg a new phenomenon became apparent; pop music from America. There had been for some time the sound of British skiffle groups like Lonnie Donegan and others, copied by a growing number of boys forming groups of their own around Swansea and the rest of the country.

The key instrument was a guitar and it seemed that if anybody was interested in music they wanted one - including me. The BBC was beginning to play more music enjoyed by the new 'teenagers' but not enough. Radio Luxembourg filled the gap and you could tune in late at night to hear the artists you missed in the day.

Then one Sunday, on the BBC programme Family Favourites, some individual requested a record by an American musician by the name of Bill Haley and his group The Comets. We'd never heard anything like it. It was called Rock Around The Clock and for British teenagers it was a revelation, heralding the start of a musical revolution. Rock & Roll was born. It wasn't that long after that day that I heard an even more exciting sound. It was another American singer; Buddy Holly and his group The Crickets with That'll be the Day. From the moment I heard it I was a fan.

Rock and Roll and the Teddy Boy era really broke out in Swansea when they showed the film Rock Around The Clock at the Rialto cinema in Wind Street just down from where we caught the bus from school. I was of course forbidden to go and see it because of the bad press it got but I went just the same without telling mater and pater. It was the kind of music which as well as making you tap your feet also made me start the habit of drumming my fingers on the table at meal times, just like a friend who actually played lead guitar and was in a group called The Hurricanes.

I thought I'd copy him because it would make me look 'with it'. Used to drive dad nuts.

"For heaven's sake stop drumming your fingers on the table boy. What's the matter with you?"

"It's music dad, music!" I'd say. But he just shook his head.

"That's not music boy, that's just a dirge of disjointed noise.

Anyone would think you've got the St Vitus' dance." "Its Rock and Roll Daddio," I replied. "It's Rock and Roll; like movin' and groovin'!"

I'd never seen him with a blank look on his face before but he definitely had one then. "What's the St Vitus' Dance, Dad? Was it one of your routines when you were young?" Whoops! He didn't like that either. Something else that annoyed him was my sense of fashion. I had an off-white sort of coloured tweed jacket. Nobody else had one that I knew so I thought it would look extra good with a black shirt and white tie.

"What?" He said. "You've joined Oswald Mosley and the black shirts now have you?"

"Who were they dad? One of your old-time music hall bands were they?" I emphasised old which really got up his nose.

"No," he replied, sighing heavily and obviously somewhat miffed at my lack of historical knowledge. "They were not, definitely, not a music hall band." He got even more miffed as to his dismay I brought much more music of the noisy kind to his ears when I got a guitar of my own and it became an even greater interest in my life. All these distractions were now intruding more into my school work which was beginning to suffer and my exam results growing steadily worse. With just a hint at sarcasm dad once told me that the little crosses put next to my work by the maths master didn't mean the same as crosses on Christmas and birthday cards. Oh, very droll dad very droll. Pythagoras had become a sworn enemy and if I'd had my way the man who invented algebra would have been hanged after his first foray at confusing things by using the alphabet as well as numbers. I had no chance.

But time passed; we the aspiring got older, maybe slightly more responsible - I wouldn't say mature - and began to differentiate between the classification of manual and office type careers and decided the ones we wanted to aim for. In the last year of school we were shown films in the assembly hall about what it was like to work in a factory, how a car was built and similar engineering themes.

Occasionally a small group would be taken out to visit companies in the area like Metal Box which was a fairly long bus ride away in Neath. Not having visited real factories before and only read about them, we were astounded at all the machinery involved; power presses in particular, and how noisy they were. It was an eye opening experience that fascinated a lot of us and drew many in to engineering while at the same time disenchanting others.

From our schoolboy perspective Swansea and the rest of the country was buzzing. We were unfamiliar with the concept of unemployment then. Everybody who wanted a job seemed to have one as far as we knew. If you didn't have one you just 'weren't working' and that was that. We didn't really dwell on the personal ramifications of the situation. I can still remember the heady excitement of those glory days following our emergence from war to rebuild our town and the rest of the country. Looking back it almost seemed to me that there was a buzz in the air. There was tremendous industrial activity all around with the docks and the industries that fed it. Coal mining was a huge concern and there were also several steelworks not that far away at Velindre, Port Talbot, Trostre and Llanelli; wages at Port Talbot rumoured to be so good that it was nicknamed Treasure Island.

Coal and steel production employed thousands together with all the support jobs in engineering and other commercial activity they generated. None of us had any reason to think that we would not get a job. Some of the most unlikely pupils in fact went on to university and became teachers. Knowing some of them as I did I found it difficult to make the mental adjustment; and thinking of the old proverb 'Ye reap what ye sew', wondered if any would be taking physics or technical drawing as their subject.

Like many of my mechanically-minded contemporaries I became more aware and took more notice of the cars, lorries, buses and everything else on our roads; wanting to know who made them and where, their design and technical details. As the last years of our school passed we watched their development as new shapes evolved and features were changed or added. Manufacturer's names were taken and small gatherings of like-minded boys both in and out of school got together to talk about the latest news. Several of us wrote to manufacturers for catalogues, brochures etc on their cranes, diggers, cars, vans, trucks tractors and any thing else Britain manufactured; in those years we literally made every thing for land, sea and air, for farming, industry, commerce and defence. The list was endless; we were a healthy industrially productive nation organising our own affairs, culturally stable with no indication of change to that dynamic. In our innocence we thought that was how it was supposed to be; that it would last forever. But as we know to our cost, it didn't. Ambitious fools were already lurking in the shadows, waiting to give it all away.

The undercurrents of change came in the last quarter of the century, tugging away with increasing turbulence and spilling into the next. Our generation, and those following shortly after, could never have anticipated how those changes, imperceptibly applied, would evolve.

None of us realised that the mechanical age in which we lived and were passing through was making history. We didn't even suspect that in those future years most of what we had learnt or what we made would be irrelevant and obsolete; our experience, training and skills suitable only for nostalgia and museums.

Now, so many years later, we have emerged from the tunnel of a full working life to retirement in the present day where that kind of prospect looks slim. During the intervening years, when we were fully occupied with our careers, the cultural fabric of our island home had also been stealthily eroded, like a slick sleight of hand card trick, transforming our thrusting industrial engine, infrastructure and sense of country into shadows of what they used to be and we seem to have lost our identity. Blinkered perhaps by the distraction of work and family matters we didn't notice that those we trusted had surrendered it to a utopian mirage; signing it away on a proposition they knew to be false and yet collaborating in the deception. So now we pay the price as it withers; relentlessly undermined with no visible attempt to redress the situation by those empowered to do so. Does the world look on, I ask myself, and wonder what happened to a once strong and proud independent nation?

It is for this reason that I believe the time through which my generation has lived has been the best that Britain ever had and is ever likely to see. Although essentially a mechanical age, it was spent in peace and hope looking forward to a promising future; a period when we were all working towards the ultimate goal of resurrecting and rebuilding our country after the ravages and savagery of war. For many of us the new 'Techno' age of today is moving too fast, requiring a mind-set that is outstripping our patience and maybe even some of our humanity.

I wonder what today's children would think if they were to experience the wonderful innocent era that we had; un spoilt and corrupted by the relentless garbage of today's multi-faceted multi-media output with, unlike members of the present day celebrity culture, role models who had really achieved something worthwhile to celebrate. We were not thrust into adulthood almost before our teens as they now are.

Today's child is heavily pressurised from almost every quarter and although inhabiting a world with gadgets and toys we could only then have dreamed about, I do not envy them. My boyhood was an innocent one with typical over-exuberant imagination finding a place in any activity that fostered it; which is probably why I was so easily led into doing what in hindsight I really couldn't have guessed the implications of at the time. I will never understand how what started out as the three of us just messing about with torches ended up causing so much trouble. Earlier I mentioned that Gordon one of my friends went missing. Things are not always what they appear to be; the following narrative suggesting a continued description of our seemingly carefree days thus far. Please bear with me. I assure you it is not. We get used to the usual pattern and habits of our lives without question and too often accept things at their face value; just like I did.

I will never know which future world events were shaped, or how, because of what we did, and, as I said at the beginning of this narrative, that thought terrifies me. My only comfort is that I did what I did in complete and utter ignorance. What follows is a record of events leading up to and subsequent to that night in late October 1957. I hope you will understand.

PART TWO

SPECIAL FORCES

We all live with our secrets. Most of them we know but then sometimes we live with secrets we didn't know we had. Royston had a secret but that was different. The secret that I have kept and lived with for so many years because I didn't know about it is however truly unique.

It had nothing to do with neighbours, family, friends or local crime and I'm telling you about it now because it needs to be told. After, and only after I have told you, I will inform the appropriate authorities because one miserable night in late October nineteen fifty seven and for several weeks afterwards two of my friends at the time, Gordon, Trevor and I, had the police and other top brass running around in desperate circles looking for us. There were a lot of police involved that night which can probably be confirmed by official records; but they didn't see what we did and if they did, they didn't know what they were looking at, because they were too busy looking for us.

We were just kids, thirteen year old schoolboys living in our fantasy world and out of nowhere it just went wrong. But it was us, with our school coded striped trouser belts clipped by a snakehead hook and our first pair of long trousers tucked into our socks left baggy at the bottom. We thought we looked real menacing. From a distance we could easily have been mistaken for Special Forces. Well in our juvenile minds, we could have.

Trevor could look particularly nasty if he gave you a squint through his extra strong goldfish glasses. I told him - you must have real good eyesight to see through those. He used to frighten my sister every time she saw him. Thinking and writing about it now, apart from the wire rimmed glasses, I suppose you could say that he wasn't far off a Hank Marvin look-alike. Same sort of stature but more nervous looking and brown hair flopping all over the place.

He always seemed to be wearing either a grey zip up jerkin or a mac, and a pair of daps instead of shoes if he could sneak out of the house without his mother seeing him. Sometimes when we weren't on a mission he'd wear the mac, even on sunny days when it was quite warm, but he never seemed to get a sweat on.

It was funny how we got to be friends with the three of us going to different schools in different parts of the town. I don't suppose if we hadn't been in the scouts we would ever have met up. But that's how it was. The real mystery was how Gordon had joined the troop living as he did in Townhill which was miles from scout HQ while Trevor and I lived locally and just a ten minute walk away. The only thing we could put it down to was that Gordon had an uncle a couple of streets away which he said he used to visit quite regularly.

This uncle wasn't a family relative though, because Gordon's parents were both Polish and 'uncle' was really a business type acquaintance of his father's. I think he and his wife must have taken a shine to Gordon when he was a toddler. With no children of their own they sort of adopted him as a nephew, and he said they spoilt him rotten.

Of the three of us I'd say he was the smartest – if you could find off duty schoolboys who dressed smartly - and brainy as well. Slicked back jet black hair some days and then parted to one side another time. Don't know why, he just played about with it that way. A roundish looking face with a broad nose gave him a bullish look that sometimes caused people to misjudge him, thinking he was a hard case when really he was quite docile. Fairly heavy in build he was the same height as me but wore a blazer most of the time except for when, like Trevor, he replaced it with some sort of jerkin. His shirt was always accompanied by a school tie which was straight and not halfway around his neck like most of our brethren. Whereas most schoolboys found it hard to keep tidy, he was the opposite. Dirt and Gordon had the same polarity and didn't cling to each other, and his shoes never seemed to be scuffed no matter what he did. It was really annoying.

Being officially in the Boy Scouts was our cover really. In our heads and unbeknown to the public at large we were Special Forces scouts and we could be exceedingly dangerous if messed with. We called ourselves Alpha One to sound extra heavy. It was a good name, and one we had decided on some time after we had started going around together. We'd been racking our brains for a while trying to come up with the right impact and then Gordon had suggested it one night on the way home after we left a scout troop meeting. Trevor was a quiet sort of individual, didn't normally push himself forward, so it was a surprise when in the ensuing conversation and exchange of ideas about conducting our covert operations he suddenly said, out of the blue, "What we need is a password like they do in films." This unexpected display of enthusiasm took us both off guard but not for long.

"Oh do we?" Gordon said, "and what's a password going to do for us, huh?"

"Well it'll be real won't it – like if I creep up on you and you just ask me friend or foe and I answer friend when I'm really a foe who's telling lies; well you might say OK and I could kill you before you realised I was fibbin' couldn't I? But if we had a password we could ask what it was and if you didn't give the right one then er, er – well, you know..." he said, trailing off at the end, not knowing how to give his idea the grand finish.

Gordon and I looked at him sort of nonplussed for a few seconds before saying to him, quite politely in the circumstances, "Trevor, you're a head case. What are you on about?"

Trevor looked hurt. "I was only saying," he said.

"But we know you, Trevor. We'd recognise you."

Determined to pursue his idea Trevor replied with a note of smugness, "What, even in the dark?"

"Yes Trevor, especially in the dark," Gordon replied, deciding to wind him up. "Your eyes glow in the dark and those glasses of yours magnify their gleam. We can always see you coming a mile off."

"Stuff you, Gordon!" Trevor said. "Just stuff you." Repeating it once again not knowing how to respond and still offended by our unsympathetic jibes.

"Don't let him get to you Trevor," I said sensing that things might get out of hand. Then to try and soothe his battered ego, "He's just trying to wind you up. Actually it's not a bad idea," and Gordon nodded in agreement.

"It might save us getting ambushed on patrol by a passing copper. If he tries to stop us and he doesn't know the password you can kick him in the shins and we'll run," he said snickering.

Trevor saw the funny side, beginning to relax and enjoy the discussion he had instigated which gave me an idea. I said, "Let me have a word with Gordon," jerking my head for him to step away from Trevor where we could plot out of his earshot.

With our backs conspiratorially turned I instructed Gordon to nod his head slowly and pretend we were talking then gave a quick look back at Trevor, now looking all forlorn as though he was standing outside the headmaster's study waiting for the cane.

Why were we being so cruel I asked myself? He wouldn't hurt a fly. We turned and walked back to him. "Trevor - congratulations," I said. "As of now, you have been appointed chief boffin for Alpha One Patrol."

He looked uncertain. Was this another insult? "What does that mean?" he said.

"Brains Trevor, it means brains," I said. "You've got the brains so you've been promoted to intelligence officer which means you come up with all the good ideas. Your first task will be to decide on challenge and response words."

You could see him grow another inch as he stood more upright with a grin on his face like a Cheshire cat. "How do you mean, challenges and responses?"

"It's simple Trevor - like saying good morning to me or Gordon as the challenge if we approached you. We would then have to respond by saying good afternoon."

"But that would be stupid," he said. "If it was morning and you said good afternoon."

Gordon and I looked at each other in exasperation and I covered my face with my hand. Our newly commissioned staff officer just wasn't getting it. Had we promoted the wrong man, I asked myself?

Gordon said, "Try and explain it to him Bernard. Make the silly sod understand."

How could I get through to him, I wondered? I struggled manfully on, trying to get a grip on Trevor's mind.

"Trevor," I said, "That was just supposed to be an example of how it works. The words don't necessarily have to be connected. They are just words. If I say a particular word as a challenge you have to say the agreed word, whatever it is, to respond. Like say we agreed that the word or words, or phrase…"

"Oh for heaven's sake don't confuse him anymore," interrupted Gordon, "we'll be here all day."

"Okay, okay," I said. "Trevor, challenge word – Yakidah – response word Marbles."

Gordon mumbled, "I'm rapidly beginning to lose mine with all this rubbish."

"What the heck is Yakidah?" asked Trevor.

"It's Welsh for Hiya," said Gordon.

I shook my head and then put my hand over my face in despair. Why had I started all this? Then I remembered I hadn't. Trevor had and I mentally reached out to throttle him. Words failed me.

"Actually," I said "it isn't Welsh for Hiya. It actually means good health and it's spelt differently to the way it sounds but I'm just not going to talk about it. Forget Yakidah. For pity's sake – let's think of something else."

After a few more minutes of fraught discussion we came up with two new challenge and response words to try: DAYLIGHT as the challenge word and MOONBEAM as the response. I thought they both sounded good and mercifully so did Gordon and Trevor.

Over the next few weeks we put the system to the test, each one of us in turn challenging and responding at every opportunity when we met up but the idea was doomed from the start. Trevor got carried away by the whole thing and challenged us in front of our other friends and acquaintances so we had to tell him in no uncertain terms that he was putting the country's security at risk.

We couldn't operate covertly, we said, if he gave our secrets and procedures away. It just became a nuisance and eventually we stopped doing it altogether.

The other thing we did was equip ourselves with what we thought was the latest Special Forces survival technology kit. A pocket knife (usually blunt), a piece of string, a pencil, an elastic band securing a box of matches (usually damp) and a packet of Spangles. If we couldn't get dynamic energy Spangles we settled for Jelly Babies or Nuttall's Mintoes. Well, we had to have some kind of food supplies to survive on. You just never knew how long a patrol was going to last around the dangerous lanes of Swansea.

We also each had one other piece of essential equipment: a torch that was powered by two batteries. Gordon, the rotten show-off, had to have one with three batteries of course and an adjustable lens that could change the beam width. We had competitions to see whose torch would cut the highest into the darkness and catch vapour trails from flying saucers in stealth mode. But they must have seen us scanning the skies and flew around us because we never ever saw even one.

We had started collecting torches the previous winter and were always on the lookout for something bigger. It seemed to be a period when manufactures were also interested in them because over a relatively short period of time we were able to upgrade to three and then four battery models with much bigger lenses that seemed to send their light beam for miles.

As well as the scout hut we sometimes used to have the odd meeting on the upper floor of a community hall in St Helen's Avenue. The ground floor had a number of small rooms , adjoining corridors and passageways which were only lit up in the day so we used to sneak down the stairs when Mostyn our scoutmaster wasn't looking and snoop around in the dark with our torches and practice creeping up on each other for a laugh. What you might call Special Forces stealth and evasion - training for if we were invading somewhere at night.

We were fearless. People were lucky not to stumble across us when we were on patrol in the lanes where we lived. We did some risky stuff and always had to make sure we weren't caught and identified. We managed to do a bunk just in time on a few occasions – of course, what I mean is we were able to skillfully conceal ourselves and melt into the night. I can remember one particular time when we were planning strategy for our next mission, sitting on the upper floor of a deserted looking garage we had found by chance and commandeered.

There were a lot of lanes with lots of garages in our area and this particular one turned up trumps. Under the cover of darkness we had snuck in around the back by climbing over a high wall. Our unit were good at climbing walls. We had to slide across some dodgy looking tiles while leaning against an adjoining sidewall and enter the upper floor through a small wooden door at the back which hadn't been secured. When we looked down to the ground floor we knew we had struck gold.

SCOUTS, SPIES, AND FLYING SAUCERS

There parked up and waiting was a gleaming black Mercedes saloon. Perfect - we had found the headquarters of the evil network we were investigating, with the getaway vehicle already in place. Since that day we had been using the loft as our own Special Forces headquarters. It was probably about three weeks later when we were there on a Saturday morning just lounging around, sitting on some old cardboard boxes, telling each other tall tales, when our reverie was dramatically shattered without warning.

There was a sudden commotion as the garage door down below started to slide open. The head honcho himself had arrived. He was on the run and was preparing to make his escape. He must have known that his cover had been blown but he didn't know by whom and that he was within a whisker of being captured.

Dilemma! What to do? Gordon, always quick with operational decisions, made a quick operational decision. Just like that.

"Leave him go," he said. "We got nowhere to put him."

Uh? I thought he was getting a bit carried away with things but then he said something really sensible, "Let's get out of yer quick!"

Even so, it was a bit of a cheek that, him giving the orders. When we first formed our unit it was me who was supposed to be the commander. Not Gordon. He could be real pushy sometimes. I'd have to discipline him about that I thought. Yeah!

Anyway, we did a tactical withdrawal, out through the side door, inching across roof tiles with our backs to the adjoining high wall, down over the wall, a drop of six feet, and we were away down the lane. We did make a bit of noise getting out. The bloke down below must have been terrified. I don't think he mistook us for pigeons either. Anyhow we managed to avoid revealing ourselves so we couldn't be identified later. Good spy-craft that. He was a lucky man. Come to think of it we never saw him either. Perhaps our spy craft was a bit one sided. Anyway, it was a typical skirmish for us and will give you, the reader, an idea of what we were about.

It is by no means the full story but the narrative which follows will reveal how and why our final mission alerted the authorities and put an end to Alpha One and its operations. This took place several weeks after the action described above which had almost turned to disaster. We lay low after our escape and didn't even turn up for scouts that week which really upset Mostyn. He was particularly annoyed at me because I had just got my tenderfoot badge to go with my other one for frying sausages on a campfire. Gave me a real ticking off he did and said my scout salute was getting sloppy as well. There was no pleasing him sometimes.

I remember getting that tenderfoot badge. It still haunts me. A special parade had been organised in front of parents at the church hall and halfway through it on a signal from Mostyn I was supposed to march up to the front with my patrol leader and salute him. He would then present me with my badge. I was dead nervous and Julian, my just as nervous patrol leader, wasn't much better. Suddenly, well before we thought it was due, Mostyn, dressed in full regalia with badges everywhere, droopy moustache and pointy hat, looked at Julian and gave some sort of macho scout leader twitch with his shoulders which we both thought was the signal to start coming forward. It was a complete cock up. We both arrived in front of Mostyn with everybody watching as he tried to make like a ventriloquist, hissing at us through clenched teeth, that he wasn't ready and to go back until he called us forward.

He'd never said anything about calling us forward before, only "on my signal." It was then that I made a personal vow. Totally demoralised and feeling like a pair of prize pratts we did an about turn and marched back to where we had started from, much to the puzzlement of the audience. When we did it for real about five minutes later it all went OK but the vow I had made remained. I would never again attend another church parade and I never did.

With memories of our escape from the spy's lair fast fading the three of us decided to organise our next fantasy mission after scouts had finished the following week. The troop meeting arrived and passed without incident, so we hung around until Mostyn had gone and then met up behind the hut. We always called it a hut, by tradition I suppose, but it was nothing of the sort really. All the scout huts or dens that I knew were usually on the upper levels of garages or old barns. I suppose calling them huts or dens made them sound more 'Scouty'.

It was at this fateful meeting that Gordon sprung a surprise on us. By now we had all got torches with four batteries, but he had done it again and got something better and he smugly sprung his surprise. He'd arrived before us and hidden it in a bush behind the boundary wall. With a big grin on his face he pulled out a six-inch search light. It had to be connected to a separate battery to operate, he told us, but it could also be connected to a Morse tapper. *WOW*!

He also bragged that he knew how to do Morse code which was pretty handy otherwise the thing would have been as much use as a chocolate saucepan. He had been practising a lot and was becoming rather good at it he said. A real dark horse sometimes, was Gordon. What were we supposed to do with that we asked? "Make contact," he said mysteriously.

"Yes Gordon," said Trevor, "but make contact with what - flying saucers again? They flew around our torch beams last time. What makes you think we can do it with a searchlight? How do you know they can read Morse code?"

"No! Blockhead!" Gordon replied, "Ships! Ships! Not flying flippin' saucers; ships."

This somehow seemed to upset Trevor who all of a sudden got rather tense and responded to the insult by telling him to go and boil his head. To his credit Gordon ignored him but it was a bad mistake. Trevor suddenly launched himself at Gordon who really should have seen it coming. For the next couple of minutes I watched and dodged them wrestling on the grass getting covered in mud while practising a mixture of coarse schoolboy swear words and insults until they ran out of steam and just lay there giggling oblivious to the inquisition that would no doubt later come from both of their parents over the state of their clothing. I could just imagine it. Trevor's mother would plead with him in exasperation; "I just washed those trousers yesterday and look at the state of them now."

"Sorry mam," he would say. "I sort of fell over and rolled down a grass bank at scouts when we were practising tying knots around a tree stump."

Gordon's father wouldn't be so passive however. His parents were Polish refugees who had come to Britain early on in the war and his father could be a hard taskmaster. I had only been to his house a couple of times and his mother, though welcoming with a ready smile, always seemed a bit edgy when his father was around. He had quite the opposite temperament and was a real misery, completely without humour. I never did get to find out exactly what his job was, only that he was some kind of engineer and vague comments about working with government factories and the armed forces. He would verbally attack Gordon with no patience at all.

"Gordon! - Gordon!" he would shout, in his deep, thickly accented voice. "Come here boy. Where have you been to get your clothes in such a mess? What do you think you are doing? I've told you before. Clothes cost money. I have to earn it to pay for them. Money doesn't grow on trees Gordon."

"Sorry Dad."

"Where does money not grow Gordon?"

"On trees dad, on trees."

And so it would go on for Gordon, poor dab. Fancy

having to put up with that all the time. Then I cheered up realizing that I had managed to avoid getting involved in one of their regular weekly wrestling matches and for once would be going home 'tidy'.

THE MISSION

Having got rid of their aggression, the discussion began again with Gordon telling us to forget about flying saucers. We are going to contact ships out in the bay, he said. That's the way they talk to each other, with searchlights, just like the Navy does. When we asked him where he had got the searchlight from, he explained that it been taken it off a breakdown truck his uncle used to own and was originally fitted on an American motor torpedo boat.

There was a surplus of marine equipment immediately after the war and his uncle had found it in a ship chandler's down by the docks. It was quite heavy and he'd had to lug it down to the hut in an old army kit bag. We pondered over this idea a few minutes wondering just how it would work. It really was an adventurous departure from what we had usually been doing. Up till then we had just been messing around in the lanes. Most of the Swansea that we were familiar with had terraced housing. Semi detached and detached houses were in the minority and wherever terraced houses didn't back onto a road directly they had lanes. There must have been hundreds if not thousands of lanes in Swansea. Miles of them, each with their characteristic alley ways and linking passages leading to other streets, derelict garages, dead ends, and hidden secrets to be uncovered. They were not put there for grubby schoolboys like us to play our games, though.

They served the valuable function of having somewhere to put household rubbish which could be collected every week by the ash men on the ash lorry. You would hear them on dustbin day early in the morning noisily going through the lanes banging the bins against the bodywork sides as they emptied the rubbish and ashes from the many coal fires then used for domestic heating. Following not so regularly a few days after them would come the rag and bone men with their horse and carts shouting out "Rag bone – rags for bargain, any old rags." They would usually take the detritus that the ash carts would refuse which could literally be anything from old boilers and cookers to bedsteads and old fireplaces. Some of the bone men could be a bit 'fly'. I remember dad getting stitched up by one on the value of an old boiler he took away.

"Don't 'ave enough cash on me now guv. Can I owe you?"

No chance with dad. "Where do you live?"

"Oxford Street. Back of Joes Café."

"The boy" - namely me - "will come with you," he said, "and you can pay him."

Gee thanks dad, I thought, but really I was quite pleased. A ride on a horse and cart sitting in the middle of all that rubbish. Fantastic! I was about eight at the time. What a tale to tell my mates. Anyway to cut a long story short I hadn't been paying full attention during negotiations and the bone man being a bit fly paid me short. There was no ride home. I had to walk but when dad found he had been diddled he took me back down there the next day, which was a Sunday morning, on the bus. It was a pity I couldn't remember the house. Put him in a foul mood and we returned home with him seething. I pitied the bone man the next time he came down our lane but there were a lot of other ones for him to visit and I certainly never saw him in ours again.

We had inspected quite a few lanes in our role as Alpha One but a new venture into marine activities could be a really interesting development as well as boosting our self importance. Swansea was a busy seaport with several large docks supporting a lot of commercial activity for ships of all sizes visiting from many parts of the world. They would sometimes anchor out in the bay waiting for the tide or a berth to discharge or take on goods. With such heavy traffic the shipping channels had to be kept clear so it was not unusual to see bucket dredgers and sand suckers in the bay keeping the water deep enough for the larger vessels. At night their masthead lights would often twinkle on the skyline announcing their nocturnal presence as they waited their turn on the incoming tide. I used to hear ships out in the bay early in the morning blowing their foghorns but had never really taken much notice of the night time seascape before. Gordon's idea excited me and I was beginning to get wild ideas of ship's captains queuing up to talk to us with their signal lamps. I also wondered at the same why they would bother. So I asked him, "What makes you think they'll take any notice of a flashing light from a beach?" "They're bound to," he said. "It won't just be a flashing light see, it'll be in Morse code and they'll be used to that."

"Fair point," said Trevor, who had by now settled down a bit and was becoming more interested, "but where are we going to do it from?"

After a few seconds Gordon suggested that we could go behind The Slip bridge off the Mumbles road. It was a good idea. It was the well known bridge landmark that straddled the main road to Mumbles, the Mumbles railway tram line and also a branch of the LMS railway that ran alongside the beach for a few miles before eventually turning off at Blackpill towards Mid Wales. I liked the Mumbles tram, or train, as we used to call it. Most people did. It was unique and made some glorious noises. When it was moving from a standing start the doors at each end would slap shut and then a loud 'mum-mum-mum-mumming' noise would begin as the traction motors wound up. A low throbbing groan would follow, increasing in intensity to a higher pitched moan and clatter of wheels passing over the tracks as it gathered pace.

When the wind was blowing in the right direction, it would carry its clatter-cla-clat and the whirr of the traction motors for miles. It also rocked very violently when it passed as crap yard at Blackpill which was about half way around the bay. Anybody sitting on the top deck had to hang on to the seat really tight or they would be flung off. I don't think anyone complained though. It was all part of the fun. I also remember an item resembling a cotton bobbin which was threaded on thick string suspended over the stairwell and drivers cab. I never did find out what that was for but it always got my attention.

We discussed the various merits of Gordon's suggested location and agreed it was ideal, having on both sides of the rails a long stone wall that would give us cover from prying eyes.

"We're going to have to call ourselves something," said Trevor, now really getting with the plot. "We can't just say we are boy scouts muckin' about can we?"

"What about sea scouts?" I said. "We can't say that either," Trevor commented. "They'll be able to check won't they?"

"What if we say it's a cadet marine patrol? That sounds good dunnit," said Gordon. We kicked around some other ideas for a few minutes eventually settling on Cadet Marine Patrol. Not that we really expected any ships to respond but at least we could try to look genuine.

"Don't forget," Trevor said dramatically, "we're going to need a call sign otherwise we'll still look like a load of idiots."

"Yeah, good thinking," Gordon and I said together. Then I added. "Sometimes your intelligence really shines through Trevor," being sarcastic actually but he took it as a compliment and his whole face lit up. He could be really sensitive sometimes. We settled on a call sign of Cadet Marine Patrol Group 1. The Group 1 we thought made it sound more authentic and we provisionally decided to initiate contact with shipping in Swansea bay after the next meeting at our own Phoenix Scout Troop HQ.

FOOTPRINTS TO NOWHERE

We couldn't do it that week because we had been invited by one of Gordon's friends to go and help them paint their den at Rainbow Troop which was twice the size of ours and had to be entered from the ground floor through a trap door at the top of a ladder. The three of us were naturally keen to help and turned up as scheduled but unfortunately their scoutmaster didn't.

There was us three from our troop and four from Rainbow. So really we should have done the job easy. Unfortunately with the absence of their esteemed leader things didn't go according to plan. It soon became evident that there was a grudge between two of them and it wasn't long before insults started flying. When the paint started flying along with them, Trevor, Gordon and I decided to leave before we became splatter victims as well.

The events which followed our departure from Rainbow troop that night gave birth to the first psychedelic scout hut in the British Commonwealth, surpassed legend and went into scouting folklore soon afterwards. When the three of us got to our HQ the next week it was evident that we were not the flavour of the month. In fact Mostyn was livid. Some lying toad had informed him that it was Phoenix Troop, namely us, who had caused all the damage. Gordon was more than indignant at the accusation and with both Trevor's input and mine into the enquiry, soon put him right on what had occurred and at what time precisely we had left the scene.

Having calmed down a bit, Mostyn, while trying not to laugh, informed us that there were now two sets of footprints, one in yellow and one in red, leading from Rainbow Troop HQ running halfway down the lane and a good way along the centre of the main road before fading away. The local plods were not best pleased either, citing defacement of public property and so on. A serious offence! He also told us that one of their four painting crew was a patrol leader and had tried to stop the others messing around. They had responded by tipping a whole can of paint over him so thoroughly that he had needed to have his head rinsed with turpentine to remove all the gloss paint. Unfortunately an unintended consequence was that it also removed most of his hair and would leave him bald for almost a month.

If I said we sniggered it would be untrue. We actually fell about laughing much to Mostyn's disgust and completely disrupted the proceedings for the night. There were serious repercussions which fortunately, he said, did not involve us. The actual words he used were that there had been an unholy row all the way down from scout headquarters.

Two of the troop were stripped of their woggles and expelled while the third was suspended for a month and given the ultimate humiliation of being demoted to cub status until he passed his tenderfoot badge again. At the end of the meeting that night when our gallant leader gave us the order to fall out we nearly fell over with relief. Funny order really - fall out - when you think about it. Just as well that we had escaped any blame that night. There was other trouble coming our way and very soon. We decided we would have to postpone our trip to The Slip for another week because only Gordon had seen the lamp working and Trevor and I both wanted to check it out and have a go at doing some Morse code for ourselves - just in case of emergency we told Gordon.

Hiding it in the hut could have caused problems if somebody was nosing around and found it, so Gordon said as long as it was OK with Trevor it made more sense to take the equipment around to his house, test it in his back lane and leave it in his garage. Trevor's garage would make a better place to store it anyway, being nearer to the Slip where we were going to signal from, and save having to lug it all the way from Gordon's uncle's house. So we carried it around, connected it all up and switched on. It was brilliant. A terrific bright light you could see for miles and the beam seemed to go on forever.

We were all chuffed to bits but didn't want to draw attention from nosey neighbours so we took it into the garage where Gordon connected the Morse-tapper to give us a demonstration and then let us have a go. If Trevor's mother or father wondered what was going on they at least didn't ask any awkward questions. They were both pretty easy going and used to schoolboy antics with both of them being teachers; his father in a boys grammar and his mother in a local junior school. So, after some practice, the following week after scouts was designated Operation Bay-Night.

That was the plan but it changed on Saturday

evening when Gordon called at the house unexpectedly just after we had finished tea. There was a little problem he said and he wanted to move the operation up to Monday night instead. Two days earlier than planned. When I asked him why he said that his uncle had not actually given him his permission to borrow the lamp and although there was no big row about it going missing he wanted it back by mid week, the following Wednesday, so not wanting to miss out after all our planning Gordon decided to re-arrange things for Monday night instead. Something he called a contingency startegy.

It was OK by me. Sounded just like the real thing, I thought: just like a real commando Special Forces urgent mission. Alpha One would be ready. It was exciting. I asked why he hadn't tried to negotiate a couple more days but he said it wasn't worth the chance that it might be demanded back right away. He'd never fallen out with his uncle before and he didn't want to start now. I agreed he'd made the right decision and it only remained for us to let Trevor know.

We both just hoped that he would be able to come. It was still early in the evening but Gordon had to get back home so he set off and I walked around to Trevor's house and told him the situation. Fortunately he was also able to change his plans accordingly but he did mention that it was lucky I had come to see him then because he wouldn't have been in the next day, Sunday after lunch, because it was his gran's birthday and she was having a family party.

ON THE BEACH

The next two days dragged. I couldn't wait for Monday night but it eventually arrived and we met up at Trevor's by the back lane entrance to his garage. He was like a dog with two tails, obviously bursting to tell us something because he had a big grin on his face. Not like the Trevor we knew at all. It turned out that when they had gone around to his gran's birthday party the day before there had been a general family gathering. He'd designed and made a birthday card for her himself as a surprise and by return she had given him ten quid to open his first bank account with.

We tried to con him into spending some of it on buying cakes for us but he said he'd promised not to waste it so we pulled his leg for a bit, told him he was being mean and reluctantly let him off the hook. Then it was down to business. We got the searchlight and other bits and pieces together, and connected it all up to test before leaving. Everything OK we made our way to The Slip taking turns carrying the lamp and the battery which was also fairly heavy and not easy to manage.

We had of course prearranged the night in a rush without getting a weather forecast and it didn't look too promising; miserable, dark and cloudy with no moonlight and the sort of on and off light drizzle that gets everywhere and thoroughly soaks you. We were not deterred however. We were Alpha One and we made our way to our theatre of operation without incident. Fortunately the heavily built steps and adjoining wall afforded some shelter or we might have decided to abandon the mission. Gordon connected up the battery, Morse tapper and the search light and we were ready to start. Snag number one. How do you start to do that kind of thing? What do you say to an unknown ship out in the bay when you don't know who they are? We had also forgotten one other really essential thing before we set up the equipment.

We hadn't checked to see if there actually were any ships out there. Duh! But we were in luck. There were about five of them, all showing a variation of lights. Some bright, some dim, either arranged in small clusters or singly but with no indication as to what they were; certainly not that we could understand anyway. Tanker, tug, fishing boat, navy? When I asked "How do we start?" I got some dirty looks.

We hadn't planned that far ahead so we had to think about it. "Do we just say Ahoy There?" said Trevor. We had forgotten all about the Cadet Marine Patrol signal we had arranged previously. Then he started to giggle and said, "Why don't we signal Hello Sailor and see what happens?" and I started to laugh until Gordon broke in, getting serious, telling us we should keep quiet or we would attract attention from the other side of the wall.

Gordon then had a real brainwave and said, "Let's signal Alpha One Calling Bay Shipping. It sounds official and important and they'll think they have to reply with a call sign like that."

It was a good idea alright. As it happened it was too authentic-sounding - if only we had realised. Perhaps thinking the same, Gordon changed his mind and said we should stick to Cadet Marine Patrol which would be more familiar, possibly confusable with existing cadet troops, and could add to our cover.

That matter resolved Gordon started flashing the Morse tapper:

```
C-A-D-E-T M-A-R-I-N-E P-A-T-R-O-L O-N-E
C-A-L-L-I-N-G B-A-Y S-H-I-P-P-I-N-G
C-A-D-E-T M-A-R-I-N-E P-A-T-R-O-L O-N-E
C-A-L-L-I-N-G B-A-Y S-H-I-P-P-I-N-G
```

The brightness of the searchlight beam cut through the darkness quite dramatically and was very visible. Far too visible. Nothing returned from the sea though.

We tried again, with no other returning beams of light to fill the blackness and then realised that we hadn't really given a reason for any shipping to respond. We had to make it easier for them to think they had to reply. So unable to think of anything else we tagged PLEASE IDENTIFY VESSEL on to the end and tried again for another five minutes or so.

We were beginning to think that we were wasting our time when suddenly we caught a flash from a ship displaying three lights that seemed to be standing at anchor not far from the dock entrance. A second flash of light and we realised that they were actually responding.

Gordon read the reply: I-D-E-N-T-I-F-Y O-F-F-I-C-E

"What's that supposed to mean?" Trevor asked. Gordon showing just how in touch he was replied, "I think he is asking on whose authority we are trying to contact shipping."

That stumped us for a few seconds and then Trevor

said "Why don't we do what Gordon suggested and use ALPHA ONE and see what happens? It sounds sort of official like dunnit'?"

After I commented that they wouldn't have a clue what it stood for we mulled over it some more, deciding that we had nothing to lose by trying, so that was what Gordon Morsed back to them: A-L-P-H-A O-N-E

We waited and watched. Nothing. Then, as we watched some more, the ship began moving from its anchorage and we thought it was the end of our contact, but then quite unexpectedly and almost catching us off guard came another burst of flashes: D-R-E-D-G-E-R D-O-C-K-I-N-G

Gordon read out aloud as they cut through the night. Much to our surprise ALPHA ONE and CADET MARINE PATROL had done the trick. We had actually succeeded in communicating with a real ship. Talk about being chuffed. Well Trevor and I were but Gordon seemed a bit disappointed and didn't look as pleased as we thought he'd be at our contact. I mean if it hadn't been for him we wouldn't have done anything like this at all.

FLIGHT

Way out in the bay, just visible through the rain from a position which had not been showing any lights before, there was a quick burst of flashes. It was so quick that it caught us completely off guard. It certainly caught Gordon because they signalled so fast that he couldn't read the message. Well at least somebody else has seen us, I said almost in unison with Trevor who had the same thought. Unknown to us at that time so had some other people, on land, and metaphoric alarm bells were going off in officialdom in a number of places with telephone calls pulling high ranking people out of their beds, homes and offices to convene urgent meetings.

We were beginning to get wet. We hadn't really prepared for the weather and none of us were wearing proper rain proof clothing. I did have my old school mac but Gordon and Trevor just wore their usual everyday knockabout jerkins. For once when he should have been wearing his mac Trevor had left it at home and the damp was beginning to penetrate, chilling the three of us.

But now a second contact had been made so CADET MARINE PATROL carried on oblivious. Gordon wasted no time at all in responding to the mystery ship and again

Morsed out: C-A-D-E-T M-A-R-I-N-E P-A-T-R-O-L. P-L-E-A-S-E R-E-P-E-A-T being tagged on at the end.

"They might not respond though, not a second time," he said anxiously." If we missed their first attempt at contact they may think we are just messing around."

Quite honestly I think it was a surprise to both me and Trevor that he could not only read the flashes but that he was so quick. We were both really impressed and told him so. He had gone up in our estimation. Half a minute passed which seemed like a week and then at a slightly slower rate came a reply; the same query we had from the dredger. We'd certainly cracked the communication procedure. It said:

I-D-E-N-T-I-F-Y O-F-F-I-C-E

Straight away, a little more excited than previously, Gordon said, "We'll use the same as before - ALPHA ONE. Either the ship out there accepts it or it doesn't."

If it didn't I guessed he meant we were off home. We'd had enough by then. We all had. I was beginning to shiver with the others not faring much better and getting wetter than I was. Just as a Mumbles train groaned and clattered its way out from the stop on the other side of the wall Gordon tapped out our reply reading it to us as he did so: A-L-P-H-A O-N-E.

He beamed it back across the water from our vantage point with the addition of a question:

W-H-A-T K-I-N-D O-F V-E-S-S-E-L

Trevor could be quite witty at times and he immediately said. If he replies EMPTY tell him to get stuffed, and we all laughed nervously. Somewhere in the distance we could hear a noise we couldn't quite identify. We should have paid more attention. We waited for a while but there was no response from out in the bay so Gordon tried again but this time just asked:

A-R-E Y-O-U T-A-N-K-E-R

Another long minute passed and then from out at sea flashes of light Morsed out:

N-E-G-A-T-I-V-E

Gordon deciphered and Trevor commented, "I think they're just messing us about."

Gordon and I both shook our heads, and then Gordon added, "Just abiding by marine protocol." Then again out from the darkness came another signal:

S-U-B-M-A-R-I-N-E

Looking ever so slightly pleased with himself Gordon relayed the information to us and we sort of crouched there cold, wet and getting hungry wondering if he was being funny. Can't be a submarine we thought. If the Navy were going to visit Swansea they would have announced it in the Evening Post and probably moored up in the King's dock. No need for them to park out in the bay. We discussed asking them to repeat the message but Gordon said if we did they would probably tell us to get stuffed.

Too risky." If it really is a sub why don't we ask them where their home port or base is?" he suggested. So that's what he Morsed out on the tapper. Again there was a waiting period. A bit longer this time as though they were considering whether they could give us an answer. At this point the noise which we had heard earlier on started ringing a bit louder and we were almost on the point of identifying it when the night carried what was to be their last communication.

Gordon read out the distant reply which left us in complete bewilderment. It was:

L-E-N-I-N-G-R-A-D.

I looked at Trevor, he looked at me and we both looked at Gordon and the three of us uttered the same thought all at once. What are all those bells ringing for and where are they coming from? This was 1957, Cold War time before the now universal mee-maw, mee-maw wailing fire engine, ambulance and police sirens. Then they just had a high pitched repeating dingaling bell.

They were getting closer and suddenly the penny dropped. The bells were tolling for us. It was the POLICE. There we were signalling a submarine out in the bay in the dark and they were signalling back. But it wasn't an officially recorded visit by a *British* submarine. It was a foreign one that had somehow got right into the bay breaching all defences against such incursions. It was an *unofficial* submarine from Leningrad and Leningrad was in that part of the world known as communist Russia. WE WERE SPIES!

Gordon and Trevor had both used a lot of schoolboy swear words and curses some days ago when we were planning the mission but just then they used some real adult ones at the same time as we all had another telepathic same thought. For pity sake - RUN LIKE HELL.

A quick flurry in the sand, disconnecting everything as fast as blind panic would allow; Gordon thrust the Morse tapper into Trevor's hands while grabbing the lamp and stuffing it into the rucksack. I picked up the battery and the three of us scarpered as quickly as we could; but not the way we had come.

Not the way we had come though. "Which way?"

Trevor yelled, panic stricken.

"Follow me." I said, "There's a gap in the wall further up." I was remembering my bait digging days with Royston nearly two years previously and thinking of the tunnel under the railway. It was a fair way to run but it was our only chance. If we tried running back across the bridge or through the railway gates at the side we would be seen.

It wasn't easy going on the sand either. We were well away from the water's edge but it was still dragging underfoot especially with the drizzle to dampen it. I just hoped that the searchers would concentrate on looking in the area where we had been and not in the direction we were heading. I stumbled a couple of times; the battery was heavy. Trevor and Gordon were sharing the weight of the lamp holding the rucksack between them. We were too slow, Gordon complained. I told him the weight of the battery wasn't helping and to my surprise and relief he just said breathlessly, "Ditch it. It doesn't matter if they find it. My father will kill me if we get caught and he finds out what we've been doing."

I'd met his father a couple of times. Not a nice person; he was probably right. I threw the battery next to the railway wall and gave them both a hand with the lamp which helped speed things up considerably. The battery was a drag. We didn't bother to look back until we reached the tunnel and when we did we saw some dim figures in the distance with torch beams scanning the beach. We wondered how good they were, and if they pointed them in our direction would they pick us out. We were definitely not going to hang about and see.

We eased our way through to the other side and

checked the main road both ways before crossing to the other side. There were parked headlights in the distance by The Slip and shadowy figures moving around but nothing coming our way. Mercifully the police's efforts to catch foreign agents were concentrated on the beach but we were long gone. It looked like Alpha One might be in the clear but we still had to melt into the night and get through the myriad streets and lanes. As we dodged through them not far from Swansea prison Trevor asked, "Where the heck is Leningrad anyway?"

Geography was not one of his good subjects. When we told him it was in Russia, you know that place that has all the rockets pointing at us, we both saw the light in his eyes go out from behind his glasses. He had taken it all as an adventure and a bit of a laugh up until then. The three of us had. But now we realised the whole thing had become deadly serious and it was turning sour. If we thought that melting into the night would be easy we were wrong. When something melts it usually begins to run and we couldn't because the lamp was too heavy - so we had to take it in turns to hold the rucksack two at a time with one in front covering to spoil the view of anyone looking to see what we were carrying. We were still even then in our fantasy world thinking stealth; an active service unit escaping from the enemy.

The authorities would be looking for a team of saboteurs perhaps. How far would their dragnet extend? In reality we were three silly schoolboys wandering around in streets where we didn't belong. It only took one young bluebottle wandering around those same streets to stop and ask us what we were doing and we'd be finished. We convinced ourselves we would go to jail. Perhaps we would meet Royston's dad and he'd take care of us. I knew all about young bluebottles; two of them had crossed my path before. We had to get away from the area as fast as possible. If we were caught, the lamp would be a dead giveaway. We would be in real trouble. I had a brainwave. Why didn't I think of it before? "How much money have we got between us?" I asked.

"Why? What are you on about?" Gordon said.

"We're not far from Oxford Street. I know these streets. We can catch a bus."

"Yeah,' Trevor said with relief in his voice, "I'm flippin' fed up with carrying this thing. Let's get a bus."

"Flippin' good idea," added Gordon.

We checked our pockets for bus fare. I had some money and Gordon had some, Trevor had none. Gordon had sufficient for Trevor as well but he didn't tell him that. I looked at Gordon and grinned; Gordon read my mind. We pulled Trevor's leg: It was just begging to be pulled. At the time Gordon was sharing the rucksack with Trevor and he suddenly let go leaving him to carry all the weigh by himself.

"Sorry Trevor," he said, "We're going to have to leave you behind. Me and Bernard are getting the bus," and we both made as though we were going to start running for one. You should have seen his face.

"Nah we can't leave him," I said laughing. "If they catch him with the lamp they might shoot him as a spy."

Trevor suddenly looked real worried so with me taking hold of the strap that Gordon had let go of we both grabbed him and started running pulling him along with us. "Come on Trevor – run you pratt. We're not leaving our intelligence officer behind." So he ran with us to catch the bus uttering some very un-schoolboy words as he did so.

"Tsk, Tsk, Trevor, baaad lugwidge. What would mummy say?"

We slowed down before getting to the bus stop because there was no point running when there wasn't one waiting so we worked out some strategy. The lamp and rucksack was OK for one of us to carry for a couple of minutes so I volunteered do that when the bus arrived and nonchalantly get on first to park it in under the stairwell with the other two following on behind me.

We would then sit as close to the stairs as possible to make sure nobody got nosey. Gordon would stay on the bus and get off at Tycoch which would give him an easier walk home. He wasn't too concerned now about getting the lamp back to his uncle and would handle any aggro over it when it was returned he said. There was obviously no point in him lugging it back home just to bring it back to scouts on Thursday so we agreed to leave it at Trevor's for the time being. We were in luck. The bus that arrived five minutes later was going to Tycoch so we got on as planned. It was past nine o'clock by now and there were only a few people sitting up the front so nobody took any notice when we got on.

It was lucky it was a seventy five. We hadn't really discussed what we would do if it was a seventy six and carried on past St Helens cricket ground to the terminus. Perhaps Gordon could have waited for a Tycoch bus while we carried on and went to Trevor's house. Anyway we were all really tired by that time and almost too far gone to care. On the journey we again reviewed our situation and decided to skip scouts for that week and meet up again the following Thursday instead to give us some breathing space. Gordon might, he said, pop down Friday or Saturday just to see us and find out if we had heard anything that might be to our immediate disadvantage.

So we left it at that, sitting in virtual silence till St Helen's where we said goodbye to him, picked up the rucksack from the stair well, also by now carrying the Morse tapper inside, and got off the bus, mightily relieved to be near to our respective homes. We made our way to Trevor's house sharing the load between us, going in via the lane entrance again and dumped the ship to shore equipment under a bench in his garage for safe keeping. Our escape and evasion completed he went into the house through his back door and I sloped off home. No more missions till things had cooled down.

Tuesday passed through the morning and afternoon in its usual way but Tuesday evening didn't. The South Wales Evening Post carried banner headlines: MYSTERY OF POLICE ACTIVITY ON THE ROAD TO MUMBLES!

There were no actual details given, only the usual police speak about secrets only known to them sort of stuff with additional comments about vehicle deployment etc. Some other low key reporting followed in the next few days. Well it was low key to start with: STRANGE LIGHTS OBSERVED AROUND SWANSEA BAY, and if anybody had seen a group of men, etc. We had a bit of a giggle over that but then the Evening Post started to get serious and mentioned the word espionage, saying things like special branch officers were investigating and conferring with a top naval commander. Even my father started paying attention. He was sitting in front of the dining room fire one night and I was kneeling on the floor messing around with my Meccano set, bits spread everywhere, when he mentioned it to my mother. He had been driving back from Mumbles in the office car and noticed a number of police vehicles hanging around doing their best to make themselves inconspicuous in unusual places. I nearly froze but managed to keep my eyes down and kept fiddling with something pretending I hadn't heard him. The next time I saw Trevor a few days later he'd obviously been worrying about it and came up with another thought. A good one actually. What if it wasn't really a submarine and just some idiot in a parked up fishing boat or tug, larking about?

Then he said something very profound but probably true. He said, with a heavy sigh, "If they catch us we're dog meat." Made me feel really good that did. If it was some clever clogs joker we just hoped he had seen the newspapers and realised the mess he'd got us into. We were confused and scared. If Mostyn found out I could see me kissing goodbye to both my tenderfoot and cooking badges; probably standing in front of the whole troop while he personally ripped them of my shirt. I wasn't too worried about the tenderfoot badge, but I was proud of the one I had for frying sausages. I kept telling my mother that I could cook but she only laughed. What if our parents found out? I could probably talk my mother around but I knew dad would have me convicted and sentenced without trial and I'd probably end up staying in for a month practicing my handwriting or something equally stupid. For heaven's sake! Why do the police always make a big deal out of nothing? It was only us having a laugh.

THE DREAM

Gordon didn't come and see us on the Friday or Saturday. We didn't hear anything from him at all. I saw Trevor at scouts on Thursday of the following week but Gordon never showed up there either which wasn't like him. He was one of the keenest even though he lived farther away from the scout hut than we did with over a mile to walk or ride.

Trevor knew where his house was so he volunteered to go and see where he had got to.

I didn't see him then till the following Monday and when we met up he was obviously puzzled. "Well," he said, "I got to his house just after tea time when he's always there. But he wasn't and neither was his mum or dad. It was queer. I rang the bell but the house sounded sort of hollow, so I looked through the front window and there was nothing there. No furniture, no curtains, no carpets, no nuthin'."

My jaw dropped. "Huh? That's weird," I said.

"Yeah, I know. I saw some of the neighbours and asked them if they knew where they had gone to and one of them said he saw a large black furniture lorry pulling away as he was getting home late on Tuesday or maybe Wednesday night the week before last. He said he knew it was one of those two nights because he usually went to see a film then with his wife." Trevor shook his head in puzzlement concluding his statement with,

"S'real funny. Nobody knew anythin'."

We both realised as he said it that it was the same week we had run from the beach and sort of looked at one another and didn't really know what to think. "If Gordon was going to move house," I said, "he would have told us for heaven's sake. Why didn't he say anything?"

"Perhaps his mum and dad wanted to surprise him," Trevor said lamely. "My father told me there are a lot of council houses up there and they probably hadn't paid the rent and done a bunk." He paused seeming to consider something else and then blurted out, "Do you think the Russians have got him?" That threw me, but I told him not to be so daft.

"Why do you think the Russians have got him, Trevor? Why would they want him anyway? How would they know it was him from all that way out in the bay? It was dark, Trevor, and it was raining."

He thought for a moment and then replied rather morosely, "They could have seen him. They got good binoculars on those Russian submarines." he said fiercely.

I was getting exasperated now but I could see that he really believed Gordon had been taken. Even my sister would have felt sorry for him. His imagination was really running riot and he was beginning to panic. I had to try and get him out of it before he blew a mental fuse.

"Trevor!" I snapped at him, "You are winding yourself up, and you're beginning to wind me up as well. Knock it off."

But he still wasn't convinced. I could see the fear in his eyes, magnified about ten times through those goldfish glasses of his. Dammit! I was to learn later that night that sometimes events can affect you more than you think. Trevor's panic had spooked me more than I realised because I began to relive our beach adventure in the wee small hours of the next morning.

We were once again signalling with our searchlight, only closer to the water's edge, when we became aware of a black shape looming towards us from the sea. Four black shadows parted from the black shape and ran up the beach in our direction. The three of us turned to run but Gordon hesitated as he tried to pick up the lamp. Before he could join us in our flight they snatched him, and while he protested loudly that he hadn't done his homework they dragged him back to the black dinghy. As they roughly threw him aboard the scene changed.

I was alone but no longer running up the beach. Instead I was sitting in a front seat on the top deck of the Mumbles train watching the wooden bobbin thing going up and down on its string. We were approaching the Blackpill scrap yard and began the usual rocking and rolling. The motion became even more violent and as I held grimly on to my seat the train gave a sudden violent lurch, jumped off the rails and slewing diagonally crashed through the scrap yard fence, ploughing through the transport detritus on the other side. There was the deafening noise of impact and suddenly the sound of shouting and a bright light came on. The bright light turned out to be the house lights; I woke up. I had been dreaming.

As I came to my senses and reality dawned I got out of my bed, much relieved that I had not been involved in any train crash and also that Gordon was probably still tucked up fast asleep in his own bed and had not been snatched and thrown into a dinghy by four silent men clad in black rubber. I looked at my bedside clock. What was all the noise about at two o'clock in the morning?

Emerging from my bedroom to meet my bleary eyed sister coming out of her's across the stairwell she asked me the same question. What's happened and why is everybody getting up?

The shouting was my father excitedly telling my mother, "It looks like a bad one this time." He had quickly put on some trousers and jumper over his pyjamas and was hurrying down the stairs towards the front door in his slippers. Mum was coming out of their bedroom fastening her dressing gown also on her way down the stairs but didn't follow him through the front door; she turned towards the kitchen. There had been a traffic accident at the crossroads just up the street from our house. This was not unusual. There was a halt sign at the junction giving precedence to traffic coming down Bernard Street hill where it crossed ours at the bottom but there were still numerous collisions when, for whatever reason, it was ignored.

"Go back to bed," my father had instructed us. "There's nothing for you to see." Sorry dad. There was always something to see when cars collided at the halt sign. We carried on into our parents' bedroom at the front of the house to take a look. Sure enough there was quite a crowd gathering around the two vehicles. A car and a van. We couldn't see much in the dark from where we were but it looked like the car, which had been coming down the hill, had been violently kissed and knocked broadside by the van and it had been quite an impact. It had been deflected into a lamp post standing on the corner of the pavement, uprooting it and knocking it over, demolishing a garden wall in the process. The top of the lamp post now lay through the ground floor front bay window of the corner house, broken glass spewing over the furniture inside the room while torn curtains lay on display hanging out of the smashed window frame. Among those on the scene were two off duty police officers who lived in the street, one of them a couple of doors up from our house and the other a few doors down. Emergency services would be a while yet it seemed and they were busily administering first aid to the victims.

The other onlookers were the newly awakened and still rather disorientated corner house owners and several of our close neighbours. Dad, realizing that his presence was superfluous, was striding purposefully back to the house having spotted us in the bedroom window. Fortunately he seemed to appreciate that this was an unusual event so he wasn't too testy when he had eventually locked the front door and climbed the stairs back to the front bedroom where we were still watching.

Mum, as ever practical, had used the time to make us all a cup of tea. What else do you do in a crisis? Dad reluctantly gave us an overview of what he had been able to find out before finally, "Packing both you kids off back to bed. Don't forget," he said, "you've both still got school in the morning." As if we didn't know.

Apparently the driver of the van was still trapped by the steering column and also concussed, having been struck on the back of the head by a very large spanner which had been lying unsecured on the floor at the rear. He was the only occupant of the van but there were four people in the car, one of whom seemed to have a broken arm. We would know more later on that day dad said. So we all went in back to bed and as I lay there trying to sleep I pondered on the nature of dreams. I wondered how it was that the abstract sound of impact of Mumbles train meets scrap-yard fence had at the same time collided and conspired with the real time impact of two vehicles outside our house to wake me from my slumbers.

I awoke reluctantly again that morning to dad's prompting. It was very hard to get out of bed and it was a Friday. I was like a wet lettuce; completely devoid of energy and very hard pressed to respond to his repeated calls to remind me that it was gone half past seven and that I would be late for breakfast and school; remembering over my fried bread, bacon and egg that the morning period was fortunately divided between art and metalwork. Would I survive? The wreckage of the car crash was still in evidence as I left to catch the bus. The van had been towed away and so had the car but workmen had only just started to remove the lamp post from the corner house. There was still quite a mess to clear up with loose bricks and other debris from the damaged garden wall and two fresh on-duty police constables were busy at the roadside with measuring tapes.

In my lateness setting off I almost physically bumped into Charlie the postman as he opened our front door to put the mail on the hall table. That was the sort of thing that happened in our street. I don't know if was standard postal delivery practice but we never gave it a second's thought and accepted it for what it was. On a Saturday morning when I was lazily lying in bed I would hear the door open, Charlie's baritone voice would drift up the stairs saying, "Oh thank you," and then the sound of the door closing. Sometimes Constance and I might spot him off duty in town with his wife and make a big thing about seeing him out of uniform shouting out, "Oh look here comes Charlie," much to his acute embarrassment and Mrs Charlie's great amusement.

Anyway, events conspired that morning and unfortunately I was still five minutes late for morning assembly because I missed the bus and had to get the next one fifteen minutes later. My form master was not very interested when I tried to explain about the accident either. He could be a right misery guts sometimes. I'm sure he would have given me detention but as luck would have it there was an extra sports period on that Friday afternoon which meant a bus ride to the playing fields at the top of Town Hill.

Surprisingly managing to endure both morning classes, without falling asleep in art or doing myself an injury in metalwork, the excitement of the 2AM awakening was beginning to take its toll and I was looking forward to a restful bus ride from Mount Pleasant to the sports field. Making myself invisible when we arrived I made sure I didn't get picked for any team events and when the coast was clear managed to skive off for the afternoon until it was time to go home. They had cleared up the mess and boarded up the corner house window by the time I climbed the three steps to the front of our house. The van driver was still in hospital while the occupants of the car had been released after treatment. I supposed that if he ever came down our street again he might be a bit more observant when it came to the halt sign. But that was the least of my worries. My thoughts again turned to the potential problem of the police looking for Trevor and me. Heaven only knew what would happen if our parents found out.

I needed to see Trevor to find out if he knew anything more so next morning being a Saturday I decided to cycle around to his house. His mother answered the door and pointed me up to his bedroom where I found him in the middle of putting a Keilcraft model aeroplane together. His dad was also interested in aircraft and was himself a keen builder so Trevor was well set up with a large board on which he had some wing plans spread and bits of balsa wood held in place with roundhead modelling pins. He was relieved to see me but worried in case I had some bad news. I reassured him that nothing further had happened but he was still strung up and said his parents were beginning to notice. When they'd asked him what was wrong he told them he was just worried about Gordon's strange disappearing act and they just repeated what his dad had said earlier, about families falling behind on the rent and doing a bunk. I was inclined to agree with them, I told him.

I brought up the subject of Gordon's uncle. It had been lurking in the back of my mind for a couple of days that we should go and see him to ask if he knew anything. They must have at least contacted him to leave a forwarding address. We could also mention that we had his lamp if we had the opportunity and see what he said. As we discussed the idea something slowly dawned on both of us. I thought that Trevor knew where his uncle lived and he thought that I knew. The fact was that neither of us had been to his house with Gordon so we didn't know. We thought we at least knew what street he lived in but again when we swapped information we were still clueless. So that put the kibosh on that strategy. The truth was that were both desperately anxious about our imagined ultimate fate. Apprehension was probably not a word either of us would have been able to spell at that moment to define our mood but it was certainly an apt description amongst all the other confused emotions we were going through and we decided there and then that we would disband ALPHA ONE and cease operations immediately. Both of us though at different times in the next two weeks sort of casually cruised around the area on our bikes to check on what was happening and noticed that there were still more police about than normal with an occasional Wolseley patrol car thrown in for good measure.

The heavy presence went on for another month or so and all sorts of rumours were being conjured up about why they had suddenly got more active along the road leading to Mumbles. All along the five miles of Swansea Bay in fact; from the Mumble to the tram terminus at Rutland Street and the funny thing was they weren't stopping people for speeding. So what was going on? It was just me and Trevor now with Gordon gone and we were having nightmares about going to prison. But what had we really done? Why all this attention just because we flashed a light at some ships in the bay?

Then a new day dawned. Mercy and deliverance! Like somebody had thrown a light switch. It all went quiet. The police had lost interest and went back to booking speeding motorists and no more was ever mentioned in the press or anywhere else about it. Events, like time, moved on. Trevor and I also lost interest and put away our torches. We never found out if Gordon put away his because he had just disappeared and no one that we knew ever heard from him again. In time I suppose we both forgot about it and just put the whole thing down to one of those crazy things you do when you're a kid. Time passed; we carried on with other friendships as well as knocking around together, but not long after the event we left scouts after losing our enthusiasm. With the loss of Gordon it just wasn't the same. We really were a close knit team and we did miss him, eventually losing regular contact with each other as well because of the natural progression of things. Sad really, I never even bothered to chase Trevor up or even came across him casually anywhere in town.

I did hear that he had moved, but to where I knew not. I tried to knuckle down a bit for school; it was fast approaching exam time, although the extra effort didn't do me any good anyway. Just one subject didn't qualify for a professorship, even though it was for physics. I was no academic. A natural inclination to mechanical things meant that that was what I wanted to be; a mechanic. Not just your usual everyday garage motor mechanic. I was going to be a digger mechanic.

Dad and I put our heads together and compiled a list of possible companies for him to send begging letters to in time for their next engineering apprentice intake. He was hoping that one of them would take me off his hands; I was looking for freedom. But I didn't tell him that. The strategy worked, and after visiting a large engineering factory in the north of England for a successful interview he eventually let me leave home at age sixteen to live in another town for the next five years and learn how to build mechanical diggers.

LENINGRAD

I am now in my seventieth year and I suppose it was maybe a couple of years ago that I first started looking back over my life and the memories of so long ago. I have sometimes wondered about friends past: about Trevor and what became of him, what career path he chose, if he has been fortunate in life and I have also wondered the same of Gordon. Had his father and mother in fact fallen on hard times and did they actually have to do a bunk, and if so to where and why hadn't Gordon ever bothered to send a card or let us know? To be honest I would have forgotten the whole episode and would not have remembered it at all if it had not been for something that occurred a few years ago.

Over fifty years had passed since those scouting days and of course I had been married for a great number of them. My wife and I had gone for a holiday to Russia, a river cruise starting in Saint Petersburg and ending in Moscow. Prior to going on a sight seeing tour we had attended a shipboard briefing lecture before disembarkation. A large port on the Baltic Sea, St Petersburg had been founded in 1703 and eventually become the imperial capital of Russia. In 1914 its name was changed to Petrograd and four years later in 1918 the central government moved to Moscow. There was yet another name change in 1924 when Petrograd was re christened Leningrad. I don't know if it's an official policy of the Russian government to confuse tourists because in 1991 they changed the name yet again, from Leningrad back to St Petersburg. But LENINGRAD? Something fluttered deep in my subconscious. What was it and why did this name ring a bell? It was like trying to climb a high wall but not having the strength to pull yourself over the top. It just would not come. The significance of Leningrad / St Petersburg being a major seaport should also have struck a chord but I just didn't link the two facts to the events of so long ago. We left St Petersburg and sailed on through Russia eventually reaching Moscow. On the second morning after we arrived we were standing in the middle of Red Square in front of Lenin's Tomb and the marble podium from which we had seen broadcast so many picture groups of the Russian leaders on black and white television during the late 1950s and 60s. I remembered scenes of thousands of troops and hundreds of tanks paraded along with intercontinental ballistic missiles with which they threatened the West. Terrifying pictures then, in total contrast to the scene in June that year when thousands of ordinary citizens from many countries mingled with each other in harmony to admire the beauty and majesty of Russian architecture.

We had been wandering around the square for half an hour or so and were standing taking in the sights when I happened to notice a group of four men to one side and slightly behind us. Their attire was more formal than tourist and one of them seemed to be looking in our direction rather intently, only to turn away on seeing me apparently noticing his gaze. I thought no more of it and the next day we flew home and carried on as normal, but somewhere, deep in my subconscious, the name LENINGRAD was still nagging away at me.

COORDINATES AND A CHRISTMAS CARD

I have for a long time believed that life is a game of chance, its outcome the result of the choices we make in response to any random encounters and events placed in front of us. I belong to the local library. Later in the following October, I was browsing away in the transport section looking for a book about steam locomotives.

Thus it was by random chance that I was looking in a particular section where somebody had mistakenly replaced a submarine book on a shelf which should only have held information about steam locomotives. How could such different means of transport be confused with one another?

SUBMARINES, SUBMARINES, SUBMARINES. The light went on. With my recent trip to Russia and the history of Saint Petersburg still floating around in my mind, my long ago memories and the present day collided with distant boyhood.

S-U-B-M-A-R-I-N-E, L-E-N-I-N-G-R-A-D, S-U-B-M-A-R-I-N-E

Swansea Bay and a rainy night in 1957. GORDON. We never did find out what really became of him. Was there really a submarine out in the bay that night? Had Leningrad really been a submarine base or the whole episode a combination of shipboard joker and a conventional family move, albeit perhaps doing a moonlight flit to avoid paying rent? My curiosity was rekindled. Maybe a bit late but I felt that I now had to at least find out a little bit more about that night. The question was - how was I going to do it? My first thoughts were to telephone one of the Royal Naval Colleges. Sounds easy enough but my calls all seemed to get diverted to a central number and answered by a secretary who helpfully transferred me to somebody else with the same idea. Tried the dockyard at Portsmouth but they couldn't help. They suggested the submarine museum who were equally unable to help because of course my enquiry related to a Russian built submarine. The curator that I spoke to however did make a useful suggestion which I had sort of tried before with only partial success.

"Yeah, try the Internet mate. Plenty of stuff there if you look."

What would we do without today's internet? Probably use the library service a lot more. So I tried again. I'd only punched in St Petersburg before and just got confirmation on name changes it had undergone over the years. It took me about half an hour messing around with different combinations of search words until, to my great surprise, The Russian Submarine Club web site suddenly announced itself. Now that was an unexpected bonus. Some browsing over the contents revealed worldwide interest and membership as well as a general history of their submarines and shipyards. But most helpfully of all it had an email address. If these guys couldn't help I would have come to a dead end.

So I enquired about submarines and Leningrad and also, aware of the sensitivity of the enquiry, asked tongue in cheek, if there was any available record of a submarine sightseeing off the west coast of Britain during the autumn of 1957. It was a few days before I got a reply but it was worth the wait. I hadn't really expected a direct answer to the last question I had posed and wasn't too disappointed when I didn't get one. But although they made a specific response with information on Leningrad and its relationship with submarines, an oblique comment in the answer, made by a commander Yuri Komolov, gave me encouragement enough to believe that just possibly there might have been a submarine around that part of the ocean during that time of year. More interesting was the information about Leningrad. Although at that time it was not a navy port it was a shipyard, building submarines at the specialist Sudomekh facility. The actual official Russian Navy Shipyard where they were based, then as now, was located in the city of Kronstadt on Kotlin Island and Kotlin Island was just off the coast of…Leningrad.

No wonder the police and other authorities had been so jumpy. I wondered if it was only us that had read the lamp signals that night. Well anyway, that was part of the mystery solved but as to the rest with the disappearance of Gordon? Again I concluded that it was just a combination of typical turnover of hard up 1950's council house tenants doing the proverbial bunk and pure schoolboy fantasy with Trevor's imagination running riot. But there was more. God! There was so much more. Out of the blue, ten days after the reply from the submarine club came another email. Plain with no explanatory text but a photo copy attachment that made me gasp and turned my blood cold. It was from an unassigned unknown email address.

But there didn't need to be an explanation. I could see what the attachment was: the log for the VOLSTANA, a Russian Quebec class submarine. The information was in Russian of course but some individual had annotated, translated and marked in ink enough relevant information for me to understand what it showed: it was the VOLSTANA's co-ordinate positions over three days and nights in late October 1957.

* * *

I didn't need to check the longitude and latitude but nevertheless I made myself do so because I just didn't want it to be true. I called a friend who had a half share in a thirty foot sailing yacht which I had never seen and which he was constantly inviting me to go and have a look at. We made an arrangement and I went over to see him the next day to check his charts. It confirmed my worst fears. The night that Alpha One had been messing around on Swansea beach had been the night the submarine Volstana had sailed from a position three and a half miles west south west off Swansea Bay after making contact with an agent signalling from the beach.

It had arrived on the Saturday afternoon two days previously and lain in deep water on the sea bed six miles out in the bay until early evening. It had then made its way to the rendezvous point and surfaced sufficient for a communications officer to mount a deck watch and acknowledge any contact. That first night it waited for two hours before having to submerge rapidly when there was a risk of discovery by a large vessel passing too close for comfort. It lay on the bottom for thirty minutes before resurfacing for another forty five minute period without contact after which it again submerged; this time to return to its original holding position six miles out on the sea bed. It sat and waited another day to repeat the whole procedure once again on Sunday night for two periods of nearly three hours each; both with a number of interruptions for rapid dives to avoid detection, finishing at 00:37 hours with no contact. On the third night contact was eventually made with an agent on the beach at 19:47 hours. It lasted for approximately seven and a half minutes and then broke off abruptly at which point the Volstana immediately submerged again, this time to maximum depth, setting course for first the English Channel and then back to Leningrad through the North Sea. What I couldn't understand and what I couldn't get my head around was the reference in the log to an agent on the beach. It was deeply puzzling until the horror of it suddenly dawned on me and when it did I was almost physically sick.

The word agent was undoubtedly a reference to us: We - the three of us – Gordon, Trevor and I - had been that agent. We had been their spies. If we had been caught by the police when they chased us off the beach it would have caused an international incident. But it still didn't make any sense. How could they think that three schoolboys playing about on the beach were signalling them in any way? We didn't even know they were there. We were just flashing the lamp out to sea for a bit of fun and they had answered; as well as, I now remembered, a sand dredger had before them. At the back of our minds as well, to reasure ouselves, Trevor and I had also thought it could have been a prank by a fishing boat.

When I thought about the implications it terrified me. In the days and weeks that followed I grew very depressed and morose. My wife couldn't begin to understand what my problem was. How on earth could I explain it to her? The whole thing was bizarre and defied explanation. How much worse could it get? It did get worse.

A week before Christmas came what I thought was the final straw to break the camel's back. Something arrived in the post that made me almost weep for my long lost friend. It was an envelope bearing a Russian postmark. Inside was a card, on the front of which was a picture with a salutation beneath written in Cyrillic with a translation in English:

РОЖДЕСТВЕНСКИЙ ПРИВЕТ ИЗ МОСКВЫ
'CHRISTMAS GREETINGS FROM MOSCOW'

But the picture was not a Christmas scene; it was of myself and my wife Janine in Red Square, standing in front of Lenin's tomb.

Behind us was the massive podium on which so many of Russia's historic leaders had posed to take the salute as thousands of troops, with their weapons of war, paraded past over the ground on which we now stood facing the camera. There was no message inside except for two words in English which simply said:

From Gordon

A FATHER'S SON

The first anonymous communication by email and confirmation of the submarine's presence was disturbing enough but I was far more unsettled by the Christmas card signed 'From Gordon.' I had to assume it was the same Gordon. My long disappeared friend. If it was, what was he doing in Moscow? Had he been on holiday? If so, and he had recognised me, why had he not come across and made himself known at the time? Surely if he was certain enough of my identity to go to the trouble of sending a card he could have at least said hello? But there you are. People change. Perhaps he was embarrassed at having left Swansea without telling us that he was going and not even bothered to contact us in the years since. That of course did not answer the key question. How the hell did he know where to send the card and how did he know my email address? When I had finished my apprenticeship I did return to Swansea for a couple of years but now live just outside Cardiff, a move I had made over forty years ago. I just could not understand it and I fretted for weeks until the middle of February when everything I had believed about him for so many years was destroyed in an instant. Brown envelopes don't normally worry me.

They're usually from the tax man or some other government enterprise, but when this one dropped through the letterbox nothing made sense ever again; cruelly changing my perspective on the life I had lived for ever. Postmarked somewhere in Hungary. No return address. Dated six days earlier.

My dear old friend,

I knew it was you the moment I saw you in the Square even after all these years. The features of the boy I knew are still there. I was so overjoyed that I wanted to walk over and embrace you but of course that could never be. The many changes that have taken place in the world over the last few decades however have made it possible for me to contact you now and explain some of the things which must have puzzled you after that night so long ago and also to tell you what has happened to me since. In the course of this letter you will learn a number of things that will no doubt shock you and I only ask that you find it in your heart not to judge me too harshly and that you will, if you can, forgive me for what I have done. I truly had no choice.

Firstly I must take you back to that night on Swansea beach in October 1957. To you and Trevor I know it was just a bit of innocent fun signalling ships in the bay, but in reality I confess to you now that it was nothing of the sort. It was in fact a cunning subterfuge devised by my father when he learnt of our collective interest in torches and how engrossed we had become with them. He spent a number of weeks preparing me for that night by teaching me the Morse code until I could almost tap it out and read it by instinct; such was his determination for the objective he had in mind to succeed. I knew you were impressed and surprised at my ability. It was course he who really supplied the lamp and composed the form of information to send.

Since the dissolution of the old Russia and the passing of over fifty years, what I will now tell you should be of no consequence. There is no easy way to tell you this. You see, my father was a spy. His job was to manipulate and take advantage of people and their circumstances, to make them work for mother Russia, no matter what harm might come to those he used. I had no idea of course. It was a complete shock to me to learn of his true identity and purpose in life. He was utterly ruthless and used me to deceive both you and Trevor on that night so long ago. You will remember that when I originally provided ALPHA ONE for our group name, you thought it to be my idea. It was in fact his. He seemed amused by our activities and took the opportunity to suggest it on a rare occasion when I was able to discuss our little gang with him. It was only when he started to prepare me for that night many months later that I realised his ulterior motive all along. ALPHA ONE was in fact his own agent call sign, already known by his controllers.

My parents were not Polish as you had believed. I remember you asking about my funny name when we first met. They were both really citizens of Russia and were infiltrated into Britain under false identities as refugees during the confusion at the start of the war with Germany. They were what your government would call sleepers, whose purpose was to blend in long term with the local community until called upon to perform a particular task deemed beneficial to mother Russia, and I was their British born son.

On the night in question the information exchanged with the submarine was not as random as it seemed, but a previously agreed pattern of coded wording. Of course as a thirteen year old schoolboy I was not privy to their meaning, although I got the impression that the situation was of sufficient importance to risk the actions we took on the beach that night. I learnt many years later that the QUEBEC 615 class submarine we communicated with had exceeded its range and had to be scuttled in the North Sea sometime after leaving the rendezvous, with the crew having been transferred to another vessel.

My part in deceiving you was not undertaken willingly but you did not know my father. He could be brutal. Far worse even than the strict disciplinarian that you briefly knew when you to came to my house. You have a saying that the best place to hide something is in plain sight. So it was with the submarine. What better cover to have than three schoolboys on the beach playing at being spies.

It worked perfectly. We got away but it was too close for comfort. When I told my father what had happened he literally went in to a frenzy. The possibility of being traced by the police and them discovering his true identity was now too great and he arranged for us to move on immediately, starting us packing that night. I of course protested; one of the few times I ever argued with my father, but he was determined and after putting my own things together I was sent to bed with a hot drink. It is sufficient to say the next thing I remember was waking up on board a ship. This is how I came to disappear so unexpectedly.

After we left Swansea in such a rush I spent a number of years travelling with my parents on various postings in America and Canada, but as I have indicated my father was a very forceful man and insisted that we return to Russia for me to join the army as soon as I was eligible. I returned to a living hell and it took many years to adjust after having spent so much time in the West.

Not long after returning, all record of my British citizenship was expunged and I was given a new identity. Along with all this of course came the difficulty of learning a completely alien language which I found very hard. It was a truly terrible time; having to endure five years of unnecessary hardship to prove that I was a true son of Russia in order to satisfy my father's warped ambitions. I was also never allowed to return to Britain under any circumstances. There really was no choice. In those days we were owned by the state and did what we were told or we did not survive, and to me he was the state and by then a ranking officer in the Kremlin. He has been dead now for over twenty years, with my mother preceding him some time before. She was far gentler and I'm not really sure that she was a spy at all but only remained with him for my sake. She had suffered ill health, not helped by him, for some time.

When I had completed my army service he had me transferred into intelligence where I spent my life in the service of my new country until I was semi-retired a few years ago. In other words my old friend, I too became a spy like my father and went to many countries to act in that capacity. My duties did not give me the opportunity to marry so I have no family but have learnt to be content.

After seeing you there in the square I had one of my colleagues take the picture while you were unaware and also had you followed back to your cruise ship. Forgive me. Old habits die hard. There was no harmful intent. I just wanted to trace you through your passport so that I could be sure, and bridge the years between us to let you know that I had not forgotten you. With today's technology and the internet most things seem to be possible. You wouldbe horrified to know just how easy for people like me.

For some reason after your visit you suddenly became interested in submarines and contacted our national submarine web site. Its purpose is quite innocent but of course it is inevitable that some correspondence is of more interest than normal and gets noted.

Your enquiry about a possible sight seeing cruise around Swansea bay was very subtle and duly flagged by comrade Commander Yuri Komolov who answered your emails. Yuri is an old friend of mine and knowing my history thought I would be interested and passed on the details.

Indeed I was and, as a token of that fateful time, I sent you a copy of the submarine log for that night as a memento. I had always wondered if such a record existed and was delight to find it in the course of my duties some years ago and kept it as a reminder of my reluctant christening as a spy. You will note that it came via a rather obscure address. It always most essential to take precautions even now.

And so my friend, I hope you will still think of me as a friend, we must come to the parting of the ways. I have had my new identity for many years now and although mostly retired, living mainly in Hungary, I still have some occasional duties in Moscow. Seeing you, even fleetingly, that day was truly my good fortune but we will never meet again. It just cannot be. I hope however that the contents of this letter will offer some solace and answers to the past however uncomfortable they may be for you. Although my life has not been at all what I would have wished I have at least survived. Russia is no longer the absolute dictatorship it was, but of course it will never be like Britain. Your people must beware though of the new Europe. It is run by dangerous fools and is heading back into a place where we in Russia have already been. Men never seem to learn from the failures of others who have gone before them. Take care my friend. Take very great care.

So I must now say goodbye. I wish you and your family peace prosperity and good health in the twilight of your years.

Your old friend,

Gordon Wasillewski

My hands were trembling and the letter fell from their grasp. As far as I was concerned an earthquake could not have shaken me more. I could hardly breath; numb with shock. I needed time to think. God! Did I ever need some time.

INFORMATION OBTAINED

I must have sat there for an hour at least, feeling sick, and too stunned to think or move. All this time, all this time, I had with all my heart believed that Gordon was in some other part of the country, safe and well living a normal life with his parents, building a career, finding a wife and building a home with children and then maybe grandchildren. How wrong could I have been? How could anyone have ever imagined the twisted road that his life had actually taken? The implications of what he had told me were terribly upsetting. It seemed that Trevor and I had both unwittingly been duped into committing treason by our friend. The whole thing on the beach was a lie to conceal messages to an enemy submarine whose country at the time had an un quantifiable number of nuclear missiles pointed threateningly in our direction.

His father's plan was simply unbelievable but extremely cunning in concept. Hiding a submarine in plain sight. Who would believe that an enemy vessel would advertise its presence so blatantly to conceal itself? Three thirteen year old schoolboy scouts on a beach claiming to be just having some fun would mislead anyone. How could they begin to know that they were communicating with a submarine of all things? It could only be that the responding ship was playing a joke. Some communications officer with a sense of humour having a laugh. If we had been caught by the police no doubt we would have been hauled up in front of some burly desk sergeant to be given a ticking off and no more would be thought about it. I could imagine the conversation, with him glowering as we explained:

"We didn't mean no harm – we was just playing at being spies and signalling ships for a bit of fun. We didn't know somebody on a tug was going to pretend they were a submarine did we?"

They might even have had a laugh about it after sending us on our way with a warning. Fate had indeed dealt Gordon an unlucky roll of the dice. To be born to parents who were spies in a foreign country where they had been for fifteen or more years. To have believed them to be part of the community and then to have so cruelly discovered what they really were. I can just imagine how troubled he must have been and how he thought his friends might react if or when they found out. He would be ostracised and labelled a spy just like them. His father was some kind of engineer, I recalled, travelling around the country working with armed forces and government production establishments. For pity's sake! Just how much damage had that man done? What kind of secrets had he passed on and what more evil had he perpetrated after we'd helped him to escape? The possibilities just didn't bear thinking about. Then I remembered the fuss when a whole spy network had come to light several years earlier with the names of Burgess and McLean prominent. Was he the unknown ghost member of this same ring which nobody knew about? If so how had he escaped scrutiny and remained undetected for so long? What about Gordon's adopted uncle? Was he involved as well?

Had he too been part of the conspiracy, if he in fact existed at all, or had Gordon knowingly manipulated us into believing in a well constructed phantom? I remembered how neither Trevor nor I had met him and didn't even know where he'd lived when we wanted to find out where Gordon had gone. The questions were endless and without answers.

Were there still spies in Swansea? Well at least not today I told myself. But when I let the cat out of the bag about what I now knew there would be a lot of questions by a lot of very belligerent government types wanting to cover departmental backsides from long ago.

While I pondered what to do I decided to check the submarine details that Gordon had mentioned. So once again it was onto the internet looking for information about the Quebec submarines. Maybe I was trying to shut stable doors too many years after the horses had bolted but now I had found out the real purpose of our beach adventure I was going to hold my own inquiry and wanted to know every last detail.

Not only for myself but also for Trevor. I owed him that much even if he didn't know anything about it – wherever he may be. Was he even still alive? I had never had any real interest in submarines before but my God! I was interested in this one. Gordon's letter had destroyed the tranquillity of my retirement and ruined some of my most precious boyhood memories. Trawling through the internet I was surprised at just how much submarine information there was and what I found out led me to draw a couple of what I thought were reasonable conclusions, assumptions, call them what you will, which served to exemplify the urgency of its mission.

Firstly - the VOLSTANA could not have been diverted from any regular patrol pattern. It was too small and had insufficient range for long patrols through the world's oceans. The class had been specifically designed as a coastal attack submarine and must have been picked because of its compactness and suitability for the bay's relatively shallow waters. An outline drawing gave its principal specifications: something just less than one hundred and eighty four feet long, displacing five hundred and forty tons submerged and powered by twin regular cycle diesel engines.

Its depth below the water line when not submerged was twelve feet six inches, which speaking nautically, was just six inches over two fathoms. Waters around Swansea bay are not very deep and I wondered how far below the surface it could get to avoid detection and how deep it would have been three or four miles out in the bay. Finding out was time consuming and it took several telephone calls to the relevant shipping, coastguard and finally docks office departments until I got lucky and a spoke to the harbour master on duty. He listened to all my questions and furnished me with all the answers I needed. I learned about spring tides and neap tides, the difference between them and when they occurred. But most importantly I found out that the eight metre difference in height at full spring tide would give a depth of around sixteen fathoms.

Plenty enough for a small submarine to hide under. Certainly enough for the VOLSTANA which only needed six fathoms to cover the radio antennae. There was one more thing I wanted to check if possible, just for my own satisfaction. That was to confirm the state of the tide on the night we were on the beach. The submarine's log had given me the date and even so long ago I remembered that it had been a particularly overcast night with no moonlight. You can still get tide forecasts for coastal towns in the local papers just as there would have been a forecast in the Swansea Evening Post all those years ago. So I checked with their archive department but it was too far back with no records for 1957. They suggested I try the museum or the guildhall both of whom were kind enough to conduct a search for me but without success. The irony was that some of their information went way back to the early twentieth century but not for the particular year I wanted.

I tried the internet yet again. It had been a very useful tool before but not his time. Again I failed to find an answer. I was getting nowhere fast! But there was one other way I could check. I remembered that spring tides were associated with phases of the moon with spring tides occurring at two of them. These were a new moon and a full moon. When I did a search against that parameter I found the answer I was looking for. There had been a new moon on the twenty-third of October giving a tide which corresponded with the submarine log. It's funny how you can seem to always remember the small details from so many years ago and not recall things from last week. Making the search triggered my memory and made me smile when I thought of Trevor turning up with a big fat grin on his face that night because of his gran's ten quid gift to him on her birthday. So there it was. The information all now tied together.The Quebec class submarine's specified range was two thousand seven hundred and fifty miles with a limit of fourteen days total endurance. It was a long way from its home port, and when I had previously gone to check its positional co-ordinates on my friends charts we had also worked out the nautical mileage and course from Leningrad to Swansea bay. If I had made a guess it would have been completely wrong. From Leningrad its course would have taken it west through the Gulf of Finland, then on through the Baltic Sea to the southernmost point of Sweden. There it would have either swung north to pass Copenhagen or travelled further west and taken the Great Belt passageway up through Denmark and then through Kattegat before turning into the North Sea to head south into the heavy swell of the English Channel.

I wondered what the protocol for submarines would have been then when sailing past neighbouring countries. Did they float by on the surface in full view or submerge to sneak past hidden beneath the waves. They would certainly have been submerged during the hours of daylight through the English Channel and on into the Bristol Channel to lie in deep water before making their rendezvous; altogether a distance of almost eighteen hundred nautical miles.

The VOLSTANA was capable of eighteen knots on the surface and sixteen submerged. Even if it was able to travel the full distance at full speed on the surface the best time it could theoretically hope for to make rendezvous would be four days and five hours. By then it would probably have rattled itself to pieces. I surmised that a top practical surface speed would be sixteen knots, made during the hours of darkness, with the possibility of fourteen knots below the waves during daylight. Travelling, say, as far as Gothenburg on the surface at sixteen knots would take around two days and leave around a thousand miles to cover the remaining distance which at fourteen knots would take another three days. If it made good time running on the surface as much as possible at night, it could have reached Swansea Bay in maybe four and a half days, hung around to make the rendezvous and then skedaddled for home.

But that was only my theory and didn't allow for any problems or deviations from plan. By the time it was ready to turn for home it was already heading into difficulties. Eight hundred and fifty miles short on fuel for its return to Leningrad, very near its limit of fourteen days' endurance and operating eighteen hundred miles away from its base, it had, according to Gordon's letter, become expendable. I wasn't so sure. I thought it was a bit more complicated and I wanted a bit more time to think things out.

DUPLICITY

Gordon's letter had mentioned something that nearly failed to register with me, but a couple of weeks later with the passage of time and a calmer mind it did, and when I put it together with the rest it hit me between the eyes. It was what he had said about his father – 'and to me he was The State and by then a ranking officer in the Kremlin.' Gordon's father was a lot higher up in the pecking order than a casual mention implied. He could only have achieved that position for one reason and that was for service to his country. He had served his country, Russia, for more than fifteen years in my country, as a spy, and had been appropriately rewarded by his government. Gordon said his father was ruthless.

He had deceived him into believing there was some kind of fatherly interest in him and his friends. He had with ulterior motive provided a name for our gang which, unbeknown to us, was really his official spy call sign, code name – whatever - to be used in a plan he was already formulating for his escape. When he was ready to put that plan into operation he had groomed his son in readiness for that night to entice Trevor and myself to assist. What a thoroughly despicable man. Although now long dead I found myself hating him for Gordon with a venom I didn't know I'd possessed. He had been ruthless enough to force his son to commit an act of espionage and then abducted him, but he did this only after first drugging him to render him unconscious to conceal and smuggle him out of his country of birth and thence into Russia, there to rob him of his identity. My poor friend Gordon. I couldn't begin to imagine the mental trauma he must have suffered. That is what spies are made of.

But Gordon's father was more than just an ordinary spy. He was special and he was no sleeper. He was active and what the press would have called a master spy. I began to wonder just how many newsworthy espionage and stolen secret headline stories had been initiated by his actions. Far too valuable an asset to lose but somehow his presence and means of contacting his controllers had been compromised. British intelligence was on to him and were searching although his identity and location were still unknown. He had planned well. If he had the slightest suspicion that he was under threat he would signal his concern by stopping all communication with his controller and a contingency plan would activate automatically. No urgent telephone calls to eavesdrop, no secret letter boxes or suspicious callers to watch. His escape plan and contact strategy with the submarine was already complete; a brilliant piece of original thinking with nothing left to organise.

Who would really have believed there was a submarine out in the bay; let alone a Russian one? What would be the chances of the signals being read and their true significance understood. Who could they ask to confirm it and if they did what could they do? By the time a search vessel was organised it would be long gone. Our contact with the sand dredger would also have caused confusion. Gordon's father knew too much and it was vital to bring him out. Once under way, and perhaps back in the English Channel, the submarine would have surfaced briefly to send a flash radio signal to a mainland receiver with agents perhaps already in place waiting with the removal vehicle seen by the neighbour. All they had to do was collect him. A brilliant escape plan brilliantly executed. Had Gordon really understood what his father did for a living, let alone realize the peril he was in and that the game was up? Even in his letter he was still under the impression that he had been imparting information to the submarine when in fact the reverse was the case. So had he been told the full truth about what was really happening? When the submarine signalled back 'LENINGRAD', it was in reality the coded instruction for a plan already in place for extraction the following night. A different name would mean a different plan and yet, although acted on immediately by his father, he didn't seem to have understood its significance or the true purpose of the submarine. At the time he must have been far too young and too shocked to understand the depths of his father's treachery, believing only what he had been told: that they had to flee because our beach activities might lead the police to their door and to the discovery of his true identity.

But his father's activities had been discovered, although they had not yet identified or located him. The submarine was his salvation; acknowledging his predicament and providing the timetable for immediate escape. It was all pre-arranged and was how they disappeared so quickly. Gordon just didn't have time to tell us anything and his father wouldn't have permitted it anyway.

And yet, in spite of everything that had happened to him he had adjusted to his new situation and made a success of his life. At the back of my mind I had been wondering how he had been able to get hold of that submarine log and suddenly it dawned on me. He must also have attained high office, in his albeit enforced profession, like his father before him. He always had been a determined little sod and had his father's genes after all. A submarine log is a classified document and to send me an archive copy of such a document he had taken a great risk. That kind of information would not have been available to general staff. He had to have had special access authority. He had also taken a lesser risk to write to an old friend and for that I was grateful; at the same time fervently hoping that in his high flying career he had not been involved in activities that would have harmed his country of birth. Somehow I felt sure he would have acted as his own censor and recused himself on that score.

One of the official reports I found said that a Quebec Class submarine had caught fire and been lost with all hands at around the time all this was taking place. No date given but I wondered if this was the same submarine that we had signalled returning to Leningrad and which Gordon said had been scuttled after transferring the crew. If it was, why would he lie about saving the crew? What sort of man had he become? The answer was of course that he was no longer the boy that I had known but a self-confessed professional spy…and spies tell lies. Or was he being considerate and avoided telling me the truth because he thought I might be troubled by this particular piece of information?

The vessel was equipped with a third diesel engine having a separate liquid oxygen supply for submerged propulsion, which must have been the cause of the fire. Closed cycle combustion systems were used to provide air independence but known to be plagued with problems. The Quebec class was so dangerous, in fact, that their crews had nicknamed them firelighters. Oxygen evaporation was also the reason for the submarine's limited duration of fourteen days and only thirty of the type were recorded as having been built before switching to the development of nuclear submarines.

I could only guess at the full story and wondered if they had met up with another vessel somewhere in the North Sea to attempt a refuel and it had all gone wrong. If this was indeed the case Gordon's father had cost the lives of many crew members. Was he really worth it? There was most certainly a lot more to their Swansea Bay visit than I could ever have imagined.

It had all of course happened many years ago now and would be of no immediate concern to the authorities except for perhaps clearing up a long forgotten police file that still lay open. With a submarine involved – if they knew about it - things might even have gone as far as the admiralty. But what could they do when they learned of the deception? Not a cotton pickin' thing! In all probability most, if not all, of the participants looking for us back then, have long since departed this world and are busy exploring the next.

Perhaps by now Gordon may also be dead. It's been five years since I received his letter and I've sat on it because I didn't really know what I should do about it. I cannot with clear conscience do that any longer. It's been playing on my mind and dragging me down.

The record needs to be put straight because for fifteen years, unknown to the authorities, Swansea had been the safe haven for a Russian master spy. A part of the city's past which nobody knows about - only me, and I am going to expose it. Somehow I can't see them having to rewrite the town's history to cover that fact going down too well.

The big question is how soon should I pass on the information, because I know what will happen when I do. The retrospective pandemonium and cover up will start; resulting in one or more overzealous glory-seeking individuals turning up on my doorstep, making excuses to come back time and time again "just to go over a few points, you understand." Well no thanks. I intend to be very busy for the years I've got left and do not want to be interviewed by anyone going over my past in the minutest detail trying to label me as a lifelong spy. I have thought about it long and hard, and come to a decision and what I *will* do is set the wheels in motion. In the next couple of weeks I shall go and see a solicitor to get a proviso that it's contents are not passed onto the authorities until some reasonable period in the future, by which time I will either be lying under the sod kicking up daisies or too gaga to remember anything worth discussing. Maybe someday it might even make a very good story.

I did have one last thought - all those years ago when I met Trevor just after we found out that Gordon had gone missing, he was distraught and utterly convinced that the Russians had taken him. He had been right all along.

EPILOGUE

This story was inspired by schoolboy years in and around the town of Swansea, and in particular the bay area, during the late autumn of 1957. Many of the events told are based on actuality, although some have been transposed in time and place with characters added to sustain continuity and background. Any resemblance of persons portrayed to individuals past or present is purely coincidental. Whether you choose to believe the events surrounding Gordon is up to you. The subject is all rather delicate and will have worrying implications for people in certain areas of authority. You'll just have to draw your own conclusions. But I know what we saw and I know what we did that night on the beach. You may well choose to dispute it. But you can prove or disprove nothing. My friends are long gone.

I am the sole witness remaining.

Bernard Andrew